Convoy of Chaos

A Car Warriors:

Autoduel Chronicles Anthology

Three Ravens Publishing
Chickamauga, GA USA

Welcome to the world of the Car Warriors: Autoduel Chronicles — Tales from the freeways of the future, where the right of way goes to the biggest guns and death sports rule the airwaves. From clandestine highway battles to prime-time arena combat, jump behind the wheel, follow the fast-paced action, and never forget to Drive Offensively!

Car Warriors Autoduel Fiction is licensed by Steve Jackson Games Incorporated and set in the *Car Wars* universe.

Stories by:

INTRODUCTION by Wil Wheaton
EASY PICKINGS by Quinn
OVER THE HILL By Jesse M. Slater
NOT MY FIRST RODEO by T.M. Gray
CRUZE CONTROL by David Bock
RADIOACTIVE RUN by Richard Cartwright
MILK RUN by Sam Robb
CARGO by Bee M Kay
TOUGH COOKIES by Douglas Goodall
ASPHALT BANDWIDTH by A. Kristina Casasent
THE WHEELS ON THE DEATH BUS GO ROUND AND ROUND by Seth Taylor
SNAFU ON SNAKE RIVER by William Joseph Roberts

Edited by: Shari Robb and Richard Cartwright
Cover art by: oldmanlogan

Ebook ISBN: 978-1-966507-46-8
Trade Paperback ISBN: 978-1-966507-47-5
Audiobook ISBN: 978-1-966507-48-2

Table of Contents

Introduction

Steve Jackson, who co-designed and published Car Wars, once told me that every tabletop game is a role-playing game, and when you play with that in mind, not only do you increase your chances of claiming victory, you open yourself to the story — my kids might call it the *vibe* — of the game. And thus, win or lose, you're probably going to have a great time.

He told me this while he had a great time kicking my ass at Munchkin, which we were playing in front of millions of gamers, on my show, Tabletop. If you want to see it for yourself, it's on YouTube.

For context, Munchkin is a hilarious satire of power gamers who steamroll their way to min/maxed victory at the cost of story and logic in RPGs. Steve was playing like a rogue who pushes a goblin into a balustrade and tells the GM that they are using backstab for an attack bonus. I was playing the game like someone who didn't want to make an embarrassing mistake in front of the designer. I was deep in my own head, analyzing every option I had and how this turn would affect the next and the next, and so on. Munchkin is usually a lot of silly fun for me, but this game was more stressful than anything else, and that's entirely my fault. This is a beloved episode of the show, viewed over four million times. My only regret is not that I lost; it's that I wasn't able to be more present and have more fun while I was playing with one of my heroes.

But it was pretty awesome to have a front row seat as Steve roleplayed the Ultimate Power Gaming Munchkin Guy with such commitment, he won by cheating. (We noticed in editing that Steve hit level 9, declared he'd reached level 10, and claimed victory. Nobody bothered to check his math, because why would we, and it turns out that the way he won is explicitly allowed by the rules. I'm not even mad. I'm impressed.)

From that day onward, I chose to treat every Tabletop game as if it were an RPG. I figured out who I was supposed to be and just let the story of the game tell me where to go, and I even won a game here and there, in no small part thanks to Steve's advice.

What does all of this have to do with Car Wars? I'm glad you asked. Car Wars is probably the most consequential tabletop game I've ever played, precisely because it was— by design—also a role-playing game. When I was 15, I looked at Car Wars and saw a pile of cardboard chits sitting atop some graph paper, accompanied by pages of charts and tables. I dismissed it out of hand. If I wanted to play a game that was my math homework in disguise, AD&D was right there, with THAC0 featuring prominently on the exam.

But my friend who introduced me to Car Wars also showed me issues of ADQ and Uncle Albert's, along with one of the AADA Road Atlases. Those books and, later, GURPS Autoduel, almost instantly transformed that pile of math homework into a real, immersive, living world. My imagination fired up and revved my creative engine to the redline. Sure, it was fun to win duels against my friends, but the real victories were the NPC drivers, gunners, Bikers, and helpless cannon fodder we met and dispatched along the way.

In 1987, I wasn't playing much D&D or 40K, but I read Dungeon and Dragon magazines, and White Dwarf. They offered updates and revisions I wanted to keep up with, and a few short stories, but their design and content was clearly from the 20th century. Uncle Albert's, the Atlases, and ADQ felt like they'd been extracted from the far-off future of 2037. They created a sense of immersion for me that I hadn't ever experienced from a tabletop game and my Autoduel Quarterly subscription and AADA membership fuel-injected my imagination for years, long after my gaming group got distracted by the new hotness.

If Car Wars didn't have Autoduel, I probably would have followed them to Fury of Dracula. We changed games back then, the way you change lanes. But I stayed. When I had time between scenes at work in my dressing room, and over entire weekends in my bedroom, I read the books, soaked up the worldbuilding and the lore. I traced my fingers along the maps in the atlases, imagining I was a duelist on my way to Sacramento for One Last Duel Before Retirement, if only I can get past these bikers. I shopped at Uncle Al's, voraciously devoured whatever fiction I could get my hands on. And when I ran out of other people's stories, I wrote my own.

And I know that I'm not the only one. This book, and the incredible response from everyone who funded it, is a testament to the enduring legacy of a classic game that was so much more than cardboard and tables (how *dare* you, 15 year-old Wil!). I am so honored to introduce it, and so excited for it to take you back to the future. Just make sure your battery is charged, your guns are loaded, and your eyes are on the horizon. It's a dangerous world out there, and you're not the only one who is driving offensively.

Have fun, friends. Let these pages reignite your love for Car Wars and Autoduel, or make your love burn even hotter. I hope your next arena battle or highway duel isn't too far off, and I hope this book inspires you to play more games.

See you on the road. I probably won't shoot at you.

Wil Wheaton

August 2025

Easy Pickings
By Quinn

I pulled up to the bar on my bike, an old model from yesteryear. It was modified, of course, with patches everywhere, dents and dings up and down the sides, and plenty of scorch marks from lasers around the rear armor. I wiped the ever-present road dust off the handlebars with a tattered rag I kept in my pocket, then dismounted. A moment later I made my way inside.

The biker bar had no name, no sign. Most establishments like this didn't have one, either. You had to know where they were, had to be a biker to coax that information out from the locals. Fortunately for me, I was. Or I was. Never mind; it's not important.

I was sweating a bit in the chilly fall air. I chalked it up to my nerves. At least I hoped it was my nerves. You never could tell what diseases were rampant out in the boonies like this, and the last thing you wanted to do out here was get sick. After all, the doctors in Birmingham don't make house calls this far out, and neither does Gold Cross.

I glanced at the entrance to the bar. There were a couple of people in a fistfight blocking the way, bashing away at each other's body armor. I could tell they weren't serious, as they both had the Skulls gang insignia on their armor and they weren't using weapons. That suited me just fine.

A few quick steps brought me over to them. I took off my helmet and shook out my gray hair, proudly displaying the necklace of handmade dog tags I wore. Making sure that they had noticed me, I looked at the necklace, then the two of them.

They stopped fighting at once. It took just a moment longer for them to clear the entrance. I nodded to them as I passed.

You know, they even held the door open for me. That's what a litany of the dead will do for you.

"Easy pickings. It was supposed to be easy pickings."

I picked up my drink off the bar and took another swig. The sweetness cascaded down my throat and into my stomach. I'd been drinking swill since I got here, and it was beginning to show. At least this batch had some taste to it.

The biker bar had a decent crowd for a Friday night. They were pouring in from a fresh kill out on I-20 somewhere, so they had cash to burn. And, boy, did they burn it. The drinks were free flowing, the music was loud, and the entertainment was very active. What the entertainment was doing I'll leave to your imagination.

I took a quick glance around to see if anyone had noticed me muttering to myself yet. The guy to my left hadn't noticed, for he was concentrating hard on finishing his gigantic bottle of algae beer before he passed out in a stupor. The woman on my right, however, had just arrived and, just maybe, noticed what I said.

I decided to act.

I tossed back the rest of the drink and slammed the glass down on the bar. It didn't shatter, thankfully, but it did roll out of my hand and down the bar toward a bunch of bikers. They saw it and laughed.

"Easy pickings," I said again, louder this time.

"Can't hold your drink, old timer?" one of the bar patrons asked, a big guy with kill markers running down his arms and laughter in his voice. He had come in with one of the many biker gangs in the area who congregated here on a sort of 'neutral ground.' His body armor showed he was a member of the Skulls. They got their namesake by mounting said human skulls to the front of the bikes, just below the lights and above the gun ports.

I slowly grabbed the glass back up and set it down next to the others. I'd been here awhile, so there were a few in my collection. Fortunately, none of them had held the real stuff, or this would be a lot more difficult to pull off.

"Yeah, I can hold my drink, and my aim, for that matter," I said, a slight slur in my voice. "That didn't help us, of course. Not last month, anyway."

The woman turned toward me; her black hair set in a ponytail. "Last month?"

I nodded. "Last month," I said softly. "Easy pickings."

The woman's eyebrow rose. "Sounds like you had a bad ride."

"You could say that, if, by 'bad ride,' you mean I'm the only survivor."

Now *that* caught the attention of the bikers around me.

The lady with the black ponytail got me another drink, and this one was the real stuff. Alcohol brewing had taken a major hit after the Grain Blight, but some places had figured out ways to get it from algae or other plants. This stuff, however, was left over from before the Blight and therefore must have cost a bundle. She handed it to me without a word while gently setting her helmet on the bar.

I took the glass in one hand and gripped one of the dog tags with the other. Without saying a word, I swallowed the drink in one gulp, feeling the familiar burn in the back of my throat.

"That's for you, Duster," I muttered, the words barely audible to those around me.

More people were stepping up to the bar, not to drink, but to find out what I had to say. If this went well, I'd be walking out of here a bit drunk but in one piece. If not, well, I hoped they would leave enough of my brains for a memory dump.

"What happened, old man?" Skulls looked at me with something that might have resembled compassion and awe. When you're in a biker gang, you're not expected to make it into your thirties without dying at least once. I looked twice as old as that, and right now, I felt every year of it.

I hesitated just a second longer, then started my story. Hopefully, they would listen and believe.

"We were tracking a big rig out of Anniston, headed to Atlanta. Our scouts had spotted it on I-20 leaving the town a few minutes before. It wasn't traveling fast, and it only had a couple of beat-up cars for escorts."

I shook my head. "That should have been our first warning, but no one thought to ask why a rig was on this route without a proper escort. We just figured it was some poor schlep trying to get a start in the business. 'Easy pickings,' Duster said."

"You know how it goes. Track your target, get ahead of it, set the ambush, then roll over them until they give up or you've smashed them up fairly good. Everybody prefers they give up, of course. No one wants to die doing this; neither they nor us. But sometimes that's inevitable."

I smiled, a chilling thing. "Like this time."

I gestured with the glass toward the steel mirror behind the bar. It was dirty, of course, and warped in places, but it served its purpose well enough. It was made from the hood of someone's car, the armor laser reflective.

"We could have used that, but who's going to get that crap out here? It's not like Detroit is down the street."

A couple of the gathered bikers nodded their heads. They were getting the gist of where this story was going, but I had a few surprises along the way for them.

"I drew the long end of the straw for once and got to pick where I was going to be in the ambush. Fortunately, I picked the back of the formation. I don't know why I did that, but it saved my life. Maybe it was my guardian angel watching over me." I grunted. "Maybe it was the pasta rumbling around in my stomach that made me get in the back. Who knows?"

All eyes in the room were on me now. Even the entertainment had stopped dancing.

"So, we'd set up in the old Talladega National Forest. You know, where that big curve is, the one with the crater on one side? That's a prime ambush spot, and we took full advantage of it. Most of us were on the south side of the freeway, while me and the mop up crew were on the other side, in case things got frisky."

I met my gaze in the mirror. "Boy, did they."

"Well, the lead escort crested the hill to see a pile of our bikes on their sides in the middle of the freeway, right next to the crater. They were old junkers we didn't need anymore. A juicy bit of salvage to tempt everyone. The escort slowed down to get the lay of the land, but it kept coming."

"Then the rig made it to the top of the hill, and there it stopped, waiting for the escort to make some sense of what was going on. Now, mind you, it pulled itself all the way up the hill so that its trailer was in full view of everything. The rig's one remaining turret (the other was a mangled wreck) even tracked on the pile of bikes on the road. A sensible precaution, to be sure, but that's what we wanted them to do. 'Any edge in a duel,' Duster always said."

"We tensed up, waiting for the signal from the lead bike. Duster was waiting for the right moment, and it wasn't long in coming."

"He had done a check on what guns the rig was carrying by judging what poked out of their gunports. It wasn't much, just a couple of machine guns on each side. Nothing we couldn't manage, and only one of the turrets looked functional. Easy pickings."

"The tail end Charlie escort came up around the rig and headed downhill to join up with the other. They looked just as beat up as the rig did, a good sign. They looked poorly armed, as well, with only a couple of recoilless rifles visible."

I wiped my brow clear of sweat. It was getting hot from the press of the bodies around me. I had the attention of everyone in the bar by now, and they were hanging on every word. Good.

"When the second escort met up with the first one near the pile of bikes, Duster gave the signal. The satchel charges we'd planted along the edge of the freeway went off, rocking the escorts back on their wheels. All sorts of crap hit their armor plates, cracking the shells, but not penetrating too deeply. We'd hoped those charges would take care of the escorts, but that was not meant to be."

"The south crew came charging out of the forest, hell bent on destruction. Our best guys, well, besides my side, led the charge, weapons blazing. They targeted both the escorts and the rig at the same time, with the most firepower concentrated on the escorts. Heck, from all the weapon fire and the dust from the satchel charges going off, you could barely see the escorts in the cloud."

"My side of the crew were just powering up their hogs when the unthinkable happened." I was staring at myself in the mirror. There wasn't a clear path to anywhere through the crowd. I was committed now.

"There was a set of popping sounds that came from the rig. At first, I thought it was the machine guns misfiring, but no, that wasn't it. It was the armor, or should I say the fake armor's release charges going off."

I shuddered for effect.

"Look. The whole outer shell of the rig just… dropped away. What we thought was just some old plastic crap they'd thrown on because that was all they could afford, actually covered up some seriously upgraded metal armor, and our gunfire was just bouncing off it like popcorn."

"That 'nonfunctional' turret I mentioned? Well, yeah, it wasn't functional, especially after the launch charges on the roof exploded and it soared into the air. The real turret came up from underneath and a pair of laser ports popped out of it. They instantly tracked in on the lead bike, which was Duster's by the way, and lit into it."

"Duster never knew what hit him. He didn't even get the chance to scream."

I took a swig from the drink that had appeared next to the empty glasses. "To Duster," I said, raising the glass to the mirror. I could see in the reflection several bikers around me doing the same thing.

I had them now.

"The hatches covering the real gun ports cracked open, and a *lot* of lasers showed themselves on the trailer. And as soon as the hatches were clear, the guns opened up in a hellish display."

"A Q truck. A godsdamn Q truck," said a voice out of the crowd behind me. I nodded.

"Exactly."

There was a moment of silence, which was only broken when a solitary voice quietly asked, "What did you do?"

"Frankly, there wasn't much I *could* do at that point." I pointed at the guy who'd asked the question. "We'd already powered up and had cleared the tree line. It would only be seconds before the truck began firing at my group, so I yelled at everyone over the radio to follow me."

"I took off toward the back of the truck, going off-road several times to take what cover I could. A couple of the rocks around me got blasted into vapor by the rig, and a bunch of my fellow riders did, too. Those that survived stuck to me like glue."

I gestured with the glass in my hand, pushing it past the others piled up on the side, like it was my bike. Everyone got the point.

"I had just cleared the rear corner of the truck when there was series of explosions behind me. I saw, in my mirrors, Charlie rush past the side of the rig, firing rockets from his sidecar. The rockets weren't much, mainly there just for show. The real purpose of the sidecar was something else."

"Cargo space," suggested another voice from behind me. This one sounded young, much too young for a place like this.

"Nope, something more important."

"What could be more important than that?"

"A getaway."

A few of the bikers looked at each other, puzzled. Others nodded their head in agreement.

"You always want to have an escape plan, just in case things go south, and if there ever was an ambush going south, it was this one."

One more sip from the glass drained it. I was feeling tipsy, which wasn't a good sign. I couldn't afford to get drunk out here, or I'd never make it out alive. So, when the bartender offered to fill my glass with the good stuff again, I waved him off. "That's enough for me. I do have to ride out of here, you know."

There was a chorus of laughs from around the room. Being caught by the cops for drunk driving was a thing of the past, a relic from bygone days. Besides, I'm sure they were thinking I would sleep it off here.

That was the farthest thing from my mind right then.

"Sounds like you had a big gang. What was their name?"

I'd been waiting for this question. "Flying Knives." I pointed to my old gang's insignia, proudly displayed on the back of my body armor. It depicted a set of knives with angel wings attached. "We usually worked I-20 from Atlanta to Augusta, but we switched it up occasionally with the other freeways in the area."

"I thought they were wiped out long ago."

"Nope. We usually rode under false flags to keep our identity secret. Over here we're known as… well, it doesn't matter anymore, does it, since I'm the only one left, and I'm too old to start them back up."

They all nodded, accepting my answer. Another hurdle crossed.

"Anyway, we, or what 'we' remained, had made it past the rig and were almost out of sight when the escorts came roaring out of the cloud of dust around them. They looked the worse for wear, but they, too, were still in fighting shape, with metal armor and lasers under the hood."

I paused for a moment. "They caught up in a hurry, lasers blasting away. Our bikes simply couldn't weather that kind of firepower, and most of them crashed, their riders burnt to a crisp. Shortly afterwards it was just me and Charlie."

"We looked at each other and nodded through our visors. I was about to turn around on a suicide run, but he beat me to it."

I closed my eyes for a moment, then spoke. "I remember his last words over the radio. 'Let them know about this rig. Let everyone know.'"

Another moment of hesitation before I continued. "Charlie slammed on his brakes, coming to a halt. The lead escort went to run him over, with the second as backup, which was what Charlie wanted."

"We had crammed the sidecar with plastic explosives, dynamite, and anything else we could find that goes boom, and when it went off it flipped both cars over. The lead rolled over and hit a rock, and the other went into the tree line. Both were wrecked."

"I turned the bike around, just on the off chance he was alive. There was nothing left, and when I mean nothing, I mean *nothing*. Just another smoking scorch mark."

"The truck was well out of range now. I looked around and realized I was the only bike left standing. There's no way I could take on a Q with just one bike, so I turned tail and ran. I didn't need to stick around to see if any of my friends were alive. It was obvious they weren't."

I shook my head. "I'm not very proud of leaving their remains behind."

"So what did you do?" It was the younger voice again.

I tossed some cash on the bar and stood up. "I rolled back into the woods and laid low for a week or two, just to get my head together. None of our gang had Gold Cross or another cloning service, so there was no one to tell. We'd never had hangers-on allowed in the gang, so no one to talk to on that end, either."

"After that, well, I've been hitting every bar I can think of in the area, letting them know about this rig. It should take some time for the truck to make what repairs it needed and get new escorts made, so I figured I had about a month for them to be ready."

I started to make my way gently through the crowd toward the front door. "So, if you see a rig with red and green stripes running down the sides and a busted front turret, especially if it's escorted by junkers, steer clear. It's a Q truck and will tear you and your gang apart."

I paused at the entrance.

"You've been warned."

With that, I stepped out into the darkness and back to my bike. I flipped the switches on the power cells and rode off into the night, alone again.

Warner Robbins was just a few miles away from me as I rode down I-75. There was a sense of safety being this close to Macon, but still, it was wise to be on your guard, especially when you're a lone biker. I suppose that's why Turbine pays me the big bucks.

I had strapped a white flag to a pole on the back of my bike, letting it flap in the breeze. Flying a flag of truce wasn't a guarantee of safety by any means, but it was respected, saying you didn't want to duel. Of course, being a biker, I ran the risk of someone simply hating what I supposedly represented and wiping me off the road. Again, big bucks. Really big bucks.

This part of the freeway was in good repair, being within spitting distance of Macon. Most of the major cities and fortress towns in the Southeast maintained the system around them when they could, and Macon did a superb job at it. I was thankful for that, for if I had to get anywhere in a hurry on my bike, the road would be smooth.

Right now, however, I was in no rush. Turbine would be waiting for me to come in. Now, if I took too long, there would be consequences, of course, but that wasn't a concern now. I was going to make it on time.

Most road signs from the days before the Blight were long gone, now. They'd been blasted to dust, burned down, or simply rusted away in the harsh weather. But a few still stood sentinel along the freeway, shining down like lighthouses in the night, calling travelers to safety and rest.

That's where I was headed, one of those signs, which lit the Dine and Dash truck stop near Warner Robbins.

Back in the old days, there was a company that built these massive stores for cars, right off the freeways. A hundred and twenty pumps for gas or more, plus a gigantic convenience store the size of an aircraft hangar, filled with food, drink, and merchandise, not to mention bathrooms. These stores averaged over sixty thousand square feet, with some of the larger ones hitting seventy thousand or more in the latter years of the company.

They were remarkable sights, meccas to the traveling public, but they didn't survive the Grain Blight and WWIII. When the gas dried up, and the Free Oil States seceded, the company just withered away into nothingness, leaving behind these massive stores abandoned all over the landscape.

That's where Dine and Dash stepped in. When things settled down and the recovery happened, they went out and reclaimed a bunch of these sites throughout the southeastern United States, or what was left of them. They threw up walls and mounted weapons on them, defending them from the hordes of scum out there in the badlands, like I used to be. They built garages and mechanic shops, charging stations, and shelters for the drivers of the big rigs that were beginning to ply the routes between the big cities.

They didn't forget the little guys, too. The charging stations replaced most of the gas pumps and were the perfect size for the traveling motorist. Car washes, a thing of the past, made an appearance once again. They even included a steady supply of gear from Uncle Al's workshops. And since most of these stops were near major cities, they were safe.

To top everything off, they lit the old signs up with new lights and logos. For the final piece, they put a rotating spotlight on the sign, so that everyone knew a safe place was nearby. And it worked. People sought out these Dine and Dash truck stops to refresh, refuel, and rest.

But I would be doing none of these things, because I had a meeting to go to.

Turbine was calling.

The turret guns tracked my every move as I approached the compound. It was a bit of overkill, of course, for the firepower those turrets could bring to bear on me far outweighed any threat I represented. Now, mind you, I didn't pose a threat at all… just a lone biker on his way down south. But it pays to be cautious in a place where everyone is armed.

I motored across the Richard P. Russell Parkway and turned onto the entrance to the compound. Once I got near the Dine and Dash, the guns stopped tracking me and turned back toward the freeway. The gunners may have been curious as to what a lone biker was doing pulling into their place, but they didn't care enough to obliterate me.

It's the small things that make you feel loved.

I swung around the walls and flipped a switch on the bike. My gun ports closed up shop. This was the custom at any truck stop or fortress town; flip your safeties on when you enter. You don't want to give anyone any ideas about shooting you before you shoot them.

I guided the bike down the lane next to the store and the charging stations, heading for the truck bays. Several of the stations were occupied with various vehicles sucking down the juice to charge their batteries. Much like me, they were buttoned up. Again, a sensible precaution.

I passed those cars by, giving them little thought. They weren't my quarry tonight. No, my target was bigger.

Much bigger.

I found what I was looking for in the farthest truck bay from the entrance. It was a nice, secluded spot, away from prying eyes. This suited me just fine, for I didn't want anyone to see what I was about to do.

There was a rig in the bay. It was big, too, with red and green stripes running down the sides of its plastic armor. The mangled turret on the front top of the trailer looked like it needed to be pulled yesterday. There were armor patches everywhere on the sides of the trailer, but curiously, there were open machine gun ports on the sides as well. They'd be just enough firepower to push off the casual attack, but wouldn't be good enough in a knockdown, drag out fight.

I pulled up into the bay and alongside the rig. At this range I could reach out and touch the sides if I wanted. Which I did, as I turned off the power to the bike. In fact, I knocked on the trailer's door three times.

A moment later the bay doors began their descent. When they touched the ground, I would be sealed in with the rig and its operators, which suited me just fine. After all, this trucking company was why I was here.

The gate touched down with a clang and a hiss, and as soon as it did, I felt a heavy weight leave my shoulders. At this point I considered myself safe.

The machine gun ports along the sides of the rig closed, then opened, then closed again, all in a rapid-fire dance. A couple of them seemed to be stuck open, because those hatches just quivered, instead of closing. Maintenance, guys, maintenance.

"Turbine," I shouted to the truck. "Get your butt out here!"

"Hold your damn horses," echoed a voice over the loudspeakers. "You know this takes me a minute to get untangled."

It took a moment or two, but Turbine managed to extract himself from the driver's seat of the truck. He was a big guy, easily over three hundred and fifty pounds, with reddish-brown hair set in a buzzcut. His body armor struggled to fit well, for several of the straps were loose and bits of the suit were cracked. He preferred it that way, saying it gave him room to move. I personally worried that it wouldn't cover him in a firefight. Not that there had been one… yet.

Turbine's piercing brown eyes stared at me. I started to squirm under his gaze.

"Did I do something wrong," I asked him.

He grunted in reply. "Hardly. How did it go?"

I handed my gloves over to him and took off my helmet. I rested it in the crook of my arm and sighed. "About as good as can be expected."

"They believed you, out on 20?"

"Hook, line, and sinker, boss."

I wiped my brow clear of sweat. It was getting hot in the bay, but that couldn't be helped now. We wanted, no, needed privacy for what we were doing.

"Good, good, all good. We'll go ahead with the delivery, then."

Turbine let out a loud whistle, and the back doors to the trailer cranked open. A couple of guys hopped out and grabbed the elevator lift from under the rig. Meanwhile, a third guy had come around from the other side of the truck and grabbed my bike. As he started to take it away, I yelled at him.

"Be careful with that! That's an expensive ride, there, David."

He turned and blew me a mocking kiss. "Don't worry, sweet stuff. Your pretty lady is in good hands." He rolled the bike onto the lift a moment later and started to raise it level with the back of the trailer.

I rolled my eyes and turned back to Turbine. "Billy," I said, "I think we're in the clear on this one, but there were a lot of gangs there. Skulls, Flames, the works. Easily enough bikers there to overwhelm us under our current armament and payload."

I took a deep breath, then let it out. "I want to take some precautions this time."

"Like what?"

"I… I don't know." I just shrugged helplessly. "Extra escorts? More guns? Thicker armor?"

"Now," Turbine said, "you know we can't do that without sacrificing our cargo space and weight capacity. As for those, we need every bit of them we can spare for this load."

"And the escorts? Can we get any more?"

"We're already set up for two. What more do you want? Besides, there's two reasons we can't: budget, and trust. Budget is obvious, but where are we going to find some duellists who can keep their mouths shut over our little operation? I mean, one word in the wrong spot and we're done for."

"And if all the bikers get together and decide to attack out of revenge?"

"Then we make a break for Anniston or the D and D just outside Birmingham and hold them off for as long as we can."

One of the guys from the back of the rig stepped up to us. "The bike's secure, Turbine. We barely got it in there with all the cargo we're carrying."

I turned to Billy. "What is this crap we're taking on, anyway?"

"Don't know, don't care. The client is going to pay us a lot of money when we deliver it to Birmingham. They left strict instructions for us not to open any of the crates, and that's exactly what we're going to do. Leave them alone." He shrugged. "We've done this before. Fairly standard stuff."

"I know," I said, watching the workhand walk to the back of the trailer. "I've just got…"

"A bad feeling about this," Turbine asked, interrupting me.

"Yeah."

"So do I. That's why I sent you out there." He patted me on the shoulder. "Besides, you've got your Gold Cross contract ready for you. So, what are you worried about? Dying? You'll be back."

"You know I don't believe that. The clone's just a copy; it isn't *me*."

Turbine shrugged again. "Yeah, but I do. Gotta protect my employees."

"We're walking a fine line on this one, boss."

"I know, but they believed you, right?"

I bowed before my audience as I walked over to the cab of the truck. "Right."

Turbine didn't hear the doubt in my voice. Oh, well, opening jitters, I guess.

I hit the button for the intercom to the trailer. "How are we looking back there?"

"For the umpteenth time, man, we're fine," Thomas exclaimed.

Another voice came over the intercom. "Yeah, just peachy!"

That was David, the guy who had packed up my bike. Turbine had hired them a while back and trusted them completely, as he did me. In fact, Billy ran his outfit with a lot of trust, and I respected him for that. Few trucking companies would do that nowadays or hire former bikers such as myself.

I fell in with Turbine several years ago, after a particularly hard life as a biker. He'd been captured by the local warlord, who held a sham trial to cover his own misdeeds, and sentenced Billy to a life of torture. I didn't agree with that, not for what Turbine had done, so naturally I broke him out of 'jail' and we shot our way out of the gang, leaving a swath of wreckage and broken lives behind.

In fact, the vehicle we used for the escape was one of our escorts. We'd repainted it, rearmed it, patched it up, and did various cosmetic things to it over the years… enough, in fact, to call it a different car. This suited us both. We didn't want any loose strings to find us.

Now, that very same car was in the lead, about one hundred yards ahead of us on I-20. We were heading westbound toward Birmingham and had crossed the Georgia/Alabama border a few minutes ago, in the late afternoon. Our other escort was still in formation, holding up the rear.

"It's too quiet," I said to Turbine. "I don't like this."

"Relax, man. We haven't seen a ganger since before we left Villa Rica." Billy was squinting, peering out the windshield through the light rain falling all around us. He kept our speed down, both because of the weather and road conditions.

"I know. We should have at least spotted a lookout or scout somewhere."

"Again, relax. Your story must have worked. There's not been a bike for miles. Heck, there's not even a recent wreck we could salvage." He smiled.

We rode on, Billy humming some tune he'd heard on the radio while I kept my eyes on all the targeting screens and cameras we had on this rig. I was certain that, if there was someone planning something nasty, they'd hit us with it soon.

We crossed over into the Talladega National Forest, or what remained of it, about thirty minutes later. There'd been some wrecks to avoid, but nothing recent. Just some old junkers no one had bothered to haul away for scrap yet.

I kept my eyes tight on the scanners. This was the stretch of road I'd talked about, and I figured if the gangs were going to spring something on us, it would be here. Poetic justice and all that.

Turns out I was right.

Our lead escort, knowing about the story I'd told the gangs, was farther ahead of us than usual. He wasn't out of reach but giving us a better lead if something happened to him. A bit brave, of course, but all part of the job.

Then he came to a halt. "Turbine, we've got a problem," came over the radio, while he linked up our screens with their cameras so we could both see the same thing.

It was the Skulls biker gang, with at least fifteen bikes, maybe more. They were sitting across our side of the freeway in a line stretching from crater to crater. Their gunports were open and their hands were on the triggers.

Billy tapped the brakes and brought us to a halt at the top of the curve. He shook his head and turned toward me. "What do you think? Anybody else out there?"

I glanced over the targeting screens and monitors. Besides the bikes, there was nothing out there. No heat signatures, either. Of course, what was there was bad enough.

"The area looks clean," I said, "But as sure as I'm breathing, there's more of them out there somewhere. They're a huge gang."

"Exactly what I'm thinking." He flipped the mike to general broadcast to the team. "Options, everyone?"

"Well," our lead driver said, "we're not getting through without a fight."

"Agreed," Thomas said. "They're just begging for us to shoot our way through. I'm not sure we should."

Tracy, our tail end Charlie escort, spoke up. "Look, why aren't they ambushing us? Why wait like this, out in the open? What do they want?"

I grabbed a mic. "I have no idea. This isn't typical of a gang, especially one as ruthless as the Skulls."

Billy put his foot gently down on the juice pedal and we began to creep forward. We weren't going fast, but even with that slow speed we were running out of options. Even so, I knew Turbine was considering something. Something radical, unless I missed my guess. And it came quickly.

"Spin up the guns," Billy ordered. "I want us ready for trouble."

I flipped a couple of switches on the gunner's panel and gripped the joysticks. Our guns went hot. I pointed them at the bikers, waiting for the order to fire. But it didn't come.

"Line up behind me," he said to the two escorts.

A confused voice came over the radio. "Excuse me, Turbine, but did you just say behind you," Tracy asked.

"Yes. Get behind me; we're going through."

"Through what?"

"Them."

Tracy couldn't contain her disbelief. "At a snail's pace?"

"Exactly."

There still was no sign of any other bikers. I knew, for my eyes hadn't left the screens since we started moving. And they were going to stay there until we were out of this mess.

The two escorts wasted no time in setting up behind our vehicle once the order had been given. They maneuvered into a line behind us and matched our speed.

Right then I noticed a heat signature flare up out in the forest. "Turbine," I exclaimed, "we've got company!"

"Figured as much." His grip tightened on the steering wheel. "We're still sticking to the plan."

"Plan? What plan?"

"This one," he said.

We crept forward, slowly encroaching on the bikes. I saw the bikers crouch down on their rides, to better hide behind the armor, but none of them opened fire. I knew, if they had, this would turn into a bloodbath on both sides.

However, they didn't move. We were a hundred feet away, then eighty. At fifty feet away they still hadn't yielded and neither had we. Eventually we came nose to nose with the bikes. Before we could roll into them, Turbine brought the rig to a halt.

"Brave suckers, I'll give them that," he said.

Right then the heat signature started to move toward us at a leisurely pace. It wouldn't take long for it to get to our rig.

I was getting more nervous by the second. "Turbine, still no one on the scanners besides the lone signature. There should be more of them. Where are they?"

As we were training our guns on the heat signature, it came out of the woods. It was a bike, of course, a big one. It had glossy red armor, its guns were painted black, and there were multiple skulls strapped all over the bike.

The rider was much the same. They were wearing thick black body armor with skull motifs on the helmet and chest plate. A rifle had been strapped to their back as well as a couple of big pistols in matching holsters. I even made out a bunch of dog tags around their neck. But the most curious thing about them was what was strapped to the side of their bike: a flag of truce.

This could only be their leader.

"What the hell," Billy said, pointing to the lone biker. "A white flag?"

I toggled my own microphone to general team broadcast and spoke into it. "Stand down, everyone. Stand down."

Again, there was a chorus of confused voices on the radio.

"That's an order," Turbine said, backing up my play. "Stand down but stay ready."

"Don't be an idiot, whoever you are," I whispered to myself. "You're dead if you do anything stupid."

Within moments their leader was in front of our truck. They made sure their bike was facing us before powering down. And with a quick flick of a switch, their gunports closed. Slowly, ever so slowly, they reached up and removed their helmet. Long, black hair in a ponytail fell out of the helmet, framing their face and neck.

It was the lady who had bought me a glass of the real stuff.

She stared up into the cab, trying to see inside. Our windows were tinted, of course, to protect from blinding attacks, and armored as well, but it still felt strange.

Billy reached for the triggers, but I stopped him. "Don't. You'll call down hell on us if you shoot her now. Remember, flag of truce?"

"Right, right."

At that moment she smiled at us, then activated her headset. Her voice boomed out over hidden speakers. "Greetings. What brings you to our little neck of the woods?"

Billy looked at me, but I shook my head. "She'll recognize my voice."

"Gotcha covered." He flipped a switch on the radio. "That will disguise it."

I gave him a quizzical glance, then shrugged. "It's our funeral if you're wrong."

"I know. Do it."

I spoke into my microphone, and a voice I didn't recognize came out of our speakers. It was low-pitched and booming.

"We're making a delivery, of course."

"Really?" She shrugged. "I've heard about you."

"Nothing but good things, I hope."

She leaned back on her bike. "Let's just say I know what you have inside that truck."

The next sentence came out of my mouth on impulse. "Oh, just a big, juicy cargo. Why, is that something you'd like to have?"

"I would, but you've got us outgunned."

"What, three to one odds in your favor not good enough?"

Turbine couldn't help but stare at me.

She nodded. "Not for a rig like yours. There's no way I'm going to order my people to get slaughtered just for fun and giggles. However, if you push the issue, I'll call the rest of the gang out of the forest and we'll see who comes out on top."

Right then a bunch more heat signatures flared to life in the woods. There must have been thirty or more. I gulped, for with our current loadouts, we were sitting ducks.

"Billy," I whispered, setting the microphone down. "I don't know…"

He put his hand on my shoulder and gave it a squeeze. "You got this. I know you do," he said, reassuring me.

I picked the mic back up reluctantly. "What do you propose, then?"

She pointed at the flag. "That. A truce. You don't shoot me, and we won't shoot you. In fact, I'll even do you a step better, but on one condition."

"What?"

"Don't come back here again, or we'll see if the Skulls can earn another notch."

Moving very slowly, she turned her bike to face down I-20 toward Birmingham and powered her bike back up. She looked over her shoulder at us and nodded, revving her engine as she did.

"She can't be serious," Turbine said. "She's going to escort us?"

"Looks that way."

"That's pure sass, then."

I took my hands off the gunner controls and leaned back into my seat. "Look, Billy, this is symbolic. Her gang's mere presence will keep all the other gangs out here off our backs. I say we go for it and accept."

"You're sure?"

"Positive."

"Then let's roll."

Billy stepped lightly on the accelerator while ordering our escorts to move out. As we started to move, the bikes parted and moved up to our point position, with their leader at the very front.

We picked up speed, leaving the area behind us. Tracy and our other car quickly spread out behind us.

"Good plan, having me go out and spread the word," I said to Billy, matching his glance.

"Naturally. Now, let's get out of here."

"Sure thing." A thought occurred to me. "You know what we would be if these gangs ever found out we *aren't* a Q truck?"

"What?"

"Easy pickings."

Billy chuckled as he hit our cruising speed. We rode off into the night, leaving dust and trouble in our wake.

Over the Hill
by Jesse M. Slater

"You're too slow, Joe!" Sagebrush Sarah Vermilion caroled as her bright yellow Conquistador Caballero sped by on the right.

"That ain't what you said last night, Red," Joe Laramie grated into the mic.

"Takin' your time might be alright for some things, loverboy, but drivin' ain't one!"

"Slow is about the only choice we have going up this grade, Sarah." Tiny Tim Holden, one of the owners and operators of Holden Brothers Trucking cut in. "You know that. But if you wanna be useful while you're showing off up there, why don't you scout out the next few overpasses?"

"Yessa, boss."

"If you shake anything loose, holler," Joe said. "I'll be right there."

Joe and Sarah had both been "perpetual contenders," always in the top ten, or top five on the autoduel circuit, where they had been friendly rivals. Joe had never been as flashy as Sarah, far less someone like Danny Cruze. Neither of them had won with anything like the regularity needed to attract the big money backers though, and they'd decided convoy duty paid better. Working for the Holdens, they had become considerably more friendly. Maybe her namesake red hair, or maybe her own natural cussedness was to blame, but sometimes being "friendly" with Sarah Vermilion was like being friendly with a porcupine.

The rest of the time, though… He had a sudden flash of memory. Sarah watching him shave that morning, before they joined the others to pre-trip the rigs, and make sure that all the damage from the previous day's adventures had been repaired. Sitting there, with her fiery curls trailing down her bare shoulders to— *Keep your mind on the job, Joe.* He shook his head. *Yeah, Sage, you need me, I'll come a-runnin'.*

Joe rolled slow, scanning both sides of the road, while behind him the twins' matching antique hot-rod tractors brought the road train along, black smoke gushing from their pipes. At the back of the train, fittingly for the wasteland of Nevada, Janis and her boys in the Combat Caboose rode like the sting in a scorpion's tail.

"It's getting steeper! Split down in three… two… one… now!" The radio crackled and Tiny Tim Holden—so named by a wag when the six-foot-five-inch, three-hundred-pound man had joined the Brotherhood—appreciated the warning. His twin, in the lead tractor of the road train, got all the views this trip. Tim, in his grandfather's antique Peterbilt, pushed up the rear. He was already in the bottom half of the eighteen-speed transmission, but a million pounds is a million pounds. He heard the *chik* of the air-shifter as he eased off the throttle. The big transmission split down the half gear, and he let the full power of his custom installed 3412 V-12 Caterpillar diesel free again.

He scanned his gauges, 1,400 rpm, right in the big motor's sweet spot. Pyrometer, oil, and coolant temps all read a little high, but that was only to be expected. Cranking out 1,500 horses at twenty-two mph would do that sort of thing. Not many truckers would venture out here. Sweet Caroline Carriers had, but after what happened to Gary… well, best not to dwell. For the Holdens, it was just another day, moving freight over Battle Mountain.

On the long flat stretches of I-80, with miles of empty country to either side, maybe a low hill here and there, each brother pulled his own train. Sometimes there was sagebrush to look at, or creosote brush. Sometimes there wasn't even that much, just bare dirt and rock. On the grades they doubled over the hump. With one set of trailers under guard at the bottom, both trucks together powered the huge loads over the mountain, before they went back to get the other.

"Grade's easing! Grab a gear… now!" With the ease of long practice, the two brothers shifted as one, even though half a dozen trailers and a million pounds of freight lay between them.

"I've got heat signatures!" The radio crackled.

"Copy that, Sarah, I'll be right there!"

"Joe!" Tim radioed sharply, "Before you go haring off, do you see anything around?"

"Not a thing, Tiny."

"You, Janis?"

"Clear here, Tiny."

"Get out of here, Joe!"

The only acknowledgment was the roar of Joe Laramie's engine as he sped off. *You'd never know that girl was a top gun herself, the way he dotes on her.*

Tim looked to his own firepower, nonetheless. Until the convoy topped the grade, they were sitting ducks. The remote turret on the roof with its quad mount .50 cals powered up. The best of old and new, a HUD lit the windscreen in front of him. The trailers blocked the view in front of him, sharply limiting his field of fire, but he scanned to the sides.

"What'cha got, Sage?" Joe asked as he flew up the desert highway. It felt good to be *moving* again, after the convoy's plodding pace.

"There's six of them, it looks like. The main two up on the bridge, with more off to either side, in the brush."

"How'd you spot them?" he asked, grabbing another gear.

"Thermal, like I said. They're glowing like candles in the dark."

"In this heat? Someone would have to try to leave that much heat signature."

"Bandits, ain't real famous for their smarts, Joe."

"A bandit that don't have some brains don't live real long, Sage." He slowed for a bend. Going 140 miles an hour worked fine on the straights, but would turn a beautiful car into a substandard airplane on these curves.

"Hell, you ought to be comin' in range. See what you think."

"Has anything moved? Have you taken any fire?"

"Of course not. They's waitin' on the train, ain't they?"

"And you're what, just sitting there watching, and they haven't done anything?" Joe drummed his fingers on the wheel. Hairs prickled the back of his neck.

"Well…"

"Come on, Sarah, let's get back. If they're not moving, the Caboose can hit them harder than we can. But I've got a bad feeling someone *did* try to leave signatures out here, to draw us off."

"We're taking fire, repeat, taking fire!" "Little" John Holden barked into the microphone. *Both perimeter cars out of pocket. Of course.* "I don't see any vehicles, but some yahoo with a MANPAT just popped up." *If these guys have rocket launchers…*

"You sound alright, John, but how's the truck?"

"Thanks for your concern, little brother. The armor took it, but you know it'll probably be expensive to make it pretty again."

John didn't have the time or the mental wherewithal to engage a target as small as a single man, even one with an anti-tank rocket. He had his hands full keeping the rig on an even keel. But he selected the area on his display, and relayed the information to Janis in the Caboose.

"Don't worry, Little John, we're on it," was her response only seconds later. Moments later, the five-inch gun—a piece of true artillery copied from the submarine deck guns of a century and a half before—began to speak. John didn't watch the resulting fireball. *If arms and legs are raining down, they can do it without me.*

From the brush on either side, armed bandit cars roared, dust and gravel spitting from their wheels. "And we've got company! Joe! Sage! Where the hell are you?"

"One minute out, boss!"

"I'm gonna dock your bonus for this!"

Several of the bandits, he counted four heavily armed cars, had raced ahead, to try to set up a block. Two more were crawling along next to his cab. "Janis! Can you clear these flies away?"

"Sorry, John. I can't guarantee hitting them and not you, the way we're all wiggling around. That's what the cars are for."

"You hear that, Joe?" When he looked down again, he saw a turret swiveling his way. *Can't have that.* He jerked the wheel hard left, and the whole massive train went that way. The bandit car, heavily armored as it was, didn't stand a chance against the mass and power of the ancient Peterbilt. The truck wiped the turret right off the side, half crushed the car, and forced it into the median.

"Son of a biiiiitch!"

The jerk John had made in the lead tractor, a hundred yards ahead of the Combat Caboose, transmitted and amplified through every step in the line of trailers, like a whip cracking. It was a miracle they didn't flip, but still a wild ride. Janis Arbruzzo-Holden let go of the butterfly trigger like a hot potato and clutched the arms of her gunner's chair. There was no sense in stitching the convoy with their own machine guns.

When the worst of the whiplash subsided, she scanned for targets. The sensors of both trucks and both cars fed data to the Caboose for a fairly complete picture on the screen. She designated targeting priorities for the five-inch. As it began to fire, lobbing its shells high over the convoy, she looked for a new home for some of her very expensive .50 caliber API, or armor piercing incendiary ammunition.

She found the target she sought, a bandit's Indra Wyvern. She didn't know where it had come from, but it hovered in her sights now, and that was what mattered. A quick press on the trigger, and a cloud of flame expanded, flecked black with the shards of armor, bits of engine, and one recognizable wheel that sailed away on the shockwave. She could hear the shrapnel on the armor, like hail on a tin roof.

"I love the smell of burning bandit in the morning!" she chortled into the radio.

"Whoever thought this roadblock idea up wasn't expecting us to be behind him," Joe drawled into the microphone. "That must have been a secondary ambush up there, with the heaters going to get our attention."

"My attention, you mean."

"No, I mean ours. I came a-runnin, too." Joe opened the red plastic guard.

"Because I hollered, not 'cause you was taken in."

"Come on, ain't no sense crying for spilt milk. Right now, it works for us. We can ram missiles up their asses; they ain't lookin' for us back here."

"Oh, right. And missiles might even blow them clear of the road, too."

"Great minds, my love, great minds," Joe rasped. "Now, you take the two on the left, I'll take the two on the right."

Sarah's voice on the radio perked up at that. "Just you make sure you've got solid lock, man of mine. I don't think ol' Little John wants to be looking down the nose cone of any misses…"

Of course he wouldn't launch without a lock, but he chuckled and said "You're as right as you are beautiful. Ready? In three, two, one!"

Two missiles from each escort car streaked toward the stationary bandits. The lighter rear armor didn't even try to slow down their heavy penetrating warheads and in mere moments, the two former rivals were treated to a spectacular bit of pyrotechnics as the fuel cells and onboard ammunition cooked off.

"John, looks like the road is clear, except for some debris."

"Consider your bonuses reinstated," John said with a sigh. It had been an effort to release his white-knuckled grip on the wheel long enough to grasp the mic. Those missiles streaking toward him… even if they had hit the bandit cars on the way… he gulped.

"Thanks, boss," came the honeyed voice of Sagebrush Sarah.

"I caught some of you two's chatter, were you saying there's another ambush up yonder?"

"Yeah. Sage saw some major IR signatures up there. But in this heat, what stands out that bright?"

"Hang on. Grade's easing. Timmy, you awake back there?" he asked.

"Huh? What? Are we there yet?"

"Pour another cup of coffee, brother, we've got work to do. Grab a gear… now!"

"Now?" Tim asked, mock querulously. "I was just pouring the coffee."

Obviously he hadn't missed his shift; the massive road train was picking up speed. A mile or two an hour, anyhow.

"Anyway. Joe. Ambush."

"Right. Too bright, can't be anything but a trap, that's my guess."

"Sage?"

"I agree, now. I just thought they was bandits at first."

"Do you think the heaters were just to pull you guys out of position? Or are there more?"

"Bandits ain't too bright," Sarah opined. "Probably designed to pull us off. But we came back, so they kinda ambushed themselves."

"I say we ought to keep on. If they had more, they'd have used them. They're not going to divide their band, just to hit us twice. They'd want to hit hard and fast and win it," Joe said.

"If you both agree, then I guess we keep on. There's not really a good way to turn around, or go around, anyhow."

"Just to be on the safe side," Tiny Tim put in, "why don't you feed the coordinates of those targets you saw to Janis?"

"Even if they were bandits," Janis said, "the boys and I can make them lie down and be good bandits."

As the coordinates came through, she ran the numbers for each shot. Eminently doable for the big five-inch. At that range, they should probably stop the road train, though, to make sure of the shots.

"If you see a spot you think you can get rolling again, why don't you stop? Give us a better shot."

"Fine, Janis. Isn't that motion stabilizer up to the job? It cost a pretty penny."

"With a smoother ride, it might do, but between your driving and Nevada roads, this is the surer shot."

"Ouch, touche!"

"First blood to Janis Arbruzzo!" Tim intoned in his best autoduel announcer voice.

"You're not helping, Tiny," she said. "The least you could have done is teach that ape how to drive before you turned him loose on an unsuspecting world."

"Me?" Tim asked. "I'm just his brother. You're his wife. Can't you tame him?"

The bickering went on, as it usually did, while the massive rig came to a halt. On a grade as steep as this, it didn't take much; it took a few thousand horsepower to keep them moving at all.

"Designate targets one through six," she said, her voice now cool and professional. "Gun crew, engage at will."

The gun was already trained in the direction of number one, and the gunner depressed his firing key the moment she spoke. The huge breech shot backwards, and the loader swung into action. Drawing a round from the ready magazine, the loader shoved it in and closed the breech. A tap on the shoulder told the gunner he was clear, and the gun barked a second time. In less than a minute, all the targets had been serviced. Janis knew from long experience the high arcing rounds tracked straight and true, but the shoulder of the mountain obscured what damage they may have done.

"We can keep hitting them, but that's about as well as we can do without spotting," she told the radio.

"Then that's as good as we'll get, for now." Tiny's voice sounded thoughtful. "We lost the last drone yesterday. I don't think we want to send the outriders off again, do we?"

"Well, let's get to it." John hung up the mic and began to shift. The lowest gear he had was just barely adequate to get the enormous weight moving. He didn't dare use too much power; a driveshaft twisted off out here would spell disaster. But then, so would a burnt clutch. It was a balancing act. But with the push from behind, the seven B-train trailers of the road train, each carrying as much freight as a standard rig weighed altogether, groaned into motion.

He set the jakes to bring the rpm down faster, and shifted, and shifted again. The fifth gear got them up to almost a jogging pace, when a fully accoutered battle rig crested the hill. It looked to have a dozen outriders, some in cars, most on motorcycles, swarming around it.

"Guys! We've got company!"

"What's up?" his brother asked. "I can't see a thing… oh, shit. I just slaved your camera. That's… big."

The battle rig looked like it had once been a Kenworth. There were probably still some Kenworth parts under all the guns and armor, but it was hard to be sure, with the sun glinting off the mirage. Its trailer looked to have been a flatbed at one time, but now had two twin-gun, superfiring turrets built onto it.

"Janis!" John shouted into the mic. "Is this what you were shooting at? I don't think it took."

"I was shooting at numbers on a map grid. I'm not responsible for this thing!"

"We're all responsible for it now, babe."

"Right. Good point."

The massive road train still only rolled about as fast as a man could run. In between splitting gears, and coordinating that with Tiny, John studied his HUD. The motorcycles shouldn't present much trouble, the train had lots of machine guns. The bikes were going to be toast. The cars weren't much more of a problem. But… the battlewagon.

John had thought the Holden Brothers to be quite forward thinking when they designed the Combat Cabooses. Five-inch guns? That'd be the first time naval artillery ever went on a road trip. Or at least he had thought so. Now he saw a purpose-built wasteland monster, and it had him badly outgunned. Not one five-inch gun, but four of the things. It really was a battleship on wheels.

Just then, he heard the reports behind him as his warrior bride opened fire. He increased the magnification on the HUD, which always made him queasy when he drove, but he needed to be able to see. She was good at her job, Janis was. She had fired a time-on-target salvo, and the three rounds—one arcing high, one almost a straight line, and one somewhere in between—all impacted together. But the solid front glacis of the battlewagon seemed undamaged.

He had to look away then, frustration and nausea combining to roil his stomach.

"No effect, honey," he said. "We'd better think of something quickly, we're not moving fast, but that thing is."

"Come on, Sage," Joe Laramie said, as he punched the throttle. "We can't do any good from back here. Maybe that thing's got a weak spot."

"It's got to," she said. "It's still a truck, no matter how big it is. Radiator? Tailpipe? Tires?"

"If it's not electric, or one of those new reactor rigs." He checked his own rig. Still two missiles, and magazines for the machine guns were full. "If that thing's a nuke, you might be calling me Glowin' Joe tonight."

"You'd enjoy that way too much."

The battlewagon moved steadily down the grade, not really flying. The outriders, though, seemed intent on closing the gap as quickly as possible. *That makes sense. If I was on one of those suicide machines, I'd hate to spend any longer in the open than I had to.* He snorted. His own speedometer, hill and all, hovered near a hundred. At that speed, it would take hardly any time at all to meet them.

"We don't want to stay and tangle with these jokers," he told her. "The train's guns can cope with them."

"Roger that," she replied. "Targets of opportunity, but break on through to the other side."

"That's right. No time to run. No time to hide. Just break on through."

Then the first line of motorcycles was on them. The machine guns made quick work of two, but the third jinked and the stream of tracers cut air behind him. Instincts from the track nearly caused Joe Laramie to throw the rig into a moonshiner's turn and go after the missed target, but his brain overrode. *Break on through,* he told himself.

In a moment, the second line of two cars and two bikes were on him. The cars targeted him with their own guns. The armor took most of it, but his windshield crazed in a dozen places. The bulletproof glass held, however, even against their high-power rounds.

From the corner of his eye, he saw the two bikers shredded to red mist as Sarah's guns took them. Joe himself held his fire, but pivoted the machine guns, usually slaved together, to opposite sides. A split second before he passed between the two, he stabbed down on the firing key, and stitched tungsten-cored 7mm rounds down the sides of both bandit buggies. *Amateurs. But what to do about that battlewagon,* he wondered.

Several of the bikes appeared to have mounted guns of their own, and they began to strafe him. In between jinking to avoid as much of the incoming fire as he could, he snatched a hand from the wheel to press the "VOX" switch. He was old enough and set firmly enough in his ways that he hated computer assistance, but there were times when it was just what the driver ordered.

"Computer," he said, "scan oncoming ironclad. Determine weaknesses, if any." *There. Let it do that work, while I focus on these putt-putts.*

One bike was deliberately targeting his wheels. Runflats or not, bullets lodged in the rubber or taking chunks out of the rim could be deadly. A wheel flying off, or even a bit out of balance, would end an autoduellist's day in a hurry. Or his life.

Joe steered into the stream of fire, taking it on the more heavily protected hood, before it tracked up his windscreen. *Damn. It's not going to take much more of that.* He felt a hot breeze fill the cabin, along with a stream of grit like a sandblaster. *Not much at all.*

The bike swerved, trying to dodge the heavy ram on Joe's grille guard. *We can't have that.* He dropped a gear and nailed the throttle. The rear end swung out hard and fast, *the beauty of 900 horsepower,* he thought, and like a six-ton flyswatter, the heavily armed and armored car reduced the biker to a crimson aerosol.

Steering into the skid, he recovered, just in time for another of the bikes to break off its headlong charge and turn in pursuit. *Maybe his buddy.* It didn't matter, though, he had things to do.

"Sage, honey? Can you scratch my back?"

"Roger, wilco. Anything else you need… scratched?"

"Not right now," he said with a chuckle. "Just a little relief from that two-wheeled flea."

"Coming right up!"

Indeed, in his mirror, he saw that she didn't even deviate from her line of attack, just swiveled a gun in the direction of the offending two-wheeler, and a line of glowing tracers stitched the biker, who slumped from the saddle. The bike of course kept going, gyroscopic forces being what they were. It did slow, with no hand on the throttle.

"Computer, how's it going? I'm going to need that targeting analysis."

"Weaknesses detected. Armor weakening under bombardment. Exhaust ports hypothesized to be in rear. Armor hypothesized thinner in rear. Cooling system hypothesized undermount or rear mount."

Stupid machine. That's about what I figured. "Clarify location of cooling, computer."

"Undermount cooling hypothesis supported by thermal imagery."

"Computer, switch HUD to thermal." Another of the pesky bikers needed killing right then, but he focused on getting the information he needed on the larger threat, and barely noticed doing it, so automatic had dealing death become.

On the thermal, he could see what the machine meant. The swirling slipstream behind the huge desert dreadnought was far hotter than it ought to be. He zoomed to see where the gradient began. *Bingo,* he thought. The heated air started right under the reactor, as he expected, but intensified just forward of the rear tractor wheels. *That's the radiator. Now, how to get at it?*

He jerked and spun the wheel as he fought his car on mental autopilot, while his mind sorted the problem. "Computer, update missiles with highlighted target."

"Updated."

"Computer, push targeting package to Unit Two."

"Transfer complete."

"Sage, I just sent you…"

"…so don't be too surprised."

"Copy plan, Joe. Godspeed," said John Holden.

John had just been treated to a virtuoso performance of automotive combat, the likes of which was rarely equaled even by the top national professionals. To clear the field of so many opponents in so little time, all while generalling a plan against the oncoming ironclad? He just had to shake his head. While the two combat cars had been madly gyrating and spitting fire at bike, car, and the odd drone, the train had kept grinding up the grade. A few leakers had made it past, but the quad mount .50s had made short work of them.

The behemoth battlewagon, though, that thing had them all worried. It hadn't started shelling the train yet, John presumed, because whoever organized this attack wanted their cargo intact. If they didn't trust their gunners to hit only the power units or the Combat Caboose, and not the valuable freight, then that would explain the continued silence of the big guns. They must be waiting to close the range.

His warrior woman had no such inhibitions, however. "Joe says his computer analysis shows your shots having effect, Jan, so keep up the good work. The tighter you can group them, the better chance they have of punching the armor."

"Roger, dear," she said. Not long after, the big gun, the sting in the tail of the train, started to speak again. She hit the hulking rig again and again, but rarely in the same place. At these ranges, and from a moving gunnery platform, even hitting the thing more often than missing was impressive, he reminded himself.

"You're hitting it," he relayed, "but not punching through. Your hits aren't well concentrated."

"You think you can do better, smart guy?" she snapped.

"I know I can't. I'm just relaying what I'm seeing."

Silence. *That's always worrisome. I'll probably regret that.* The next salvo, however, was another time-on-target strike clustered very tightly indeed. *Do I dare compliment her? Do I dare not?*

It seemed to have stirred the bandits in their thumping great ironclad. A few seconds later, all four of the battlewagon's big guns spoke. He'd been watching for it, and steered as far across the roadway as he could. Three of the shells landed where the train had been. The fourth dug a crater mere feet in front of the long nose of the custom Pete.

"BRACE—" was all he had time for, before the rig bounced down into the hole. It bounced out again, but it set up a terrible swaying and jerking in the trailers behind.

"I think you rang its bell, Jan," he said, when he had the rig more or less under control again.

"Whatever that was sure rang mine!"

With the four big barrels of the battlewagon pointed at the train, the two outriders had made their move. They had swung off the road and vanished into the sagebrush, while the gargantuan rig had its eyes on the train. When the shot presented, the two seasoned autoduellists salvoed their remaining missiles into the sides of the battlewagon. Clouds of steam joined the fireballs of the missiles.

For almost thirty seconds, the monstrous thing continued to close on the road train. John's heart beat harder, he couldn't get much closer to that thing. Even an incompetent fool of a gunner would have to be able to hit the power units and not the cargo at some point.

Then the great beast of the desert ground to a halt. John would have whooped, but he had things to do. "Everyone hold on, the big ironclad is out of action, but it's still blocking the road. Here we go!"

With that he steered deliberately, steadily into the median. They weren't traveling fast, but it was a desperate gamble. His tractor and the first few trailers swayed to the left, then swung like inverted pendula back to the right when he started up the far side. The trailers still coming down swayed in opposition and the whole train groaned at the incredible shearing force applied to frames, to couplers, to fifth wheels and kingpins.

By a miracle nothing actually sheared off, and they were up on the eastbound side of I-80. Fortunately, no other traffic came their way. For some reason not many people passed this way anymore. The bandits, the relief convoys like his, and that was about it. Even in the days before the blight, this had been desperately empty country, but now it was desperately empty except for bloodthirsty bandits. What infrastructure and support there once may have been were long gone.

As the rig passed the battlewagon, its turrets didn't even swivel to follow them. Whatever was out must have disabled their hydraulics too, he thought with grim satisfaction.

"Well done, outriders!" he said into the microphone. "Consider your bonuses doubled, after that show. That was truly fantastic."

"I'll hold you to that, boss," Joe Laramie growled.

"Eh, money is nice and all," said Sarah, "but right now I want a bonus I can drink!"

The rest of the ascent had been business as usual. A long slow climb, and lots of empty country to look at. Joe and Sarah took their conversation off the main channel. The others hadn't had much interest in their plans for that liquid bonus (in both senses of liquidity) but they'd had a lot to talk about. Especially about what might happen after that bonus, if they could make Reno that night.

"I want a nice long soak. Let's get a room with real plumbing, and we can wash this damned desert off," Sarah said. "Then, after that, we'll see if there's a bottle of champagne left in the town. You and me, lover."

"That sounds nice, Sage, but bubbles? Really? You don't want to put the cash into something… you know, solid? Like getting out of the life?"

"Getting out? What would we do if we couldn't do this? Raise cockatiels?"

"Raise cocka-whats?"

"If you two can spare us a moment," Janis's cool, professional voice cut in. *Damn.* Well, it was still a Holden frequency, after all. They weren't *that* private.

"What's up, Jan?"

"That big battlewagon is behind us."

"What? That thing shouldn't be on the road again this fast."

"I told you, you should have blasted it on the way by, Jan."

"They were helpless, Sage. There's a difference between shooting someone in the heat of battle, and cold murder."

"Cold murder is the practical choice sometimes, my dear," said John.

"Well, it's back there, and it's firing. We didn't hurt it as bad as we thought, or they fixed it somehow. Does it really matter?" Janis's voice showed the strain.

"Save the junior debate club for Reno," growled Joe. "What are we going to do about it, now?"

"I've got a clear shot, pretty much point blank," said Janis. That meant they were close enough the big gun didn't need any extra elevation. She could aim straight at the target, just like a rifle.

That was the norm with small arms, but when artillery reached point blank, someone had screwed up badly. *In this case, that's us,* Joe thought. *We were too busy making plans for a hot date, and we weren't watching six as well as we ought to.*

"And we're almost to the crest of the grade," added John. "The pace might pick up a bit from here."

Tiny Tim piped up for the first time in a while. "Joe, Sage, you take positions at four and eight. That way you're clear of Janis and her gun, and can make sure that big bastard didn't bring any friends. When we top the hill, we'll get going."

"Don't you want someone clearing the way?" Joe dropped back, but both cars to the rear seemed odd.

"Just stay out of the way. The road's pretty straight, and it'd be a strange ambush that picked the downhill side. Nah, we'll just make a run for the other train. They won't want to tangle with four duellists, two armed Cabooses, and a company of merc guards. We've just gotta get there."

"You make it sound so easy, Boss," Sarah chimed in. Joe could see she was already in position, though.

Joe Laramie's skin prickled. He tried to scan ahead, thinking some bandit might still be waiting there. The Caboose's big five-inch went to rapid fire, and his car rocked from the concussive muzzle blasts. He scanned his mirrors, the rear cameras, and the HUD, but he didn't see any auxiliaries around the battlewagon. No more combat cars, no more silly putt-putts. His missiles, the only thing he had heavy enough to touch something like that were expended. He felt useless and exposed, just hanging back there.

Tim Holden felt the road start to tilt down, and suddenly they were accelerating, as the back of the rig went over the crest.

"I'm not gonna call 'em," his brother's voice crackled from the radio. "Just wind 'em out and jake shift. Don't worry about the half gears."

"Roger!" *Drive like we're empty, got it. With the hill's help, it should work.*

The massive rig shot down the hill, picking up speed like a racer. In no time at all, he hit top gear, bouncing off the red line. They were rolling over a hundred miles an hour, and still the battlewagon kept pace.

"That's all I've got!" he called into the mic.

"Are you ready for wild ride, little brother?"

"What in hell do you call this?" Terrifying, Tim called it. He couldn't see anything ahead, but the rear of the trailer he pushed. Behind he saw the flashes of the battlewagon's guns. On either side the sagebrush and power poles flashed by at an alarming rate. Every bump, every sway, every jiggle of the enormous conglomeration of equipment magnified. *If he thinks it's wild up there…*

"Kick it into Georgia overdrive, then."

"Are you crazy?"

"Yes. Aren't you? I thought that's why we took this job. We're the only ones crazy enough to do it."

"Dammit, John. Fine. Georgia overdrive." Tim stomped down on the clutch and slid the shifter into neutral. Without the engines to restrain them, the mighty road train went right on accelerating. He ran out of speedometer; he didn't know how fast they were going, but John was going to owe him a very large bottle of something very strong, and very old. Preferably from Scotland.

Joe gaped in astonishment when the massive train slingshotted forward. The fire from the battlewagon intensified, but it was dropping behind. It landed several shots on the Combat Caboose, but Janis's armor held.

Joe let out a long breath he hadn't known he was holding. It looked like they had gotten aw—

From the corner of his eye he saw, literally *saw* one of the battlewagon's shells miss wide of the Caboose. It arced in, and he saw it land directly on Sagebrush Sarah Vermilion. The beautiful, fiery, passionate woman whom he had come to treasure, even to love in these few days, snuffed out like a candle. The yellow speedster vanished for a moment in the fireball. When he saw it again it was cartwheeling down the road.

A howl of anguish rose up in his throat, but he choked it back. No time for that now. There'd be time for that when they got off this accursed mountain. Then he could mourn, then he could wait. In a few months, the Gold Cross membership would pay off, and she'd…

The howl did break loose that time. She'd be born again, and she'd remember nothing. All that had happened, all they had been to each other on this trip had all happened *on this trip*. Since their last upload.

That was the last straw in Joe Laramie's mind.

He spun the car into a moonshiner's turn. He didn't even think, his hands on the wheel and his feet on the pedals worked of their own accord after the years, the decades of grueling practice had burned the responses into his muscles, his synapses.

"Janis," he said, clicking to a private freq, "when we meet again, tell us… about us, will you?"

"Where are you going, Joe?"

He made no answer. That thing would not claim any more of his friends, not if Joe Laramie could help it.

"Computer, radar plot projectiles. Display on HUD."

The computer made no acknowledgment, but suddenly there were arcing tracks on his display. Ballistics was a simple science for a computer like his. "Project impacts." They now showed their dashed trails ahead, with likely impact points. He drove like he had never driven before. Into a hail of fire, the results of which he had just seen, but he jinked and jerked the car around all of it. No shell touched him. He shot past the battlewagon so quickly that its machine guns had little time to bear. If any hit, he didn't notice.

Again, he slewed the car into the turn, this time to catch the desert dreadnought. From the rear, maybe it would be more vulnerable. Even something that big couldn't be armored everywhere, could it? He found a likely spot, a bit of skirting that covered the rear tires, and depressed the trigger. Tracers arced from his guns, and between every pair of tracers, five rounds of AP. He watched his magazine levels fall. He braced to see the tires blow. The wheels come bouncing off. The huge trailer with turrets mounted sway out of control and flip the truck.

None of it happened. Even here, this crazy, monstrous rig was armored, and armored heavily enough to withstand his guns. Their indicators flashed red, but still he fired, hoping to bore through, if he couldn't punch through.

Nothing. His guns clocked out. Empty. And all for nothing. NOTHING! He roared incoherently and punched the wheel. Then he remembered: out of the corner of his eye as he'd flashed by, he'd seen the hole in the skirting that the missiles had torn.

Now he steered right and sped alongside the massive truck. "Computer, steer parallel to target. Computer, open driver door."

With those accomplished, he leaped for the hole in the skirting. He had no weapons remaining, none but himself. A moment later, he thought, and he wouldn't have had that. Heavy machine gun rounds from the battlewagon strafed through his car, and with the door open, there was no armor to stop them.

Pity, he thought. That had been a good car. But he wouldn't need it anymore.

He looked to see where he had landed. He was on an armored belly pan under the trailer. *They even armored the belly. Who armors the belly?*

He looked around and saw the perfect target, right in front of him. The air lines. No dangling pigtails like a civilian rig. No, these were armored, and run inside an armored compartment. But that's what they were: air lines. A minute's work with his screwdriver, and the armor was pried away. A quick slash with the mono-molecular ceramic blade of his knife, and the air gushed into his face. For a moment. Then, with no air in the red line, all the brakes on the trailer locked at once.

"My God," came Janis's soft voice over the radio. "Oh my God."

Tim was watching too, in the display relayed from the Caboose's cameras. Their inveterate pursuer first seemed to stand on the brakes, but then the throttle as well. Tim didn't know what they had in that thing for a powerplant, but it overpowered six axles of brakes, and dragged that huge, armed and armored thing until several tires wore through and exploded. The huge ironclad lurched to the side, slewed around, and then seemed to be in slow motion as it tumbled, over and over.

"What the hell did he do that for? We were getting away!" John demanded, over the radio.

"If you don't know, I'm certainly not telling you," Janis snapped.

"Because of her? Dammit! Forget Gold Cross. Hell, forget New-U, too. I ought to send both their contracts to Clones-R-Us, for that. Such a stupid—"

"Guys, I don't think we have time for this," Tim put in. "Look at *our* tires!"

Tim had an excellent view up the side of the train, every time it took a slight bend to the left. Most of the tires were running in a purple haze. They weren't rated for anything like this speed, and especially not at this load, nor on a hot day in the Nevada desert. They were hot, and only minutes, or maybe seconds, from failing.

"We've got to back it down!"

"Tim, we're still four or five miles from the bottom."

"We're going to end up just like that battlewagon if we start cooking off tires, John. We need to slow down."

"But we're going too fast to get back in gear!"

"I know, damn it. I told you you were crazy. This is why! We've got to try, though."

"Well, OK. Turn on the magnets, and see what that gets us."

The magnets, what had once been called regenerative braking, did help. They stopped the runaway, but without the engine and its jakes, not much more.

"We're going to have to try the service brakes too, John."

"OK, mountain drill. Brake hard for five, then off."

On the first application, they lost an appreciable amount of speed. The gauge still did not help. They let the brakes cool for a few seconds and tried again. Again and again, they braked, and each time they had to push harder for less result.

They were down to 120 MPH, however. "We're just going to have to go for it!" Every time they rested the brakes, the speed climbed again.

"Right. One last go. We've got to get back in gear and get the jakes working. Aaaand…. NOW!"

As one, the brothers stepped on the brake. The application gauge spiked, and speed started to bleed off. But energy can be neither created nor destroyed, only transformed. In the case of brakes, the tremendous amount of kinetic energy contained in the runaway rig transformed into heat, through the friction of the brakes.

They could only absorb so much heat. The rotors were glowing red, and every time the pads touched them, they just smoked. Every wheel on the truck rolled with white smoke, and the smell of burning brakes and hot rubber was enough to choke Tim to the point of retching, even with the cab sealed tight.

But they were down to 106. "Now or never, John!" he shouted, between coughing fits.

"Now, then!"

Together, they revved their huge Caterpillar diesels to the max and jammed the shifters into gear. It wasn't a pretty shift. Gears clashed and the trucks rocked, but they went into gear. No driveshaft twisted off, and the transmissions did not shatter. Then they were off the throttle, and the jakes began to crackle. A more welcome sound Tim Holden did not think he had ever heard.

Now, he thought, reaching for his map, *where can we limp that would have 136 tires, sixty-four sets of brake pads, and a really, really nice bottle of scotch? We are gonna need it. Tonight, we drink to Joe and Sage.*

Not My First Rodeo
By T.M. Gray

Mara RidgeBear looked out the kitchen window at the slowly turning windmill across the pastures, open phone forgotten in her hand.

Would it never stop raining?

First, the call from Goldcross three weeks ago saying they had activated her husband Zane's insurance policy for cloning because he died in the Cody Annual Rodeo and AutoDuel. Seth, their eldest, had brought the rest of the kids home in the convoy with their two closest neighbors. The other kids had already taken part in CARAD's horse and motorcycle divisions, as well as the 4H and FFA judging.

A week ago, TC broke her arm falling off the water tower while helping her brother.

And now this.

"Mrs. RidgeBear? Are you there? Ms. Mara?"

The tinny voice from the phone brought her back. She lifted it and spoke.

"Yes, I'm here, Maple. Did they say why they were moving the cattle auction up so early?"

"No. Maybe? They said something about the rain, or the train? I don't remember. Papa wants to know what we are going to do without Mr. Zane to lead the convoy to the stockyards in Cheyenne. Mrs. RidgeBear?"

Maple was sixteen, the same age as her twins, but as a girl, she was far more inclined to worry. Mara made a snap decision.

"Let your father and the other neighbors know I will lead the convoy. I'll let the Cattle Association know, too." Mara didn't wait for the answer, but hung up. She didn't want to second guess herself; it had been a long time since she had rode shotgun with Zane.

She went over lists in her mind. Some feeder steers would be a little under ideal weight, but if they had an easy ride, they shouldn't lose too much from stress.

And we need the money.

GoldShield still needed a large final payment for physical therapy and all the other little expenses for when Zane's new body finished growing. Cloning was hard to think about, so she mostly didn't. Sometimes she worried how he might see her from his new 25-year-old body, while hers showed that she had six kids and lots of ranch work under her belt in their twenty-year marriage.

She shook the thoughts away, picked up the two-way handset, and called a meeting. Three days prep instead of two months was going to be tight.

Mara was thankful once again that her parents, Oma and Opa, lived with them. They would preside over the ranch while she and the older kids were gone. It might only be two days, but the farm chores and watching for varmits—both animal and human—waited for no one.

Sam, their only hired hand, and twelve-year-old TC with the extra guard dogs, including Zane's herding dog, Anna, would stay to help them.

TC had strict instructions to stay away from the water tower while they were gone. Seth had maintained it since his father's death. The tower was crucial for the ranch, not only to provide water for the house, paddocks, and barn, but also for the experimental algae tanks.

That was another of Zane's ideas, to grow their own algae and then convert it to ethanol to supplement the gas and diesel they used in hybrid with the electric batteries. They used the remains of the algae after processing to feed animals around the ranch. Over all, they were pretty self-sufficient, as any rural family had to be.

And now that also included Mara taking up the reins for the annual cattle drive.

Her Uncle Nick would go with them. He was still a crack shot and would man the mini-guns on the twenty-six-foot trailer that Mara would be pulling. They agreed Seth would drive his 'Dueling Hummer as a convoy escort. Jesse and James, the twins, would each pull one of the twenty-two-foot trailers, while Mike, their fifteen-year-old brother, would be a backup driver and guard when he wasn't driving.

Bri, seventeen, and a self-taught wiz with computers and robotics, would operate the mobile base comms and drones from Seth's Hummer. They would travel about mid-pack, to give the best relay and response time.

A new neighbor, Brandon, had volunteered to escort. He had a monster truck outfitted for AutoRodeo and he had even done a couple of amateur AutoDuels over in Deseret. Mara didn't know how well he would deal with the slow pace of the convoy. He had already made a bit of a fuss about being near the end of the convoy order during the Town Hall meeting.

Matt, an older neighbor with lots of driving experience, both in war and in the 'Duels, was another of the support drivers. His vehicle was far more practical, both heavily armed and armored. It made Mara feel a little safer that he would be along, especially since Zane wouldn't be there with her. Of course, if Zane were here, she would stay back, watching the home front as usual.

Counting the neighbors, including David SellsBirds, his daughter Maple, and two of his sons, they had nearly twenty vehicles between cattle haulers and support vehicles. That would hopefully make the gangers and rustlers think twice about attacking. She and Opa agreed taking the cattle drive south through Rawlins would be best, despite the highway crossing the Continental Divide several times and the roads being rarely maintained.

Pre-dawn, the convoy lined up along the highway. Mara cradled a steaming mug filled with her favorite mint tea that grew in the greenhouse. She wore her usual jeans, t-shirt and boots with a jacket thrown over. You never knew what kind of wild storms would blow up without notice in the mountains.

She saw a few wives and children hugging loved ones. She had been in those groups before, wondering if this might be their last hug.

It's a dangerous world out there.

She glanced over to where her kids were doing the last checks on vehicle lights and saw Uncle Nick climb the ladder to the machine gun nest. They would run on gas and algae-ethanol until the sun came up. Afterwards solar panels would store energy in batteries to run hybrid later in the day.

Hopefully, there would be enough sun. It was a delicate balance to get there on time and spend the least amount of expensive gas doing it.

Mara walked over to the cab where Bri was putting a backpack and cooler up in between the seats for her.

"Thank you, Bri. I really appreciate it."

"Can't have you starving, Mom!"

Mara grinned and Uncle Nick looked over the side and down at them.

"Hey! What about me? I'm far more likely to starve up here, if the crows don't get me first! And I have to put up with your mother's driving."

Bri laughed, and Mara shook a finger at him in mock displeasure.

Since the door was open, her American Shepherd bounced his way up to the passenger seat.

"You riding shotgun with me today, Toddy?" His tongue lolled and his eyes were bright. He loved to travel.

Bri gave her mom a brief hug before she trotted off to join Seth down the line. Mara looked up at Uncle Nick.

"You going to be okay, Uncle?"

He looked down at her, his eyes showing he understood that her question was as much for herself as him.

"This ain't my first rodeo, Mara. Mount up, the sun's gonna rise in an hour. Everything will look brighter then."

Mara rolled her eyes at his pun and grinned, which was his goal. She climbed up into the tall seat and scuffled Toddy's head.

"This is MamaBear, lock and load'em, we're a go. Let's get this bull-hauler train on the road," she called out over the CB. She eased the big rig into gear smoothly, mindful of the cattle in the back. They were doing this.

I am doing this. For my friends and family.

Fred BlackEagle of the Eastern Shoshone watched through his rifle scope as the eight ganger motorcycles, loud enough to wake the dead, moved up from Sand Draw toward Sweetwater Station at the intersection of old 135 and 257/789. They stopped on the side of the road. He saw one pull out a radio to contact their two advanced scouts that had gone to the old rest stop.

Fred got a message through his ear buds.

"Two gangers dead. Rides handled."

That was the signal. Fred motioned with a finger. The targets were already pre-selected. Eight waiting snipers fired one round each. Six bodies fell immediately. Two others, likely already dead but not yet fallen, were shot again with finality.

Two minutes later, two of his men covered the distance to the bodies and signaled. All enemies dead.

He sent on his comms for extra men to come get the ganger rides. Lastly, he called his men at Sweetwater rest stop.

"Put me through to the RidgeBear base unit."

Soon Fred heard the sweet voice of Zane RidgeBear's oldest daughter, Bri.

"Hello, NoShadowWoman. This is Fred BlackEagle."

"Hello, War Leader BlackEagle, go ahead."

"You are clear through Sweetwater Station. Let your mother know we repaid part of the debts owed to Zane RidgeBear. When you return, let my wife know and we will clear the end of your path home as well."

"Thank you, War Leader BlackEagle, we are so very grateful. Thank you, Uncle." Bri spoke respectfully, but with gratitude in her voice. She was doing her best to hold back tears.

"It is good, NoShadowWoman. Be safe and be blessed to both go and return. Be careful; if you keep crying you might get a shadow and how would the sun feel?"

She heard the humor in his voice.

"Also," he said. "Wave to the young men who will ride by you between Lander and the Station. They celebrate victory today! BlackEagle, out."

She smiled through tears over at Seth in the driver's seat.

He grinned back at her. He had also heard the messages. Then he reached out a gloved knuckle and caught a tear from her cheek.

"Better dry those up Sis, before those young men see you all red-faced and it makes them run away," he teased. "Besides, you'll rust my ride here if you keep that up."

She laughed and punched him in the shoulder. She picked up the CB mike and relayed the messages.

The sun attempted to peek over the distant mountains, but the clouds fought back and let loose a gully washer before they were thirty miles outside Lander. Mara was happy that they didn't have to watch for gangers for this part of the journey. But the storm made the roads even slipperier, and visibility was sketchy. She worried about her Uncle Nick up in the gunner pod and hoped he didn't drown.

Toddy stood with his front feet on the dashboard and his back feet on the edge of the seat. He peered through the rain-soaked windshield; his ears flicked back and forth in time with the wipers. He growled low a few times at shadows off the sides of the road, but a quick glance satisfied her that they were elk or bison that wouldn't approach the convoy, anyway. She reached out and petted his head a moment before she took the wheel again at ten and two.

As they climbed into the mountains, the rain lessened, then turned to snow.

Would the solar panels ever see the sun? Only forty miles to go to Sweetwater Station. And only 250 miles after that. I hope the boys are alright back there. So many things to worry about. I don't know how Zane does it.

After a short break at Sweetwater Station, which gave them time to stretch their legs and clear the slush off the solar panels, Mara gathered everyone together. Even with small snow flurries still spinning in the wind that never seemed to cease up here, folks were in a decent mood.

Which is good, as we still have most of the trip and the danger ahead of us.

Seth was still teasing his sister about the young Native men that had been waving rifles over their heads as they passed the Hummer. Bri was blushing mightily.

Mara checked on the younger boys, Jesse, Mike, and James. They were looking bright-eyed and excited.

"All good?"

"Of course. This is amazing, Mom." Mike was particularly happy, as he normally wouldn't have gotten to go on the convoy till next year. She grinned at his exuberance. She turned as Uncle Nick came up, stretching his back and shoulders.

"You doing okay?"

"I'm fine. I'd rather cold than heat, anyway. You can throw on another jacket or put a blanket on your lap in the cold, but in the heat you can only get so naked without someone having fits."

He continued after the laughs and boos stopped.

"We need to get back on the road. Once we head down the mountain, the rain and sleet should ease up. This time of year can go from cold and snow to blazing hot to a windstorm in the blink of an eye, just…"

"Wait five minutes!" Everyone joined in.

Mara waved to the kids and whistled for the dog. He was there as she opened the door. She climbed in and gave two quick pulls on the air horn to let everyone know to get ready to head back out. In ten minutes, they were back on the highway.

We might actually manage this.

The mixed rain and snow had stopped, but left a heavy fog that had been a slog for the last ten miles. It thinned some as she rounded a long downhill turn. She saw the lights of an oncoming semi blink off and back on again and automatically slowed more, although the weight of the truck wanted to push her faster.

The black semi passed. Its windows were completely shaded so that she couldn't see the driver or anyone that might be riding shotgun. The custom paint job would have thrilled Zane, though. Skeletons and hooded grim reapers all up and down the sides of both the trailer and the cab itself, with gun ports near the rear. The writing on the cab declared it *"The Grim Reaper"* in fanciful script. It gave her a bit of a shiver.

The other vehicles from the convoy were stacked up behind her, and somewhere near the back, someone even honked a horn, but she stubbornly maintained the slower pace.

Flashing headlights always mean trouble ahead.

They made it down that grade and up the next hill. This one had an old 'steep grade' warning sign at the top of it, nearly blank from the scrubbing winds and weather. Only a half visible 8% along with part of a symbol of a truck on a triangle remained. She was going slowly enough at this point that gearing down wasn't even necessary. The fog had thickened again, and she was getting a prickly feeling up the back of her neck.

Was the fog what the trucker was warning about?

Fog swallowed her cab. The headlights cut through but not far. Toddy barked once.

"What are you doing, MamaBear? This ain't as bad as that freak blizzard earlier." She recognized Brandon's voice over the CB. "Look, I've got good roll bar lights. I'll pass up to the front and lead now."

She checked her left side mirror. She could see his headlights, pinpoints in the fog, already moved over into the left lane. With the slope, he gained speed fast.

"Negative, Brandon. I've got a bad feeling about this," she replied. He moved on past her anyway at a pace that would have been suspect even if the weather was clear and the roads well-maintained, monster truck or not. He turned on his search lights once he was past, and she watched his taillights quickly dwindle.

He left plenty of space, at least.

His taillights suddenly flared and then disappeared at an angle.

Mara applied her own brakes and downshifted to a crawl. In seconds her headlights illuminated the huge boulders, bushes, and mud of a landslide that covered the road completely and was still dropping rocks over the shoulder.

No sign of Brandon's truck.

She mentally thanked the Lord and that trucker for the warning. She set the parking brake and called Bri.

"Send up a drone, see if you can find Brandon."

Bri opened the connection with the scout drone and slid on her VR HUD. She launched it following the path of the landslide to start. It didn't take long to find his truck on its side, more than half-buried in rock, mud, and scree. The top roll bars and roof were completely crushed in, and an enormous boulder sat on it.

She realized that it could have been her mother, or even herself, if the convoy had been going faster.

She debated going in closer. It could be bloody carnage, or he might still be alive. 'Dueling trucks were very tough.

Bri blinked twice to click on the emojis and comments which scrolled quickly down the left side of her HUD, bringing them up to center. She realized they were discussing the brutal crash, and some were sending jeers and Super Tips. Brandon must have had his cameras on and streaming before the landslide hit him.

A light blinked in her periphery to the right .and she glanced over at it. A satellite beacon had just come online. She blinked twice to click it and it read "GoldCross".

Bri was sad, though she barely knew Brandon, especially because it reminded her of her dad being gone.

She flew the drone back to the convoy just in time to see Matt's escort Humvee ram back and forth through the landslide that covered the roadway. The reinforced front end knocked big rocks and scree out of the way with ear deafening crashes. She paused to enjoy the show and forgot to report in until her mother spoke to her through the headphones.

"Bri? Did you find him?"

"Oh, yeah, sorry, Mom. I didn't get too close with the drone, but I noticed his beacon come on to notify GoldCross. I guess he didn't make it. But it was a really big boulder. I don't think he even knew what hit him."

Mara was saddened by how easily people were desensitized to death when it happened through a screen and there was cloning on the other side. Even Bri had sounded more consoling than upset.

What's the purpose of life anymore? Is there a value? Or is a life just the cost of cloning, brain taping, storage, and physical therapy?

Toddy jumped into her lap and pressed against her in comfort. She hugged him and buried her face in his soft fur for a moment. If she died, there would be no coming back. The worth of her life was nothing, calculated on that scale.

She looked up and dried her tears. Another neighbor's pickup had switched out with Matt's vehicle; it had a snowplow blade welded onto the front.

Dave lowered the blade and pushed the mud and smaller rocks quickly off over the side. He honked and most of the other trucks honked in reply as he spun around on the narrow road and pulled out of the way for the convoy to pass, and to regain his place in the order.

The entire ordeal took less than fifteen minutes. Mara prayed that the rest of the journey out of the mountains would be quiet.

Hopefully no more losses.

She put the rig into gear and drove across the muddied road. Even over the sound of the engines and air brakes, she could hear the low thump-thump of a GoldCross helicopter coming in fast.

Nick was sweating like crazy in the homemade swivel pod on top of the big trailer. At least the air was clear up here, unlike down in the midst of the cattle cars. True to his statement back at Sweetwater Station, all the cool was gone, and the metal trailer top multiplied the heat of the sun to blast-furnace levels, it seemed. He wished he had more ice water.

He scanned the horizon, the roads, and the draws on each side. Even with drones up, he was the first to notice the off-road buggies erupt out of one of the draws about 300 feet on the north-east side. He keyed his mike and called out.

"Four dirt-bugs about ten o'clock!" They moved as fast as the terrain would allow, and for souped up dirt-bugs, that was pretty fast.

Nick spotted one of the raiders with an old-fashioned RPG trained on a large overhang of dirt and rock a few dozen yards in front of the caravan, a blockade waiting to happen. He turned his homemade mini-gun pod to face them and engaged the weapon.

The tracer rounds of Nick's first burst intersected the buggy, its driver, and finally, the gas cans stored on the driver's side. Unfortunately, the rocket was already launched before driver and gunner were fried and became one with the seat.

"Rocket live!" Nick yelled over the comms. The sound of incoming small arms fire highlighted his warning.

"It's high," Seth yelled. He opened up on the nearest dirt-bug. Bri was already on the CB.

"It went over. Hold course."

Seth left the road to intercept the oncoming dirt-bugs in the sandy field. He lit one up, causing it to spew bodies as it hit a rock and flipped end-over-end.

With his view atop the lead trailer, Nick noticed that the remaining idiots slowed too much as they turned around for another strafing run. A rookie move. They should have done a spin-drift at speed.

His beloved mini-gun Dillon Aero M134DH routed a couple hundred rounds directly into the main compartment of the dirt-bug in the back.

"Sayonara asshats!" Nick yelled as he rotated the pod for the next shot.

Maple Sellsbirds had been excited to be allowed to ride shotgun with her dad and see the RidgeBear boys. She had seen dangerous people before, and RodeoDuels at the fairgrounds, but a personal attack was new to her. Maple saw the shattered glass hit her dad through the driver's window. She could tell from his lips that he had yelled that he was okay, but she couldn't hear him past the ringing in her ears. Despite everything, her dad kept the rig and trailer on the road and steady.

Maple didn't think twice. She rolled her window down and grabbed her elk rifle from the middle console holder. She sat up on the window ledge with her toes hooked under the seat and leaned on the cab roof, bi-pod arms down.

Outside the cab, the wind blew furiously; but it often did in Wyoming. Maple focused through her scope on the dirt-buggy that had shot at her dad. Then on the back of the driver's head, a target bigger than an elk's heart.

The movements of the rig, wind, dirt-buggy and driver bouncing in it seemed to gel into a beautiful clear pattern in Maple's head. She waited one second, then two, then a soft pull back.

A few hundred yards away, the driver's head exploded as the 300 Win-mag round passed through it. The wheel jerked to the right and the dirt-bug hit a rock big enough to flip it, spinning it crazily through the air. Target down.

Seth lined up the mini-gun, but before he shot, bodies flew and the dirt-bug smashed as it rolled and flipped.

He slowed, not expecting to see survivors, but he intended to be sure. His dad always said if low-life scum would attack a large, armored caravan, they would certainly attack others less able to defend themselves, so leave nothing on the back trail.

Beside him, Bri declared there was no further movement visible through her drones. Seth took a big breath and let it out slowly, it was hard being the man of the house sometimes. He spun the Humvee around and sped up to rejoin the convoy.

In the Sellsbird's rig, Maple slid back into the seat and re-stowed her elk rifle, securing it by habit. Then she leaned forward, put her head in her hands and cried.

David reached his arm over and massaged the back of his oldest child's neck. She had shot at a person, not an animal. Certainly she hit them. He cried with her, both proud and sorry to his very soul for the loss of her youth.

Mara breathed a sigh of relief when the 'Welcome to Rawlins' sign finally came into view. It had been sunshine all the way from Muddy Gap, which had let them switch over to the electric engines for those vehicles which had them. The only "shade" they had encountered had been the run-in with the dirt-bugs.

They had stopped soon after the attack, to make sure the wounded were cared for, mostly David's glass cuts and a clearly traumatized Maple. The bullet had gone through the headrest of her seat and out the top of the cab. It missed her by inches. Some other stray bullets had impacted various vehicles, and miraculously, only one cow had been injured by shrapnel.

Mara tried to get Maple to ride in one of the other vehicles that didn't have a broken window, but she was adamant that she wanted to stay with her dad. The Shoshone were a proud and tough people, as she knew from her husband's stubbornness.

Up ahead, a few blocks before the interchange to I-80, she saw several bull-haulers and escort vehicles, as well as another tanker truck pulled up on the side of the highway. A few people with rifles pointed at the ground blocked the road; they were at the ready, but not directly threatening. Mara slowed to decide whether to run them down or stop. The bull-haulers could be folks who wanted to join, but it might also be a raider trap.

Toddy braced his paws against the dashboard, barked, and wagged his tail. That decided her. She stopped about fifty feet away.

One figure, ball cap pulled low against the bright sun, handed their rifle over to another, waved, and trotted up beside her cab. Mara rolled her window down and Toddy hopped over onto her lap and half out the window. She grabbed his collar to keep him from jumping out.

"Hey, Toddy-boy! Good to see you, too!" The voice was feminine, and Mara recognized one of Bri's friends from their online home school co-op.

"Oh, Tandy! You almost got yourself shot!"

Tandy pulled off her cap and ruffled Toddy's ears a moment before she spoke, eyes bright with unshed tears.

"Ms. Mara, there's been a lot of shooting lately. My mom's in the hospital and my Da's back at the ranch with a busted leg. People are just being plain stupid down here about cattle. That's why when we heard that you all were coming this way instead of through Casper, we made up our minds to join up with y'all, if you'll have us. We got some escort vehicles, as you can see." Tandy pointed back at the parked vehicles. "I'm driving that Army Surplus APC over there."

"I don't see why not. A bigger presence at this point can only help discourage rustlers."

"Great! I'll let them know. Where do you want us in the order?" Tandy hopped down from the step.

Uncle Nick had walked up between the solar panels on the trailer and squatted down, a gloved hand on the top of the cab. He piped up before Mara even had a chance to ask.

"Well now, ain't that some dang fine cannon fodder we got here."

Tandy shaded her eyes with her cap. "Uncle Nick! Aren't you too old to be up there? Can you even see to the edge of the road?"

Nick guffawed at her dig and climbed down the ladder.

"I'll take care of this, Mara. Let me go see who's here. We were planning to take an hour's rest in Rawlins, anyway. Just let everyone know to pull over here for now."

"We brought some extra drinks and picnic food we can share out with everyone," Tandy said. She turned and waved at the rest of the group and threw two thumbs up.

Mara got on the radio and shared the new plan. Another fifteen experienced drivers with armored and armed vehicles would certainly help.

Buster "Il-Stenn" Jackson grinned. He could almost feel the terror of the algae-suckers in the old pickup truck and trailer. He and his bros, all Carnivore Brotherhood, were so deep in their tequila, they almost hadn't noticed as it sped down 487 past the southern junction with 77.

They had shot a fellow last week near Casper for his bootleg booze. Then decided they didn't want to share the case of tequila with the War Dogs—or anyone else. They had often discussed getting out of town to an old Carnivore hide near Chalk Mountain, so it was an idea whose time had come.

The four men had looked at each other with wide eyes and barked like jackals. They finished off the tequila and tossed the bottles on the side of the road. They gunned their rides and took off after their prey. The battered silver trailer and old blue truck was speeding like the devil himself was after them. Buster was sure the driver underestimated the horrible fate that awaited. He and his boys were bored, and he knew some fun and torture would be in order before the night was up.

Buster sped up to the driver's side window and caught sight of a scared blond woman, whitened knuckles gripped the steering wheel. In the passenger seat was a terrified teen brunette with a blanket on her lap. He leered at them and then reduced the throttle to fall back behind them to where his boys were riding.

"Two women!" He watched their faces light up with anticipation of some real fun. "Both pretty and one innocent and young," he yelled again.

"Let's scare 'em some more, Il-Stenn," Crusher called back.

His brothers-in-mayhem knew the game, had no fear, and with shark-like grins, began to play. Excitement coursed through him as he drew and aimed his smaller pistol.

"Let the games begin!"

Bee Hoeffler's husband had been shot dead on a side road in Casper not even a week ago, probably by gangs trying to steal the black market hooch he peddled. That left her and her two daughters, fourteen-year-old Sarah and nine-year-old Nancy, without any income except the twelve cattle they had raised to sell. That meant they had to get the cattle to the auction in Cheyenne. In Cheyenne, they could live with her mother. It would be safer than Casper, especially with her husband gone now. If she could sell eight feeders at auction, it would leave the young bull and her three best breeders to produce with. That meant she and her daughters could likely live a far better life. She had to try.

She had the old 2004 Dodge Ram 1500 she had inherited from her dad, which still sported some armor from his old 'Dueling days. Since word of the early auction in Cheyenne had leaked to the gangbangers in and near Casper, I-25 was no longer a viable option for a single-family, small feeder-calf operation like theirs. She figured it was a "hail Mary" play to haul down 487 to Medicine Bow and hope to meet up with some other ranchers on the drive near there for safety in numbers. She prayed, prepared, packed, and they went.

Two miles past the southern 77 turn off, Bee first glimpsed motorcycles approaching steadily from behind. With a pang of terror for herself and her daughters, Bee pressed harder on the gas. It was bad for the cattle, but things would be even worse if they were caught.

"Nancy, get on the floor. Sarah, cover her with the blanket," Bee spoke firmly. It wasn't but a minute when the first biker caught up to the window. As a woman and mother, Bee recognized the evil leer on the gang banger's face, and it ratcheted her fear up a thousand notches. She grabbed the mic of the old CB radio. The sound of bullets hitting the trailer's armor, *ping, ping, ping,* drove the terror deeper into her soul. She prayed as she keyed the mic.

"Anyone! Please! We need help! Oh, God! Please someone answer!" The voice of a woman came over the radio base. Seth looked over, concern furrowed his brow. Bri clicked the hover/follow switch and shoved the drone controller over to him, even though he was driving. They were almost at Medicine Bow.

"Go ahead, we hear you," Bri said into the mic. "Where are you?"

"We are on 487 headed south about fifteen miles out of Medicine Bow. Please send help! I am going as fast as I can with a full cattle trailer, and we have bikers chasing us. My daughters and I hear the bullets hitting!" The voice sounded terrified but determined.

Seth flipped his own auto-drive switch for a second and ditched the drone as carefully as he could into the bed of one of the convoy pickups filled with extra hay. He started to call his mother on the Humvee's smaller radio as Bri gathered information from the woman, but MamaBear's voice came over even before he could get through.

"Seth, please go help them. I know it could be a setup. We'll stop up in Medicine Bow and for now, it looks clear to there."

"Done," said Seth and slid to a stop at the side of the road.

"Get out now, Bri." As she started to balk, Seth continued. "Get out and get in with the SellsBirds. Take the drone controller and go!"

Bri got out with the controller and ran toward the slowed truck where her idiot brother had ditched the drone. She was eager to reopen contact with the terrified mother and her daughters. Hopefully, someone had told the woman help was on the way.

Matt pulled up beside Seth in his own tricked out Humvee. Seth waved him on. They turned north onto 487 and gunned it. Seth admired Matt's Humvee. Its armor, roll bars, and old-style cattle catcher were epic and made the vehicle look like something from an old movie that somehow mixed outer space with apocalypse.

Seth caught up with the conversation on the radio as they headed north. The woman had calmed some, but it was only seconds before she screamed at an extremely loud gunshot followed by silence. A moment later, she came back on.

"One of the gang bangers got beside me and tried to open the door handle. I shot him through the window with my husband's old 357."

Seth heard folks cheer, but MamaBear took over the conversation.

"Cool it! Stay off the channel. Hun, can you see our trucks coming your way?"

Seth could tell that at these speeds they would meet in the roughs area about 7 or 8 miles out from Medicine Bow and keyed his own mic.

"We're on our way ma'am. We'll intercept you and the gangers in about one to two minutes. We'll likely come out of those hills in front of you about the time you get to them. You'll see both of our vehicles then. Just keep your rig steady straddling the yellow lines, don't swerve and don't stop. We'll go around you. My mother, her handle is MamaBear, is the older lady who is talking to you. The younger one is my sister Bri. We got you. Keep coming."

"Okay, but the bullets are faster now, and they seem bigger. I think we just lost a back tire on the trailer," the woman's voice quavered, clearly trying to hold it together for her family.

Seth finally saw the old blue Dodge Ram barrel down the road at them.

"You're almost here. Don't stop."

"Okay." She sounded a little steadier to Seth.

"Matt," Seth said. "I'll slow on the left and ready the mini-gun for a strafe as soon as the trailer passes. That'll handle any followers who were too close to the trailer. You just do you, man."

Matt floored it, staying in the right lane. He could see a biker move up again on the side of the old Dodge.

"If you don't survive, Seth, at least you won't have to answer to your mother for calling her the 'older lady'!" Matt snickered and let go of the mic.

Time for some payback. He hated gangers.

Il-Stenn was angrier than a hornet. The slitch had shot Scar as he had tried to get in and Scar and his ride were roadkill. He was going to make them pay, in screams and more screams, until they were as silent as Scar was now. He would make the younger one his personal bar decoration until she aged out or got dead. He took aim at another tire on the damned over-armored trailer and…

The rounds from Seth's mini-gun ripped Il-Stenn mostly in half before the sound could register in his alcohol and anger-fogged brain. His ride flipped along behind the trailer for quite a way before it stopped in a fiery ball.

Crusher also caught lead poisoning from Seth's short, quick strafe. As he died, his custom fat-ape handlebars jerked left and steered the Hog into the rocks a couple of dozen feet off-road behind Seth's Humvee. Its impact was followed by an even more spectacular explosion. How the dang thing stayed upright that long, Seth would never know.

Mortal-Combat Feinstein was drunk-focused on getting a shot off close enough to scare the woman to stop, rather than wreck the entire rig and lose the cattle and the women. He held his course and fired once and giggled as he heard a scream when the side mirror shattered.

He readied another shot but had not seen the vehicle approach in his lane, partially hidden by a dip in the road. When he did glance up, he had less than half a second before he became airborne, catapulting over the cow-catcher rig on Matt's Humvee. He smashed into and rolled up the armor cover over Matt's windshield and somersaulted bonelessly through the air over the back of the Humvee before "Mortal-Combat" took his fatality on the unyielding pavement below.

Matt grinned wickedly and keyed his mic, glee apparent in his tone.

"One less piece of gang banger excrement in the world, Seth."

"Two dead here," Seth responded. "Too bad we didn't get any vid of this; I didn't think to turn it on."

"And that is why you are still an amateur, boyo," Matt teased. "Better luck next time."

The boy is getting better and better each year, though, just like his old man, Zane.

Seth switched his CB back to the woman's channel.

"Is everyone okay in there, Ma'am?"

"I…I think so. None of us are hurt badly or shot or anything. Just some glass cuts. Thank you both! Thank you so much!"

Seth could hear the sob in her voice. Bri's voice cut in as soon as the woman's hand let go of the mic.

Seth heard her begin to soothe the woman, much as she would a scared animal or young child. Seth switched channels.

"Hey Matt," Seth said in a chipper voice. "How about you use that fancy scraper of yours to get any big pieces of trash off to the side of the road and I'll get out and kick off anything else I see?"

"My pleasure," Matt said mildly. "Glad to honor the last wish of a soon to be fallen battle-brother when your mom gets ya, Seth." Matt left the mic keyed long enough for Seth to hear the mock-evil laughter begin.

Seth called the older man a few choice names. They did a quick sweep and headed back to Medicine Bow and the convoy.

"This is MamaBear. We are on the final leg. Let's not lose focus. I've been informed there's another convoy about twenty strong that will meet us in Laramie in about fifteen minutes. Their scouts reported the ramp at 210 we intended to take is completely blocked by a huge pile up and fire and is impassable for at least twenty-four hours. So, it'll be I-80 the rest of the way to Cheyenne. The Cattleman's League knows we are coming and once we reach the city limits, we'll have escorts waiting to get us to the stockyards for the auction."

Mara paused for a moment and gathered her thoughts. The news of 210 being closed had been very unwelcome. And she was very displeased that the escorts wouldn't come past the city limits to help them.

"But every other scum raider, rustler, and wanna-be 'Dueller knows that, too. I-80 is likely to be a fifty-mile obstacle course crossed with a running battlefield. Eyes sharp, hands on the wheels, pedal to the metal, MamaBear out."

The Laramie convoy of bull-haulers and armed escorts waited in the old Walmart parking lot. Mara had led her group there through the slower but safer Business 80. They pulled into the cleared lot, forty vehicles strong now, having picked up a few more singletons along the way. This had become an 'epic convoy', as Jesse had happily declared over the radio just a bit ago.

Mara put the rig in park and got out to stretch and meet the leader. He was a tough old rancher and trucker, marked by his Brotherhood vest and Karhart ball cap. Mara held out a hand, which he grasped firmly, but not crushingly.

"Any new word on the 210 bypass?"

"Nah, it's down for weeks. The fires have melted a lot of the asphalt, so it's going to need major repair, or more likely a completely new ramp," he answered as he released her hand.

"I'm Rick Overton, I know your husband, Zane. He's a good one, and so is your boy there. I recognize him, too." His cap bill pointed over to Seth, who then joined them.

The two shook hands.

"Good to see you again, Mr. Overton. Dad always spoke highly of you." Seth was taller than the older man by about a hand's breadth.

"He's okay even if he's leading you astray from real rodeo life." Overton smiled.

Seth grinned at him.

"Well, are you wanting to lead the convoy now?" Mara thought he might, since he was far more experienced, and could see that Zane wasn't leading.

"No ma'am. Seems like you've done just fine and we don't want to go stompin' around in a finely running machine and monkey it up. We'll just tack onto your six, just like we talked about before. And if we pick up any other strays, we'll slide them into the rocking chair between us. Got some heavy artillery with us, too, and that'll keep the back door safe."

Mara was a tad relieved, as well as a bit sad. It might have been nice to step out of the responsibility of leading and just go along for the ride. But she had come to enjoy the excitement of running everything and seeing it work.

"Thank you, Rick. I really appreciate that."

"Oh, something else that we just got wind of y'all should know. There's one and maybe two singletons gone missing along the Interstate. No word where. Likely dead or worse. So, we know the rustlers are active and serious. They'll try to trick weaker drivers and high-value targets out of the line, where they can attack them easier."

"So, keep everyone moving and in their place. Got it, Rick," Mara replied.

"Should we run a rescue?" Seth asked.

"No, son. If they didn't kill folks straight out, they've taken them to their hides, and no tellin' where those are. They'll kill and eat the cattle, or sell 'em on the black-market. They move contraband fast around here. Plenty of cartel around, not just gangers. Best to get your own load to market and that means keep on the gas."

Seth looked disappointed but nodded his head.

"Thank you again for the warning, Rick. I see that there are some porta-potties there and I'm in need before getting back on the road. I have a feeling it will be the only time my bladder is happy till Cheyenne." Mara tried to sound cheerful, and both men laughed.

When she was back in her cab, she took a moment to bow her head in a quick prayer. Afterwards she felt a little guilty that she had mostly asked for safety for herself and her family. So she prayed again, adding that everyone in the convoy was family now, too.

She put the rig in gear, gave a short blast of the air horn, and circled out of the parking lot and onto the last bit of B-80 before merging with I-80. She automatically checked the radio, lights, and computer. As ready as could be for the worst. Hoping for the best.

The 210 exit was just as much of a mess as Rick reported. No trouble, other than occasional potshots from hidden gangers in abandoned vehicles along the side of the road. At the size this convoy had grown, over seventy strong, the shots were more like giving the truckers the bird. Mara was very happy about that.

The old interstate ran fairly straight along a ridge and visibility was decent overall. The sun was behind them and bits of chatter came over the radio, mostly about two more singletons they had picked up and slotted right between the two groups.

Mara almost started to relax and enjoy the drive but something niggled at the back of her mind, maybe some mother-sense. She kept her eyes on the road and all around.

Shaine St. Michaels moved carefully over the sandy, broken ground near old US-30 and I-80. Earlier he had worried about avoiding stinging insects and the puncture vine that grew in profusion near the sides of the road near the old Vedauwoo Volunteer Fire Department. But after he heard the screaming of women and girls being held prisoner, bugs and weeds didn't bother him much at all.

He had wanted to jump up and run to help them as soon as he heard their cries. The evil laughter that came from the gangers when one of their victims screamed only made it worse. He'd let a few tears fall. Then at the memories those sounds invoked, anger gripped his heart and seemed to ice his body and will.

Shaine's mother, father, two brothers and sister had been captured by similar filth when he was thirteen. But they had been lucky; they were killed right after they were captured and before the torture could start, by crossfire between two rival gangs fighting over the truck and trailer. He had barely escaped.

That was four years ago.

He had heard a few weeks back that several gangs had banded together and taken up living in the same place his family had died. Old junk vehicles and parts had been stacked and partially buried to make a suitable cover for firing at the vehicles that came down I-80. So he had begun stashing weapons and explosives in the desert back behind it for his final revenge.

This morning, he heard they had captured a couple of families. Folks in the cafe where he worked said there was nothing they could—or would—do for strangers, especially against the gangs. Shaine felt like something broke inside when he heard that.

He loaded his old dirt bike with the last of the weapons he had acquired and left Cheyenne within thirty minutes. When he got close, he left the bike, took the Army surplus duffle bag and began the low crawl across the desert ground.

Finally, he moved into position in a little ditch behind a mostly buried set of engine blocks. He pulled out the weapons from the duffle bag. All four barrels of the last crazy weapon he had stolen were loaded with different kinds of mini-rocket grenades. If explosives worked for the gangers, they could probably work against them. He tucked the other gear around him to be ready to grab.

He waited impatiently for the gangers to start an attack on new vehicles. At least then, they would leave the prisoners alone for a while. They were being held in a little square of pushed together vehicles and welded sheet metal, right near the two still loaded cattle trailers.

Shaine finally heard the first lazy shots from the gangers. He didn't have ear protectors, like his mother would want, but he was pretty sure it wouldn't make a difference as he didn't expect to survive this.

He selected his first target through the scope.

The convoy picked up speed as it approached the exit ramps near the mostly destroyed Vedauwoo FD buildings. There were even more trashed vehicles stacked along the road up ahead. The perfect place for an ambush, and Mara's niggling got stronger.

Driving interference in the rightmost lane, Seth, Matt, and Tandy with her APC, were ready to respond as needed.

Bri had eight drones up, so she had to use the tablet instead of the VR HUD. She reported her findings.

"Confirmed, sides are full of bogies behind cover. Currently, overpass is clear. Highway is clear."

About that time, small-round fire splattered into the convoy. The drivers hardly flinched.

"Pour it on and don't stop," MamaBear said as soon as Bri finished. "Matt, Seth and Tandy, do what you need to do to get us through, and please be safe."

Everyone on the radios knew very clearly that 'safe' would not be the *modus operandi* for those three vehicles. The three escorts swerved and headed down the off-ramp.

"What the—!" Bri's tablet screen nearly whited out as a huge fireball affected the cameras of the drones. It was followed by several minor explosions. She was sure that the area holding the fuel stores had been hit from behind, rather than from the road.

"We may have an ally! I'll send a drone," she continued.

Seth gave a curt nod and Matt and Tandy both acknowledged, even as all three vehicles rained fire and destruction on the gangers, who were now more exposed.

Bri swerved a drone back behind the emplacements. Desert scrub shouldn't be able to hide something big enough to cause those kinds of explosions. Another explosion rocked the area of gangers furthest from the convoy. Her mom's rig was almost parallel to the place the fuel reserves had been destroyed. Bright fire flared high and black smoke billowed across the highway. It was a fitting celebration of destruction against those who would attack truckers bringing food and caring for their families.

Shaine was overjoyed to see the resultant series of explosions had destroyed fuel and gangers. He scanned through the scope to pick his next target and was surprised when he saw heavily armored small vehicles leave the relative safety of the highway and race toward the gangers nearest the off-ramp.

To the right, at the far end of the spur nearest Cheyenne, gangers stood up to see the explosions. With their attention captured for the moment, he rolled quickly into a better position, aimed at that area, and fired another rocket. To Shaine's delight, as it reached the gangers behind the overturned line of vehicles, it detonated in the air. Even from this distance the destruction was spectacular.

A drone flew in fast and low over Shaine's position and he grabbed the first handgun he could reach and aimed. It was a flare gun, but it would take out the drone.

The drone had stopped on a dime and had a camera rather than a weapon pointed at him. He decided to trust it and moved the gun off the line. He yelled "innocents" toward the drone three times and hoped the operator could hear him.

Shaine shot the flare gun at the biggest piece of an old billboard sign above and to the side of where the prisoners were being held. By the grace of God, the flare struck the sign and created a dazzling beacon.

The drone rose straight up so fast that he lost track of it. He shrugged and turned to look for the next largest grouping of enemies.

Vengeance is mine today.

Reefer was mad as hell at the destruction pouring in from all sides. Nobody from the Laramie cartels had reported anything as large as this convoy. He had never considered that a cattle convoy would be this heavily armed. But somehow a frackin' army had surrounded him and his crew. *Time to ExFil.*

While he booked toward an arroyo where some of the best rides were stashed, he grabbed one of his favorite toys from his belt, armed it, and reared back to throw the thermobaric grenade toward the area the rockets seemed to come from.

As it left his hand in an ascending arc, mini-gun fire ripped through Reefer Tuck, leader of the Blood Snakes, from a pod on top of a large tractor trailer as it sped by. The grenade flew about a hundred feet, where it burst just above the ground with minimal damage to anyone—except for fleeing gangers.

"There's a guy with guns back behind a berm at about 150 yards!" Bri tried to speak calmly, but knew she failed; it was just too exciting.

"I think he's the one that caused the explosions. And now he's saying something to the camera. But the microphone can't pick it out from the noise. And he's kinda cute. And now he's motioning off in another direction and… WTF! He just shot a flare in the direction that he was waving. Holy shite! I'm going up."

Bri wished she had time to smack her brother, who chuckled at her even as he drove and fired.

Seth fired a devastating burst into several fleeing gangers. The flare burned bright in the distance.

"Don't shoot at the enclosure," Bri yelled. "I see a bunch of people bound up and lying on the ground in there! I can't tell how many are alive for sure."

Overton's voice came over their headphones.

"Most of the gangers are running for their mangy lives. We can come back and get the prisoners later. We need to keep moving while we have the advantage—"

"Matt, you have the most space, go get the prisoners out of there." MamaBear's voice cut through like a drill sergeant. "Tandy, get the guy with the guns who's helping us. We aren't leaving anyone behind. Seth, cover fire as needed. Don't leave any of those friggin' wretches alive unless they surrender."

Seth's eyes widened. His mother almost cussed.

Shaine didn't know what instinct caused him to flatten face first into the ground, but he was glad that he had. The most awful booming sound he had ever heard was followed by showered debris. It took him a few ear-ringing seconds to look toward the battle again.

The gangers had fared much worse. A few still staggered to the little arroyo where the gang leaders had stashed their rides.

From her drone's eye view, Bri saw their new ally had aimed the crazy four-barrel launcher at a group of fleeing gangers. She could also see Tandy's APC was right in the path.

"Tandy, turn away now! Turn away!" Bri was thankful to see Tandy swerve away from the retreating gangers and curve around to retrieve the shooter.

Shaine vaguely remembered that the second barrel had the same sort of grenade in it as the previous barrel. It looked like the ones who had survived the blast didn't care whose ride they grabbed. He made sure they never rode again. The SAGM grenade hovered just over where the scum had leaped down into the arroyo and detonated. Nothing much was left of either motorcycles or gangers. Shaine pumped his fist once in a 'yes!"

That one's for you, Mom and Dad.

A very military-looking vehicle braked beside him, weapons trained and then swiveled away. A hatch opened and a girl wearing a backwards facing ball cap looked out, surprising him. She motioned him to get in.

Shaine grabbed up the launcher and pistol belts and clumsily climbed in. His balance seemed a little off. The girl motioned him to sit and said something. Shaine smiled but couldn't hear her. He never really heard much of anything from that side ever again.

Bri watched through the drone as the young guy got into the APC. Another drone was trained on the prisoner area while a third followed as Mr. Matt's cowcatcher ran into several gangers and flung them through the air like a zombie video game. He skidded to a stop by the prisoner area, leaned out the window, and with precision aim, shot two gangers right in the head who were trying to drag a kicking and screaming girl away. It was movie-level epic.

Matt got out of the Beast and pick up the bound teen girl, who continued to scream and struggle while he put her into the back seat. He deftly added two more women and four children, stacked in almost like cord wood. The last prisoner Matt retrieved was an older man covered in enough blood that it was a miracle he was alive. Matt placed him in the passenger seat before he got back in and sped for the road.

Two bodies remained in the pen.

Bri checked each of the drone's feeds. Nothing moved, except the upset cattle in the trailers.

"MamaBear, this is CommsBase One. Everyone has completed their missions and are returning to position. Two casualties in the prison pen. But there's two small cattle singletons with livestock that really need rescuing, too."

"Anyone want to go back and pick up those trailers?" MamaBear came back on the radio immediately.

Four young men from the Laramie convoy excitedly volunteered to help; bummed they missed out on the big fight. The convoy had slowed, which would allow them to catch up easily, if they were worth their salt in hooking up the trailers.

"Put the other bodies in the back of your vehicles, too, please," Mara said quietly. "People deserve to see their loved ones put to rest."

"Yes, ma'am," a subdued voice came back.

No GoldCross helicopter winging to the rescue here.

With the ambush destroyed, the rest of the ride into Cheyenne was smooth, and they met up with the Stockyard escorts just as they crossed the city line.

Mara dove into the whirlwind of unloading, organizing, and paperwork that was far more familiar to her. She bid Overton and his cohort goodbye and thanks. She made sure that Bee and her girls were safely escorted to her mother's place after their cattle were dealt with. The rescued families were thankful, but grieved two holes in their lives. She had even invited Shaine to come back with them to work on the ranch, assuring him they could use another hand. He had happily agreed after he realized that she wasn't joking.

Mara was conflicted—but ultimately grateful—that money had come not only from the auction but also from viewers who had seen the big battle that several of the convoy drivers had broadcast. With the final insurance payments sent, she and Zane could figure out their new relationship when he got back. As a wonderful bonus, the ranch would be good to go for another year with funds still remaining.

After a night in a hotel on the Stockyard grounds, they hooked the empty trailers up for the drive back home.

Toddy jumped up into the cab and Uncle Nick climbed the ladder with a thermos of hot GreenKaf under one arm. He watched Mara as she checked the back gate and the solar lines.

"You sure you're gonna be okay leading this convoy back up? I know BlackEagle will clear it from Sweetwater Station back to Lander, but there's a lot of road in between. I could drive and that young Shaine could man the mini-gun."

Mara straightened up, feeling more confident than she had in a long time. She looked up at him and smiled.

"I got this, Uncle Nick. It's not my first rodeo."

Cruze Control
By: David Bock

Daniel Cruze leaned against the side of the trailer, arms crossed over his chest. The trailer was emblazoned with his likeness and his catch phrase "Cruze Control!" in big, exciting orange and red letters. He watched the team mechanics working on the tractor while the sun beat down on them. Sweat trickled along his spine, causing an itch he couldn't reach through his body armor. He uncrossed his arms and shifted his shoulders, trying to get some relief.

Above him, the turrets on the trailer whined ceaselessly, scanning the likely approaches. This was not a safe section of highway to loiter. Not that many areas on the road could be considered safe.

A growing hum filled the air. A convoy of trucks, flanked by their escorts, blew past his three vehicles. A buffet of warm air slapped them, followed by a cloud of dust and debris. The mechanics cursed as they tried vainly to protect the open electronics bay.

For the umpteenth time, he checked his watch. If they didn't get moving soon, he'd miss the start of the competition and have to forfeit his match against Mark Groenten. That would be a serious blow to his reputation as well as his bank balance.

Ten minutes later he'd had enough.

"Leo, open the trailer and get my car out. We can't wait any longer."

His manager looked at him, worry written plainly on his expressive face. He chewed on the ends of his mustache.

"You sure, Daniel? They should have the truck fixed—"

Daniel held up his arm and pointed to his watch.

"Leo, we should have been moving half an hour ago. Even if they got it fixed right now, I'd be lucky to get to the arena before check-in closes."

"But what about the support crew?" He gestured at the team huddled around the tractor's engine compartment, like acolytes with a holy relic.

"No time! They can follow along later. Worse comes to worse, I'll hire some local mechanics."

"Daniel!" Leo sounded offended. "Do you know what that'll cost?"

"Yes, less than a forfeit. Now get moving."

Ten minutes later, still too long for Daniel's frayed patience, his car was rolled out of the trailer and down the ramp. The crew gave it a final check.

Leo walked up, struggling to fasten a set of body armor a size too small, as Daniel was giving the car his own personal once over.

"Leo, what in the nine levels of hell do you think you're doing?"

"If you're going, I'm going with you. No way am I letting my best client go off to a duel all on his lonesome." Leo's chin jutted forward and his moustache practically bristled. Daniel realized this was one fight he couldn't win. He smiled fondly at the fireplug of a man.

"Welcome aboard Leo, glad to have you with me."

Out on the open road, as their speed increased, Daniel's tension eased. His shoulders relaxed and he rolled his head, causing a slight popping noise. He checked the nav system again.

"If all goes well, we should get there well before check-in closes."

Leo nodded, face pale as he held on tightly to one of the handles on the edge of the roll cage. Daniel glanced over at him in concern.

"You okay, Leo? You look kind of—"

"The road! Watch the road!" Leo's voice had a shrill edge.

As they came around the gentle curve at a smooth 100 mph, Daniel realized they'd already caught up with the convoy that'd blown past them earlier. He eased back on the throttle, and made sure he would pass well to the outside of the escort vehicles. No need to cause additional concern to any already itchy trigger fingers. Convoys were prime targets for raiders and bandits on the largely lawless highways.

"Leo, switch on the radio and hit the seeker button. The blue one, lower left."

After a few moments of alternating silence and static, the system determined the convoy's channel.

"—car coming up on the left. Looks like he's just passing through. Over."

"Roger. Seems to be giving us a wide berth. Over."

"Yup. Stay alert, this could be a distraction. Nice looking car though. Out."

Daniel grinned at that; the Hammer Head was an aesthetically pleasing design. Especially with the additions his team had made, and the custom paint job. He keyed his mike.

"Thanks. This is Daniel Cruze passing on your left. Just playing through on my way to Midvale Arena. Over."

There was a moment of silence, then the radio crackled to life again.

"No crap? The Daniel Cruze, as in 'It's time for some Cruze Control!' Daniel Cruze? Um, over."

Grinning wider, Daniel hit the transmit key again.

"One and the same. Over." He noted the company logo as they pulled level with one of the trucks. The name 'Gertrude' was painted on the driver's door in fancy script. "I'll leave word at the gate for comp tickets for anyone with Sweet Caroline Carriers. Always good to meet more fans. Over."

"Nice! Thanks Mister Cruze. Over." He punctuated this transmission with three blasts from the truck's air horns. *Baahh, baahh, baahh.*

"I'm Daniel to my fans. Y'all be safe. Out."

The normal byplay, along with their reduced speed, seemed to help Leo relax. He settled back in his seat, smiling slightly.

They'd passed the first flanking car and were approaching the lead escort vehicle when it erupted in flames and spun off the road. Simultaneously, what sounded like a hailstorm echoed through the car. Alerts lit up his dashboard.

A word that would have shocked Daniel's fans escaped his lips as he downshifted, trying to get out of the line of fire. No joy. Whoever the gunner was, he'd locked on the Hammer Head and seemed determined to take them out.

Daniel rapidly executed a few more evasive maneuvers. Whoever the gunner was, he was good. Well, his mama always told him a good offense is the best defense. Activating the targeting computer, he spun the wheel and headed directly toward the source of machine gun fire. Not expecting this, the gunner overcorrected and rounds spattered the tarmac to his right. All the swaying had Leo desperately clinging to the roll cage handles, muttering prayers.

After a brief scan, the system beeped and put an aiming indicator on the heads-up display. Teeth bared in an eager grin, Daniel adjusted his trajectory and loosed off two rockets. He spun the wheel away from the explosions and cut back along the convoy as several vehicles erupted onto the highway from the overgrown verge a mile or so behind the last truck.

None of them were factory combat vehicles. Two appeared to be up-armored farm trucks, three were modified family sedans, and the last looked like a trike, or a motorcycle with a sidecar. That driver was either insanely brave or suicidal. Open vehicles had a very short lifespan in combat. He keyed his mike.

"Convoy, convoy, convoy. This is Daniel, any of these guys back here friends of yours? Over."

Even before they had a chance to respond over the radio, the tail end truck's rear turret answered his question. A stream of tracers from a medium autocannon sliced right through one of the sedans. It staggered, turned sideways, then flipped, rolled, and burst into flames. The bandits scattered for a moment, then opened fire on the convoy. One of them scored a solid hit on the turret. With the brief attention he could spare, it looked like the shot had damaged its traverse mechanism.

Daniel lined up with the HUD target indicator and fired two more rockets, both aimed at one of the farm trucks. He had two rockets left, so he switched firing controls to his machine guns while prepping a little surprise. He could only use this once.

He drove directly toward the oncoming attackers. The Hammer Head shuddered as he peppered them with a few bursts of fifty caliber armor piercing tracer rounds. He wanted to keep their attention on his car. Thankfully, their accuracy was nothing to brag about, and most of the return fire went wide. When there was about fifty yards separating them, Daniel cranked the wheel. As he cut across their path, he hit the button to release an oil slick. He then continued his turn to head back toward the convoy.

They had almost no time to react, and since they were jinking to avoid fire both from him and the now limited arc of the tail end Charlie, most of them hit the oil perfectly. The trike spun in front of one of the remaining sedans, taking them both out of the fight in a tangled snarl of metal and flesh. The other sedan went skidding off the road and slid to a stop facing backwards, narrowly avoiding a rollover. Not a fatality, but at the very least delayed before he could catch up, if he even tried.

The driver of the remaining farm truck knew his business. He kept his wheels straight, accepting a few hits from the truck turret until he was through the oil. He then gently drifted onto the shoulder and drove through the grass for a couple dozen yards, wiping most of the oil off his tires. At that point, he hit the accelerator and came racing up their trail.

A flash from the truck bed was followed by a large blast impacting the roadway next to Daniel's car. Shattered asphalt pounded them, ringing the compartment like a bell.

"What the hell was that?" Leo's voice was loud and shrill.

In all the excitement, Daniel had forgotten his manager in the passenger seat.

"That was an anti-tank gun, Leo. I wonder where they got one of those?"

"How can you be so calm?"

Daniel grinned at Leo's exclamation.

"You just hang on Leo, everything will be fine."

As he wrenched the wheel back and forth, three more shots cratered the blacktop, only one even coming close.

Daniel flipped switches and slowly eased up on the accelerator, letting the farm truck close the distance.

"What are you doing? That guy can blow a hole right though us!"

"It's okay, Leo. I know what I'm doing."

When the rear camera showed the attacker was in the right position, Daniel yanked the emergency brake handle and spun the wheel. The car swapped ends in a perfect Bootlegger Reverse. As the Hammer Head's nose came around, Daniel fired his last two rockets. One glanced off the side of the truck and detonated some distance behind it, the other was a direct hit on the cab.

Flames flashed from every scam in the driver's compartment followed by a large secondary explosion. Armor panels flew away from the blast like startled birds. A body, or at least most of one, was flung out of the truck bed. The burning remains of the truck rolled slowly to a stop.

Daniel turned back around, more gently this time, and headed to catch up with the other vehicles.

"Convoy, convoy, convoy. This is Daniel, approaching on your six. No more bandits from this end. How's everything up there? Over."

"Bandits routed. We lost one escort totaled, two others and one tractor damaged. Much thanks for the assist. Over," replied a voice he hadn't heard before.

"Damn, Mister Cruze. That was some fancy driving! We caught it all on the gun camera. You took out five of them by yourself!"

Daniel recognized this one.

"Hey, I told you, I'm Daniel to my fans. This section of road seems pretty hot. You mind if I tag along with you until we get to Midvale? Over."

"We'd be glad to escort you the rest of the way, Mister Cruze, I mean Daniel. Out." The first voice again, this time with a barely suppressed chuckle.

The rest of the trip was uneventful.

Once through the gates and inside the city barrier, they could all finally relax. Daniel exchanged friendly farewells with the convoy crew, along with promises to meet up later for drinks they insisted he wouldn't be allowed to pay for. With final wishes for good fortune, he peeled off and headed to the arena.

He pulled up at the check-in gate and finally got out of the car. It had only been a few hours, but his body told him it had been days. Leo stumbled out the other side, holding onto the car and swaying.

A tall, slender fellow in overalls and body armor, carrying a clipboard, approached them.

"Hi, I'm Daniel Cruze, here to check in."

"I'm sorry Mister Cruze, registration closed ten minutes ago." The regretful tone in his voice seemed genuine.

"Yeah, about that, I was caught in an ambush on my way here." He gestured at the car, finally taking note of the number of bullet craters from the machine gunner. It didn't look like any of the armor panels were salvageable, he'd have to replace the entire side. Damn.

"I'll also need to purchase some seventy mike-mike rockets, an oil cartridge, and some fifty caliber APT rounds before the match."

"I'm sorry sir." The clerk swallowed nervously. "But the rules are very explicit. Check in closes at start minus two hours. No exceptions, no excuses."

"Damn," Daniel muttered. Louder, "Leo! Can you come over here, please?"

As Leo came staggering around the front of the Hammer Head, Daniel gestured to the registrar and faded back. If anyone could get them in, it was Leo. He wasn't considered the best manager in the business for nothing.

An hour later, Daniel was sitting in the arena bar slowly nursing an Alabama Slammer while Leo groused beside him.

"Those stuck up, no good chazers. I'll black-list their arena, that's what I'll do! No self-respecting duellist will ever fight here again!" He shot back the rest of his Jack and Coke and slammed the glass down on the bar, signaling to the bartender for another.

"Take it easy, Leo. Rules are rules. If they made an exception for me, they'd have to do it for everyone." He took another small sip of his drink and sighed. He'd been counting on this prize. None of the other drivers were really in his league, though Groenten came close. A solid win here might have bumped him up to the next class. Now? He was out expenses and with a big repair bill to boot. He sighed again.

There was a commotion at the entrance to the bar.

"Hey, there he is fellas! Mister Cruze, I mean Daniel! C'mon guys."

Daniel turned around to see a group of men and women making their way through the doorway of the bar. They were all smiling in his direction and some of them were waving to make sure they'd gotten his attention. A bouncer tried to head them off, but two of the larger members of the group pulled him aside for a private discussion. The rest were soon clustered around Daniel, all talking at once and trying to shake his hand or pat him on the shoulder.

"Amazing driving!"

"The way you took out that last truck was awesome!"

"I really liked the twofer with the car and trike."

One of the truckers waved to get the bartender's attention and ordered a round for the group, then pointed at Daniel and Leo.

"And these guys don't pay for another drink tonight. Put 'em on my tab." He slapped a credit card with the Sweet Caroline Carriers logo on the bar top. The rest of the evening was a kaleidoscope of conversation, camaraderie, commiseration, and cocktails. Lots and lots of cocktails.

Daniel was jolted awake the next day by someone pounding on his hotel room door. *When did I get a hotel room?*

"Just a minute." He clamped his hands to the sides of his head to keep it from exploding and staggered into the bathroom. After relieving himself, he took some analgesics and washed them down with three glasses of water.

Only slightly steadier, and the throbbing in his head syncopating with the person outside knocking, he made his way to the hotel room door.

"Who is it?"

"Midvale police. Are you Daniel Cruze? We need to talk to you. Would you please open the door, sir?"

At least they're being polite. I couldn't have done anything too bad.

Daniel unlatched and opened the door. On the other side were two officers in MVPD uniforms looking serious. The two strangers exchanged glances and one of them checked his notepad.

"Are you Daniel Cruze, sir?"

"Yes, what's left of him at least." Daniel attempted a rueful grin. No response from the police officers. *Oh boy.*

"And are you associated with Leopold Blum?"

"Leopold? You mean Leo? Yes, he's my manager." Daniel tried desperately to get his mind tracking. Something serious had clearly happened. He didn't have time for either a hangover or morning muzziness.

"Yes sir. There's been an incident. Would you please get dressed and come with us?"

"Hey, I'm a little bit out of it this morning. Could you guys tell me what's going on?"

"Yes sir. We're headed to Midvale General Hospital."

"What!" A chill raced down Daniel's spine.

"Apparently your manager," he checked his notebook again, "Leopold Blum, was assaulted at approximately 3:35 this morning while attempting to access the bonded arena garage."

"Assaulted? What? Is Leo okay?"

"You'll have to talk to the doctors about that, sir."

"Why was he there?"

"That's what we were hoping you could tell us, sir."

Daniel threw on some clothes and accompanied the officers to their patrol car. During the short drive to the hospital, he sat in silence, his stomach a twisted knot, thoughts racing inside his still pounding head.

The police car pulled into the parking lot of a large medical complex. The officer driving parked it at an aggressive angle in front of a 'No Parking Anytime' sign. The other officer got out and opened Daniel's door.

"Come with me please, sir." He pointed to the main doors. Numbly, expecting the worst, Daniel followed him through the entrance.

The officer led him through the confusing maze of corridors. He was clearly well-familiar with the hospital layout. Arriving at the ICU, he leaned over the counter of the nurse's station and spoke softly to the woman on the other side. She nodded and pointed up the hallway.

"Please follow me, sir." The officer made a 'come along' gesture.

"What's going on? Where's Leo? How badly was he hurt?" Daniel's heart began to pound and sweat prickled his skin. This couldn't be happening.

"The doctor should already be waiting for us in Mister Blum's room, sir. He'll be able to explain the medical side of things."

The officer pushed open a door and waved Daniel through. There was indeed a man in a doctor's lab coat standing next to a hospital bed, but Daniel barely noticed him. Leo was lying there swathed in bandages, one arm and one leg splinted. What was visible of his face around the gauze was gray and drawn. He was clearly unconscious.

"Oh, Leo! What happened?"

The doctor stepped forward, hand extended.

"Mister Cruze? I'm Doctor Clifford and I'm the attending for Mister Blum. Are you the next of kin?"

Another chill raced down Daniel's spine at those words.

"What? Why? No, he's my manager and my friend. How bad is it, doc?"

"Due to his head injury, we're keeping Mister Blum in a medically induced coma. As such, he's unable to make medical decisions for himself. Do you have a way to contact his family? The officers didn't find anything in his personal effects."

"I…" Daniel paused to get his thoughts in order. A medical device beeped softly in the corner. "He's mentioned a daughter, but I got the impression they weren't close. Other than that, I don't know. His business partner might know more."

The police officer stepped forward, pulling the pad out of his breast pocket.

"Business partner? Do you have his contact information?"

"Um, his name is Max, Max Bialystock." Daniel fumbled out his wallet and gave the officer one of Leo's business cards.

"Thank you, sir."

"Will one of you please tell me what's going on here?" Daniel tried to keep his voice calm, but by the end of his question, he knew he was talking too loudly.

"Sorry, sorry." He closed his eyes, took a deep breath, and turned to the doctor. "Can you please tell me my friend's condition?"

"Without approval from next of kin, I'm afraid I can't tell you much." The doctor smiled in what seemed like honest sympathy, or a well-practiced bedside manner.

"Wait." Daniel dug through his wallet again and pulled out a folded piece of paper. "Does this help?"

It was a limited medical Power of Attorney. Leo had one for Daniel as well. It was part of Leo's standard contract requirements prior to travel. The road was a dangerous place.

"Of course, Mister Cruze, my apologies. In layman's terms, Mister Blum took quite a beating. He has fractures of his left arm and right leg, two fractured ribs, and a minor fracture of his skull. In addition to a variety of abrasions and contusions. He's stable and, as I said, we have him in a medically induced coma so he can rest."

"Then he'll be okay?" Daniel hated the way his voice shook.

"We're confident he should make a complete recovery in time. Our only real point of concern is the head injury. We're keeping a close eye on him for any signs of swelling or intracranial bleeding."

It wasn't an act. Doctor Clifford had an excellent bedside manner. Daniel started to relax for the first time since he opened his hotel room door that morning.

"Thank you, doc. Please take good care of him."

"We will Mister Cruze, we will." The doctor's smile broadened. "In the meantime, if you have a moment, some of our staff are fans and would love to meet you."

The officers returned Daniel to his hotel with a 'suggestion' not to leave town. As if he would with poor Leo lying there in that hospital bed. He'd looked so small without the usual animation of his personality shining through. Daniel swallowed past a lump in his throat, his eyes prickling, and headed up to his room.

When he opened the door, he found a folded piece of paper had been slipped inside the room, just beyond the threshold. It was a sheet torn from a spiral bound notebook. The ragged bits from where it was pulled from the wire were still partially attached.

Daniel looked up and down the empty hallway before entering his room and closing the door behind him. He turned the deadbolt and flipped the door block, for all the good they would do against a determined intruder. Picking up the paper, he sat on the edge of the still rumpled bed and turned on the light.

Whoever it was from had lousy handwriting, which wasn't helped by being written with what looked like a felt tip marker. It took him a moment to figure out the text. The first line read,

"You owe us and you'll pay."

Daniel's throat tightened as he started to reach for the phone.

"If you contact the police, your friend dies. We put him in the hospital, we can put him in the morgue."

A selection of profanity drifted through Daniel's mind. None of it seemed sufficient for the circumstances.

"You messed up. Now you'll pay. You'll be contacted with instructions. No police or your friend is a dead man and so are you."

Daniel stared blankly at the paper for a few moments. He had no idea what to do. Sure, he'd had the occasional overzealous fan, or fan of a defeated challenger get threatening before. But nothing like this. He'd let Leo handle those situations, but he had no idea what his manager had done. Only that they'd gone away.

"Dammit, Leo. What did I get us into?"

Dispirited, Daniel put the note in his pocket and headed to the hotel restaurant. He wasn't hungry, but he knew he needed to eat something.

He was halfway through his real-meat burger and fries when he remembered his crew. They certainly should have gotten the truck fixed and finished the drive to the arena sometime last night. With a sinking feeling, he realized they'd be looking for Leo, not him. When they couldn't find the team manager, what would they do? At this point, Daniel was so frazzled he couldn't even remember any of their last names. He could only imagine calling hotels asking for "Jimmy or Mike." He could try tracking the truck. There couldn't be too many forty foot van trailers with his name on the side. As soon as he got back to his room, he'd start making phone calls.

It didn't take Daniel long to locate the team. They were stuck in a holding area just inside the gates. Apparently, when Leo left with Daniel, he had the papers on him to pass the truck and escort cars. Without those, the city security force wouldn't let them inside to wander freely. Daniel had no idea where Leo would have kept the documents. Best to start by checking in the Hammer Head, then work from there.

It took his ID, some charm, and a refusal to accept no for an answer, before the arena garage guard finally let Daniel in to visit his vehicle. When he got to the bay, he realized why the guard might have been so reluctant. Someone had vandalized his car.

Thankfully, whoever it was hadn't been able to bypass the security locks and get inside the vehicle. However, they'd still done significant damage. They'd slashed the tires enough times even the run-flats were ruined. All the windows had been painted over, they'd pried up the headlight covers and smashed the lenses, and they'd finished things off by painting rude words on the doors and hood.

Daniel stood there for a moment, rage bubbling under his calm exterior, the only sign a slight twitch in one cheek. More than ever, he really missed Leo. This was exactly the kind of situation the man loved, a chance to scold or yell at someone until he got what he wanted.

After a few moments contemplating the damage to his once beautiful car, Daniel turned on his heel and went to find someone in authority.

He finally worked his way up to Mister Maynard, facilities manager for the arena.

"I'm sorry Mister Cruze. As the contract clearly states, Midvale Arena Garage, LLC is not responsible for any damages to cars left overnight in our facility." The bespectacled man explained, leaning back in his plush leather armchair with a self-satisfied expression.

"I see." Daniel's voice was soft and calm. His cheek had started twitching again. "Is that your last word on the situation?"

"I have no more say in this matter than you do." He raised his hands, apparently in an implication of helplessness.

"Very well, Mister…" He pointedly glanced at the man's business card, "Maynard. I'll make sure to tell the reporter I'm meeting with this evening that your organization can't, or won't, take responsibility for gangs of vandals rampaging through your facility. I'm sure it'll make a nice headline."

The other man snapped upright in his seat, his mouth dropping open beneath widening eyes. Leo would have been amused.

"Now see here, Mister Cruze–"

"Good day, Mister Maynard."

"Just a moment. Please–"

"I won't waste any more of your time right now. If you learn anything more about the vandalism, I can be reached at the Golden Oaks Arms, room 714." He walked out and closed the door softly, cutting off the other man's sputtering. Daniel knew Leo probably would have handled it better, but his friend wasn't here. He took in and released a deep breath and headed back toward his hotel.

On the walk over, deep in useless thoughts, his reverie was broken by a loud call.

"Hey, Mister Cruze, I mean Daniel, wait up!"

He turned around and saw several members of Sweet Caroline Carriers hurrying to catch up to him. He stopped and waited for them.

"Nice to see some friendly faces, guys. What's up? How're your injured crew members doing?"

"Pretty good, pretty good. Though it's gonna' be a while afore Gary gets behind the wheel again. Thanks for askin'." The big guy, Daniel was pretty sure his name was Jock, gave him a searching look. "You okay, Mister Daniel? You look like you just had to put down your dog."

"Not *quite* that bad, but I've had a string of bad luck since I got here." Daniel spent a few moments catching them up on what had happened in the past day. The expressions on their faces flowed from surprise, through shock, to anger.

"That no good, penny-pinching, son-of-a—"

"Poor Mister Leo!"

"Where do they get off treating you that way?"

"Your beautiful car!"

After a few more moments of outbursts, another of the convoy members–Marianne, he thought–focused their attention with a sharp whistle.

"Right. Mister Daniel, you're coming with us. You need to meet with Mister Cartwright. He's the company rep here in Midvale. He'll know what to do." So saying, she turned and started marching off, confident they would all follow. Which they did.

Just over an hour later, Daniel was sitting in a comfortable chair, drink in hand, across from a heavyset man with gray hair and a flowing moustache. He spoke slowly and calmly, but had eyes that would drill diamonds. Daniel had explained the situation as best he could, including missing duel check-in due to the ambush on the convoy, the attack on Leo, the note, and the vandalism to his car.

Mister Cartwright muttered to himself as he flipped through a copy of the arena garage contract from company files.

"'Incidental damage.' Incidental? Maynard, you slimy toad."

With a sigh, he leaned back in his chair and picked up his own drink, a lowball glass of bourbon. He took a small sip and looked across the table at Daniel.

"Here's the deal Mister Cruze, do you mind if I call you Daniel?"

Daniel nodded with a friendly smile. He had no idea what to expect.

"Excellent, please call me Richard. Anyway, here's the deal. Their contract protects them from incidental damages, like backing your car into a wall or some such. Intentional damage, such as the vandalism you described, is a whole 'nother animal."

Daniel let out a breath and felt himself relax for the first time in over a day.

"That's the good news." Richard leaned forward, a tight smile on his face. "The bad news is, unless you've got a clever lawyer, they can tie you up in legal knots from now until doomsday." He paused until Daniel nodded in understanding. The tension started to return.

"Here's what I can do. Sweet Caroline Carriers can provide legal representation in this lawsuit, in exchange for your services as a convoy escort on two or three runs." At Daniel's expression, Richard held up a hand. "Now hold on, let me finish." Again he waited until Daniel nodded.

"Like I said, we can do that, but it still might take months to get things resolved, then however long to get your car repaired and arena-ready. Instead, what I propose is we cover those repairs to your car in exchange for the aforementioned escort duties. With the abilities you so ably demonstrated on the run here, it shouldn't present you with much of a challenge, and will help keep your skills sharp." He paused to take another sip of bourbon and smiled at the glass before continuing. "In addition, we may be able to coordinate your escort schedule to locations with arenas and time them to get you there for some duels. But the needs of the cargo will take precedence. In the meantime, I'll have a couple members of our security team posted near Mister Blum's hospital room to prevent any—unpleasantness. Regardless of any other agreement, I'll expedite the release of your transport crew. As a show of good faith." He jotted a note on the scratch pad by his phone.

"I, um, that's very generous, Richard. Do you mind if I confer with my manager before answering?" Daniel knew he was completely out of his depth.

"Of course," Richard smiled and leaned back in his chair, raising his glass of bourbon in an exaggerated toast. "Take what time you need, just not too much, eh?"

Daniel sat at Leo's bedside and described the current situation, the truck, escort cars, and crew in the holding area; the vandalism to the Hammer Head; and the suspiciously generous offer from Sweet Caroline Carriers. Throughout it all, Leo lay there quietly, the only sound the beeping from some piece of equipment in the corner, and the rhythmic hissing of the oxygen cannula under Leo's nose. He was still sedated, but talking it out to him helped Daniel organize his own thoughts.

"Leo, I think I know what I should do, but I don't know if it really *is* the thing I should do. I need your help, old friend. I need your advice." Daniel rested his hand on Leo's arm and lowered his head. Other than the hospital noises, they sat together in silence for several minutes.

"Pzzz." The mumbled word hissed softly from Leo's lips.

"Leo? Leo, are you awake?" Daniel jumped up and ran to the doorway. "Nurse, nurse, I think he's waking up!" He hurried back to the bed and gently took Leo's hand. "Stay with me, Leo."

"Puzzz."

"What is it, Leo? What are you trying to say?"

His eyes still closed, Leo worked his mouth and licked his lips.

"Putz." His voice was thin and scratchy, but the word was clear enough. Daniel laughed in delight.

"I love you too, pal."

Moments later, the room was crowded with medical personnel, two of whom gently ushered Daniel out, while the rest clustered around their patient. They led him to a small waiting area and promised the doctor would be out to talk with him shortly. Then they were gone, leaving Daniel alone with his thoughts.

True to the orderlies' word, it wasn't long before the doctor strolled into the alcove where Daniel was sitting.

"Mister Cruze?" Daniel stood up and nodded. The doctor gestured for him to sit again, and sat across from him. "I'm Doctor Barrett. Mister Blum is awake and relatively cognizant of his situation and surroundings. His short-term memory is a little spotty, but that's to be expected both from the type of injury combined with the remains of the sedation we had him on."

"Is he going to be okay?"

The doctor smiled and nodded.

"While there are few certainties with this type of head injury, we're quite confident he'll make a full recovery. But he's going to be with us for a while."

"Can I see him?"

"Of course, but not right now. Come back in a few hours. He's pretty tired, and will be for some time. I'll leave word with the nurse's station that you can come back outside of regular visiting hours."

"Thank you so much, doctor. He, he means a lot to me."

"I understand. We'll take good care of him." The doctor stood up and led him toward the exit.

Daniel headed back to the hotel. After everything that'd happened today, what he needed was a hot shower. He put together a to-do list as he walked. Item number one was asking Leo about entry papers for the team. A group of figures stepping out of an alley pulled him from his reverie. They headed toward him with what came across as ill intent. He slipped his pistol out, holding it down by his side. They might have nothing to do with him, and he'd hate to make a potentially lethal mistake.

"Hey, folks. What's up?" There was no answer as the four people started to spread out, still heading right toward him.

"I'm gonna' ask y'all to stop right there." Daniel hated the way he sometimes slipped into his childhood accent under stress. He raised the gun and brought it to a compressed ready position in front of his sternum. His vision started to narrow, but not so much that he didn't notice two of the flanking figures hesitated at the sight of his pistol.

"Last warnin'. Git, or else."

At a snarled command from the one in the middle, two of the figures produced clubs, another a length of chain, and the apparent leader a large knife.

"Aw hell." Daniel pushed the gun straight out at the man with a knife and started to take up the slack in the trigger.

"Remember, you wanted this."

Training and instincts took over. Daniel put two shots center of mass in the leader, then swung to the one with the chain and put two in him as well. Both dropped groaning to the ground. He transitioned to one of the club wielders, but that man dropped his weapon and held up his hands while backing away.

"No, no, no, no!" He turned and ran.

Before Daniel could swing to the fourth figure, he'd closed enough to strike Daniel on the forearm with his club. Hard enough to cause Daniel's hand to spasm and drop the gun. He dodged the next blow, this one aimed at his head, but the breeze from its passage ruffled his hair.

Daniel was by no means an unarmed combat expert. He preferred to do his fighting from inside a car. But he'd learned the basics, and one of the things he remembered was in this type of situation, close with the attacker, get inside their weapon, then attack with all the aggression he could muster.

He took a blow to the shoulder that partially numbed one arm, but then he was inside his assailant's swing. Daniel drove in a couple of solid body blows, then realized the thug was wearing a ballistic vest. As his attacker tried to backpedal, Daniel got a lucky punch to his neck. With a strangled "*Urk!*" the other man dropped to the ground, clutching his throat. His head made a satisfying thunk against the pavement when Daniel put the boot in, then he went limp.

Daniel tried to massage feeling back into his arm as he retrieved and holstered his pistol. He checked on the other two thugs. They were also wearing ballistic vests, and both were still alive, though not happy. The handgun he carried threw a heavy slug. While it wouldn't penetrate a vest, that energy had to go somewhere. In this case, it was absorbed by his assailants' rib cages.

While he was standing there, wondering what to do next, an MVPD patrol car raced up, lights flashing and siren blaring. Two officers exited the car, guns out, but not aimed. Daniel carefully and slowly spread his hands and moved his arms away from his sides.

Daniel spent the next several hours sitting in an interrogation room, telling the same story over and over to various officers. Eventually, a detective came in with two cups of coffee. He set them down on the table, pulled out a key, and uncuffed him. Then he pushed one of the cups toward Daniel and sat down, sipping from the other one.

"Sorry for keeping you waiting so long Mister Cruze, but we finally got enough of the story from your three attackers. The fourth one is in the wind, but we're pretty sure who he is. Security video from a nearby business clarified the timeline. Looks like an open and shut case of self-defense, you're free to go. Thanks for not going Mozambique on the two you dropped—saved us a ton of paperwork."

"You're welcome, I guess. Is there anything you can tell me about why they attacked me? It seemed more than just a group of muggers picking the wrong victim." Daniel took a sip of the coffee, grimaced, and put the cup down.

"I can't officially comment on an open investigation, but off the record…" He looked at Daniel and raised his eyebrows.

Daniel nodded.

"Off the record, it looks like one of your fellow duellists hired them. That's all I can say right now."

Daniel leaned back in the chair and stared at the detective in shock. Sure, it was a very competitive business, but hiring goons to incapacitate or kill your opponent outside the arena just wasn't done. He wondered who was really the target of that highway ambush.

"Um, wow. That's—yeah. All I ask is if and when you get confirmation, you report them to the AADA. They'll pull his ticket so fast it'll make his head spin."

The detective nodded and wrote something in his notebook. After tucking it back in his pocket, he stood and extended his hand.

"Again, sorry for keeping you so late, Mister Cruze. And while this isn't an official request, it might be better if you didn't hang around Midvale right now."

"I understand. I need to head back to the hospital and talk to my manager about that very thing."

"Right, right, the attack in the arena garage. This crew was responsible for that as well. One of them admitted it in exchange for a plea deal."

Daniel took a deep breath, attempting to find his calm.

The detective banged on the interrogation room door and led Daniel out toward the lobby.

After a quick shower and change of clothes at the hotel, Daniel hurried to the elevator. He needed to talk to Leo. Waiting for him in the lobby were Jock and three other members of Sweet Caroline Carriers.

"With Mister Cartwright's compliments. He heard about the recent bother and told us to keep an eye on you. Where we headed?"

Daniel opened his mouth to argue, then saw the set of Jock's jaw and surrendered to the inevitable. He'd just think of them like the escorts for his truck.

"Thanks, Jock. I'm headed over to the hospital to check on Leo."

"Right, hospital it is, form up guys,"

Surrounded by the four large truckers, he headed for the lobby doors.

They had to cool their heels in the corridor for a bit once they got to Leo's room. Medical people were in there doing whatever they needed to do for their patient. For all Daniel knew, Leo was getting a sponge bath. His four escorts greeted the two men loitering in the hallway. Those must be the guards Mister Cartwright had mentioned.

Eventually, the door opened and several people filed out. Before going into the room, Daniel stepped over to Jock.

"You mind waiting out here? I need to talk about some private stuff with Leo."

"No problem, Mister Daniel. We'll be here when you're done."

After a deep, calming breath, Daniel walked into the room. Leo's appearance was noticeably improved. Though an arm and leg were still in casts supported by wires, and his head was still swathed in bandages, the eye that peeped from under the gauze was almost its normal bright and intelligent self.

"Evening, Daniel. What brings you here?" An impish grin curled up one side of Leo's mouth.

While still scratchy and weaker than Daniel liked, Leo's tone was much livelier than the last time he'd heard him speak. *Was it only this morning?*

"Hey, Leo. How're you feelin? You're looking better than when I was in before."

"Yeah, I still feel like hammered drek, though the folks here have been taking good care of me. Doctor Clifford is a real mench, and one of those nurses would make a great future ex-Missus Blum." The corner of his mouth curled up again, and he chuckled. This triggered a coughing fit. With his good hand, Leo waved for the pitcher of water on his bedside table. Daniel filled the associated cup and held it so Leo could guide the straw to his mouth. After nearly draining the glass, he leaned back with a sigh.

"I had the weirdest dream while I was out. I dreamt you were going to quit dueling to sign on as a convoy escort."

"Um, yeah. About that." Daniel cleared his throat and Leo's one visible eye narrowed suspiciously.

"Are you telling me that wasn't a dream?"

"Ah, no. Not exactly." Daniel was experiencing the same sensation as when he'd been caught shirking his chores as a kid.

"Um," he cleared his throat again. "Well, with the missed duel, the damage to the Hammer Head, both from the ambush and the vandalism, your injuries, and the attempted attack on me tonight, I was—"

"Wait, vandalism? Attack on you? What the hell haven't you told me?"

"Right, sorry. Let me catch you up." Without going into excessive detail, Daniel recounted recent events. When he was done, Leo lay there staring at him, like Odin considering a particularly sheepish Thor.

"So, you missed a duel. So what? Your car got damaged. Boo hoo. For this you want to throw everything away?" Leo's one unrestrained hand gestured angrily. "Because some schmuck sore loser had me beaten up, and you had to knock some sense into a few thugs, you want to toss your career in the trash?" Daniel made calming motions with his hands.

"Hey, Leo. Take it easy. You're blowing this out of proportion. Nothing's decided. Mister Cartwright made an offer, and I wanted to talk it over with you is all."

"Mister Cartwright. You get your Mister Cartwright over here. He and I need to have a *conversation*." Leo's emphasis on the last word made Daniel distinctly uneasy.

"Okay, Leo. I'll give him a call. You just relax, buddy. You don't want to pop any stitches, or something." Still making placating gestures, Daniel backed out of the room, closing the door behind him. He leaned his head against it for a moment and sighed heavily. *That could have gone better.*

When he turned around, Jock and the other five employees of Sweet Caroline Carriers he'd left in the hall were standing in an arc around the doorway.

"Uh, you want me to call Mister Cartwright, Mister Daniel?"

"Ah, you heard?"

"Yeah, I think the whole floor heard some of that."

"Cripes." Daniel rubbed his eyes. "Yeah, if you could give him a call, I'd really appreciate it."

Daniel patted the other man on the shoulder. He glanced at the hospital room door, but considering Leo's current mood, decided to leave him alone for a bit. Instead, he walked to the waiting area and collapsed in one of the chairs.

About an hour later, the elevator opened and Mister Cartwright strolled out. He headed straight for the nurses station where Daniel, Jock, and the others were waiting.

"Good evening, gentlemen. Daniel, you look like a small boy who's been caught with his hand in the cookie jar." He smiled charmingly.

"Ah, yeah. Leo didn't take my explanation of the situation and your offer too calmly. I hope I didn't poison that well."

"Don't worry, my boy." He clapped Daniel on the shoulder and led him toward the door to Leo's room. "I'm sure two rational men can come to a reasonable understanding."

Daniel opened the door and they entered the room. He made introductions, and Richard took the visitor's chair next to the bed. Leo fixed Daniel with his one uncovered eye.

"Daniel, why don't you wait in the hall while Mister Cartwright and I make nice-nice." Though the words were joking, his tone wasn't. At all.

"Um, okay Leo. Sure. I'll just wait—" He closed the door behind him as he left the room.

While Daniel paced the hospital hallway like an expectant father, he listened to the voices coming from Leo's room. Mostly all he could hear sounded like low mutterings, the words indistinguishable. Occasionally, one or both the men would raise their voices, and he could hear them clearly.

"Are you out of your mind? Do you have any idea how much Daniel brings in per annum?"

"Mister Blum!" The rest of the reply was unintelligible.

After what seemed like an eternity, the sounds of laughter drifted from the room. Moments later, the door opened and Mister Cartwright strolled out.

"You just rest up and heal, Leo. I'll stop by later this week to continue our conversation."

"Don't forget the backgammon board."

"I won't, don't worry." He closed the door softly and turned to Daniel.

"Well, my boy. It seems we have an agreement after all." Richard clapped him on the shoulder. "If your Mister Blum ever decides to retire from managing autoduellists, I'll snap him up in an instant to negotiate our contracts."

Daniel let out a long sigh as Mister Cartwright led him back to the seating area.

"I'll get my mechanics in for an estimate on repair times for your car, but I don't think that'll be more than a few weeks at most. If you can get me a schedule for accredited duels after that, we can work out convoy escort details."

After Mister Cartwright left, Daniel went back into the hospital room. Leo was lying there looking like the cat who'd bested the canary two falls out of three.

"Well, Daniel. I think I got a reasonably good deal for us."

Daniel mentally translated that to '*I let him keep his pants.*'

"You'll drive with three convoys as escort, to locations of my, I mean our, choosing. Between convoys, you'll be free to compete in duels. Sweet Caroline Carriers will be responsible for maintaining the truck that transports your car and pit crew. And," Leo waved his hand like a magician, "we get one percent of the profit of those three convoys. Net, not gross."

Leo buffed his nails on his hospital gown and looked up at Daniel with a big grin.

"We may come out of this better than if you'd just stuck to duels." Leo's eyes focused on something only he could see. "This may be a whole new untapped market."

He shook his head and looked at Daniel again. The smile was gone.

"By the way, Richard managed to find out who beat me up, vandalized your car, and attacked you. I think you and some of your new friends should go and have a chat with him."

Daniel leaned against the building wall, arms crossed. Several members of Sweet Caroline Carriers lounged nearby, trying to act nonchalant.

He pushed himself upright as the door to the secluded nightclub opened. Music spilled out into the alley, along with a group of four men and five women. Daniel approached them openly, a friendly grin on his face.

"Hey, aren't you Mark Groenten, the autoduellist?"

"Yeah, I am. You wanna autograph or somein'?" The smaller man tried to focus on Daniel's face.

"Or something, yes. I'm Daniel Cruze."

There was a moment of silence, while Groenten tried to process this through a haze of alcohol.

"Cruze? Cruze? Hey, you're that guy. Why ain't you in the hopsital? Hospital."

The women, being professionals of a sort, picked up on the tension and slipped back into the club. Whatever was about to happen, they wanted no part of it. The three men with Groenten exchanged concerned glances.

"If you want somein done right, you gotta do it yoursef." He lunged for Daniel, hands outstretched to grab. Easily sidestepping, Daniel stuck out a leg and Groenten tumbled to the ground. His followers started to advance on Daniel.

"Look behind you." Daniel smiled pleasantly and pointed past them.

Six members of Sweet Caroline Carriers stood in line abreast across the alley. Come alongs and crowbars in their hands. They held them with the ease of men who know how to use their tools, both for official and unofficial duties.

There was a brief scuffle. When it was over, three of them held Groenten's toadies, while two others stepped forward to pin Groenten to the ground. The last one handed Daniel what the truckers called a tire thumper. Basically, a short, weighted club.

Adrenaline and fear had cleared the intoxicants from Groenten's brain.

"Wh-what are you gonna do? They weren't supposed to kill anyone. Just keep you out of the arena for a while." He pulled vainly at the two husky truckers holding him down. "What are you gonna do to me?" His voice had gotten shrill.

"Like you said, keep you out of the arena for a while." He raised the club high.

"Leo sends his regards."

Daniel ran a final system check. The Sweet Caroline Carriers mechanics had done a fantastic job repairing the vandalism and combat damage to the Hammer Head. They'd even made a few improvements, though it would take him a while to get used to the new corporate paint job. He keyed the radio.

"This is Escort One, ready to roll."

The replies came back quickly.

"Escort Two, ready."

"Escort Three, all green."

"Carrier One is go."

"Carrier Two, ready."

"Tail-End Charlie, good to go."

The convoy boss in Carrier One came back on.

"Okay folks, this should be a milk run, but maintain your spacing and no one get sloppy. Roll 'em out!"

This was punctuated by three quick blasts of his air horn. *Baahh, baahh, baahh.*

Daniel in the lead, the vehicles pulled out of the lot and rolled toward the city gates.

Radioactive Run
By Richard Cartwright

"**G**ive 'em a broadside, Mr. Gerald!"

"Firing guns One, Three, and Five," Matt Gerald replied from the gunner's station. Old-timers still called it the passenger seat. The tractor trailer shuddered from the fire from the M230/G3s as JG flicked the steering wheel to keep the rig she called *Amanda* between the lines. A fireball erupted on the driver's side of the trailer *Amanda* was towing.

"Tango One is out of the fight and Gold Cross has some new customers. You know, JG, that was funny the first couple of times. After about the five hundredth, it loses something."

"Nah, Matt, always funny," JG snarked back.

"Attention incoming convoy 78-143. Transponder and recognition codes accepted. This is Oak Ridge Gate Control. Single up tight. We're about to sweep out the trash. Thirty-second warning," barked a contralto voice from the speakers.

JG jumped on the convoy channel. "Blockers single up. Don't let the raiders get between us."

"Roger Lead One. Blocker One copies." Hillbilly Reynolds was in the lead as Blocker One, driving his ancient 1970 Barracuda about twenty yards ahead of *Amanda*. Looks could be deceiving; about the only thing remaining of the 20th century in that car was the outer shell. Over the years, Reynolds had upgraded everything else to the current autoduellist tech, including a roof-mounted gun turret and a pop-up rack of anti-auto missiles.

"Blocker Two, copy. Kissing your ass, Follow Two."

"In your dreams, Blocker Two."

"Cut the chatter," JG ordered as they approached the kill box.

A couple of the more agile pursuit cars went skidding as they attempted to slow down and turn away. The heavier cars tried to fall in behind the convoy to avoid the hell fire to come.

Two blue beams of coherent light bracketed the onrushing tractor trailers and their escorts. One of the raiders drifted into the beam. The

Amex Duelbuggy vanished in a bright sphere of destruction followed by a rumble and shockwave that had the end of the fifty-foot trailer skidding to the right.

JG turned the wheel to correct the skid. She idly wondered what kind of ordnance it had been carrying, as the rear camera monitor dimmed to mute the flash. The backup periscope eyepiece glowed a bit, so the explosion must have been something.

"Follow One and Blocker Two, finish off any hangers on. We don't need a surcharge for cleanup from gate control."

"Blocker Two, loading rear cannon. Engag—holy sludge!"

JG selected the rear feed from Follow One, named *Moria* by her driver and gunner, just in time to see the two sets of gun emplacements on either side of the highway retracting back into their camouflaged boxes, muzzles still glowing. "That's new," she observed.

"No kidding," chirped Oz, the gunner for Blocker Two. "Six inches closer, and it would have singed my paint."

"That was impressive. Makes me wonder why we keep Oz and Kiwi on the payroll," cracked Taz, *Moria's* driver and Kiwi's partner.

"Convoy 78-143, please surrender vehicle control to Oak Ridge gate control at this time."

JG accepted the request from the gate computer system and took her hands off the wheel as the tractor slowed.

The rig approached the fortified gate area, bristling with railguns and other weapons. The two giant Hellbore laser emplacements flanked the gate. A suited tech was standing inside one of them checking the tube for wear.

"Good girl, Amanda," JG murmured as she patted the dash of her vehicle. "We're going to drop the load and book you in for a spa day."

"You know, naming your truck isn't too odd. But talking to it is a little weird," Matt observed.

JG's phone beeped. The cabin system chimed "Incoming call from Specialist Ilona Reed for—"

"Accept!" Matt barked the command before JG could send it to voicemail. She flipped him the bird.

"Hey, snuggle bunny," crooned the contralto voice that had been all business a few minutes ago. "I am off at 1830. Meet me at my quarters? I just got my chocolate allotment. Not to mention a quart of strawberries for taking an extra shift."

Matt snickered.

"Did Matt accept the call again?" Ilona asked, humor in her voice.

"He did. I'll try to be there. We have to get unloaded, and then I have to get *Amanda* over to the depot so they can start the overhaul and refuel."

"She'll be there. I'll take care of the depot check in. She gets bitchy at anything standing in the way of her and strawberries," Matt chuckled.

"Thank you, dear. I would invite you to join us, but Yolanda told me at lunch that she's looking forward to your… visit," Ilona shot back.

"Gotta go. JG will be there. See you later. End call." Matt almost babbled. His face flushed red as JG gave him her best snarky look.

"Blushing? Where's my macho gunner and co-driver?"

"Don't judge. It works for us. It's not like you don't have a guy or girl at every terminal."

It was JG's turn to blush. "That's just stress relief. Ilona's special. We're looking for the right man for both of us to settle down with. Anyway, there's receiving."

Expedited unloading of their algae-based foodstuffs pleasantly surprised JG. But the pronouncement of the depot manager had her suspicious.

"No mistake. Your convoy will be fully refurbished and rearmed by 1600 hours tomorrow."

"That can't be right. *Amanda's* due for an overhaul and reactor refuel. That's a three-day job, minimum." JG pointed out. "We're not paying for expedited service." *Not that we could afford to.*

They ran decently in the black, but the five-year reactor overhaul and refuel were going to take a bite out of the company's savings. As it was, they had been operating *Amanda* deeper in the yellow than she had liked for the last month, so they could make sure that Oak Ridge, which had the best prices and highest quality work in the country, got the job.

"Of course not. Your total cost will be no more than the quoted estimate. As for the overhaul and refuel, we're slipping in a new, fully fueled OR 5800 and swapping out the OR 4810 you have right now. That's only an eight-hour job. Plus, a new ordnance loadout. You must be in good with the Fairy Godmother Department at Admin." The white-coated manager beamed as she looked down at her tablet. "Oh, I almost forgot. Director Bock would like to meet with you at your earliest convenience."

"Don't tell me, let me guess. All this was authorized by Director Bock?"

The blond manager gave her a weather girl smile. "How did you guess?" She reached into a pocket and pulled out a guide disk that she tossed in the air. It righted itself and emitted a soft hum from its fans, hovering expectantly. "Just follow the drone and you will be at the director's office in no time."

"I read an article in *Overdrive* a couple of weeks ago about the OR5800s. The specs look sweet. Twice the power delivery of the 5500s and four times what we could get out of our 4810 new. Closer to five now. Seven-year fuel cycle. Nine with a plutonium mix. That's all an estimate, though. The post said that they're still in testing and at least three months away from wide deployment." Matt shoved his hands in his cargo shorts as they followed the flying guide.

"Say anything about price?" She tried to keep the worry out of her voice.

Matt sighed. "JG, 'around 130k fully fueled.' The core price for our 4810 would be twenty-two at best. Probably less, since the inner containment vessel has to be replaced. That's why we've been running at seventy percent output. The original estimate for the refuel and refurb was thirty-seven thousand. The ordnance upgrade was worth about ten, twelve thousand."

"So Director Bock has authorized an upgrade worth at least sixty-one thousand more than we are being billed. I don't think the Fairy Godmother Department likes us *that* much."

"Yeah. I have a feeling that the Sodomy and Lash division is going to get involved."

"Indeed. And here we are." JG pointed to the flashing green light of the now stationary drone hovering before a pair of dark wooden doors with a brass nameplate emblazoned with "D. Bock - Operations Director."

Matt opened the door and made a courtly gesture, his brown eyes twinkling. "After you, boss."

She stole a glance at her reflection in the polished brass plate. Green eyes and a button nose, framed by brown hair in need of a cut, looked back. No makeup and she hadn't had time for a bath during the layover in Knoxville. Screw it. She doubted Bock was interested in her looks or scent. Smiling at Matt, she strode in. "Thank you, kind sir."

"Come on through. My assistant's gone home for the day," a voice called through an open door on the far end of the unoccupied reception room.

The director's office had a set of chairs and a loveseat with end tables. A large wooden desk was centered on the far glass wall that overlooked the Oak Ridge complex of new and old construction. The line of modular nuclear reactors running along the banks of the Clinch River were off to one side, while a mix of office buildings and factories occupied the middle. Off in the distance were the geodesic domes that were both the hope of a Blight-free future and a current source of revenue, second only to the fuel reprocessing and modular reactors that powered the large tractor trailer rigs like *Amanda*. The domes reminded her of a pillow talk conversation with Ilona.

"Before the Grain Blight, the nerds were working on a project with the University of Tennessee Arboretum regarding seed irradiation. The scientists had a warehouse full of seeds from all over the world, all in sealed packages. When things started going to hell, all the national labs like Los Alamos relocated to Oak Ridge because it had the most reliable sources of power from the old TVA system."

"I remember my granddad talking about the moves," JG had replied, her hand stroking Ilona's jet-black hair. "They had Army escorts and diesel-powered tractors. Some of the convoys stretched for a mile or more."

JG snapped out of her reverie as Bock stood and came around his desk. He stuck out his hand. "Thank you for coming. I apologize for the abrupt summons, but time is of the essence. Please have a seat. I've got water and green tea if you like."

"No thanks," JG replied, taking the proffered hand. She hated algae tea.

"None for me, thank you," Matt said as he shook hands in turn and sat down, looking expectantly at Bock.

Bock sat in one of the overstuffed chairs and looked at JG. His dark eyes were penetrating. He stroked his bushy salt and pepper goatee, so at odds with his shiny bald head.

"Ms. Graham. We're impressed with your operation. You're always on time, your cargos are never short, and you provide excellent value for the money. All the companies we talked to say you're the best. We appreciate your patronage of our repair and refurbishment services. And our security chief has nothing but good things to say about your crew whenever you lay over here."

I wonder if this is what Texas Toast feels like all buttered up before going in the skillet.

"I'll get right to the point. We need a high priority shipment transported to the Sequoyah Nuclear Plant outside of Chattanooga. It has to be delivered no later than 11:59 PM tomorrow."

"We're not set up to haul nuclear materials," JG interjected.

"We know. You will be hauling two Type B casks. Loaded, they are just within your maximum gross tonnage, one hundred and forty tons per unit. That's why it was critical to replace your 4800 series reactor. Your other unit's OR 5200 is more than up to the task. Of course, we will pay for exclusive use of both trailers for the eighty-six miles of the trip."

"It's going to be a lot more than that. I-40 to 75. Then—"

"Route 153." Matt jumped in, cutting JG off. He had pulled out his tablet. "Then across Chickamauga Dam to either Hixson Pike or down to US 27. We don't have any intel on conditions beyond the dam. Assuming we can pull out by five or six in the evening, we would be crossing Chickamauga by dusk at the earliest. I don't fancy the idea of traveling on unknown roads in the dark." Matt mused. "I don't think we could guarantee the delivery time."

"Fortunately, you have a vetted route," Bock interjected. "Madame Curie, route to Sequoyah, please." A holo map appeared in the air over the coffee table. "You leave out the main gate and get on I-40 west to the Rockwood exit, where you go south on 27 down to the Sequoyah Road exit. From there, it's a straight shot to the plant. I can also confirm that the way from 27 to 153 is passable. Oak Ridge and the Tennessee Titan Association jointly maintain the roads to facilitate fuel and equipment deliveries between here, Watts Bar, and Sequoyah. The average transit time is far less than the route you were thinking. You'll have nuclear materials placards, so the possibly of thieves is minimal. Our former contractor normally made the run in a bit less than three hours, and rarely—if ever— had any trouble."

JG did the math. The income worked out to about two thousand per unit, with the exclusive use of both rigs. Even with the deadhead costs to Atlanta or Knoxville to pick up another load, they would likely clear two grand.

"Director Bock. I don't mean to sound ungrateful, but Oak Ridge is paying essentially sixty-five thousand with the upgrades, for a four thousand dollar job. It just seems too good to be true. I'm curious. What happened to your regular carrier?" JG asked.

"The owner retired suddenly and sold his equipment to Lifoods."

"Just how sudden was this retirement?" Matt interjected, cocking his head to the side.

"An hour after the Lifoods crew arrived with the bills of sale. He transmitted the contract termination fee from Los Disneys." Bock's jaw twitched with agitation.

"If this shipment is not received within the allotted time, Oak Ridge will be in breach of its contract with the Tennessee Titans to supply reprocessed fuel rods and other services to the organization and its nuclear plants. The consequences would be so dire as to make sixty-five thousand loose change in comparison."

"And if we decline?" JG asked carefully. She thought Matt's eyes were going to bug out.

"Then we will do the work, per the original estimate. It won't be a priority. At all." Bock's eyes narrowed. The "at all" wasn't friendly.

JG remembered Ilona telling her about a Beedle Tools convoy team that had been in for maintenance. Those yahoo slushboxes were out at one of the Oak Ridge bars, got drunk, and tried to treat a group of women having a TGIF party like a bunch of hoopties. Suddenly, a three-day job turned into thirty days, and they lost their gig with Beedle.

The threat was clear. JG and her crew had to be in Greensboro in ten days to pick up a load of heavy weapons at Roncone Arms and join up with an eight-truck convoy making deliveries to bases down the east coast ending in Tampa. JG had done everything short of fracking the broker to get the gig. If they did well, it would mean more contracts, along with a vendor discount on Roncone products. The OR 5800 could easily drive a set of Roncone Starburst lasers. She had read that the company was adapting them for mobile use. It would give them a huge edge against rando autoduellist wannabes and garden variety thieves. Any edge that kept her people safer in a dangerous business wasn't to be overlooked. She smiled thinly at Bock.

"I see. Graham Hauling will be glad to accept the contract."

"Who's calling at this ungodly hour?" Ilona mumbled as JG reached over her to grab the phone playing "Eastbound and Down." She silenced the immortal tones of Jerry Reed and barked at the caller.

"Matt, this better be good!"

"It's 12:30 in the afternoon. About time you got up. And the shop has completed the work. The foreman said Bock not only authorized OT, but a bonus if they could beat their estimated completion time. We need to kick the tires and light the fires."

"I knew that I should have never gotten you that vid of *Independence Day*. On my way."

Ilona was already up and dressing. "Hit the shower. I'll make us egg burritos. I need to report in anyway."

JG showered and dressed in record time. Ilona still had enough time to whip up breakfast burritos and brew some dandelion coffee. The walk to the vehicle shops let JG soak in a little of the springtime sun. It felt so good that she unzipped her coverall almost to the belly button. The wildflowers that had managed to beat the blight graced the air with their fragrance.

"Okay, what's up? You've been pensive since I got back from Bock's office," JG asked her lover.

"I would deny it, but we agreed never to lie to each other." Ilona blew out a breath. "The rumor mill is saying that your run to Sequoyah has a lot on the line. Oak Ridge and the Tennessee Titans have had a strained relationship from the start. My grandparents came from Los Alamos. They always talked about some of the things that they brought with them. Things that make really big booms. That's part of the reason that the TTA left us alone to start with.

"Along with fuel to keep the nuke plants running. Don't they sell electricity to get the things they need to stay the law of the lawless lands?" JG said.

"Right."

"But it galls the TTA that they are beholden to a bunch of geeks who are a power in their own right." Ilona nodded at JG's observation.

"Word is that if we miss this delivery window, the TTA will be entitled to free fuel deliveries for the next two fueling cycles. That's forty percent of our annual revenue."

JG winced at Ilona's words. And winced again when the realization hit her.

"The TTA was behind the previous company leaving the delivery hanging," Ilona said.

"Like I heard in one of your old movies, 'they made him an offer he couldn't refuse'," JG snorted.

"I bet they brokered the equipment sale to Lifoods. Oak Ridge couldn't afford to piss off their major food supplier by claiming the equipment."

"Indeed. Five more years and we might be able to feed ourselves and sell some excess. Right now, we need algae foodstuffs so we can sell all we raise to the rich bastards so we can afford the materials to build more clean room domes." Ilona laughed mirthlessly. "Who knew that folks who were pros at using clean rooms and handling radioactive stuff could be farmers too?"

The sidewalk they had been walking along forked. The left went to the shops. The right, to the security center. Ilona reached for JG's zipper and slid it up to the top.

"Don't want anyone else getting interested in the goods. I'm going to try and pick up another shift in the domes, so..." she pulled a box out of her combat utilities and handed it to JG. "Two strawberries. Come back to me and there'll be more. Be careful, love." She leaned in and kissed JG.

JG returned the kiss with interest till Matt's voice boomed. "Didn't y'all get a room already?"

Breaking contact, JG flipped the bird in the direction of his voice. "Frack you very much, Matt," she muttered as Ilona chuckled and headed towards security.

Turning, JG saw Matt sauntering up, holding hands with a statuesque black-haired woman with the mix of Caucasian, native American, and black features that marked her as Melungeon.

"I don't think you've met Yolanda, JG. Yolanda Harris, meet Jasmine Graham. But call her JG. Everybody does."

The woman was close to JG's five feet eleven inches, and had a business-like handshake. "So pleased to meet you. I've heard so much about you." She had the same Appalachian twang that JG lapsed into when she was home for any length of time. Growing up in the trucking business had exposed JG to a lot of regional accents. She tended to sound like wherever she was at the time.

"All good, I hope. Matt, I'll start the inspection on *Amanda*. Do we have anything on a load time?"

"As soon as we pull up to the dock. Oh... I authorized some mods. No extra cost. The armorer here wanted to field test some new toys."

"You made changes to *Amanda?* And you didn't clear it with me?" JG gave Matt her sweetest Southern girl smile and butter-wouldn't-melt-in-her-mouth tone to convey just how truly pissed she was.

Matt threw up his hands while Yolanda snickered. "Just look at it and give it a chance. I am going to walk Yolanda to admin. Turns out she's Bock's assistant."

"Ok, take your time."

Matt winced. JG hid a smile. *You know you're in trouble, gunner of mine.*

The arrival of the other half of her convey crew distracted JG from planning revenge on her gunner.

"Why is Matt moving like his hair's on fire and his a—"

"Language, Oz!" Taz's voice barked at her son.

My mystery employees. Good people. If they pretty much keep to themselves on their own time, it's not my business.

"Mom, I'm nearly twenty. I've heard the words, and I am sure JG has too."

JG took in Oz, Taz, Kiwi, and Highlander. No last names. The quartet hired on as a group, bringing along "*Mongrel,*" a car that was a little of this and a bit of that. It had some very sharp teeth, mainly twin rear-firing 90mms that Oz called his "cannons." They gave *Mongrel* a vague 1950s Caddy finned look, coupled with a roof-mounted machine gun.

The group's past was shrouded in mystery, although the vague Aussie accents that JG recognized from the *Crocodile Dundee* movies had led to a question in the interview that Taz had answered.

"We're from way west of here looking to leave our troubles behind and seeking honest work." Her tone was friendly but made it plain that was all to be said on the subject.

"So what happened with Matt, JG?"

Oz's repeated question snapped JG out of her reverie. She related the bones of the story to a round of chuckles

"Anything that makes us more profitable is fine in my book. The sooner we get *Moria* paid off, the sooner we can start saving for our own overhaul," Taz said.

Taz and her crew also brought a fair bit of cash that was enough to put a large down payment on the late model Frost Giant they called *Moria*. Graham Trucking held the note on the balance.

It had been a good investment in JG's opinion. Taz was a careful driver that had no problem with JG in charge. *Mongrel* was the perfect rear blocker with its rear-facing weapons and had saved both rigs more than once. "Most convoy raiders don't want to fire on a trailer and risk damaging the cargo. The way the weapons are mounted means *Mongrel* doesn't have that problem," Highlander had explained when showing off the car for the first time to JG.

They arrived at the shop a moment later. Taz and her crew peeled off toward *Moria* while JG headed for *Amanda*.

The aromas of oil, paint, rubber, and the ozone lightning smell of electronics hit JG's nostrils. The beeps of test equipment, the whirr of power tools, the screech of metal on metal, and the occasional curse assaulted her ears. She walked onto the shop floor, ignoring the "No Customers Past This Point" sign to reach her rig.

What did Matt let them do to you, baby?

She scrutinized her orange, black and white modified Republic Frost Giant. The change caught her eye at once. Two black twin-mounted tubes that looked like miniature versions of cannons she had seen in pictures from the First Civil War had replaced the GAU-26s mounted behind the driver and gunner positions over the sleeper area.

"What do you think? Roncone Arms Starburst 15MX. That's their fixed close-in weapons system, modified for mobile platforms. That's why the M designation and X for experimental."

The voice belonged to a freckle-faced, lanky man about JG's age, with brown hair in desperate need of a comb and cut. He was the walking image of the nerds portrayed in the eighties vids that were JG's kryptonite.

"Travis Osbourne. Shop armorer and resident genius of the Oak Ridge motor pool and shop." He stuck out his hand. JG took it automatically. The matter-of-fact delivery of a phrase that would be a boast for most people struck her. She got the feeling that he could deliver on the description.

"Pleased to meet you. I think. Tell me what you got my gunner to agree to."

"Oh, you won't regret it. When Director Bock authorized the install of the OR 5800— good move by the way; that 4810 was on its last legs—I suggested that we toss in the 15MXs. Roncone's been bugging us for some field test reports, and we just haven't had anything with the juice to power those bad boys. Ten megawatts per pair, thirty-second burst with a ten second recharge. Five megawatts in continuous alternating fire. They can fire a maximum burst of twenty megawatts each. But they will need two minutes to cool and recharge. Might have to flip a breaker or two as well. Not good in a fight, I would think." Travis talked as fast as her replaced Gatling guns chewed through belts of 30mm.

Honestly, she had thought mounting lasers on a ten-wheel tractor had been a fun "what if." Now that she had some real performance numbers, it sounded like overkill. But on the road, she'd rather have overkill than be killed.

"Hey, is it true that Hillbilly Reynolds is one of your blockers?"

The conversational shift jarred JG a bit. "Indeed."

"He was a real up-and-coming autoduellist on the circuit. No one seems to know why he walked away."

"The love of a good woman." Rhonda, his gunner, had persuaded him to retire from competition in favor of the relatively safer job of convoy blocker. In his interview, Hillbilly had told JG that the look on Rhonda's face when she saw him in a hospital bed after a near fatal competition had decided him to find a safer way to make a living. JG wasn't sure convoy blocking was that much safer than autoduelling, but she provided full Gold Cross cloning benefits for all her employees. Travis didn't need to know all that.

When the armorer caught on that she wasn't going to elaborate, he started rattling off information on the minutiae of the new reactor, the reinforced power conduits, and *Amanda's* new specs, while dogging JG's steps as she tried to do a walkaround of the rig.

"You'll be able to maintain a top speed, fully loaded, of ninety miles an hour on decent interstates and maintained roads like 27. Realistically, that's more like fifty miles per hour, with weapons firing. We also took the liberty of reinforcing the pilot at the front." He pointed to the mounted blade, reminiscent of the old cow catchers on steam locomotives. Today the V moved away road obstructions and helped cool the reactor.

"It's going to run hotter too. You hit a deer with that, and it will be medium well by the time you come to a complete stop." The nerd snickered at his joke. JG rolled her eyes.

Moving down the line of the trailer, JG was happy to see that they hadn't messed with the M230/G3s. She had gladly lowered the ceiling of the trailer to accommodate the control runs and ammo pods to service the six autocannons spaced around the top of the trailer. They provided tried and true point defense that she knew worked.

"What are those, Travis?" JG motioned to two broad silver strips, one running from the bottom wind skirt and the other three feet above the first. They didn't look decorative.

"That's... something I came up with. A lot of convoy operators talk about their trailer blind spots." Travis blushed.

"Yeah, that's why you gotta have blockers. There's a gap between the trailer wall and the maximum depression of the top guns that raiders can sneak into. Nobody's been able to develop gun pods you can economically mount to cover the gaps without giving up cargo space or the ability to slide in containerized freight. With the mods to accommodate the M230s, we barely have the top clearance for standard containers."

Travis nodded enthusiastically. "Think of these as electric fences. When energized, you brush up against a car and they get thirty thousand milliamperes. Even if the electronics are shielded, that will probably trip some breakers and take the car out of the fight for a bit. Won't do the passengers any good either."

"Won't the charge just conduct around the shell of the vehicle and go to ground?"

"When powered up, these quills—" he pointed to a line of what looked like icepick blades folded back into the strip, "—stick out and punch through the shell. That's why I call it the 'Porcupine System.' I also wired in the Starburst capacitors to allow you to trigger a directed EMP to take out any hardened targets. I call it the 'Death Blossom' from one of my favorite movies."

"The *Last Starfighter*? I love that movie!" JG couldn't hide her excitement.

"Wow! You too?" Travis visibly had to collect himself. "Like in the movie, the Death Blossom drains the capacitors. It takes two minutes for the capacitor to recharge. In the meantime, the Starbursts are reduced to one megawatt continuous fire."

They chatted about eighties movies, and had tentatively agreed to pool their vids for a watch party the next time she was in Oak Ridge, when Travis got a call requiring his presence. As he hurried away, JG reached under her seat for the steel-capped hickory stick that had been in her family for three generations. She wandered around the truck, inspecting the outer rubber tread of the steel, Kevlar, and graphene woven tires, listening for the thump of full inflation. She had splurged for the air leveling model and the front run flats that had gotten them through more than one sticky situation. Satisfied, she swung into the cab, her air ride seat contouring to her weight and shape.

"Good afternoon, JG. All systems are nominal. Since my last run, I have acquired a new OG5800 power plant, two twin-mount Roncone Arms Starburst 15MX laser cannons, and multiple other upgrades. Would you like details?" the AI's alto voice sounded over the internal comm system.

"Good afternoon to you too, Amanda. Not at this time. Start us up."

A deep hum began, and JG felt a slight vibration coming up from the floorboard through her well-worn cowboy boots. The gunner's side door opened to reveal Matt's head, followed by the rest of him climbing up through the door and settling into his station. Two sets of cherry red lip prints adorned his cheeks.

"I see Yolanda marked her territory," JG remarked dryly.

Matt pulled down the sun visor and checked his face in the mounted mirror. Cursing, he wiped his face with his sleeve. "She did that deliberately. I thought she was putting it on thick this morning."

"Of course she did," JG chuckled. "Checkout?"

"Board is all green. I can't wait to get on the road and test the Starbursts under field conditions. Travis and I did a test fire on the range yesterday, and they not only melted a three-inch steel plate like a pat of butter in a hot skillet, they gouged a hole in the backstop berm. And that was the one-megawatt setting! So, what did you think of the lasers?"

He sounds like a kid on Christmas morning. Boys and their toys.

"Killing you has been deferred. For now." She smiled. "Well, let's be about it then. Amanda, send provisional acceptance of the work—subject to test drive—to the shop manager and advise that we are pulling out."

"Done, JG." The big bay door started rolling up as JG pressed on the accelerator slightly to move the tractor forward toward the opening.

Taz and Highlander, *Moria's* driver and gunner, were just pulling away from the Y-12 shipping dock after receiving the cask containing the nuclear fuel rods. *Amanda* was to carry an empty cask that Sequoyah had requested for their second reactor, citing damage to the one on site, according to Bock.

Matt hopped out and opened the rear trailer doors. JG backed in, watching the rear camera after declining *Amanda's* offer to use the autonomous backing function.

"Okay, be sure to center it. I want the weight evenly distributed." JG called out as the lowboy forklift eased the transport cask into the trailer. There was just enough space between the walls of the trailer for a slim person to slip by. She waited to hear the screeching sound of the top of the container scraping the ceiling, but the warehouseman knew his business.

"Yes ma'am." The lowboy operator couldn't quite hide the "bitch, please," from his voice, but JG decided she deserved it. Matt sniggered.

A moment later, the forklift pulled back. There was a "click" as the cargo hooks extended and engaged the floor, wall, and ceiling anchor points.

"Matt, I'll pull the rig forward so you and—" JG glanced quickly at the warehouseman's name tag as he climbed down from the forklift "—Mr. Newberry can get the doors shut and sealed."

JG swung into the cab and pressed the ignition. She inched forward enough to allow Newberry and Matt to lock and seal the doors. Waiting for Matt to get in the cab, she decided to double-check the weights. "Amanda, please get gross and tare weight."

"Gross weight is 130,000 pounds, ten thousand pounds below max weight. Tare is forty-one thousand. Total shipment weight is eighty-nine thousand pounds."

That didn't make any sense. The transport cask's empty weight should have been eighty thousand pounds. A hundred and thirty thousand pounds is very close to the weight of a full load of fuel rods.

"What is *Moira's* gross weight?"

"128,000 pounds gross," Amanda reported, relaying the information from Taz's rig.

"Amanda, please call up manifests for both loads."

"Here you go, JG," Amanda replied.

"One B type transport cask for nuclear transport, eighty thousand pounds empty weight," JG read to herself.

"I don't like that look on your face," Matt observed as he buckled into his station

"You won't like what I'm thinking right now, either. I'll be back," she growled as she opened her door.

"JG, Director Bock is in a meeting right now and can't be disturbed." Yolanda said, standing to try to block JG from storming into Bock's inner sanctum.

His conference was apparently with a sub sandwich and a bottle of Coke. Bock had just taken a bite and was chewing frantically to clear his throat to speak. JG didn't give him the chance.

"What the hell is inside that cask?" JG spat out. Bock swallowed and sighed.

"Yolanda, it's all right, please give me and JG the room." JG heard the door shut behind her.

"I'm waiting, Bock. You're in fracking breach of contract for trying to put undeclared cargo in my trailer. Give me one good reason why I shouldn't back up our trailers and push those loads back on the dock."

"I would ask you to sit down, but you need to get on the road. So, short version. You're carrying a load of depleted uranium ingots for the

Tennessee Titan Association. That's why they're being such hard cases about breach of contract. They're about to be in breach themselves to the buyer of the depleted uranium. We didn't disclose it to you because we think we have a spy amongst us. We don't know who. TTA? Possibly the Free Mountain Society? But honestly it could be anybody, even Sturgis."

"Okay, I can sort of buy that. But you damn well should have told me. I won't endanger my crew without knowing what we are going into. I don't care how big a barrel you think you have us over."

"The fewer people who know about the DU, the better. Nobody is going to knock over a load of enriched fuel rods, there's just no market for it. Depleted uranium is another animal. And we didn't lie to you. We contracted with you to transport a nuclear materials cask. If you wanted to ask what's in it, you should've."

She could see that Bock realized he had gone too far with that last statement. His face flushed, and he held up his hands placatingly.

"Okay, that last was uncalled for, and I can understand why you're pissed off. Let me sweeten the deal a bit. First, I will have TTA send out an escort to meet up with you. At our expense. Second, I will have a courier meet you at your truck with a package. It will fit in your sleeper. Call it a peace offering. Open it up, and if you're still dissatisfied with the job, we'll talk further."

"It better be pretty damn good, Bock."

Sure enough, by the time JG got back to her idling rig, there was a woman with her hands full of a large box. As JG thumbed the tablet resting on top of the box and took possession of it, she found it was surprisingly light for its size.

"Wait a minute. Take this back for a second. I want to open it."

"Yes ma'am, Director Bock thought you might."

Cracking the seal released a familiar smell. Peeking in, JG smiled. "As an apology, that will do nicely." She resealed the box and hoisted it up to Matt to stow away in the sleeper area.

"Damn. We should have spent more time blasting rock faces. While I like dull, I thought we would a get a *little* action," Matt grumped as they pulled through Sale Creek.

"You know how much thirty mill rounds cost. Every shot not fired increases our profit margin. And quarterly bonuses, I might add."

"Where's your sense of adventure?"

"I left it with our savings balance after the bill from Oak Ridge was settled. Yeah, we made out with the upgrades, but our rainy-day fund is pretty dry right now. At least we're making good time. For a secondary, this road is remarkably well maintained."

"It really is. Better than Atlanta." Matt blew out a breath. "I was looking at our route. If we're getting ambushed, it's going to be here. Amanda, please display the map marked 'Ambush One'."

"Hold on. Let's get everyone in the circuit." JG had previously briefed Taz, her gunner Highlander, Kiwi and Oz, along with her own blocker Hillbilly and Rhonda in an all-hands circuit as soon as they were on I-40, with a promise to keep them informed.

The heads-up display projected a map with 27 intersecting state Route 111. A crazy quilt of ramps and lanes had JG squinting at the projection. "Amanda, show our route using street projection." The display switched from a map projection to a driver's eye video rushing past an exit under a bridge and merging into a long straightaway lane. "Amanda, halt projection."

"Yeah, the map view's confusing. I was about to do that myself," Matt said. "Amanda, start video 100 yards from exit to state Route 111. Set speed to an effective ten miles per hour."

The video moved more slowly this time. Matt pointed to the upper right of the projection. "If I were planning this ambush, I would have missiles set up here on the curve, just out of sight, using the woods and overgrowth as cover. As we come barreling through, they could fire at the tractor, and we would have no time to counter."

"We can run lead to flush them out," Hillbilly interjected, bearded face popping up in a video box in the corner of the map display. "Lay down some fire to keep them from popping off a missile."

"True. What are our alternative routes? I thought I saw a way around this. Amanda, play view back to the last turnoff. No, not that one, the last one on the northbound side. There, that one." She pointed to a road marked "Dayton Pike."

Matt grimaced. "Yeah, I considered that. Problem is there's a couple of bridges with low weight limits. One is only twenty-three tons. The other is forty. I might risk that one going fast, but the twenty-three ton? No way. Not to mention, we have no idea what condition that road is in. The bridges might be out for all we know. Route 27 is the only way we can go."

"Into an ambush. So, what is your cunning plan? Because I know you have one." JG smiled at her gunner.

"Of course I have a cunning plan. I'm full of cunning plans. It's why you hired me."

"I've come to find out that's not the only thing you're full of. Okay, hit me with your plan."

"Okay, see the forest growth here…"

"Blocker One, confirm there's an old Bradley on the ramp about two hundred feet from—crap, that guy's got a tube! Rhonda, get him! Oh frack—" A missile streaking into their line of vison struck the Barracuda, converting it into a fireball.

Matt hadn't waited for an order to fire. A hum and flash of foliage going up was the only indication that the system was operating.

Shooting past the exit, JG spotted the Bradley fighting vehicle midway up the ramp. It looked deformed, like a plastic toy put in the oven. Glancing back to the road in front of her, JG saw the scorch where Blocker One was hit. Pieces of twentieth century Detroit iron clanged as the cowcatcher shoved the fragments of Hillbilly and Rhonda's car aside. *Amanda* rolled over the remains.

Hillbilly so loved that car. JG pushed the grief down. *Later.* "All units. Fire everything as the guns bear!"

"Lasers still recharging. We're only going to have the chain guns for the first half of the transit before the lasers are back online," Matt interjected, his voice unnaturally calm.

JG braced herself for the hail of metal rain striking the cab as it cleared the overpass. *Odd.* There wasn't nearly as much as she was expecting.

Glancing to her left, she saw the pack of cars and trikes moving down the on-ramp to 27, gaining speed with every second. JG swerved into the left lane.

"Taz, slide into the right lane. Let's block 'em. Kiwi, follow, and Oz, keep 'em from tailgating," Matt barked out.

One of the cars was flying a blue flag with a green stylized mountain logo and a big, orange "FMS" emblazoned on the front. JG took note. Then she heard a hum and saw a flash. *The new lasers.*

The flag, along with the rest of the car, caught fire, along with several of its fellows. By the time they were in line with the next overpass and had to cease fire to maintain the bridge truce, the Free Mountain Force was down to three cars and two cycles.

JG and Matt could see relief ahead in the form of a long bridge. No one fought on bridges. Damage to ground-supported pavement was relatively easy and quick to fix. Rebuilding a bridge, not so much. So bridges were never fired upon or endangered in any way. "Thank God. We're almost to—oh frack! It's a causeway. We're so screwed!" Matt cursed.

The road ahead had water on both sides. The line of scrub trees running on either side of the highway shattered the illusion of safety. That wasn't a bridge, it was a road built on raised earth. A land bridge. They would be fair game. "I had planned for Kiwi to peel off at the Tsati-Terrace exit. But there's no way they're going to make it that far under constant attack. And what are we gonna do without a rear blocker? They'll be able to board us from behind."

Kiwi's voice cut in. "Dammit! Front tire blew. I can't hold it! We're going—"

A thump from the back and Taz's wail jerked JG's attention to her aft camera.

Mongrel had careened into the Jersey barrier and exploded. One of the cycles swerved into the lead FMS car, causing both to veer off the road into a copse of trees, out of sight. Two cars and a cycle remained.

"Taz, floor it. Take the lead. Just do it!" JG slowed slightly, dropping in behind *Moria's* trailer.

"What are you doing?" Matt nearly screamed.

"Trying to save our asses. Are the capacitors full?"

"Uhhh, yeah. But they're in our blind spot. I can't get a lock." Matt's face lit up. "Porcupine?"

"Exactly. Those two cars are heavily armored. We're going to need the EMP burst. Ok, I am going to hit the brakes. Trigger Porcupine as soon as they are close."

JG stood on the brakes. Tires squealed and smoke trailed from all the tires. *Moria* jumped out ahead of them.

"Now!" she cried.

Red lights erupted along JG's instrument panel and went dark for a second. Her sideview mirror reflected a blue flash of lightning leaping across the gap between the trailer and the pursuing vehicles. The cars glowed. The electric charge contorted the cycle rider who still hung on the machine like a raccoon struck by lightning on a pole. JG realized that the muscles in his fingers must have spasmed around the handlebars.

Then the reboot cycle started as JG left off the brakes and floored the accelerator. The rig continued to coast for a few seconds, and then the electric motors engaged and they started to pick up speed. The cameras rebooted.

The first armored car was slowing to a stop, scraping along the Jersey barrier. The cycle was falling behind, clearly out of the fight.

The last armored car had shrugged off the EMP. Matt was pouring fire from the trailer guns, but the rounds were visibly bouncing off the armor. The driver was easing back into the gun's blind spot. This surviving armored car could disable the trailer at its leisure.

But before the FMS car could exploit its advantage, a figure in blue popped up from the northbound side of the Jersey barrier and shouldered a tube that belched flame from one end. A missile flashed from the other. It flew true to the final pursuer, piercing through the armor and blowing the roof off the car.

"We're in the clear! There's a pack of cars in TTA colors taking station on me. Get in the right lane, JG. The TTA guys are lined up in the left lane." Taz's voice boomed through the convoy circuit. "Better late than never," she added bitterly. Matt excused himself to the tiny bathroom in the sleeper area. He was wiping his mouth as he came out.

The rest of the drive to the plant was anticlimactic. Sequoyah Road was wide and paralleled by an old rail line, hinting that it had been purposely built to support the original construction and ongoing maintenance.

Once they arrived at the plant, a blue-clad guard directed JG to the left with the muzzle of his rifle to a road marked "Sequoyah Receiving." Taz followed a cart with a blue blinking strobe through the main gate to one of two buildings with a cylinder on top. Two giant cooling towers loomed over the complex.

"You ok?" JG knew that her gunner was usually fine once he puked up his guts after a fight. But they had never taken losses like this before. Matt smiled thinly.

"I will be. I've never been so scared in my entire life. We've been in some tight spots. But nothing like this. I can't believe you're still so calm."

"Trust me. As soon as I am backed into the dock and powered down, I will be having a nervous breakdown."

"Well, I will leave you to it. I'll meet the guy to open the trailer doors."

The shakes were kind enough to hold off long enough for JG to answer the call of nature after shutting the rig down. Once her hands were a little more under her control, she savored the two strawberries that Ilona had given her as she stared out the windshield at the afternoon sky.

She tried not to think about what this job had cost. *Gold Cross makes it so easy to be ok with death. You get vaporized in a fireball and a few months later, you're back. But you're still dead. At least for a little while. And you never get back the memories you make after they tape you. None of them will ever remember today's run.*

In the privacy of her rig, JG shed the tears she could never show her coworkers for the loss of the memories.

"Incoming call from a Karen Bolgeo. She says she is the plant manager." *Amanda* piped up.

JG wiped the last of her tears away and hoped her face wasn't too blotchy.

"Put her through." The face of an attractive dark-haired woman appeared in the heads-up display.

"Ms. Graham, thank you for taking my call. We have notified Oak Ridge that the shipments have been received on time and per the manifests, despite your losses. I apologize we were not available sooner. We intended to have control of the 111/27 interchange when you arrived, but got delayed responding to a reported raid on an area market."

"It all worked out. Graham Trucking has excellent Gold Cross coverage for its employees. They'll be back."

"Good to hear. We have a load of spent fuel rods and an empty—" JG couldn't miss the emphasis on 'empty' "—transport cask going back to Oak Ridge. I can offer three thousand, plus escort to Oak Ridge for the load. Interested?"

That would solve a lot of problems, JG thought. Without blockers, she was going to have to withdraw from the Greensboro job, anyway. It would be months before Gold Cross had Kiwi, Oz, Hillbilly, and Rhonda's clones grown and rebooted.

Bolgeo apparently took JG's musing for hesitation as she added. "In fact, I can detach two of my cars and their crews to you till your regular team is back. I understand that you have an upcoming trip to Greensboro and points south on behalf of Roncone Arms. Pay them normal scale, paint them in your colors for the duration, and then restore them to TTA livery at the conclusion of the agreement."

"Very generous. I accept. I assume that their spying will be discreet." JG smiled.

"I am shocked, shocked that you would think such a thing." Bolgeo's image smiled back. "One more thing. Personal. My great-great grandmother is very partial to chocolate-covered strawberries. She has a birthday in two days, and I understand you might have some available."

JG looked back at the crate of chocolate-covered strawberries just out of camera range, deciding how much it would take to part with a portion. "I might. Let's talk..."

"Attention incoming convoy 78-147. Transponder and recognition codes accepted. This is Oak Ridge Gate control. You have been cleared for expedited delivery, Dock Four. Welcome back." JG didn't recognize the baritone voice. Off to her right, out of the corner of her eye, she could see the sun setting on the mountain ridge. She shook her head. Hard to believe that she had pulled out through the same gate a little less than eight hours ago.

Matt was snoring softly at his station. She had tried to get him to use the bunk in the sleeper area, but he had insisted that he "only needed to rest his eyes." Throwing up and exhaustion after a battle seemed to be the price Matt paid for his unnatural calm and general unflappability in a fight.

She let him doze and met the warehouseman herself. She needed to stretch her legs anyway. Walking out of the gathering gloom into the brightly lit dock area, she encountered an elderly bald black man with "Idlette" on his name tag instead of the pale, roly-poly Newberry.

"Evening Mizz Graham. Heard you had a rough run. We had a bit of excitement here about an hour after you left. Nothing like what y'all had on the road, but security came and hauled off Jase Newberry. Handcuffs and everything. Darndest thing. Nobody knows why."

JG was pretty sure she knew. She wondered how the raiders had known which truck was carrying the DU. Newberry had to have known the cask was heavy.

The warehouseman passed a tablet over the electronic seals while he was talking. After determining that the seals hadn't been tampered with, he thumbed the screen and offered it to JG, who did the same. The seals released with a click.

For a change, she let *Amanda* back the trailer up and exchanged pleasantries as the forklift snagged out the transport cask with the prominent dent in one side. Crane accident according to Karen Bolgeo. Which reminded her, she needed to do something about the Fifteen Hundred Dollars bulging in her hip pocket. The TTA had a strong preference for cash transactions, even for a quart of chocolate-covered strawberries.

Walking back to the cab, her phone buzzed. She pulled it out and saw four messages. The first was from the Oak Ridge Gold Cross office. The clones for Hillbilly, Rhonda, Kiwi, and Oz had been successfully started. Because Graham Trucking was a Diamond member, the company premium would not increase.

The second was from Travis, who insisted JG drop *Amanda* off for a comprehensive checkup. He'd also scored a copy of *Wargames* and wondered if she and her friend would like to watch it at his apartment Friday night.

The third was from Ilona, who promised JG stew, strawberries, and a back rub as soon as she could get to her apartment.

The last message was from Bock, who wanted to meet with her in the morning about additional business opportunities.

Matt was up, looking at his own phone as JG swung into the cab. "Can you drop me by Yolanda's apartment on your way to truck parking?"

"Sure. Gold Cross texted me that they started Hillbilly, Rhonda, Kiwi, and Oz's clones. And Bock wants to discuss "additional business opportunities.""

"You know, we could do worse than establishing a home base here," Matt observed.

"Certainly something to think about."

Milk Run
By Sam Robb

"**O**rder up!"

Jackie grabbed plates full of fresh eggs and hot, sizzling bacon off the serving bench and carried them out to the patrons waiting at the dinner tables. Sure, they were a bunch of thugs, likely thieves, and possible murderers. At the Last Waffle Haus, though, they were her customers, and she served them with a smile.

"Here y'go, Mongo." She sat the plate down in front of the hulking bald man with a wink. "Double eggs and bacon, fresh off the griddle."

The rusty chains attached to every part of the ganger's leather jacket jangled as he picked up his cutlery. The butter knife and fork looked tiny in his hairy, oversized hands. His broad smile was a mix of broken teeth, facial scars, and metal implants.

"Mongo say thanks."

Jackie nodded and worked her way over to the counter. When she slid her last plate into place in front of another regular, Tiffany, the junior waitress, sidled up to her.

"Hey, Jacks." Her voice was low. "See the eight-top? They finished up a while ago, but ain't movin'."

Jackie checked them out. Seven obvious gangers. Crewcuts, long coats, and low voices as they talked over empty plates, nursing their drinks. "They aren't causing trouble, are they?"

Tiff shrugged and popped her bubble gum. "Nah. They're just putting off some real down vibes, is all."

"Wannabes. Let 'em sit. We're not even half full. They can have free refills on the algae caff, so long as we don't need the table. Just keep an eye on them." She nodded back at Mongo. "What about tall, dark, and scary, there? He's been around a lot lately."

"I think he's sweet on me. You know that dumb guy stuff of his is an act, right?" Tiff directed her 100-watt smile Mongo's way. The ganger gave her a shy wave in return before turning his attention back to breakfast.

"Are you serious, Tiff? I'm pretty sure he's wanted by three separate city PDs."

"If he keeps being sweet to me, they won't be the only ones who'll want him," Tiff said with a sly smile.

Jackie shook her head and turned back to the kitchen. She found herself face-to-face with Hank, the chief line cook. Well, face-to-chest. He was a good foot taller than her, not that it mattered most times. She popped up on her toes and gave her husband a quick kiss, then frowned when she realized he was wearing light body armor instead of his apron.

"Hank Krasnov. What's going on?"

Hank shifted his body to put his back to the patrons. Despite—or perhaps, because of—their sketchy clientele, the Haus was agreed-upon neutral territory. Right off the road on old Route 40 near Holbrook, they were the only place to get an honest-to-goodness non-algae meal for two hundred miles in any direction. Which meant the gangers left them alone. Mostly. As long as they kept serving real bacon and eggs.

That didn't mean they talked about their business in front of them.

"I have to make the supply run." She knew he could crank up the volume well enough to stop Mongo in his tracks, but he pitched his voice low and soft.

"What? I thought Pops was going."

"Threw out his back shifting a pallet again." Hank grimaced. "I stood him up at the grill. He'll be fine there, but there's no way he's managing the trip out to meet up with Amos."

Jackie wasn't sure where Amos Yoder and his kin came from. They were some old-school religious folks called the Aimish or some such that had a compound up around Navajo territory. From the stories Pops told, he and Amos' father had done a thing or two in their youth. When Pops opened the Haus, the senior Yoder had already settled down and started a farm. They continued their hell-raising association into slightly milder days and still helped each other out.

"Can't you put it off?"

Hank shook his head. "Amos is expecting someone. If I don't make the meetup, we'll run short of real protein before the end of the month. I don't want to see that happen again."

"Oof. Yeah." That had been a rough week. "I understand. Still… be careful out there, will you?"

"Of course." Hank raised an eyebrow. "Female intuition?"

"Dork boy." She smacked him. "Can't say. Something feels off, though."

"Hmm." Hank frowned. "You can take the girl out of the arena, but you can't take the arena out of the girl. I'll listen to you, Little Miss Autoduellist."

"You'd better. Make sure *Bessie* has a full charge and she's tuned up before you take her out, you hear?"

"Already done. Listen. It's a milk run. A couple of hours out, a couple of hours back. Promise."

She smacked him again. "How many times have I told you? Don't tempt Murphy." She made up for the kinetic admonition by standing on her tiptoes for a longer kiss. "I'll hold you to that promise. Now git. I want you back before dark."

Twenty minutes later, most of the morning customers had left except for Mongo, the eight-top, and some guy sitting near the front door looking wistfully out at the desert. Jackie closed off the left-hand side of the diner and started clearing tables.

She paused. There was a faint but familiar rumble, the sound of Hank pulling *Bessie* out of their reinforced garage. Their former-armored-car turned transport was a pain to handle and a brute to drive, but she appreciated the protection it offered. Especially now, since the idea of Hank being wrapped in armor and bulletproof glass made her feel good. The patrons of the Haus left them alone, but not everyone out on the high plains desert was a customer of theirs.

"Hey, Waldo. Can we order some real coffee for once?"

"Shut up, Lem." The leader of the gang at the eight-top ran his hand through short, spiked hair. "And I told you, call me Crash."

"Fine. How long are we going to sit here, *Crash*? At least Benny gets to be outside."

"Benny's outside because he's a moron I can't trust to do anything other than watch for the supply truck to leave. Are you a moron? Didn't think so." Crash glanced sideways at the nearly empty counter. Just past the dumb ogre, Old Man Krasnov was still puttering around in the kitchen.

"Yeah, alright. I get it. He's just a kid. But—"

"No buts. We're sitting here until the old man heads out. International Breakfast Sandwich wants to know where this place is getting their supplies. *Los Muertos* is going to find out for them. And when we do?" Crash smirked. "I've got a little surprise for them, a can opener that'll pop their stupid supply truck right open for us."

Fast Eddie rolled his eyes. "We never agreed on our name. None of us are even Mexican, for crying out loud." He picked up his empty cup and stared into it with a sigh. "Why can't we use English?"

"Shut up. Spanish is cool, and you're not." Crash ground his teeth together and keyed the radio hooked up to his earpiece. "Benny. Still nothing?"

"Hey, Waldo! I mean, Crash." Benny's voice was as cheerful as ever. "I haven't seen the old man leave yet. He probably won't for a while, I don't think."

Something in Benny's tone made Crash pause. He stopped and keyed the mic again, speaking slowly. "Benny. Why do you say that?"

"Well, the other guy took their truck out." Benny sounded vaguely confused. "You know, the old man's kid. That would make him the young man, right? No way the old man can take the truck out until he gets back, I wouldn't think."

"Benny…" Crash worked his mouth for a moment, unable to find suitable words, until he finally hissed, "You *idiot*."

"Aw, Crash." Benny's voice was heavy with hurt. "You promised me you wouldn't say that anymore. You know it makes me homesick."

"Idiot!" Crash waved the others at the table up. "When did he leave?"

"About ten minutes ago, maybe?"

"You—you—augh!" Crash killed the mic and knocked the empty cup out of Eddie's hand. "Come on. Krasnov's kid is already on the road. Mort, Hombres, you take the door. The rest of you, follow me."

Jackie was wiping down the last of the tables when Tiffany shouted. "Hey! Where do you think you're going? Jacks! We got runners!"

Jackie turned to look at the eight-top Tiffany had pointed out earlier. They were up and moving for the door with purpose. Five exited, heading for the parking lot. The last two turned around at the door, pulling sawed-off shotguns out from under their long coats. The larger of the two raised his voice as they waved their modified scatterguns slowly across the diner.

"Sit down, shut up, and nobody gets hurt."

"Yeah." The smaller one sneered. "You two brats? Sit your butts down. Take a load off. Might improve your attitudes."

Jackie leaned over, peering past them at the parking lot. The five thugs stopped near a trio of beat-up yellow dune buggies where a blonde guy waited for them. The leader of the band started yelling and waving his hands around. In the end, they piled into their buggies. Instead of heading back to Route 40, they took off into the desert.

In the same direction that Hank had left moments before.

"Hey. Toots!" The small thug waved his shotgun at her. "I said sit down."

Jackie stiffened. Tiff immediately put a hand on her arm. "Jacks, maybe not."

"This is *my* home." Jackie spoke quietly, but a hard edge lurked beneath her words. She narrowed her eyes and lifted her chin along with her voice. "Free breakfast for two weeks. Bacon, eggs, *and* coffee. Not algae, either. The real stuff. Deal?"

The two thugs glanced at each other. The larger one chuckled. "Do you really think you can buy us off with *breakfast*?"

"I wasn't talking to you," Jackie said, ice in her voice.

Mongo spun around on his stool, throwing his empty plate like a China frisbee. It caught the small thug in the throat with a sickening crunch. The man dropped his gun and grabbed his neck, making frantic choking sounds.

"Son of a—" The larger thug swung around toward Mongo. Before he could get his gun all the way up, the big man who had been sitting quietly near the door whipped around in a blur, bringing up a baseball bat. The bat slammed into the barrel of the twelve-gauge, levering it straight up. The thug pulled the trigger in shock, sending buckshot through the ceiling immediately above the door just before the bat took him across the temple, dropping him like a rock.

The man at the door looked down at the two thugs, then gave each one of them an extra whack with the bat before turning to look at Mongo. The oversized ganger gave him a nod before turning back to Jackie.

"Deal. Sorry about the plate. I mean, Mongo sorry." Mongo looked at the man by the door. "Split it fifty-fifty? You can have my coffee."

"Sounds fine to me. I'll take a cup now, ma'am, if you don't mind."

"Tiff here will get you one." Jackie ripped off her apron and threw it at the junior waitress. "You've got the floor, Tiff."

"Where are you going?"

"After the idiots tailing my husband."

Jackie hit the garage at a run. Crow, her old border collie, raised his head expectantly when the door slammed open.

"Hey, boy! Want to go for a ride?"

Crow jumped to his feet, barking. She yanked open her locker and pulled out her old super-novex suit. It took her less than a minute to strip down and suit up.

"Check it out, boy. Still got it." OK, maybe it was a bit tighter around the hips. For someone who hadn't raced for five years, that was still pretty frackin' good.

Crow plopped his furry butt down and made an inquisitive little growl, quivering with excitement.

"Don't worry. I won't forget you." She pulled out two helmets. The first was hers, a hard shell. The second was softer, made to fit a canine head, and festooned with electronics. She slipped it over Crow's skull and tightened the straps. Crow jumped to his feet, barking excitedly, spinning circles in place before her, eager for her to activate the camera drones slaved to his helmet.

"Easy, boy! Give me a minute."

Once she had his helmet on, she donned hers. The corner feed in her HUD was dead for now. Once they were out and she could deploy the drones, it would show her whatever Crow was looking at—and the border collie looked *everywhere*. Jackie didn't know if it was his herding instincts or if he was just the world's biggest canine fan of autoduelling, but her pupper would make sure that nothing within sight escaped his notice. Or hers.

Crow was already sitting in the passenger seat of her arctic-blue four-by-four when she slipped behind the wheel and strapped them both in. She'd taken the side doors and the hard top off years ago, to reduce weight and increase her speed and maneuverability. Other drivers went for maximum protection. She preferred to be a zippy little angel of destruction.

The autocannon, she'd left in place. A quick check of her steering wheel controls had it swinging around in a 180-degree arc, covering the front and sides of her stripped-down truck. She finished her check by confirming her "emergency" weapon, a rocket-propelled grenade launcher, was in place. A rack mounted in front of Crow held a couple of rounds for the RPG. Completing the ensemble, her favorite high-capacity slug-thrower sat in the console holster, ready for use. She even had a light anti-vehicle mine loaded up in the under-carriage dispenser.

A girl's gotta be prepared, after all.

"Ready, boy?"

Crow barked enthusiastically. She popped the ignition, and the engine fired up with a satisfying whine. Moments later, she was outside and turning to head into the desert. She punched another button once they were clear of the garage, launching a pair of drones with a low hum. Not the half dozen she and Crow used to play with, but it would do. Her HUD display flickered to life as the eyes connected with her on-board systems, including Crow's helmet. She grinned as her pupper barked excitedly, whipping his head around to both take in and show her the surrounding sights.

Her hand hovered over the last button, the most important one. The one she'd always punched before she started a duel.

Why not? I need to be in that frame of mind.

She jabbed the RECORD button. The drones swooped and spun, taking in the scenery around her as she picked up speed, heading out into the desert.

"Hey folks! Been a minute, hasn't it? We're back though! I'm your host, Jack Frost, here with Pupper Crow. We've got a special show for today as we hunt down some idiots who thought they could mess with my family. This is going to be *fun*! Now, what do you say I quit yammering, and we get this show on the road?"

She stopped talking right as her theme song started playing. A shiver ran down her spine with the first burr of the electric guitar. It was an old song—older than her, older than anyone she knew—but it was perfect.

She stomped on the accelerator, tearing into the desert, listening to Tom Petty sing the opening lines of "American Girl".

Crow wiggled down into his seat, tense with excitement. Going for a RIDE on the Metal Couch was always exciting. This time, though? She put on Her Skin! The musky, plastic scent of the material when She pulled it out of the locker brought memories slamming into him. Sweat and noise and terror and adrenaline and excitement and speed.

Speed! Moving faster than he could run, faster than he ever thought he could move. Then—then!—She put on his Eyes! They weren't there yet, not really, but he knew they would come as soon as She started talking. He shook with anticipation. Soon! Racing, cornering, swooping. Moving even faster than She did! But more than that, even better than that: the Skin and the Eyes and the RIDE all together meant one thing…

It was time to HERD!

Jackie knew this area of the desert like the back of her hand. More importantly, she knew where Hank was heading. *Bessie* was an over-armored ironclad and had to stick to the beds that had once been part of old back roads. The thugs in the buggies might have to follow his tracks, but *she* could ignore the roads and beeline over the hills and through the canyons to intercept them.

She hoped.

She navigated smoothly around the rocks embedded in the hard-packed soil of the wash. The tracks she followed crossed over those small boulders as often as not. It took her twenty minutes to spot the dust cloud ahead of her. Crow barked excitedly and the pair of drones zoomed off ahead of them.

"Here we go, folks." Slipping back into her old banter was comfortable, like pulling on a favorite sweatshirt. "Now, that may look like they're laying smoke, but I just think they don't know how to handle themselves out here. You can see from the tracks that they're not used to this arena. You know what I say: respect the road, and the road will respect you. We're going to teach them that, aren't we, Crow?"

Her pupper yipped excitedly. The drones were close enough to the dust cloud that she could make out the three buggies tearing across the wash. She flipped between the drone feeds until she found what she wanted.

"There we go. Crow. Down, boy. Stay!"

Crow did his best to lie flat in his seat. He couldn't get too far down, since he was still strapped in. However, the helmet he was wearing still translated and transmitted his movements to the drones up ahead. They slowed a bit to linger just behind the dust cloud, giving her a partially obscured view of the three buggies they were chasing.

Take them out. She started to reach for the RPG, then stopped. She knew this wasn't an arena dustup. There wasn't a pizza truck on call to come fish her out of the wreckage if she pancaked. Out here in the high desert, it was better to shoot first and ask for forgiveness posthumously. Still… she'd seen their buggies and their driving.

Maybe not sitting ducks, but darned close. Her heart raced in that old familiar way.

She grinned. "Looks like y'all are in for a spitball fight today, folks. From the looks of it, these bozos have a pair of gangers in each buggy. Maybe some hand-held weaponry, but that's about it. Which is why Crow and I are gonna give 'em a tap on the shoulder, let 'em know we're here, and have some fun. What do you say, boy?"

Crow, still crouched down, whined in anticipation. Jackie merged the autocannon sights with the feed from one of his drones. She was running smooth while the bozos ahead of her bounced all over the place.

"Let's say hello." She lined up her shot and tapped the firing button, sending a short burst down range.

"I think there's someone behind us," Benny said. The blonde man turned, trying to see over his shoulder.

"Eyes on the road! Shut up and drive." Crash held tight to the roll cage as Benny bounced over yet another rock with a bone-rattling *thump*. "There's nobody behind us."

The air filled with the unmistakable crack of lead passing them at high speed. Autocannon rounds stitched the ground between them and Lem's buggy. The CB radio burst into life.

"What was that?"

"Dude, is someone shooting at us?"

Benny jerked the wheel left to avoid a rock, then yanked the wheel back to avoid running into Lem's buggy. "Told you there was someone behind us."

Crash let go of the roll cage with one hand and grabbed the CB mic. "Spread out! Dodge! Don't let them shoot you!"

The radio crackled. "Ah, hon." The voice that came across the airwaves was smooth, confident, and definitely female. "I ain't gonna shoot y'all no more. That was just to get your attention and let you know that we're playing a game." She chuckled. "Well. *I'm* playing a game. It's called 'Fish in a Barrel'."

Benny's eyes widened. The buggy slowed as he took his foot off the accelerator. "I know that voice. That's Jack Frost!"

"What? Why are you slowing down? Go!"

Benny shook himself and leaned forward, urging the buggy to speed up. "She's an old autoduellist. Oh, man. I wonder what she's doing out here? Was she at the diner and you didn't tell me? I could have gotten her autograph!"

Crash blinked, trying to process everything, then grabbed Benny's shoulder. "Are you telling me this is one of the *waitresses*? Idiot!" He grabbed the CB mic. "Lem. You and Teeny peel off and take care of the *chava* who thinks she's got the *cojones* to take on the *Muertos*. *Humo que puede!*"

"Um. Say that in English?"

"Smoke that tin can!" Crash bellowed. He jabbed the CB mic at Benny. "You! Drive!"

Jackie shook her head. Off in the distance, one of the dust clouds peeled off to her left and slowly circled around until it was heading her way.

"Did y'all see that turn right there, folks? Nothing wrong with a nice slow loop like that, I mean. Unless someone's trying to turn you into scrap. Crow. Up! Attention."

Crow popped up, mouth open in a doggie grin. Off in the distance, the drones swooped around and up in lazy loops. They ended up above and behind the buggy headed their way. Jackie stepped on the accelerator. Rocks, brush, and even one extremely startled lizard zipped by as the distance between her and the other vehicle shrank rapidly. Jackie waited until the goggle-wearing gunner in the yellow buggy pulled out an oversized rifle. The man steadied the rifle on the dash; or at least, tried to. Jackie grinned when they hit a rock and the rifle bounced up, smacking the driver on the side of the head.

"Poor fellows. That had to hurt. You can see they're barely dodging. Could take 'em with the autocannons, but I've got another plan in mind for them. Let's start off by showing them how you do a high-speed turn."

Jackie reached across her steering wheel with her left hand. With her right, she downshifted, then switched to the handbrake and yanked it hard. At the same time, she stomped on the clutch and spun the wheel.

Crow lifted his head and howled in delight. Her arctic-blue four-by spun around in a tight 180-degree turn, kicking up a cloud of gravel and dust. She lifted her head and shouted with him, then released the handbrake and mashed the accelerator down, putting the ganger's buggy behind them.

A little sloppy, but it'll do.

A faint POP sounded behind her, then another. Her helmet, and the wind whipping past her, muted the crack of bullets passing her, but she still knew they were there. She reached over and pressed Crow down so he was hidden by the up-armored seat. Her shoulders itched, and she wiggled down in her own seat as she heard another pair of gunshots. Her reinforced super-novex suit would protect her from a shot at anything past point-blank range, but it would still hurt like hell.

"Alright! Now we've got 'em just where we want them, folks." She missed dodging an oversized rock, making her truck bounce and rattle. "Sorry boy. Now, there's a canyon up ahead that's a perfect place for us to play a game of tag. Let's let these bozos know they're it."

Jackie jinked and jived, heading for the hills. "Crow! Look up ahead, boy. See the canyon?"

Crow barked, and the drones above them raced ahead.

She knew he *loved* when they zipped through canyons. They'd even done this particular one last week. Jackie could easily imagine the footage his drones were getting as they zoomed over the route in smooth, easy motions. She hit a dip and practically bounced out of it, rising to that infinitesimal moment of weightlessness that made her scream in excitement before her tires let go of the air and kissed the ground again.

Something went SPANG off her back panel. Jackie swore and yanked the wheel hard, veering off in one direction before angling back toward the canyon mouth.

"Oh, folks, that there was the sound of those bozos sealing their fate. Here we go. Crow, herd 'em on in!"

She caromed off a bank like a blue pinball, sliding into the mouth of the canyon, easily twice as wide as her truck. A second later, the heat of the sun disappeared, replaced by the cool air nestled between the sheer rock walls. She took her foot off the accelerator, slowing down to keep an eye on the canyon entrance behind her.

"Come on…" Would they be stupid enough to follow?

The sound of the other buggy's tires on the canyon floor said yes. She pushed her pedal to the floor as the yellow buggy practically jumped through the canyon mouth behind her; the gunner leaning forward eagerly, rifle steadied on the dash. One—two—three shots rang out, the sounds racing up and down the canyon, creating echoes that built upon one another. Sparks and chips of stone leaped from the walls, showering down where she had been moments before.

"Alright. Here's where it gets tricky." Crow's drones followed the other buggy, zipping around unnoticed behind it. "There's a sharp turn right here, and I need to slow down for it. Crow! Ready boy? Herd 'em!"

Crow growled excitedly. A glance in the rearview mirror showed the gunner lining up another shot. One of Crow's drones zipped directly overhead, forcing him to duck, rifle forgotten. The driver handled it better, but still slowed and swerved as the second drone followed the first.

"Perfect! Good boy." Jackie slowed, braking and spinning her wheel hard to make the over ninety-degree turn. The canyon beyond ran straight for a quarter mile before exiting into the scorching sun again. As soon as they were out of sight around the turn, Jackie grinned.

"Let's leave them a present, now. Y'all know what's coming, but they sure don't!"

With that, she yanked the quick-release lever next to her seat. The mine nestled securely under her back bumper dropped behind her. It bounced a bit before settling down, a mottled tan lump lying flat against the dark soil of the canyon.

She slowed to a crawl, turning to watch behind her, waiting for the yellow buggy to take the turn. Which it did a little too fast. She winced reflexively as they bounced off one wall and into another. Crow's drones swooped up and around the turn gracefully right behind them, precisely as they drove over her cow patty.

A sudden flash exploded underneath their buggy, lighting up the canyon. A deafening roar filled her ears before the audio filters in her helmet cut in, saving her hearing. The mines she favored weren't immensely powerful, but they were meant to disable another duellist's vehicle.

An *armored* vehicle.

Crow's drone feed and her helmet's HUD cut through the smoke and chaos to let her see what was going on. The fireball threw the frame of the light, *un*-armored buggy seven feet straight up, shredding the undercarriage. Their engine, on the other hand, kept moving forward, spewing oil as it bounced down the canyon like a demented bowling ball. The tires each shot off in their own direction, hitting the rock walls hard enough that she *felt* them pop. She watched the drive shaft separate from the undercarriage and drop, catching the dirt and tossing the buggy forward.

When the engineless, tireless, chewed-up chassis came down, it did so nose-first. The impact threw the driver and gunner forward. Jackie winced as their heads bounced off the dash. Then winced *again* as the tail end of the vehicle came crashing down, whipping them backward and cracking their skulls against the remains of the roll cage.

Jackie's CB crackled into life. "Lem! What happened? Did you get her?"

Jackie watched in amazement as the driver levered himself out of his side of the shattered vehicle. He took two steps before collapsing, going down face-first into the ground. She doubted he would ever get up again. After that ride, he had to have more broken bones than Mongo's plate on wing night. She looked up at the drones hovering overhead and smiled before keying the mic.

"That would be a negative, sugah. You want to give up now, or make it best of three?"

She listened to the sputtering at the other end of the channel before she killed the volume and peeled out of the canyon, heading back to the two other buggies.

Crash slammed the channel selector on the CB. "Eddie! Where are you?"

"Up ahead of you. I found the tracks."

"Good, whatever. Turn around."

"What?"

"Turn. Around. NOW." Crash's eye twitched. "Something happened to Lem."

"You want me to go find him?"

"No! Let him walk home. I want you to go take out the waitress."

Benny glanced over at him. "You sure that's a good idea, Crash? I mean, she's an autoduellist. She was pretty good, back in… um… the day, and, well… um." Crash's eye twitched madly. Benny decided that was a bad sign and put his own eyes back on the road. The CB crackled back to life.

"You, uh…" Eddie cleared his throat. "You feeling alright, man?"

"I feel just dandy, Eddie. Just dandy. But I'd feel a lot better if you would TURN AROUND AND GO TURN THE STUPID BLUE THING BEHIND US INTO SCRAP!"

"Right! Right. Turning around now."

Crash slumped in his seat, breathing heavily while Benny hunched his shoulders and tried to pretend he wasn't there at all.

Jackie bounced over the landscape, dodging brush that dotted the slope of a small hill. Five minutes later, she rounded a spur of rock and spied a buggy in the distance, hauling ass away from her.

"Hey, folks! Here we go with round two. I'm plumb outta mines now, so we're going to have to do this the old-fashioned way." She switched her HUD from Crow's drones over to the targeting sight on the autocannon and tried to draw a bead on the buggy careening across the plain ahead of her.

"Long shot. I should close the distance. What do you think, buddy?"

Crow's bark was one of alarm, not agreement, mixed with a shout from right behind her. She ripped her attention away from the autocannon just as the second dune buggy slammed into her rear bumper.

The impact threw her backward, bouncing her off the seat. It forced the breath from her lungs, making her gasp like a fish out of water. Her vision blurred and she fought to find the wheel, her four-by-four fishtailing and slowing.

Crow's alarm bark warned her again, and she yanked the wheel right out of pure instinct. Instead of driving into her back end again, the yellow buggy scraped down her side. She pulled left, battering the other vehicle as it passed. She glimpsed the other driver fighting to keep control while the gunner tried to angle his shotgun back at her.

Jackie slammed on her brakes. Her tires jittered, making her ride shiver. She broke contact with the other vehicle, making her and the other driver both fight for control. Their disengagement caused both vehicles to slew around wildly. The gunner in the yellow buggy flailed around, trying to keep his balance. Five rapid-fire shots rang out as the auto-shotgun emptied its magazine wildly in every direction except—thankfully!—hers.

She tore through some underbrush and her truck dropped without warning into a depression. It must have only been a few feet, but the impact nearly rattled her teeth loose. It also robbed her of momentum right as she bounced into an overgrown patch of California juniper. She plowed through, the thick branches whipping at her and slowing her even more in passing. The fall and the thick undergrowth left her barely moving when she finally exited juniper patch. She pushed the pedal to the floor, but her engine emitted a familiar high-pitched whine and cut out.

"Things are not looking good, folks." She slammed the starter. Her engine revved, trying to spin up, but refused to catch, dying almost immediately. She looked around. The other buggy had left her far behind, racing off into the distance. She watched the yellow buggy start to swing around in a wide arc. The gunner used the roll cage to pull himself to his feet, head whipping around wildly until he located her, pointing and yelling. The driver tightened his turn and a second later, the yellow buggy was racing back, headed straight for her.

"They think I'm an easy mark now that I'm dead in the water." She unstrapped, freeing herself from her five-point harness. "What do you think, Crow?"

One second to disconnect her harness. One to grab the RPG from the rack in front of Crow. Another to roll out of the car and pop up to a kneeling position, ready to fire.

Like riding a bicycle. She grinned, braced herself, and pulled the trigger.

A burst of flame speared out the rear of the tube. It didn't have much of a kick, but she was wobbly enough that it still nearly knocked her over. She found her balance just in time to watch the rocket fly true, dead on for the hood of the buggy trying to run her down. It moved so fast that the driver didn't have time to react as the deadly warhead arrowed toward him.

Which saved his life. The RPG roared just over the hood, between the driver and gunner, under the roll bar, and over the back of the buggy before it sailed off into the distance.

The buggy screeched to a halt ten yards from her. It was close enough to her that the rumble of the tires on the earth shook her bones. There was a whiff of odor in the air, the distinctive scent of brake shoes smoking. The eyes of the driver and the gunner were both wide and white with terror.

Jackie raised the empty RPG launcher, settled it on her shoulder, and sighted on the buggy.

The driver threw it into reverse and must have pulled hard on the wheel. The gunner lost his auto shotgun as the buggy whipped around in reverse, slammed to a stop, then accelerated away from her to make a beeline for the horizon. She stared as it ran, finally letting the grenade launcher drop from her shoulder when it rounded a hill.

"Good choice, boys." She stood and tossed the launcher into the back, next to the autocannon, before sliding into her seat and tapping the ignition. This time, the engine started right up. *Of course.* She reached over and gave Crow a good skritch until her hands stopped shaking. She breathed deeply, then put her hands back on the wheel once more and gunned the engine.

Crash had twisted around completely so he could look out over the back bumper.

Benny cleared his throat. "What's going on back there?"

Crash ignored him, spinning around to grab the CB mic. "Eddie! Where are you going? She's right there. She's just a waitress, for crying out loud!"

"She's a grinding *loon*, is what she is! That was a rocket, man. She tried to blow us up!"

Eddie's voice shook. That was more disturbing to Benny than the explosions. Eddie *never* got scared.

"What?" Crash ignored Eddie's obvious distress. "You're running? You do that and you'll never work with me again."

"You know what? Deal. See you later. Benny, don't let him get you killed. Eddie out."

Crash stared at the CB mic in his hand, then ripped it out of the dash and threw it behind him.

Benny shrunk down in his seat. "You OK, Crash?"

"No! Those losers—" He shuddered, getting control of himself. "Today sucks, but you know what? Bad as it's been, it's about to get a whole *lot* worse for her." Crash's face twisted in a snarl. "I was saving this for that armored beast, but Miss Wannabe Duellist is begging for it."

Crash twisted around, kneeling in his seat, and reached into the back of the buggy. He hauled out a three-foot long metal dumbbell and dropped it onto his shoulder.

"What's that?"

Crash cackled and slapped the side of the tube. A flat wire sight popped up in response. "Waitress-be-Gone." He giggled again. "Gets the job done. Hold us steady, Benny. You hit a rock or anything and I'll use this on you." He leaned into the sight and shifted the barrel, trying to draw a bead on the battered arctic-blue vehicle behind him.

Jackie grinned at the traffic on the CB. "Did you hear that, folks? Sounds like we've got a runner. Two down, one to go. Let's finish this." She turned to head for the last remaining buggy. Her grin faded as she saw the gunner in the other vehicle rummaging around in the back of his buggy. "What are you doing now?" she muttered.

The gunner in the last remaining buggy turned and lifted something. It was larger than a rifle, by far. It wasn't until he slammed it down on his shoulder and popped up the wire sight that what she was seeing clicked.

"OK, that's bad." Jackie kept up her narration out of habit. She jerked the wheel hard left, bouncing up out of the seat, tires scrabbling for purchase on the hard-packed earth. "It looks like Mr. Bozo here wants to play rough."

She started jinking erratically; left, then right, then right again. She'd always had problems with this sort of thing. Crow made for an excellent cinematographer, but he was a crappy gunner. She locked the autocannon forward and tried to nudge the barrel down to account for their separation before mashing the firing button.

A burst of fire speared out and chewed up the ground two-thirds of the way between her and the buggy ahead of her.

"Come on…" she nudged the sights on the autocannon up and let loose with another burst.

Benny shouted in surprise as a burst of autocannon fire screamed past them on the left. "She's shooting at us! Why is she shooting at us?"

"Shut. UP!" Crash screamed. Crash braced himself against the roll bar behind the seat and pulled the sights down on the stripped-down four-by-four behind them, lips peeled back from his teeth in a feral grin.

"Bye-bye, bi—"

His words disappeared in an explosion of heat and the roar of the knock-off javelin launching its heat-seeking anti-armor round toward Jackie's truck.

"INCOMING!"

Jackie wasn't even conscious of shouting. Nor of spinning her wheel, or slamming her hand across the buttons on her console. She felt the distinctive CLICK of each anti-missile defense switch under her palm as they engaged, and the tug of her tires as they bit into the earth, attempting to whip her buggy into a tight arc.

There was a timeless pause, mid-turn, when everything seemed to slow to a stop. The missile hung in the air, silhouetted in its own expanding exhaust flame, giving her enough time to think. *Can I finish the turn? Did I unload the chaff, or—*

An explosion from behind the autocannon pushed her to the left. A pair of anti-missile rounds, flare and chaff, popped off and exploded immediately between her and the incoming ordnance at the same time. Intense heat washed over her as the cloud of aluminum strips obscured the missile headed her way.

Crow howled.

"Come on, girl!" She fought with her ride, trying to get it back on track. "Work with me!"

The world exploded.

Dirt and gravel fountained up as the missile augered into the ground and detonated a few yards behind her. Her truck slewed left, then right, then back again. She fought desperately to keep control. Five seconds later, she emerged from the cloud of debris, covered in dirt and shouting in triumph.

"YESSSS—"

The shout turned into a scream. An enormous chunk of rock caught her back left tire. The tire exploded into shreds of reinforced rubber, causing the whole side of the four-by-four to sag. Jackie disengaged the clutch, reaching for the brakes, but found herself unable to reach to them as her truck flipped, flinging her sideways.

Right. I undid my belts.

That was her last rational thought. Her hand slipped off the steering wheel and she was airborne, tumbling, until impact with the ground took her breath away along with her consciousness.

Head over heels. Crow felt the straps holding him in, keeping him from bouncing. He knew this was Bad. It had happened before. He would stop rolling and then She would cut him loose and they would wait for the big noisy box full of Bad smells to come and take them away from all the noise. She would be angry, but not at him. He would have to push up against Her and remind her that everything was OK because She still had him.

He stopped looking through his Eyes and waited for the turning to stop.

When the Metal Couch stopped moving, he was in the wrong place. The ground was on his side, but he wasn't lying down. The straps were still holding him. It was all very strange. He whined and looked left, which was all wrong, because that was up now.

Her couch was empty. She wasn't there. She was always there!

Crow whimpered, whipping his head around. Trying to see where She was, to see—

Eyes. He could find her with his Eyes. He looked through them again. Where were they? He swooped around. There! Far away, the yellow thing they were chasing. Past that, he saw something: himself, in the Metal Couch.

He whined and pushed his Eyes forward, toward where She had to be.

"Yes!" Crash pumped his fist at the fountain of dirt behind them. "I got her! I got her!"

At least, that's what Crash thought he was saying. The roar of the anti-armor round had left his ears ringing. He could see Benny's mouth moving, but couldn't make out what he was saying.

No big loss.

To the right side of the explosion, there was a flash of blue as the waitress' truck rolled, tumbling until it slowed and came to a rest on the passenger side.

"NNnnnnnGAAAH!" Crash smacked Benny on the shoulder. "Turn around! Go back!"

"WHAT?"

"GO BACK!" Crash pointed. "NOW!"

Benny slowed and turned, taking them back the way they had come.

Thirty seconds later, Benny slammed to a halt next to the arctic blue four-by-four sitting on its side. Crash was out of their buggy in a flash, eyes wide. His head whipped around, searching.

"Where is she? Benny. Do you see her?"

"Jackie? No." Benny killed the engine and clambered out his side of the buggy. "There's Crow, though. That's her dog! She always rode with him."

"SHUT UP!" Crash picked up a rock and threw it at Benny. The blonde man ducked, even though the stone went wide. "I don't want to hear about the dog, I don't want to hear about some washed-up duellist, and I don't want to hear you anymore. Unless you see that waitress, keep your mouth SHUT!"

Benny stepped back and raised his arm, pointing past Crash.

Crash spun around. A hundred yards away, a figure in a blue body suit stirred feebly.

Crash snarled and stalked across the hard-packed earth of the high desert.

Jackie came to slowly. There was pressure, then pain. Then her higher mental gears kicked in. *I really need to stop doing that.*

It wasn't the first time she'd been thrown from a car. That was the point of the super-novex, to keep her in one piece. More or less. *Don't move.* She took inventory of her situation. Sky up above, so she could still see. The coppery taste of blood in her mouth was strangely familiar and almost comforting. She wiggled her fingers and toes. No problem. Nothing to do then except lie still and wait for the pizza truck.

… except she couldn't lie still, could she? There was no ambulance coming. Someone else was, though. They'd been chasing someone, hadn't they?

She groaned, tried to roll over, and blacked out for a moment. The pain made her vision waver. When she could finally focus, a shadow fell over her. She looked up through the faceplate of her helmet. The ugly thug from the eight-top looked down on her, eyes wide.

"It is you." He giggled. "What, you think some cheap imitation novex makes you a duellist? You thought you could take on *Los Muertos*?"

She coughed. Despite the blood in her mouth, her throat was dry. "Who?" She finally croaked.

The thug blinked, then kicked her in the side. His punt wasn't anything compared to the tumble she'd just taken, but it caused enough pain that she missed his ranting. She didn't miss the oversized hand-cannon pointed in her general direction, though.

"…*Muertos*. Ha! Benny thought you were some sort of celebrity."

Jackie froze. Super-novex might protect against road rash, but it wouldn't do much for her if he opened up with that gun at this range.

"You're just a dumb waitress, aren't you?"

Spots danced in front of her eyes. No. Not spots. Something was flying toward them, *fast*. A familiar low hum filled the air.

The laugh bubbled up from inside her. It hurt, but she couldn't stop it. Then the thug's face screwed up in rage, and she didn't *want* to stop it. She ignored the pain and raised her hand, pointing at him, gasping out four words amidst the laughter.

"Smile—for the—camera!"

His rage faded to puzzlement, but just for a fraction of a second before Crow's two drones intersected his head at 100 miles per hour.

She must have blacked out there for a second. She came to, staring at the sky, Crow nuzzling at her and whining. Jackie reached up and used him to help roll over onto her hands and knees, head down.

"Good boy." She laid a hand over him. "How'd you get out of your straps?"

"I kinda let him out."

Jackie whipped her head up, then winced. The round-faced blonde thug stood next to her four-by. He had his hands clasped together, wringing them nervously around something.

"I hope you don't mind. He looked like he wanted to be let out, so I did."

Jackie carefully levered herself up to wobbly feet. The kid didn't seem to care, so she took a moment to check herself out. *No permanent damage, thankfully.* "From my ride?"

The kid shot a glance at her truck and hunched his shoulders, shrinking into himself. "Sorry about that. I mean, I didn't do it. I didn't shoot at you none. That was Waldo, there. Only he calls himself Crash. Called, I mean. He's past tense now."

"He's Crashed, you mean?" Jackie fought the urge to giggle. She knew if she started, she might not stop.

"I guess." The blonde blinked rapidly. She watched his mental gears try to re-engage his original train of thought. "What I meant, it was like you call yourself Jack, when you're really a Jackie. I'm, uh, kind of a fan, by the way. I mean, who wouldn't be? You *are* Jack Frost, aren't you?"

He's babbling. Neurons fired, memories of a life lived a long time ago and a long way away. She undid her helmet, pulled it off, and carefully shook out her hair. Not bad, she thought; and if she had to stop and spit out some blood, well. That's what the fans expected, wasn't it?

"The one and only." She turned up her smile. "What's your name, sugah?"

The poor kid *blushed.* She almost felt sorry for him.

"Benny, ma'am. I was kind of wondering if I could, um." He thrust his hand forward. In it was a pen, and a coffee-stained paper placemat from the Haus. "Could I get your autograph?"

She looked down at Crow. He cocked his head at her, his tail giving a tentative wag that turned into a flurry of happiness. She sighed.

"Tell you what—Benny, was it? Tell you what, Benny. Help me get my ride right side up and follow me back to the Haus. Then I'll give you your autograph, and you can tell me exactly what in tarnation is going on here. Deal?"

Benny grinned. "Deal."

She made it back to the Haus half an hour before Hank did. That gave her enough time to pull into the garage and peel herself out of her supernovex. She tossed it into the back of her truck next to the autocannon and threw a sheet over it. Crow jumped from the passenger seat of the four-by to the concrete floor of the garage, plopped down, and promptly fell asleep.

"Good boy." She gave him a skritch. He twitched, already deep asleep and no doubt dreaming of the day's excitement.

She was at the front of the Haus, tying on her apron, when she heard *Bessie's* distinctive rumble. Benny was in the corner, head back and mouth open, sound asleep after her impromptu interrogation. Tiffany caught her looking Benny's way and smirked.

"No rest for the wicked, eh?"

"You know it." She jabbed a finger at Tiffany. "Not a word to Hank."

"Oooh. Looks like you had an exciting ride. You've still got a little, you know." She gestured at her cheek. "Right there."

Jackie peeled a bit of ballistic gel off her face and flicked it into the garbage. By the time Hank wandered back into the Haus, she'd already picked up two orders and was busy cleaning tables. Hank strolled over and hugged her from behind. She could tell she'd have bruises tomorrow, but the painkillers were doing their job. At least, she could lean back into him without groaning.

"No problems?"

"Not a one. Well. I heard someone out there playing 'American Girl' on one of the CB channels. Could have sworn I caught a flash of blue in my rear-view mirror at one point, too. Anything you want to tell me about?"

She turned in his embrace and stomped a foot. "You weren't supposed to know!" At his look, she sighed. "Not right away."

"Kind of hard to miss." He lowered his voice. "I listened in. Thank you."

"Well." She grinned. "It felt good to get out again. And Crow caught some amazing footage. We can sell that on the fan networks for a pretty chunk of change."

Hank let go of her and stepped back. "That might be a recurring thing. I suspect they weren't just after me. They wanted Amos."

"Not them. International Breakfast Sandwich. That's what Benny said." At Hank's raised eyebrow, she pointed at the kid sleeping in the corner of the diner. "Long story, but he decided he likes us better. We can ply him with bacon and get the complete story when he wakes up."

Hank shook his head. "You girls and your strays. We need to find out what he knows. If we can't keep Amos and his family safe from IBS, we can kiss our supply lines goodbye. You may have to come with me for a while."

Her heart skipped a beat. "Me and Crow, you mean. Maybe."

"What do you mean, maybe? I can tell you're already itching to get out there again."

"I got lucky today. They weren't expecting me. Next time will be *very* different unless we prepare. We need to up-armor my truck, for one. Top off our ammo and expendables. I can hammer on my old ride until it's usable, but we'll really need at least three runners to do a proper screen." She glanced over at Tiff, leaning on the counter and chatting with Mongo. "We could put Tiff's new boyfriend in my old ride with Benny, then maybe—"

Hank held up both hands, laughing. "Whoa there! All great ideas. Save that enthusiasm for when we have a chance to talk it over with Pops, though. It's still his diner, after all."

Jackie grinned. "OK, OK. I'm a little excited. Do you think he'll go for it?"

Hank paused, then nodded. "I think so. Especially since I agree with you. I get the feeling it's time we expanded this operation."

Cargo
By Bee M Kay

"I frackin' don't care! My contractions are coming every three minutes and you... Augh!"

Yorick Mayes glanced at his vid phone and watched his wife double over. Rick winced in sympathy. "Amy, honey, we passed the Sturbridge I-84 connection a few minutes ago. We won't be much longer. Thelma, what's our ETA?"

"At our current speed, our estimated arrival time is in one hour, twenty-one minutes, at sixteen hundred-" the on-board AI answered.

"Thanks," Rick cut her off. "I'll be home soon, Amy. Just hold out a little bit longer."

Static crackled from the vidscreen's loudspeakers.

Dang. He hated to see her like that, hated even more that he was unable to help her, because he was stuck at work. He was hauling a case of Uncle Al's Vindictive Piston Oil—the limited edition with the casket-shaped transport box and exclusive printed-on skull design —through the countryside in his GMC van.

Well, he and Amy owned the van. But his gunner-wife hadn't done any runs with him since they had learned she was pregnant.

This job, though, was heaven-sent. They needed the money. Badly.

Between paying off the loans for the van, repairs, hospital bills and just living their lives, they were technically broke. No gunner meant no risky stuff. As a result, new jobs had trickled down to the speed of cold molasses, especially when regular customers switched to other transport companies.

Of course, he had tried hiring replacements for Amy, but as a business, they were just too small to afford it. The profit margin had dropped to near zero with an extra salary to pay and made their bad situation worse.

And then, there were their Gold Cross plans. The suckers at GC wanted two thousand per update recording, on top of an annual memory storage fee of one thousand per person for their 'clone on demand' plan. And that was not counting the ten thousand it would cost to actually start a new clone! Both his and Amy's brain tape updates were done monthly; money they simply couldn't afford. Maybe less was more. He had to talk to Amy about this after the baby was born.

Once the hospital bill for *that* stay had arrived. Darn it.

He sighed. Better a few months of lost memories than minimal housing and junk food on the table.

Dang. I better cross my fingers and not jinx things. Rick tugged at the collar of his body armor and focused on the street instead, or rather, the Groove Hauler convoy that drove before, beside, and behind him. Between the three heavy-duty semis, two smaller trucks, Rick, and the escorts, there were thirteen vehicles. He had paid passage with them because safety lay in numbers.

On screen, Amy sat up straight again. She pulled the camera closer, exhaustion written over her face. "You better hurry. Mom says she's taking me to the hospital now." She touched her lips with one finger and reached for the camera. "Love you."

Yorick mimicked the gesture. "Love you, too."

"Augh, friggin'—"

Her next contraction set in, then the screen went dark.

"Signal lost," Thelma announced.

"Call her back."

"Unable to comply. The connection to the phone provider is jammed."

Rick slammed his fist on the steering wheel. "Darn it!"

"Mommy Shark here. Attention! Incoming raiders," the convoy's foreman, Frank, crackled over the radio on their assigned channel. "I repeat, incoming raiders. Initiate Formation Fishtank. Acknowledge with status. Over."

"Thelma, combat mode." Rick reached for the helmet he had stored on the passenger seat, put it on, and opened the gun compartment. Handguns, a portable rocket launcher, and a mortar tube lined up for a worst-case scenario. Meanwhile, Thelma prepped the van: its autocannon and auto defense mechanisms activated. Rick folded down the steel plate windshield armor, all but closing the field of vision through the front window.

"10-4 on Fishtank. Shark One is armed and ready, over," Trailer Truck Number One called in.

"Okay on the fishies. Shark Two is armed and ready to rumble! Over," the second rig reported.

"Affirmative for Fishtank. Baby Shark is armed and ready. Over," Rick said.

'Fishtank', a standard formation, consisted of two heavily armed rigs leading the convoy, the trucks and Yorick's van in the middle, and the third rig bringing up the rear. The escorts zoomed ahead and alongside them. Frank Miller operated the convoy and owned two of the rigs. A no-nonsense man when it came to safety drills, he ensured everyone on the team knew by heart what to do at all times, especially when under attack. Rick had done enough trips with the Groove Haulers in the past couple of years to know the moves inside and out. The convoy's internal communications were encrypted, of course; you didn't want the enemy listening in on your plans. Call signs and code were standard, nevertheless, helping to avoid misunderstandings.

"They put up a roadblock, but surveillance says it's not very solid. Shark One will try to ram through it first, to save ammunition. But don't take chances," Frank instructed.

Great. If Shark One—a heavily reinforced Freightliner Cascadia with armor and weapons enough to make most raiders turn on their heels and run—should fail to make an impression, Rick would be right in the middle of the melee. He detected drones homing in on the rig and the truck ahead of him. "Thelma, acquire targets. Take out the flying pests!"

"Affirmative."

The autocannon mounted to Rick's GMC spat bursts of explosive-tip, copper-plated steel bullets. One of drones got hit. It emitted sparks, tumbled off course, and crashed down on the streets below. The other crashed into the rear of the truck, exploding in a burst of flames. As far as Rick could tell, the truck's armor held. Not that he had time to worry about that.

A grasshopper buggy accelerated next to him, with one of the escort vehicles in hot pursuit. But the escort wasn't firing at the grasshopper. Their machine gun, a Vulcan MG, hauled bullets into something behind them.

"Holy Reboot!" Rick muttered. A battered pirate Ripsaw tank barreled after it. The Vulcan's rounds did zilch to the heavily armored tank. Instead, the Ripsaw's M240 machine gun blasted a few precise rounds at the escort. It scored a lucky hit and the vehicle's engine belched out flames and black smoke briefly before it detonated.

One of the other drivers screamed, "Shark Eight is out, repeat, Eight is out!"

Frank's voice radiated unnatural calm. "Keep formation."

Rick sighed. *Damn!* But one could not stop, salvage, and mourn in the middle of an attack.

"Keep formation," Frank repeated, "Sharks Six and Ten, take care of the Ripsaw. Everyone, they have several Pickups with cannons running along the old highway. Be careful."

Rick growled. The old highway had been replaced by the interstate and still ran parallel to the newer road in many places. Some sections were in good enough shape for use by the bandits to run this kind of attack.

Ka-WOOM!

"They have a howitzer!" someone yelled. "Susi, Max, break up, break up!"

The rig ahead of Rick swerved desperately when the shell hit the street next to it, narrowly avoiding the explosion's fireball. Rick stepped on the pedal and followed suit. The escort vehicles swarmed to shield them from the attackers, but one could only do so much about rockets and shell rounds.

Ka-woom-Katacha-whOOM!

The shockwave hit Rick's van square in the side, pushing him almost off the road, as the next explosion shredded the asphalt. Gravel pelted the van as it zigzagged out of control, plunged down into the crater, and catapulted into the air. Time slowed to a crawl. The van arched high, leaving the interstate, and Rick screamed at the same moment it crashed through a thicket and into the ground with the sickening sound of tearing metal.

Darkness.

Shades of gray swirled in eternal lines, before soothing white noise crept into his mind, snatched away by the shrill *Whee-oo! Whee-oo! Whee-oo!* of the alarm klaxon blaring through the haze in Yorick Mayes' skull. The acrid smell of smoke stung his nose.

A voice fizzled in and out over the rioting klaxon. "…Mommy… calling… Mommy Shark… come in, Baby Shark, repeat…"

He knew that voice. The convoy's foreman… Frank? Yorick sat up, the motion rewarded by sharp pain stabbing into his brain from his left shoulder. His eyes snapped open. "Ow!"

A thin beam of sunlight pierced through the shattered remains of the windshield. Dust particles danced through the air in the slice of light. The world outside felt strangely off-kilter; rocks, dirt, and splintered glass took up most of his view. And the blasted klaxon continued to scream at him with a vengeance.

Yorick blinked.

Fragments of memories drifted by.

Amy… lovely Amy… his wife Amy… Waiting for him back home… Just a quick delivery run, then he'd be with her…

…her and the baby…

He'd miss the baby being born… Amy laughing at something Frank said over the radio… Frank… The Convoy? Right, they'd made good progress and had just passed Southbridge on the Interstate 84 when…

"Baby Shark! Are you deaf? Rick! Answer me!" the voice from the radio demanded.

Tarnation! The raiders… there had been raiders, right? And they had attacked Groove Hauler's convoy. The road gained instant giant potholes and… Rick gulped in air, all the haze in his head gone. *Frack.*

"Rick! Answer me!" the voice from the radio demanded again.

"I'm fine," he croaked, fumbling for the seatbelt buckle. His fingers trembled so badly, he only managed to click the lock open after two attempts.

Frack! What was wrong with him? This wasn't the first and it wouldn't be the last crash he'd been in. He slipped out of the seat and to his feet. His stomach lurched. His vision went dark and grizzled like a dying TV screen, the noise of the klaxon seemed suddenly miles away. He grabbed the back rest of his seat. It was the only thing that kept him upright.

"Not now," he snapped. "I won't faint now."

After a couple of steadying breaths, his body chose to obey. His shoulder pulsed in pain, but Rick ignored it. "Baby Shark to Mommy Shark, I'm fine. Copy?"

The fire alert klaxon drowned out the reply. Darn it. He'd totally forgotten about that. "Thelma, turn off the blasted fire alert."

"Confirmed."

The wails of the klaxon died in a strangled yelp. Rick sighed. "Thanks."

"Mommy Shark to Baby Shark…"

"I'm here, Frank," he croaked. "Baby Shark to Mommy Shark, do you copy?"

"…explosion and smoke…" Static frazzled Frank's voice, making him hard to understand. "…must be dead…"

"Blast it! I'm fine! Don't you hear me?" Of course they couldn't hear him. They must be out of reach by now and likely thought him dead. Wonderful. He was on his own. *Frack.* He wouldn't make it back to Amy in time to see his son or daughter being born, and as the cherry on top, he'd miss the triple bonus for delivering the cargo on time. *Double frack.* He just hoped that the rear end of the convoy had made it through the section of torn street in one piece. "Thelma, start the emergency transponder signal."

"Confirmed. Transponder signal initiated. Warning. Ammunition temperature is above normal levels," Thelma informed him. "Immediate action is required."

Uh-oh. On top of whatever was left of a thousand rounds of their MG-ammo, a handful of rockets and mortars filled the sealed ammunition bank.

Rick fingered for the release of the emergency kit. He needed a mask. If his van had been fully equipped, automatic fire extinguishing systems would've already taken care of any flames.

Unfortunately, his van wasn't fully equipped. Yorick and Amy had settled for the bare minimum in equipment for their Hauler-Flex van, because they couldn't afford any better. The upgrade to automatic systems and the addition of a recoilless rifle to the setup that he had planned for after this trip? *Pointless now.*

The van was schrott, kaput, busted.

They were broker than broke.

They were bankrupt.

He'd have to hire out as driver to a convoy again and go back into racing.

We'll have to move in with Amy's parents for a while. A smile pulled at the corner of his mouth. *She's going to kill me…*

At least, he'd survived the crash. *What use is it that we have a GC plan, when there's not enough money in our savings to pay for starting a clone anyway?*

"Warning," Thelma's voice tore through the whirlwind of thoughts. "Immediate action is required."

"Wha—" Smoke began to haze the air in the driver's section of the van. Rick sighed. He must be deeper in shock than he had thought, not firing on all cylinders, because none of the post-crash stuff held any importance until...

"Argh! I'm doing it again! Thelma, show me the location of the fire."

Rick shook his head, but it didn't help to dispel the growing sense of detachment.

The vehicle's schematics lit up on the screen in front of him. A red blob blinked near Amy's gunner seat in the rear of the vehicle.

There was no way he'd give up the GMC without a fight. Rick grabbed a face mask from the emergency box between the seats and put it on. Then, he reached under the driver's seat, pressed on the clip of the fire extinguisher fastened there, pulled it out of its storage space, and yanked the safety pin.

Thin trails of smoke crawled through the cargo compartment. He struggled through the inside of the van, squeezing past the cargo. The armor had taken the brunt of the impact, but the roof looked like a giant had stomped on it.

Amy would not be happy about this.

Rick reached the gunner's seat in the rear end of the vehicle. No sign of the fire, but thick swaths of smoke swirled above him.

"Immediate action is required," Thelma demanded

He kicked open the small utility door next to the ammunition storage that the AI had marked on screen.

Flames roared out of the compartment.

The heat bit into his skin. Rick took a step back, ignored the pain and aimed the nozzle at the fire before he pressed the release. A cloud of extinguishing powder whooshed through the ammunition compartment's opening. A few moments later, the chemicals had done their job, and the visible flames were gone. But the danger was far from over. He'd have to remove the ammunition and tear open the paneling to vanquish the still smoldering fire because the van had enough wiring, plastic, and electronic parts in this section to feed it.

Rick had neither the tools nor the time to do that. He sighed. "Inform me if the ammo gets to critical levels again, Thelma. I'll get the cargo outside."

"Affirmative."

He ignored the pain in his shoulder, put down the empty fire extinguisher and fingered for the release of the cask's safety belt. When he pried the box from the floor, his shoulder screamed bloody murder. The pain sent another dizzy spell through him, and the load almost slipped from his hands. Belatedly, he remembered that he still needed to open the door. "Great job, Rick, just great."

He put down the cask, turned around, grabbed the handle of the van's slide door, and pulled.

Nothing happened.

He tried again.

The door didn't budge.

A quick examination told him that the impact had mangled the mechanism. *Not good.* He went for the back door. *Dang. Also jammed.*

"Ammunition temperature is beyond safety limits," Thelma said now. "Evacuation recommended."

"Yeah, yeah."

What now? The driver's side door was blocked by the thicket, because of the angle at which the van had landed. The exit on the passenger side, however, opened easily enough. There was his escape!

Rick put a foot on the emergency box that sat between the front seats and dragged himself upwards. He was half out of the door when he remembered the cask of merchandize.

Frack!

He looked back down into the belly of the van and froze. Smoke hazed the air, thickening with every moment as the fire grew stronger. Rick hesitated. *Going back in there is madness. But without the money for the delivery…*

He sighed, took a deep breath and dove back, then lugged the cask toward the opened passenger door. *Why does the frackin' thing have to be so frackin' heavy!?*

Fumes bit into his eyes and lungs; he coughed, but kept pushing the box up. It was a tight fit at best, and the cursed thing just got stuck half-way through.

"Son of a…!"

Rick tried to rattle the cask loose, but it was no good.

"Temperature critical," Thelma announced.

He needed more leverage. Standing on the edge of the driver's seat now, Rick pressed his entire upper body against the cask. It slid up a few more inches. Thick smoke billowed past him. *One more try.* He slammed upwards. Agony burnt through his shoulder, sending him into a dizzy spell on impact, but his cargo popped out of the opening at last.

Rick climbed up behind it and somehow managed to drag the cask from the chassis to the ground next to the van without breaking the goods. He leaned against the metal frame, heaving for air as if he'd run a mile.

Thelma's muffled voice sounded from inside the vehicle, "Temperature critical. Explosion imminent. Evacuate at once. I repeat, evacuate at once."

"Poo on a stick!" He put his full weight into hauling the box toward the embankment of the Interstate. Twenty feet, thirty…

Dizziness washed over him. He lost balance, stumbled over the cask, and fell hard. Liquid agony blazed through his shoulder when he tried to get back to his feet.

He screamed in frustration. Or pain. Or both.

He didn't care any longer.

He looked back at the van, then up the embankment. Was he far enough away from the vehicle to get through the inevitable explosion unscathed?

Rick tried to get up but dizziness knocked him back down.

Drat. At least Amy was safe. If she'd been in the gunner's seat… He pushed the thought away. *Gosh, Amy…*

But at least he had made it out of the van.

Rescue would arrive soon; with the raiders gone, the emergency transponder signal would get someone here, and if his luck held, he'd be back with Amy in time to see his son or daughter born.

WHOOOOM!

The shockwave from the van's explosion hit brutally. The skin of Rick's back singed through the protective clothing. He hurled face first into the dirt, his body a molten mass of misery.

He must've passed out, because the next thing he knew, someone rolled him to his back, so he lay flat in the grass. He opened his eyes, fighting to see through the slowly receding rim of darkness that clouded his vision.

A stranger stared down at him, and asked in a worried tone of voice, "Hey, Yorick, dude, you okay?"

Rick sat up, looked at the smoldering carnage that used to be his transporter and sighed. The van's roof now had a huge, ragged hole, courtesy of the detonation in the ammunition storage. "My van exploded."

The man followed his line of sight, then looked back at Rick and gave a sharp nod. "Yeah. Looks like you took quite a bang. You hurt?"

"Yeah, I'm…" Rick stopped mid-sentence. He should be crying from pain, what with his shoulder busted and his back burnt from the fireball. But except for the creepy, dark halo that framed everything in sight, he felt… Comfortable? He quickly took inventory, but nothing seemed to be out of place or out of function. Weird. "No, seems I'm good."

"Great! I heard your distress signal, and then saw the smoke column. You need a lift?"

He nodded. "I was on the way to Springfield. You going that direction?"

The man grinned and held out a skinny hand. "I am now, Yorick."

"Thanks, man."

Rick grabbed the hand and was pulled to his feet swiftly. A few inches shorter than him, the stranger looked like skin and bones clad in black clothing—from his protective armor to his hoodie, jeans, and boots. A fellow trucker, perhaps? Rick pointed at the cask of Vindictive Oil. "Do you have space for my cargo, too?"

The man frowned. "That casket? I'm not an undertaker."

Rick grimaced. "It's just some special edition Uncle Al's merchandise, Mister… I'm sorry, I seem to have misplaced your name. We've met before?"

"Mortimer Graves. At your service." The man bowed. "Just call me Morty. And to answer your question… yes, Yorick, we did meet, in the Hartfort Arena, six years ago."

Rick frowned. "I'm sorry. I don't remember anything from that day."

Morty's expression showed sympathy. "I know. You died."

Rick shuddered involuntarily. He—that was, the original Yorick—had been killed by an enemy grenade during his first professional autoduel race in the Arena in Hartfort. Fortunately, his sponsor had insisted on a Gold Cross plan, and Yorick-The-Clone had been started straight away. He'd awakened in a much younger clone body just a few months later, with a few weeks' worth of memories missing from before the accident.

"Yes… I'm Yorick two-point-oh." Rick forced a smile. "Well, then, pleasure to meet you again, Morty."

A few minutes later, they had carried the box up to the interstate. A quick look around confirmed no other wrecks; he had been the only Groove Hauler victim of the craters in the asphalt. *Something to be grateful for. I hope the rest of them made it to town.*

Morty's rig turned out to be a dusty, time-worn, black 587 Peterbilt, with an equally dusty and time-worn black trailer. The weapons Rick could see at a glance were no joke. Several turrets sat on the length of the trailer's roof; MGs, cannons, rocket launchers and some fancy weapons systems he couldn't identify immediately. Rick gave a low whistle. "Nice setup, dude."

On the sides of the truck and trailer, hooded skeletons with scythes and the artfully drawn words "The Grim Reaper" perfected the image. It was a common motif—many teams and convoys had death-related names and themes. Cargo hauling was a risky occupation.

"Let's put the box into the trailer," Morty said. "How did you get it out of your van? That thing weights a ton!"

"Business secret," Rick laughed, then sobered. "My wife's having our baby right now and I'm not coming back empty-handed."

"Then let me help you with that." Mortimer opened the trailer's doors. "Here you go."

Rick noticed the usual plethora of spare parts and ammunition boxes he'd expect a trucker to lug along on a cross-country run. The cargo, itself, consisted of three regular sized, weirdly shaped lava lamps that poked out of a strapping system in the middle of the trailer. One was switched off, but in two of them, the glowing bubbles in the lamps danced up and down slowly. They sent a soft glow into the otherwise dark space. "You're on your way to pick-up?"

"Well, I'm not running empty." The man pointed at the lamps. "There's those two, and you as well. But, yeah, I need to step on it, my next customer's waiting."

Morty assigned a spot near the doors for Rick's cask. After they secured the merchandize properly, the two men hopped off the trailer and closed the doors. When they reached the Peterbilt, Morty gestured for Rick to climb into the semi-tractor's passenger seat.

Rick squeezed past the MG mount and into the cabin. Unlike the exterior, the interior looked spic-and-span clean and very comfortable. An hourglass, sand in the bottom bulb, dangled from the radio mount. It was too large for a key chain. *Nice touch for the Grim Reaper theme.* A screen that showed images from the rig's external surveillance camera system sat on the dashboard, so that both driver and passenger could see it.

The gunner's seat spelled 'Put Your Ass Here And You'll Never Want To Get Up Again'. He strapped himself into it and fastened the seatbelt. The darkness encroaching on his vision pulsed, but he ignored it. He'd get a full checkup once he was in Springfield and had made sure that Amy and the baby were okay.

Meanwhile, Morty had boarded as well, and moments later, the engine roared to life.

Rick felt the reassuring vibrations in every fiber, and the full, rumbling sound of the semi spread a sense of safety through him.

"Welcome back, Morty," the *Grim Reaper* AI's sugar-laden voice greeted them. "And who's our lovely fare today?"

"Corvy, this is Yorick Mayes." Morty performed a quick introduction. "He rides with us to Springfield."

"Understood, Morty," the AI said. "Hello, Yorick Mayes. Welcome aboard. We have an assortment of beverages and snacks in the fridge for your convenience, but let me know if you need something else."

Rick suppressed a chuckle. "Sure thing, Corvy. Pleasure to meet you."

Mortimer expertly curved his rig around the craters in the street and accelerated to cruising speed. He switched gears and activated the cruise control.

"You travel this road often?" Rick wanted to know after they had driven a while.

"More often than I like. It's been busy lately."

"There's been an uptick in traffic ever since they started building the new autoduel arena in Springfield."

"Yeah, there's that, too."

"Got myself quite a few good contracts out of it," Rick said. "Today's trip was an emergency run. Triple standard fare."

Morty's eyes went wide as saucers. "What?"

Rick grinned. "Yeah! The casket you helped me with? That's an extra-large, limited-edition cask of Uncle Al's Vindictive Piston Oil. The autoduellist who ordered it sounded really desperate. No idea what he's planning to do with all that oil, though."

Morty sighed. "The things people do for money…"

Rick shot him a side glance. "No pain, no gain. And it's less risky nowadays with the whole clone business."

"Perhaps. But there has to be someone who picks up the pieces after they depart… Gold Cross clone or not."

"I'm just grateful that you were there to pick me up, man!" Rick smiled. "So, do you often go without a gunner and escort?"

Morty gave him a toothy grin. "Most criminal elements are clever enough to stay away from me. I have a certain… reputation."

Rick frowned. "Well, that's… reassuring."

He'd never heard stories, heroic or otherwise, of a trucker with the handle of "Grim Reaper" in any of the truck stops he visited. And Mortimer Graves certainly was not one of the Knights of the Brotherhood. Those guys and gals were celebrities in the trucker world for the help and assistance they gave their fellow drivers.

"Doesn't mean that there are no fools who think they can't get a lick in and steal my cargo," Morty said, and pointed at the surveillance screen.

Rick only saw dust and speed-blurred landscape.

Morty pressed a button on the steering wheel, and with the cruise control now disengaged, the semi picked up speed. "You've got any experience as a gunner?"

"Four years riding shotgun on cattle convoys in Wyoming."

"That'll do. Corvy, acknowledge Yorick Hayes as part of the 273rd Grim Reaper Brigade and our new assigned gunner."

"Affirmative." The AI's sugar-sweet voice switched to a more business-like tone. "Yorick Hayes, welcome aboard the *Grim Reaper* as our new gunner. I have an MG at the front, two automatic cannons, rocket launchers, and a mortar in the trailer for your usage. The regular collection of passive defense systems is available for your entertainment."

"Uh… Thanks?"

Morty looked grim. "Corvy, battle mode."

"Battle mode confirmed."

Rick still made out nothing but dust and empty road behind them. "Er, no offense, but…"

A high, keening sound pierced the sky. It sounded like something from a horror movie, a skin-crawling mixture of insane seagulls' calls and a circular saw screaming its way through metal. Rick clutched his ears, but the infernal noise shredded through him, resonating with every cell right down to his bones.

"That's a sound weapon?" he yelled at Morty.

"Banshees!" Morty yelled back, and with an expression even more grim than before, stepped on the pedal. The rig's engine roared and the vehicle sprang forward. "Take them out as soon as they're in range."

"On it." Rick checked Corvy's progress in arming the weapons and readied the MG next to his seat. In the rear camera image, he watched a bunch of dark shapes blur into existence from the thick cloud of dust the rig trailed behind it. The camera automatically zoomed in, bringing them into focus. He made out people on motorcycles. The bikers pulled up on both sides of the Peterbilt's cabin at a ludicrous speed.

Deranged, whining howls tore at Rick's nerves. The banshees, long white hair streaming freely in the wind, clad in outlandish leather suits and wearing what must be twisted masks, homed in on the *Grim Reaper.* As they got closer and the surveillance image got sharper, he realized that their faces were... not human? Rick's insides cramped. "No frackin' way!"

It got worse. The motorcycles had sidecars from which the raiders were free to attack. Rick knew that bikers usually weren't much of a threat to a convoy or rig. But these guys had what looked like large rocket or large caliber mortar launchers on the side cars. How was that even possible?

WHOAFF! Bright flames exploded from the nearest launchers—no, strike that, they were huge flamethrowers!—over the front window.

"Yorick Mayes!" Morty screamed and cuffed Rick's arm. "Don't dawdle, take them out!"

Rick shook himself out of his stupor. The shrieks and wails got even louder, and the passenger door's armored glass window cracked in a spectacular spiderweb.

"Darn it!"

No frackin' way he'd have any raider shoot his vehicle from under his ass twice in a day. "Corvy, auto-target the bikers and fire at will."

"Affirmative."

The twin autocannons roared to life, each burst *Ka-tcha-ka-tcha-ka-tcha!-*ing into the enemy.

Rick added his own deadly rounds to it, hitting the riders of the two motorcycles next to him. A glance in the side mirror showed the vehicles as they slammed into each other, fell back, and then they and their side cars cartwheeled into fireballs.

Three more bikes crashed into the carnage before the trailer's dust cloud swallowed them. A distant *CHA-WHOOM!* shook the semi moments later, but he had no time to celebrate.

"Morty, they're trying to board the trailer!" Rick sent another round of lead into the attackers.

"Oh, they won't dare." Morty swerved the rig from one lane to the other. "The trailer's iron-plated. Keeps them out."

Rick shrugged. Iron plating was useless. Even steel plating had never kept raiders from boarding. But Morty apparently had dealt with these banshees before, and obviously felt he knew how to handle them. Their attackers, equally obviously, didn't care about anything the *Grim Reaper* threw at them. Rick focused on the ones who tried to jump on the tractor, mowing down one attacker after the other with short MG bursts. There was only so much ammunition in the MG's storage, better not find out the hard way how much they had left.

Corvy had no such reservations. The autocannons kept rattling like there was no tomorrow, and a small fortune of mortar shells and rockets whooshed into their pursuers. A brief look at the rear camera confirmed that none of the raiders had made it up onto the trailer—yet. They were pretty darned close though. Rick noticed that some hooks and grapples had latched to the doors, and frowned. What were they thinking? The rig blazed down the road at over a hundred miles an hour. To cross over to the trailer at this speed would be sheer insanity. Then, the first banshee stepped up on the rope. She seemed to fly toward the trailer, and reached for the trailer door handle.

"Corvy, rear defense!" Rick snapped.

"Target acquired."

Several dozen eardrum shattering explosions later, the banshees had fallen back at least three hundred yards.

"We're near the I-90 Chicopee crossing," Morty said. "If we keep them at bay until after the bridge, they'll fall off."

"What, more iron plating on the bridge?"

The MG's bullets hit another banshee and she tumbled from her motorcycle.

"No, Ludlow is in Gremlin territory."

"Playing one gang against the other? Smart."

The banshees had switched from using flamethrowers to guns. Rick heard the bullets hacking into the armor.

CRAAACK!

The already damaged passenger side window gave way, and bullets lodged themselves into the ceiling of the cabin. The wind rushed in, driving dust and tears into Rick's eyes. He kept firing in the direction he'd last seen the banshee motorcycles.

"Son of a…!" Morty checked his side mirror and grimaced. "Corvy, give 'em an earful!"

"Engaging loudspeakers. Please state your choice of music."

"Iron Maiden," Morty yelled. "You know the song."

Guitar riffs and drums boomed through the cabin. *"Alright!"* the singers chimed in. Another explosion shook the truck. The unearthly wail, which had threatened to rattle everything apart, became tortured before it broke off entirely. Had Corvy hit whatever sound weapon the cretins had dragged along?

The band finished the chorus of the song. The banshees shrank away, fell back, or veered to the side, putting as much distance between themselves and the rig as possible.

A few moments later, the semi rattled over the Chicopee bridge, and Rick could no longer see any of the raiders. The airstream from the broken window rampaged through the cabin, blowing more dirt into Rick's face. The heavy metal music still played at a deafening volume. Morty checked the rear camera, and apparently certain they had left the banshees behind, began to decelerate.

"Corvy, end song and run system check."

"Confirmed."

The infernal noise stopped. Since they had slowed to a normal speed, and the frequency at which sand and insects pelted his face became bearable, Rick finally dared to open his mouth again. "Whoa. I've driven this road a hundred times, but those banshees? Never even heard of them!"

"They usually keep a low profile and stay away from the living." Morty looked at the broken side window and sighed. He switched on the cruise control. "Hold the wheel for a moment, will you?"

"Sure." Rick grabbed the wheel to keep the rig on the road, while Morty half-climbed out of the seat, reached behind him into the sleeping cab, and pulled out some window plastic, thick, clear tape and a pair of scissors. Rick smiled in relief. "I see you are prepared."

"You bet." Morty slipped back into his seat and pointed at the materials. "Now, if you'd kindly take the supplies and—"

"Yeah, yeah," Rick interrupted him and grabbed the scissors. "Less blabbin', more fixing."

Half an hour later, the truck pulled into the Gold Cross hospital entryway. Mortimer stopped the *Grim Reaper* near the visitor's entrance, and Rick was happy to disembark. He felt a bit queasy and the dark rim that impaired his vision had become worse now that the adrenaline had worn off.

"Thanks, I'll find my way from here," he said, shaking Morty's hand. "I hope we will meet again sometime."

Morty grinned, reached for the hourglass that dangled from the radio's mounting bracket, and turned it so that the sand began to run down from the top bulb again. "Be careful what you wish for."

"Well, you better be off. I've got a wife to see, and your next cargo's waiting."

They bid their farewells and Rick jumped down to the street and shut the door. He almost had a heart attack when the Peterbilt honked goodbye before it rolled back to the road. He walked a few steps toward the hospital's entrance, and the familiar sound of the tractor's engine suddenly faded.

Rick frowned. He turned to look at the rig rolling down the street.

But the semi faded out of vision, too.

He blinked.

No. Way. Rigs didn't simply vanish.

The dark rim ate away at his vision, and a wave of dizziness washed over him. He really needed to get himself into the hospital and let the doctors run a few tests before he collapsed on the sidewalk.

Then, he remembered that the cargo he had rescued from his crashed van was still in the back of Mortimer's trailer.

Great, just great. So much for getting the triple fee.

Once he'd made sure Amy and the baby were okay, he'd have to track down Morty, contact him and retrieve the goods.

But now…

Now, all he wanted was to go inside…

…find out the number of Amy's room, hug…

…hug and kiss her, and…

…and the street scene lost color, shapes blurred, and the darkness that had lurked at the borders now pounced in. His balance ceased to exist. Rick stumbled and bile rose in his throat. He crashed into something hard. The air smelled of disinfectants and soft voices muttered something he couldn't quite make out.

Everything was a mess of blurred, convoluted shapes, with him stuck in the middle, unable to move, or even think straight. *Crap.*

He heard someone say, "Push, Mrs. Mayes! Push hard! Once more!"

Mrs. Mayes? As in Amy Mayes?!

A wail tore through his eardrums.

Rick tensed. Banshees, in Springfield?

Another voice said, "Congratulation, Mrs. Mayes! It's a boy! You know what you'll call him?"

"Benjamin," Amy's voice whispered.

And for a moment, the fuzzy shapes sharpened, and he finally recognized Amy. She lay on a delivery table close by, with a newborn on her chest. Rick stared at the wonder before him, just an arm's length away, his heart swelling with warmth. He reached out to his family, almost touching Amy and… in the blink of an eye, everything washed out of focus again and his hand plunked into nothing.

Rick screamed in frustration.

The sounds of the delivery room faded and the blurred world around Rick went pitch dark. He felt as if he was floating. The sensation faded after a while, and he tasted the faint scent of oil and machinery.

His vision slowly came back, but it was like being inside of a long, dark tunnel. He stood in an aisle of what looked like a huge warehouse with an automated storage system. To the left and right stood huge racking systems, partially filled with tall, transparent cylinders. The cylinders were perhaps eight feet tall, about three or four feet wide and attached to pipes and cables. Human looking shapes in various stages of development floated inside a cloudy liquid.

Cloning pods.

Holy Reboot.

He shuddered.

How had he ended up in a cloning facility? Nausea crept up his throat. He had to get back to the hospital, to Amy and his son.

An automated forklift, carrying a cloning pod, drove into the aisle. Rick pressed into the shadows of the rack behind him, but the vehicle ignored him, following a line on the ground. It stopped in front of one of the empty berths, lifted the pod into it with precise moves, and the utility connections snapped into place automatically.

A bright green light pulsed at the top of the cylinder for a few moments, then dimmed, and the status monitor screen next to the cloning pod switched on.

The forklift, its job completed, rolled back to where it had come from.

Who was in that pod? He couldn't tell, and didn't care.

I have to deliver the cargo and get back to Amy!

He wanted to run for the exit. But he couldn't.

Something pulled him back to that blasted clone pod, like a magnet.

He staggered the few steps from the aisle to the pod, forcing himself to get away, but the pull proved stronger. Finally, he gave up. Whatever this was, it wouldn't stop until he had gone to the pod. He read the information on the status monitor screen.

Remaining Growth Time: 180 days 128 hours 39 minutes 55 seconds.

Condition: Green.

7346-A-90555-Springfield-Mayes-Yorick.

"My clone?!"

Frack.

"How can they start my clone? I'm not dead!"

And that was when Morty's amused voice whispered out of nowhere, "Alas, poor Yorick, that's where you're wrong."

Rick spun around.

The air next to him blurred. Vapor condensed and concentrated into the shape of a human.

It solidified into the familiar features of Mortimer Graves. His almost skull-like face, his dark eyes like saucers in their sunken sockets, and the smile he plastered on it made him look like someone straight from the Blight years of the past.

Morty's looks hadn't bothered Rick before. Of course, he had wondered what illness had wasted the man so much. But now, the undead vibe of the trucker sent a chill down Rick's spine.

"You?"

Morty grinned and put an old and apparently heavy leather knapsack on the ground. "Yes, me. I told you we'd meet again. I'm here to pick you up for your shift as my gunner."

"What?! You're kidding me, right? Your frackin' gunner?" Rick stared at Morty, then once more at the monitor screen, then at the man again. "Wait… I'm really dead?"

It didn't make sense. And how could he be a gunner in anyone's rig if he was a goner?

"How? I made it out of the van before it exploded!"

"That you did, my friend, but a piece of shrapnel caught you in the neck and finished you off. Didn't take long for you to bleed out."

Rick struggled with grasping the full scope of this news. "I'm dead."

"Well, technically speaking, you're not dead any longer." Morty pointed at the cloning pod. "Your clone's growing in there. In a few months, the body will mature to twenty-five years of age. They'll upload your memories from the brain tape and you'll wake up again to be with lovely Amy and little Ben."

That much was true, and it calmed him a bit. But it still didn't explain anything. "And we're here, why?"

"Because I can't just drop you off at the Afterlife Hub. You have a clone." Morty sighed, bowed down to the knapsack and opened it. "Listen. You passed the tests and the higher-ups in Afterlife decided…"

"Whoa there! You're telling me the Grim Reaper is real, and it's you?"

"Not *the* Grim Reaper. Only one of them. Proud member of the 273rd Grim Reaper Brigade. We're legion." Morty gave him a scary grin-grimace. "Anyway, there's rules. While you spent the past few weeks in storage in my trailer waiting for transfer, you fell under my protection."

Rick's stomach plummeted through the floor. Or at least, it felt like that as he kept listening to Morty.

"But since they started your clone, regular rules apply, and the supervisors thought you made a great addition to our ranks." Morty's grin looked painful. "Congrats, you've been conscripted into the Grim Reaper Brigade's service until it's time for your clone to wake up."

Rick stared at him. Maybe they had both lost their minds. "As a gunner."

"Yes. My cargo's attracting too much unwanted attention."

"Like from banshees and gremlins?"

Rick saw Morty reach into the backpack and pull out a ball of light.

"Amongst others. The Brigade pays well, but it's a risky job. My last gunner… Wendigos ambushed us. After they were done with eating my cargo…" The Grim-trucker-Reaper studied the glowing ball he held between the tips of his bony fingers for a moment. "Rescue came too late. They had my gunner, that poor soul, for lunch."

Horror crept into every fiber of Rick's being. "I'm not going with you."

Morty looked up again, and Rick thought he detected sadness and guilt in the man's eyes.

"You don't understand, Yorick. It's not like you or I have a say in this."

"No, Morty… *You* don't understand," Rick growled and balled his fists. "You, nor anyone else, will keep me away from Amy and my son."

The Reaper sighed. It sounded like one of these long-suffering sighs that came from the very bottom of the soul. "Let me connect you to your new body first."

Tendrils of light shot out of the ball. Some zigzagged toward the clone pod, some toward Rick, and struck like a bolt of lightning. But it was something entirely different. Rick's entire body began to tingle for a moment. When the sensation ebbed, a weird feeling of safety —like being anchored in an underground shelter during the midst of a hurricane— spread through him. He *belonged*. The feeling grew so profound that he knew that it had been missing ever since Morty had picked him up. A soft, glowing, thin band of light now bound him to the clone inside the pod.

"There. A nice, strong attachment." Morty stuffed the now dark ball back into the knapsack. "We should leave. Our next cargo's waiting."

Rick shook his head. "I already told you; I won't come."

"And I repeat: you don't have a choice, Yorick."

Morty snapped his fingers and the next thing Rick knew, they were back in the cabin of Morty's Peterbilt. Curiously enough, it was parked on the sidewalk outside of the Gold Cross hospital in Springfield, just where the trucker had dropped him off.

"You're kidnapping me?" Rick roared. "And you think I'll cooperate with you? Dream on!"

"We better hurry." Morty pointed at the hourglass that dangled from the radio mount. Most of the sand had already run through to the bottom bulb.

"Welcome back," Corvy greeted them. "Cargo pickup confirmed, coordinates 42.2 degrees north, 72.94 degrees west. Four regular units, two storage units."

"Thanks, Corvy." Morty started the engine and the semi rolled down the road. "The Brigade isn't your enemy, Yorik. Even as a conscript, you can provide for your family while your clone's growing."

Tarnation. Morty obviously knew what carrot to dangle to get his interest. "You mean I get paid in real world money for riding shotgun with you?"

Morty named a figure per run that Rick was entitled to. Less than he had hoped for, but it would keep Amy from having to take on jobs again mere weeks after giving birth. Though… "Wait a sec. How does that even work? Reapers still ain't real… not really real… Ah, crap! You know what I mean!"

Morty grimaced. "Instant karma."

Rick raised an eyebrow. "Seriously? You're sounding less convincing by the minute, bro."

The other man shrugged. "You'll understand when you wake up. And you know, there are other perks, if…"

"If I don't get eaten by Wendigos?"

It was a low blow, but it gave Rick a certain satisfaction to see Morty wince.

"There are other perks if you sign up as a regular after your conscription ends… or before that date, if you find you like the job."

"Yeah, fat chance of that happening, Morty."

As they drove down the road, out of town and into the sunset, the last houses of Springfield whooshed by before they entered the westbound I-90. Perhaps this conscript thing wasn't so bad after all. Instead of being a waste of space in the cloning pod, he could help his wife and son. However, he refused to play by the Brigade's rules.

"I have two conditions, Morty."

"Oh?" Morty kept his eyes on the road. "They are…?"

"We will check up on Amy and Ben once per week, minimum."

"We can't."

"Because…?"

"The universe doesn't like it when Reapers meddle with the living."

Rick crossed his arms. "Then, forget it. I'm not going to fire a single shot if we get attacked."

Morty shot him a pained look. "You've no idea what you're asking. That karma thing…" He let out a defeated sigh and focused back on the road. "I already broke the rules by letting you see your kid's birth. I can't keep running solo. If they hand me my derriere on a plate, so what?" He nodded once. "I agree, if you promise to keep the visits strictly invisible and silent."

"As long as I can see them and make sure they're okay," Rick agreed.

The Peterbilt barreled down the interstate, way too fast considering the sun had slunk below the horizon by now.

"Any improvements on his condition?" Morty asked.

Rick frowned. "What?"

"I said, what's your second condition?" Morty repeated, shooting him a concerned look.

"Oh, yes, remember the casket I had with me when you picked me up?"

"Yes. I no longer have it."

"You ditched it?"

"I'm not an uncouth thief, man!" Morty grumbled. "Crap. The bugger's brainwaves are still erratic."

"Mr. Mayes is hallucinating again," Corvy announced.

Morty shrugged. "I know! I'll have to re-upload the last data segments again."

Corvy snapped, "May I remind you that it's against safety regulations, and you already tried it how many times now? Four?"

"Hey, I'm here, you know?" Rick waved a hand at Morty. "What are you talking about?"

Morty ignored him and instead sighed. "You know the only other option is to wipe his brain, and there's no guarantee that *that* works out."

"Well, it could be a hardware defect. His brain's obviously not connecting the synapses to store the memories correctly," Corvy suggested.

"Possible," Morty admitted. "His memories are a mess and he's increasingly delusional."

"Wait, what?" Rick winced when the rig's comfy gunner's seat faded into the soft reclining chair of a GC Reboot room. Patches of wet pressed against his scalp and temples, and the low hum of machinery filtered into his thoughts.

A lady wearing a lab coat stood next to the recliner. She raised her hand and shone a small flashlight into Rick's eyes. She turned to someone behind her. Rick followed her line of view and saw… Morty? Only, the guy no longer looked the part of a modern, semi-driving Grim Reaper. The black attire and protective amor was no more. *And what's with that smart Gold Cross medical technician outfit he's wearing instead?!*

"I know it's against your ethics, Mortimer… But you might have no other choice but to scrap this one."

"Hey! What are you doing? Who are you?" Rick tried to get up, but found himself struggling against restraints.

"Please relax, Mr. Mayes. You're probably feeling a bit confused, but that's perfectly normal in your situation. I'm Corvina Crowder, and you're in the Springfield Gold Cross Hospital Clone Reboot unit. You'll be right as rain in a moment. Just take a deep breath and let us do our job."

The lady *did* sound like Corvy. That didn't make things any better in Rick's books.

"Uploading begins in three, two, one," the man who looked like Morty said.

The wet patches on his head thrummed with energy.

"No! Stop!"

"Reboot!"

His brain exploded into fireworks.

Rick screamed.

Darkness.

A faint spot of warmth and light shone in the distance, but he was stuck.

Yorick pulled in a labored breath. Nausea swirled through every fiber of his being; the irrational fear of being trapped in molasses and pulled slowly under the surface sent a bolt of panic through him. He struggled toward the light. The sense of safety it radiated drew him in.

A long, painful wail sent him into high alert.

Holy Reboot! Banshees? Not banshees again!

Rick's eyes flew open.

He was neither in the street, nor the warehouse or Morty's trailer truck, but in a hospital room. A Gold Cross logo graced the wall.

Amy sat on a chair next to his bed, busying herself with a bawling baby she held lovingly in her arms. She reached into a bag next to her chair and pulled a toy from it, cooing while she handed it to the baby. At once, the crying stopped. The infant began to babble and then giggled in excitement.

Warmth and awe spread through him.

Amy. His Amy.

Oh, how he had missed her!

Safe. She was safe. And positively no banshees anywhere.

He let out a sigh of relief, then frowned. *Strange.* What happened to Morty? And then, there was that warehouse interlude, and the baby Amy held was way too large to be a newborn. Something didn't add up.

Was any of this real? It felt more like a fever dream, there-but-not-there, a twisted image of the world seen through the lens of some kind of drug-induced state. A bit like the involutory trip he'd experienced when the nurses in the hospital had pumped him full of pain relievers after he had broken his shoulder as a teenager…

Only… This was way more bizarre.

"Amy?" Rick finally managed to say, his voice hoarse.

She looked up from the baby, and their eyes found each other.

This was no dream.

"Amy."

Her eyes glistened, then she smiled, so broad and delicious, like he had rarely seen her smile before.

"Rick! You're awake!" She stated the obvious, scrambling to his side, the baby held tightly to her chest.

"You're all right?" Rick whispered. His vision blurred, and Amy's calloused hand caressed his cheek. His breathing hitched and he swallowed hard. He looked up into her face. "You and the baby…"

"We're fine."

Holding her and kissing her was one thing, but the child, squished between them, protested with an indignant howl. Rick hesitated briefly, unwilling to let Amy out of his grasp again.

But when the baby began to struggle against them, Amy pulled back with a slight sob. "Sorry, sweetums. Mama scared you?"

She smooched the baby's forehead and gently stroked his back.

The child must've been born months ago. *I missed all that time.* Rick forced his lips into a crooked smile. "Is that…"

"Yes, honey, this is our son." Her smile was genuine, and it softened as she addressed the boy. "Benjamin, this is Daddy."

Rick's heart galloped madly, like one of those racehorses at the Kentucky Derby.

He gently reached out to the infant. "Ben?"

Ben's small face screwed up in fear, and he stared at Rick wide-eyed. Lips pooched in a pout, he turned away with a cry, burying himself in Amy's shoulder, his tiny hands still clinging tightly to the toy.

"There, there," Amy soothed. "Sorry. He's just getting into that shy-of-strangers phase."

"And I'm a stranger." Rick's chest constricted. "I'm sorry I was late."

"Six months late!" she said. "But you tried. That's all that counts." She laughed. "Even though I cursed you to the inferno and back when I was in the delivery room, Yorick Mayes."

"I'll make up for it." He smiled, but then he remembered what she had said. Six months late. He sighed. "When… I mean, I am a clone, yes?"

Amy froze. "You left us the day Ben was born."

"How…?"

Her expression went blank for a moment, and he could tell she steeled herself. When she spoke again, she had gone serious, very serious. "A courier run with the Groove Haulers went sour. The raiders got you. The van's a total loss, too. Of course, you don't remember any of that."

Rick blinked. There were fragments of memories that shouldn't be there: the van destroyed, monsters, explosions, lava lamps, the Grim Reaper, and his truck. But everything was so disjointed and frazzled that it confused the heck out of him. "Morty ain't real, then?"

"Who? Morty… Oh, you mean Mortimer Graves? He's real, all right. He's the GC Reboot Technician in charge of your case. He said he'd drop by for a check-up later today."

Rick nodded. "That's him. I woke up during Reboot."

"A nice man. He came by when they put you into this room and warned me you might wake up a bit confused because they'd had a problem with your memory tape." She tousled Ben's hair. "Some corrupted sections? Anyway, they sorted it out, and here you are."

Rick relaxed. Now, that made a lot more sense. His brand-new brain still needed to get its act together after the messed-up memory restore, and all the gunner-for-the-Grim-Reaper-Brigade madness must have been just a nightmare. He smiled. "So, I'm the Yorik three-point-oh update. It's a pleasure to meet you, Mrs. Mayes, and Ben."

"You're looking even younger than when I met you." She settled little Ben on the bed and sat down next to Rick. "There's one more thing. The cargo…"

"It disintegrated with the me and the van?"

Amy grimaced. "Your sense of humor hasn't updated, for sure." She gave him a thoughtful look. "The van exploded, all right, but you got out okay. A piece of shrapnel from the explosion nicked an artery in your neck. The coroner said you didn't suffer." She sighed and leaned into him. "They didn't find the cargo, and we thought it was gone. But when I called the company about it, they said some trucker dropped off the cask just in time. They think he was from the GC salvage team, because he told them you couldn't make it."

And there was no way that Morty, the Grim Reaper, would ditch a case full of Uncle Al's Vindictive Piston Oil if it bought him a gunner.

Nonsense. Morty was just the GC technician. The Grim Reaper didn't exist. *He searched for connections in a string of coincidences.* Still… Rick shivered. "Without the triple fee…"

Amy grinned. "Indeed. How do you think your cash-strapped wife paid for your clone so quickly, huh?"

Tough Cookies
by Douglas Goodall

A pleasantly artificial voice called out, "Giles Jordan, room three-eleven."

That was my cue. Room three-eleven had no door, only a screwed-on sign showing the room number. A little card with the name 'Stephanie' sat in a slot, indicating the room was more permanent than the staff.

"How can Motorways Transport Insurance help you today, Mr. George," said the less pleasantly artificial woman behind the desk. She was no android, but she had so much makeup you couldn't be sure.

"Mr. Jordan," I said. "I had a policy on my Mule. One hundred thousand dollars for the truck and two hundred thousand for the cargo."

"Yes, sir, our records indicate that the contract was signed in December of last year."

"And when my truck was attacked, and I barely managed to make it to El Paso with my life, you refused to honor that contract."

Her smile grew larger and more forced. "On the contrary, our records show you received twenty thousand dollars yesterday."

"The policy was for one hundred thousand."

"As you'll note in paragraph fifty-one, the policy pays less on a sliding scale based on the unnecessary risks the driver took when—"

"And you didn't pay a cent for the load."

"Our records show that the cargo was delivered, not lost."

"I made it to the warehouse, but some of the load was damaged, and they're holding me responsible for—"

"Our policy pays for lost cargo, not damaged cargo. When drivers take unnecessary risks—"

"Driving is inherently risky. That's why you sell insurance. I can't help being attacked by a cycle gang!"

The agent's smile grew even more forced, and she started focusing on a spot above my left ear. "Your truck's telemetry indicated that you were going over one hundred fifty miles per hour, much higher than the recommended speed. Indeed, higher than the top speed of a Mule.

Additionally, the telemetry shows that you were airborne for three seconds on two occasions and crashed through multiple barriers. Reckless driving such as this automatically activates the unnecessary risk clause."

"So if I just pulled over and let the cycle gang murder me, I'd be golden."

The agent typed something briefly, then paused as if listening. She probably was. "In that circumstance, since you took no action to defend your cargo, paragraph sixty-four indicates that we—"

"Suppose I shot a few gang members and drove just a tiny bit dangerously. Enough to piss them off, but not enough to get away. What then?"

"Paragraph sixty-four indicates—"

"Let me speak to your supervisor."

She gave me her first genuine smile. "Mr. Wilson is unavailable at this time."

I stood and hit the desk with both palms. "Let me speak to your supervisor, or I'll see you in court."

She scooted back a little in her chair, typed a little, then paused again, waiting for her lines. "Our records indicate that you do not have the resources to see us in court. Motorways thanks you for your business. Have a nice day."

She swiveled her chair away and stared at her screen. I could tell she was still paying close attention to me, but what was the point? I wasn't a big transport corp. I was an owner-operator who lost his truck and his savings. They knew I couldn't make them pay, so they didn't.

There was no door to slam. They stole that from me, too. What was left of the insurance money went to the three nearest bars.

The next evening I was in a cheap motel, nursing a headache, and reading want-ads. I was looking for either a job or a cheap used truck. What I found was a whole lot of nothing. I called up a few and left a message anyway, explaining my situation. Going back home wasn't an option. Couldn't be an option. Deseret. Cattle. My brothers. All the I-told-you-sos. My mom parading the plainest, dullest, most desperate women past me until I went mad and picked one.

Disgusted with myself and my prospects, I took a shower. Afterwards, there was a message on my phone. I listened to it, then listened to it again to be sure.

American Nippon wanted an experienced long hauler to drive a Scorpion, a nice longnose sleeper rig, with a refrigerated trailer from El

Paso up to Billings. The pay wasn't that good, but the driver could keep the truck "or a cash equivalent" after the job.

I-25 was good driving once you got out of New Mexico. There might be a little trouble between Colorado Springs and Cheyenne, but the gangs there picked on the weak, not on convoys. The job was too good. I called back and said yes. I was told to meet the team for a briefing at the Montigo Institute of Technology tomorrow at seven. It was too good, but what choice did I have? Raising cows?

"Jaylene, I want you to drive for me."

That was what my dad said after I pulled off that Amateur Night victory at the Double Drum. I was head over heels. It was only my second night, and it wasn't luck, let me tell you. A girl couldn't get any happier.

As they were handing out the prize money – not even enough to repair my Firecracker – my dad pushed his way through the crowd. He had his serious face on, and I reckoned he was going to chew me out. Instead, he asked me to be his driver.

I thought he meant real AADA matches, that he was coming out of retirement. I got even happier. See, my dad was Oceanus Price. Even a pro would sign up to drive for him. Sure, he didn't win as much as some, but he worked the crowd. Everybody loved my dad. I have a dozen half-brothers and another dozen half-sisters to prove that. Everyone's got an Oceanus Price t-shirt or toy car.

But he didn't want me to duel. He wanted us to do escort work. Not that kind of escort work, although he was so popular that might've paid better. No, he wanted me to drive him around in slow truck convoys just in case some pecker took a pot-shot at us. Then he could turn on the cameras, man the turret, and shoot them back. I reckoned the number of BLUD and wannabes seeing his car's colors would make him a liability in a convoy, and it kind of did, but everyone loved my dad.

We got plenty of work, and my dad sold the footage for a decent bonus. We had a dozen boring escorts, a few ambushes, a couple run-and-guns. There was one ball-hoot through a mountain pass up in Colorado that led right into a minefield. And I mean a field full of mines. But this latest job started out different. The briefing was in a college classroom. This was some high-class college, too, really putting on the dog. It had plush carpet, upholstered chairs with fold-out desks, and a modern entertainment system.

We got there last, so there wasn't time for proper introductions. I didn't care after a quick glance. A few times one of the other drivers caught my eye, and I tried to have a little off-road fun. My dad didn't like that, either. He always showed up just in time to keep me a perfect lady.

Leon Russell and Ethan Porter were a team. They were dressed in fatigues, like they wanted to still be in the army or marines or whatever. I assumed they drove the red-white-and-blue Fourth of July minibus we parked next to. They were both alright, but they didn't pay me any mind. The truck driver was Giles. The client's client. The box-of-rocks we had to keep alive. He gave me a quick up-and-down when we came in, then shook his head. Whatever that meant. He was the most boring, average guy you could imagine. The last one was Teresa Ochoa. My dad nodded when she introduced herself, said he'd heard of her, and kissed her hand. She was mature, confident, beautiful, and I tried real hard not to hate her. I stopped trying—not when my dad started flirting with her, because he was always doing that—but when she started waving her thick eyelashes back at him.

Finally, the client came in. Because it was American Nippon, we got a suit and a translator. They bowed at us. We were all sitting down. No one was going to bow back, but they did stuff that way. The middle-aged man said something in Japanese, and the younger one repeated it in English. "Thank you for your patronage. You may call me Mr. Yoritomo. We are pleased you arrived for the briefing." I wondered if it sounded that dull in the original Japanese. The younger man hooked up a laptop to the classroom projector and started one of those business slideshows on convoy strategy. The real basic stuff: go through obstacles or turn around, keep moving at all costs, evacuate wounded instead of trying to give aid on the spot, respond with maximum aggression if you can't get away…

Five slides in my dad surprised me by speaking up. "Show of hands, fellas," he said. "How many here never defended a convoy? Yeah, how many been in less than ten convoys?" Even I'd done more than that. "So let's skip this stuff everyone knows and get to the details. What are we carrying, who's in charge, what's the road conditions, who do we have to pay off, how do we communicate, that stuff."

The suits talked a bunch to each other. I should've brought my micro so I could zone out with a game, but I hadn't rigged the new one to not cut out after twenty-five minutes. Besides, I didn't want another lecture on how I was going to burn out my brain or whatever.

Eventually the translator spoke again. "We apologize for the miscommunication. We acknowledge and value your experience as drivers. The refrigerated trailer is carrying medical supplies and frozen genetic samples from the Montigo Institute. We purchased these supplies and require them to be delivered to our headquarters in Billings, Montana. Mr. Russell will kindly direct the convoy. All vehicles will be outfitted with a point-to-point laser system for secure communications in line of sight of Mr. Russell's vehicle. We are pleased to announce that we are unaware of unusual hazards along I-25. We statistically expect one combat encounter before arriving in Billings. Additionally, rival interests may attempt to stop the shipment. This is a light convoy for the value of the shipment, but we believe a larger one would attract a proportionate response." Boy, I hated how suits talked.

There were a few questions, but either the suits didn't answer, like who the "rival interests" were, or they gave boring answers. Then it was Leon's turn, since he was "in charge" to question the credentials of everyone else. Like "why is a little girl coming along?" Because I'm Oceanus Price's daughter, and I can drive circles around your fat Fourth of July. And "what are Teresa's qualifications?" Teresa said she grew up in Wyoming, and everyone laughed. I didn't get it. My dad said he knew her by reputation, and I didn't think it was only because he wanted to get in her suit skirt. Giles said he rode a convoy with her once before and she was a pro. And then "who's this Giles?" Well, he's been a trucker a super long time. He did tell a story, probably half made up, about his last job and the tricks he pulled to get away from some hawgs.

We all went out to check vehicles. Everyone knows my dad's. He spent a lot of time in the thirties and forties, but he got sponsored up to the seventies in his last season and kept the car. It's a sleek, custom model with dual heavy rockets in front, an anti-tank turret on top, and it can drop spikes and mines.

Leon and Ethan would be in that Fourth of July. They even had a name for it. "Betsy." It—I guess I should call it her—was heavy on rockets, both fixed and turreted. Once it ran out of rockets, though, reloading would take a while.

Teresa had a vehicle that looked like it started out as a Timeslip with a higher suspension and off-road tires. It had a Vulcan turret up top and a complicated looking drop pod in the rear. There were a dozen fake blast-away ports, but maybe they weren't all fake. You never knew.

The refrigerated trailer was armored, and had solid tires, but it didn't have any weapons. Not even a drop pod. The truck part only had three rockets up top and fléchette guns on the sides, so, yeah, it obviously needed us to babysit.

I usually hoped our jobs saw at least a little action. It was the only excitement I would get with my dad around. But this time I was hoping for an easy run. We were a match for most hawg gangs, but not for pros. My dad said it would take an hour or so to get started, so I got in the driver's seat, dug out my micro, and spent the prescribed twenty-five minutes with the new remake of Astrodome 2060. It was awesome.

"Hey, Giles," Leon said over the radio when we set out. "How do you like your new truck?"

"I love it," I said. It had a good power plant, the latest updated electronics, solid tires, decent armor, and comfortable seats. It was lightly armed, but that's what a trailer gunner or escort was for.

I-25 was rough in spots. Burned out cars. Potholes. Old battles that were never paved over. Traffic was light. Leon spent some time on the point-to-point laser coming up with animal-themed code words to use in case of trouble.

We made good time, given the road, and we spent the first night in Pueblo. It was only late afternoon, but Leon said we shouldn't risk Colorado Springs to Cheyenne at night.

The escort drivers rented rooms at a motel, but I stayed in the parking lot and tried out the sleeper berth. It wasn't bad. I got some sleep, anyway.

I woke suddenly, certain I'd heard something, but not sure what it was. The sleeper made it hard to get dressed in a hurry. It was a brisk morning, not yet dawn. The only sound at first was a wobbly maid's cart being pulled around the motel by a cleaning lady. Then I heard a whisper, but angry, like a whispered argument. It sounded like it was coming from the back of the trailer, so I walked over there and saw Teresa. She had one hand on her hip and one holding the phone far in front of her. "You're up early," I said.

She jumped and turned to me. Her eyes dared me to accuse her of something. I just stood there like I had nothing better to do. "I needed to take a personal call," she said. "There's no reception in my room."

I nodded. I didn't trust my voice not to sound suspicious. She walked back to the hotel and I looked over the truck. The locks were still in place. They were biometric, keyed to me and Leon. You could get in the truck, but only by cutting the door off or hacking the lock. Both required tools Teresa couldn't conceal in that skirt.

The motel had a little restaurant attached. It wasn't fancy enough to be a chain. We all ate breakfast, bright and early. When we'd all eaten a little, Leon clapped his hands and piped up. "Alright! We had an easy day yesterday. Let's hope that continues. Colorado doesn't allow dropped weapons. It sucks, but we're going to unload and disarm them now before we leave. We'll stop a bit north of Colorado Springs and reload them. The road isn't patrolled much north of there. We might need the weapons, and I think it's worth the risk of a fine. Got it?"

Everyone nodded or murmured affirmatives.

"I expected some action yesterday," Oceanus said. He seemed disappointed. His daughter didn't say much, just picked at her food and buried her overly made-up face in her phone.

The sky was clear and sunny when we set out. Nothing happened until about fifty miles south of Denver. A patrol car had been checking us out for a few minutes when it turned on its emergency lights and hit the siren. Leon came on the point-to-point comms. "Alright, I don't know what he wants, but let's not start any trouble. Remember jackrabbit to run, aardvark to attack."

When we all pulled over the officer got out of his car very slowly and walked up to Teresa's car in the rear. She kept her mic on, so we all heard what was said. "Looks like you and your friends here have some mine launchers, maybe some spike launchers. We don't allow those in Colorado."

"They've been disabled, officer," Teresa said.

"Oh, have they? You don't mind if I inspect them? Because from where I'm standing it looks like the minivan disarmed and unloaded theirs, but you and that show-dog up front must have forgotten to. You just sit tight. I'll check on the other vehicles."

He walked up to mine, gave it a show of an inspection, then up to *Betsy* and did the same. When he got to Oceanus' car in front, he found what he was looking for. Oceanus kept his mic on, too.

"So you've got a mine launcher back there. And it's loaded. I'll bet it isn't disarmed."

"Oh, but it is," Oceanus said. There was a clicking noise. "See? I flipped the switch, but no mines."

"That's not good enough for the state of Colorado. So where's this little caravan headed?"

"Montana," Oceanus said.

"Who you working for? Phelps? Nippon?" Oceanus must have nodded or something. "God damn foreigners," the cop said. "You'd take their money? What're you transporting?"

"Medical supplies," Jaylene said.

"Oh, real humanitarians, are we? Now what have we got here." I saw him lean further down, resting his arms on the window and sticking his butt out in the road. "Puppy dog! If you ask real nice, I'll let you go with a fine. How about it?"

"Please let us go with a fine, officer," Oceanus said. It sounded like he was gritting his teeth.

"I wasn't asking you," the cop said.

"She's my daughter," Oceanus said.

"She's old enough to ask for something she wants."

There was a dangerous silence. I saw *Betsy's* rocket turret twitch a little, although a rocket wouldn't do much good right at that moment.

"Please, Officer, can you please let us go with just a fine?" Jaylene asked.

"Well, since you asked so nicely, yes." The cop stood back up. "Now who here holds the purse strings?"

Ethan leaned out his window and said, "That would be me, Officer."

The cop walked over to *Betsy* and collected a wad of cash. "Ah, now, this is a little too much," he said. "For this, I'm gonna escort you to the other side of Denver and make sure none of those mines accidentally fall onto Colorado's good roads."

He got back in his patrol car. "What an asshole," Teresa said over the laser comm as we pulled out. Everyone chuckled a little in relief. True to his word, at least, he escorted us through Denver. Things got a bit tense when two more patrol cars joined the escort between Denver and Colorado Springs. Leon managed to get them on the radio. The cop said, "We're just making sure you stay out of trouble."

They followed us through Colorado Springs, farther than patrols usually go on I-25. A nuke hit the city back in the war. There wasn't much left. A little north of Colorado Springs, Leon said, "Something's up. I haven't decoded their encryption, but there's suddenly a lot of chatter from all three patrol cars."

A few minutes later all three cars slowed, let us pass them, and then they turned around.

"I don't know whether to be happy they're gone or not," I said.

"Let's pull over quick and reload those dropped weapons," Leon said.

Oceanus only had to put a fuse in to re-arm his, and neither my truck nor my trailer had any. Ethan and Teresa had to get out and reload by hand. Leon stayed up in the turret, keeping watch.

"Nothing suspicious up ahead on radar or telescope, but the road seems rather empty in Fort Collins. Oceanus and Jaylene," Leon said, "scout up ahead a bit. See if there's something waiting for us."

I'd been itching for a real drive, not this molasses, since yesterday morning. We were dead stopped on the side of the road, but my dad's car went zero to one-twenty in ten seconds. I grinned wide and let the g-force push me back, back into the seat. It felt so good. There were some bad potholes, but I dodged them easy. There was a little traffic, but they might as well have been sitting still.

Of course the best fun I'd had in weeks couldn't last. I-25 went around the east side of Fort Collins. We were almost out of the city when I saw a few cars coming back south. Then I saw a jam up ahead. I didn't want to get jammed myself, so I slowed up a bit. There were two big rigs and a few pickups blocking both sides of a bridge. There was no way to go around.

They were sending all the cars on both sides back to a parking lot where it looked like they were getting searched.

We couldn't get caught up in whatever that was. I hit the brakes and spun around into the grassy median. There was a fence, or the remains of a fence, so I couldn't just slide over to the southbound lanes. There was a gap in the fence a mile or so back, so I drove fast as I could in the grass. The gap came into view just moments before the target lock warning went off.

I swerved through the gap in the fence and an explosion just behind us lifted the back of the car and liketa spin us around. I kept it straight.

"Oh, it's on," my dad said. He flipped a switch and the record lights came on. There were cameras in the car, not just outside.

I heard a chopper behind us, but it was higher than the rear cam, so I couldn't see it. The turret started clicking as my dad lined up a shot. I tried to speed up, but the cars the blockade let through were in the way. Half were driving crazy, giving me a hard time, like they'd never seen a rocket blow a chunk out of the road before. My dad started firing, slow and steady. The target lock warning came on again. I swerved again and the driver who was right behind me had a real bad day. It liketa blinded me between the rocket and the power plant. The other cars were giving us some room now. I heard the chopper getting closer and my dad was shooting faster.

I wondered if this was some shakedown or if they set up the barricade to catch us. It didn't matter right at the moment. I saw some splatter off the asphalt in front of us and heard a couple bangs on the car's hood and trunk. The chopper must be out of rockets and switching to guns. I saw another gap in the fence and took it. The right tire hit something, bouncing me so hard I liketa hit my head on the roof. I heard my dad curse at me.

Once I was going the wrong way on the northbound side, I slammed the juice, and we were off again. I heard my dad say on the radio, "Jackrabbit, jackrabbit. I repeat, jackrabbit. Barricade, taking fire. Get off 25."

The chopper was so close I could see the grass blowing, but they couldn't match our speed now that the road was clear. My dad kept firing and then said, "Got 'em." I heard a soft, distant boom. Another warning light came on. The right motor was running a temperature. I must've hit something going over that fence that jammed up in the wheel. I took the next off-ramp, let off the accelerator a little, and turned right on the first big street.

"Where's the convoy?" I asked. "Can we give them directions?"

I heard a roar behind me, coming up fast. The rear cam showed a pair of Run n' Guns using their rocket boosters. Both had the standard anti-tank gun. Lightly armed, but still bad news. I couldn't outrun them, but one thing about four-wheel-drive electrics, they sure could turn. I hit the brakes, then maxed the steering wheel left, slid around the intersection, liketa bumped the curb, and slammed the juice. I grinned as the g-force squashed me into the seat. The Run n' Guns shot past on the rear cam, and I turned left before they were back in sight. They weren't dumb, so I took a few more quick turns, kind of heading back the way we came for a piece.

"The convoy's taking 287," my dad said. "Just keep heading west."

Things went okay until I heard the Run n' Guns again up ahead. I saw them turn out of a side-street a few blocks in front of us. I didn't want to ram even a little car going that fast, but I had a couple heavy rockets in front, so I let them both loose. They started firing on us, and I heard my dad firing his turret.

Holes appeared in our windshield. I heard the shots come through the car and got a little spray of laminate chips on my face. I didn't think I was hit. I swerved left again, just as I saw the rockets hit. One of the Run n' Guns flipped forwards. I didn't see what happened to the other one. I slid onto 287. It was in even worse shape than I-25. We were bouncing like an air hammer on a trampoline. I saw the convoy in the distance up ahead and slowed up a bit. They weren't going more than fifty.

My dad told them about the blockade on the laser comm. I just breathed slow and easy, trying to let the excitement flow out of me. Then I saw another two vehicles coming up quick behind us. Anyone would recognize that silhouette anywhere. "Pair of Joseph Specials behind us," I said. We could outrun those easy. But the big rig couldn't.

My dad started shooting. I heard Leon over the laser comm. "There's an old lake up ahead where the road curves left. Drop spikes and oil just before the turn. Be ready for it."

"Roger," my dad said. I was driving too hard to say much. And too thirsty. Combat always made me so thirsty, but there was never time to get a drink.

The road was in good shape here, and the convoy sped up to eighty. We caught up before the Old Joes were in range. They'd been trying to shoot us the whole time, but their shots were going wide, way wide. Teresa's turret pinged our hood a few times, and it didn't look like she was hitting the Specials at all. Her little Vulcan had even shorter range than their anti-tank guns.

I got a little left of *Betsy* and out of Teresa's line of fire. She plinked us a couple more times anyway. "What the hell, Teresa," my dad said. The turn was coming up. As soon as I saw *Betsy's* drop pod activate, I pulled out of the way, dropped spikes, and started the turn. The turn was rough for the big rig at that speed, but the Joseph Specials ran right into the trap. Neither had good tires, and they both lost control. One hit a remaining section of guard rail and flipped. The other just sailed right off the road and into the mud.

"You okay honey?" my dad asked.

"Fine, fine. Right motor's hot. How about you?"

"All smooth back here."

I passed the convoy to take up our front position again. The road got way worse, and we slowed to maybe forty. At least the front passenger motor cooled a bit now that we were going at a snail's pace.

"Well, that was worth a few views, at least," my dad said, turning the cameras back off.

"Oceanus! What the hell are you doing?" Leon screamed.

"Saving your butts, what does it look like?"

"I'm not talking about your driving," Leon said. "You're recording?"

"Gotta keep my ratings up," Dad said. He always loved the cameras.

"This is supposed to be a secret convoy," Leon said with an edge in his voice.

"Yeah, well," my dad said, "tell that to whoever set up the roadblock. I don't see what the problem is. No one's going to see the footage until after we're in Billings."

"We'll talk about this tonight. Meantime, let's see if we can get to Laramie and patch up."

I felt useless in my truck. All I could do was keep going. I had three powerful heavy rockets I could fire forward. I could disable lighter vehicles with fléchette guns to the sides. But all the action had been behind us. There wasn't a thing I could do. I never got used to it. When my truck got attacked, it was either the trailer gunner or the escorts that got me out of trouble. A running battle like when I came into El Paso was rare. I only took solo loads if I was desperate, and I only survived that one due to the drug-fueled incompetence of the gang.

We kept on 287 while Leon checked the route. From the last reports, it was drivable, if slowly, all the way to Casper. There were unpredictable cycle gangs and bandits in the area.

We were heading through a small town when a cycle gang came up behind us, quick. They were all off the road to our left. Given the state of the road, they were probably better off on the dirt. Maybe we would be, too. None of them fired on us before they passed us. They wore a sort of double-headed vulture symbol I hadn't seen before. It looked like a mockery of the Byzantine double eagle.

"We should shoot them now," Oceanus said.

"Negative," Leon said. "Not our job to clean them up."

"They're gonna set up an ambush."

"How do you know this?"

"Just a feeling," Oceanus said.

"Just a feeling? Or you just want more combat to record?"

"I'm just telling you," Oceanus said, "they're going to ambush us. I can feel it."

"I don't like him advertising our position," I said, "but I have the same feeling."

The gang was too far ahead of us now, so the discussion was moot. I didn't like the way they looked at us, though. Their gazes weren't long and intense, like they were sizing us up. They were quick side glance, as if they already knew who we were. The dirt they were kicking up and their face paint reminded me of a bull getting introduced to the herd. They were going to be trouble.

Their cycles were a mix of older models, all electric. The legally required noisemakers were disabled, so the only sound they made as they passed was the whir of their tires on the dirt, the wind rushing around them, and the hooing and hawing they did as they passed.

We forgot about the gang when a pair of copters came up quick on our right. They were firing rockets at us before we knew they were even there. One rocket went just over *Betsy* and the other hit it. I couldn't get a lock on them. These were military copters, either from theft or surplus. Oceanus fired back first. He had the reflexes you'd expect from an AADA star. Leon shot one of the copters down with a rocket pretty quick, too, but the second set of rockets hit *Betsy* and the entire right side of the minivan blew open and started pouring smoke.

Oceanus got the other copter with his anti-tank gun. A lucky shot, I guess, and one I was thankful for. We were driving through a ghost town, and the laser comms were down. Leon wasn't answering the radio, either. Ethan got on the radio and said he was going to pull over and see what the damage was. I knew he wanted to go to check on Leon, but I wasn't about to quote convoy tactics at him. Besides, the smoke coming out of *Betsy* was getting worse. We needed to put that fire out.

The area was hilly, and the road kept cutting through the hills. Ethan was slowing down before a gap with a tall cliffside to our left and a shorter one to our right. I heard a loud hissing sound. I didn't place it at once, but I realized it was the sound of electric tires spinning up on dirt.

"Cycles starting up on our left," I said at the same time several others tried to talk. Oceanus and Jaylene were in the lead and hadn't slowed yet. They had just entered the gap between the cliffs when the first cycle soared off the left cliff, over the road, and landed on the right. There was an explosion right next to Oceanus' car, and it flipped up on its right side and slid into the cliff with a bang.

Betsy started accelerating again. Another dozen cycles leaped over the gap, sailing gracefully above *Betsy* and then above me. As they flew overhead, they tossed mines, spikes, Molotovs, grenades, and who knows what down on us. I couldn't do a damn thing about it. I can't fire rockets straight up. I didn't have anything that could aim at them. Dirt from their tires rained onto my windshield.

I spared a brief glance to see how far Teresa was behind us, but she wasn't there at all. What the hell? With Oceanus' car out, she had the best weapon for handling cycles, and she was gone. There were explosions all around. I swear one hit my trailer. I couldn't focus for a second, and my ears were ringing, but I kept the rig under control and made it through the gap. Oceanus and Jaylene were out, maybe dead. That car surely wasn't going anywhere.

With Teresa gone, the convoy was just me in the Scorpion and Ethan in *Betsy*. And *Betsy* was not in good shape.

A couple of the cycle gang missed the jump, but most of them made it across unscathed. I tried to spot where they had gone and saw a cloud of dust. No, two clouds of dust. I fiddled with the unfamiliar controls of the Scorpion and managed to zoom in on them. Teresa was off-road to the right and the cycle gang was about a half mile behind her. I saw another gap in the road up ahead. This one had the higher hill on the right side. The cycle gang was going to do the same thing again. But what the hell was Teresa doing?

I was about to call Ethan, but realized he was already trying to say something. I just couldn't hear him properly. I said, "Can't hear. Ears ringing. Teresa's off-road to the right. Cycle gang's just behind her. The gang is gonna jump the next hill about a mile ahead. No idea what Teresa's doing."

We might not make it through the second gap, but I wasn't sure what we could do about it. I think Ethan was saying something about not being able to use his weapons. Then I had an idea. Two ideas. My rockets only fired forward, but they were guided. It was time to find out how well they could turn. I slowed a bit and fiddled with the weapons controls. I tried to get the computer to estimate the range to the cycle gang, and I launched two rockets just ahead of where they were going to be, using the near and far estimates. The blast took out five or six of them, and as many more piled into them from behind. It worked great. Better than I expected. There were still about ten left.

As we started to approach the next gap, I had the computer calculate shooting a rocket at the top of the cliff. I thought I had a pretty good lock on it. The *Betsy* started pulling through the gap, and I braked hard. When I thought the cycle gang was committed, I launched the rocket and hit the juice. The first three cycles soared out over the road before the rocket hit the middle of the cliff. It hit too low, but the top of the cliff was falling, and not where they expected it to be. The rest of the cycle gang either fell into the road or crashed onto the cliff on the other side. But those first cycles dropped mines right in front of *Betsy*. Her front end popped up, and one tire flew off. Then she landed and came to a dead stop as the tire bounced off down the road. I was too close. I swerved to the right and missed hitting *Betsy*. It was a mistake. Not because I ran over a couple of the gang members—screw them—but because my rocket had started an avalanche. Thirty feet of rock and dirt was sliding into the road, and I drove right into it.

"Dad? Dad!" I was hanging in the driver's seat, the seatbelt holding me up, pressing into my ribs on the right side. My right arm was just dangling. I tried to turn my head to see my dad, but I couldn't move far enough. I tried to unbuckle my seatbelt, but I couldn't get my right arm to move very far. I heard Ethan on the radio saying something about there being a traitor and not having any weapons. I could worry about that later.

I got the seatbelt undone with my left hand and held on to it while I pulled my legs up and slid my feet down onto the passenger side window. I turned to the rear of the car and wished I hadn't. Part of the turret had slammed back into his head. One eye stared blankly back at me, and his mouth hung open.

"Dad," I cried. "Oh God, oh Jesus, Dad."

I closed my eyes. I had to get out. I couldn't do anything for him. I had to get out. I tried to open the door that was now above me, but I kept trying to open it with my right hand, and it wasn't working. I closed my eyes again and took a deep breath. It didn't help much. I turned off the car with my left hand and pocketed the keys. Then I got the window rolled down and tried to pull myself up, one-handed. I eventually got my feet on the center console, the handbrake, and finally the steering wheel and flopped out onto the side of the car. Or the top, depending. I pulled myself up a little further, then slid off onto the road. My arm hadn't hurt at first, but it was starting to ache something terrible. I could make a fist, so it wasn't paralyzed. I just couldn't move it right.

My dad was dead. Our car was wrecked. I was all alone somewhere in Colorado or whatever was north of that. And I had one working arm. Think, Jaylene, think.

Dad always had supplies in the trunk. I got the trunk open and got our emergency pack. It was the kind of luggage that has wheels. Not that it would roll well on this road, but it had a change of clothes, some snack food, and water for a day. No, scratch that, two days. It was just me now. I had my 7mm pistol like usual, but wasn't sure how well I could draw it left-handed.

I couldn't go back. There was no help in Fort Collins. I started walking as fast as I felt I was able to, pulling the luggage behind me with my good arm. That place Leon talked about… Laramie? It couldn't be more than two days walk, could it?

Thank God for seatbelts and good armor. I woke up. I wiped a disturbing amount of blood off my face and looked around. I couldn't see anything going on through the windows. Just empty road and a lot of dirt.

I opened the door and slid out onto the ground, almost losing my balance. I drew my pistol and looked around. The *Betsy* to my left was on fire and had a huge hole in the side. One of their rocket pods must have blown. Leon was probably dead inside. Where was Ethan? At least a few of the cycle gang made it. Where were they? Where was Teresa?

I stumbled partway around the wreck and saw Ethan on the ground with a rifle next to him. I didn't see anything immediately wrong, but somehow I knew he wasn't getting up. Looking around more, I saw several members of the cycle gang, all equally dead. Was I alone?

I still couldn't hear well. The world was silent and calm, a strange contrast to the signs of violence all around. I went back to the rig and thought I'd walk around the trailer and check for damage. I couldn't hear the reefer unit, but then realized, well, I couldn't hear. I put a hand out and felt the side of the trailer. It wasn't running. Crap. The load would be thawing in a few hours.

My hearing was getting a little better. I thought I heard Teresa yelling. I walked around the back of the trailer and almost ran into her. She had her back to me.

"I did everything you asked! At the cost of my reputation. Of course there are no survivors. I just told you I can't figure out how to open the truck. Maybe. Maybe I could rig up a rocket launcher, but you need to get someone here pronto. I don't care. No, I don't care!" It was then that her pacing led her to turn and see me. There was a short pause, and she dropped her phone and went for her gun.

"Before you shoot," I said, holding up my hands, "tell me why you did it."

"Do you know what's in that truck?" I shook my head. "Wheat. Blight-resistant wheat seeds. I did a lot of work for ConTexCo, a lot of work for the Denver Algae Consortium. They don't want the seeds to arrive. I can't say no to them. They know all about me."

She raised the pistol. I ducked before she fired and rolled under the trailer.

Gunfire up ahead. I tried to go faster, half-jogging, even though every bounce hurt my arm. There was more gunfire, then more, then a huge explosion. There were a couple shots after that and then nothing. I saw smoke, and I thought it wasn't far. I crested a short hill and there it all was. *Betsy* was down and out, smoke pouring out of her. It looked like the cliff collapsed onto the big rig. Teresa's car was parked behind it. What was going on?

I kept moving forward. There was someone behind the big rig. Just a blur way out here. From the color, I assumed it was Teresa. She was trying to do something to the trailer. Open it? I was close enough to see her better. She gave up on the trailer and got out her phone. Then she had a conniption fit, pacing back and forth, waving her arms all over.

The door of the Scorpion opened and Mr. Average came out. He seemed wobbly. I kept getting closer. He wandered around, then went around the trailer. I wasn't sure what was going on, but I left the luggage behind and started jogging as fast as I could. I managed to get my pistol out in my left hand. Maybe I should've spent more time trying to shoot left-handed. Every time I did, it was a disaster.

Teresa drew her gun on him, and they said something to one another. The truck driver rolled under his trailer. Teresa squatted down to shoot at him. I heard three gunshots. I guess the truck driver – Giles, that was his name – had a gun, too. They both had pretty good cover from each other, but Teresa was wide open to me. I didn't know what was going on, but I wasn't going to let her shoot him. I was close enough. I knelt down, aimed, and fired.

I was shooting left-handed, and with only one hand. I assumed I was going to miss. I fired again and again, trying my best to aim every one. Teresa turned after my second shot, but I got her with the third and sixth.

A shot rang out. The good news was I could hear it. The better news was that it didn't hit me. Nine more shots came, about evenly spaced. They weren't close enough to be from Teresa. After the shots stopped, I peeked out from under the trailer. I didn't see anything, so I slid out and got into a crouch. I snuck up to where Teresa was and saw...a shoe. And then a foot. And a leg. And the rest of her.

I holstered my pistol and looked around for my savior. I saw Jaylene, her obnoxious makeup streaked all down her face, holding a pistol and walking toward me on the road.

"Hi," I said when she got close. "Thanks for that. How you doing?" She said something, but I couldn't quite make it out. I shook my head and pointed at my ear. "Sorry," I said, "I can't hear well right now."

We just stood there and stared, awkward and tired. "I should try to call our employer," I said. For that, I'd need to get to Leon. *Betsy* was still smoldering, but I figured if she hadn't blown up yet, she wasn't going to. All the doors to the trailer were locked. I climbed into the burning hole and looked around. I saw a narrow way to the turret compartment, and found what was left of Leon, but I couldn't get him out. It took a lot of twisting around, but I managed to pull his phone out of his pocket. Luckily, it was the new kind that can be unlocked with a thumbprint, and Leon's hand was handy. There was a "Mr. Yoritomo" there, quotes included. I copied the number into my phone. I was about to call when I realized I couldn't hear well enough to make the call.

Jaylene was sitting on the side of the road, holding her legs, her 7mm still dangling in her left hand. Come to think of it, I didn't think she was left-handed. I looked again and saw her right arm was just hanging lifeless.

"Something wrong with your arm?" I asked. "Can I take a look at it?" I was no doctor, but I'd had to set broken bones a few times growing up. It was hours to the nearest doctor from the ranch. I got out my emergency kit and made her a splint. I tried to ask some yes or no questions while I was about it. I learned her father was dead. Her car was wrecked. He didn't have Gold Cross anymore. She wanted to go back and bury him if we could.

I asked if she could call Mr. Yoritomo and tell him the truck was damaged, and all our cars were out of commission, but we could probably take a couple of the coolers in Teresa's car if he told us which ones were the most important.

She made the call, and we managed to get the info across, even if she had to yell at me a few times. I figured the truck could wait for now. Better to leave it locked until right before we had to leave. I got Teresa's keys, packed up both our emergency kits in the trunk, and drove back to Oceanus' car. He was a mess. I couldn't get him out of the car. The car was really jammed into the cliffside, too. I couldn't roll it back upright.

"How about a viking funeral?" I asked. I had to explain to her what that was. None of our cars were gas, but there was dry brush all around, and I had a few fire starters. I managed it, and we watched the car light up. Jaylene said a few words. I'd like to think it was a spectacle worthy of him, but it went unrecorded.

We drove back to the truck. I unlocked the trailer and found the coolers Mr. Yoritomo wanted. We packed them in Teresa's car in the trunk, surrounded by the most frozen of the remaining goods. Teresa's car had off-road tires and suspension, so I went off-road most of the trip. It was smoother than the road itself.

We stopped in Laramie. Jaylene got a proper cast and painkillers. I recharged Teresa's car and got some fresh ice for the coolers in the trunk. I was exhausted, but I knew we had to make it to Billings before the load thawed out. I drove all night and Jaylene slept fitfully in the passenger seat. With both our emergency kits we had food, water, and caffeine. We took the back roads, going through the reservation. No one challenged us. I was glad. I wasn't sure I could drive this car and shoot at the same time.

I called Mr. Yoritomo again when we got near Billings. He told me how to get to the American Nippon headquarters and where to park. I unlocked the trunk and picked up the coolers.

Jaylene opened the passenger door and got out. I was just about to go wake her up. "It was a lousy job," I said, "but we're here. Want to talk to Mr. Yoritomo?"

She shook her head. "No," she said quietly, "I don't rightly know if I'd curl up like roly-poly or strangle him."

"I don't rightly know what I'm going to do myself. I'll see if I can get you paid for both yourself and your father."

She nodded. She could get an award for the quietest teen girl. That was fine with me.

Some suits met me and took the coolers. Another suit led me to a small meeting room. About the time I was sure they had forgotten about me, Mr. Yoritomo arrived with the same translator.

"We are pleased that you delivered the cargo safely," the translator said. "American Nippon hired four convoys to bring the samples. Regrettably, all of them failed except for you."

"Well, I'm not too pleased with how more than half of us died."

"There is no shame in dying to complete an important job."

"There's no fun in it, either. Look, the least you can do is give Jaylene a double share. She lost her dad out there."

There was some conversation in Japanese. "We are pleased to grant Oceanus' share to his daughter. We can offer more than that. Ethan and Leon had Gold Cross. Their clones will be paid their share. The payments for those in the other convoys who died without Gold Cross and without next-of-kin will be split between yourself and Jaylene Price. Tell me, do you know what you brought us?"

"Teresa said they were blight-resistant wheat seeds. Can you really grow wheat here again?"

"We regret that these are only test candidates. These are a small, but crucial step. For your success, please accept the bonus, the value of the Scorpion that was lost, and this small gift."

I raised an eyebrow. "Thanks," I said, "I didn't expect—" and I wasn't sure what else to say. Corps didn't just give you a bonus like that. I'd have to look at the contract again. Mr. Yoritomo smiled and pushed a fancy, lacquered wooden box across the table. The translator took it, treating it with great care, and handed it to me. I wasn't sure what it was, and wasn't sure if I was supposed to open it here or not.

"We are pleased to announce that the funds have been transferred. We would be honored to work with you again in the future."

I gave them a little bow and walked out the door. I wandered around lost for just a minute before another suit showed up to lead me out. When I got back to the car, Jaylene was waiting. She'd cleaned herself up and changed her clothes while I was in the meeting. I told her everything.

"What are you going to do now?" she asked.

"I have enough money to buy a new rig. I liked that Scorpion. I'll probably get one of those and look for more work. How about you?"

"I don't rightly know. I got the payment. It's... a lot more than I... I could buy a car and get in the AADA for real. Hell, I could buy three cars. I'd have to win, though. People don't love me the way they loved my dad."

"Well, if you'd rather be a trailer gunner, I suspect there will be a job opening in a few days."

She nodded but didn't look at me. Probably for the best. I wasn't sure we'd get along over the long haul. I had nothing better to do, so I opened the box. There were two dozen cookies in the box. Chocolate chip by the looks of them.

"What is it?" Jaylene asked.

"A bonus," I said, tilting the box so she could see inside. "Cookies. I think they're made with real wheat."

"How is that possible?" She peered into the box and took a deep breath.

"Oh, they still have wheat in labs and such. Australia's still got it. I've had real bread before, but everyone says it isn't as good as it was before. Maybe they have to treat the flour somehow to keep the blight from attacking it. These are probably worth a fortune if they're made with lab wheat. I don't know who would buy them, though."

"Sell them? Hell, no! We earned these cookies." She grabbed one.

"So we did," I said, and took a bite of heaven.

Asphalt Bandwidth
by A. Kristina Casasent

Dee stood behind her fiancé who sat in the driver's seat, steering the bus northward. "Jay, you promised we'd talk about this."

Jay considered the armored compact car that had just pulled in front of him and the petite woman directly behind him. Absently, one of his tattooed hands stroked the blond wispy almost-beard that matched the color of his short hair. He decided the bulbous lime-green car with the 75mm cannon headed the wrong way down the freeway toward them was less dangerous. Definitely better to deal with that one first and put off the other as long as possible.

He swerved the bus to avoid a mine the heads-up display highlighted, calling back to his fiancée, "We can discuss it later. We have another intercept ahead. This one has a 75mm. Get the drones out. And wake up Kay! Tell him there's trouble."

Jay then took the bus through a smooth, if wide, U-turn to buy Dee and his brother Kay time to react. The lack of traffic on the big freeway made the turn something other than a fancy attempt at creating an accident.

The lime-green compact charged the big bus. Muzzle-flare and a highway sign popping off its pole announced the first round fired.

Jay watched on the inside monitor as Dee sprinted for her console near the back of the bus, where the drone section was installed. The interior running lights shone on her short electric blue hair. As she passed the turret midway through, she grabbed the engineer's boot hanging out of it and shook it. "Kay! Get moving. Your brother says there's a 75mm up ahead!"

The armor on the bus would resist the anti-tank rifle for a while. But it could disable the transport with a lucky hit much too quickly. And then Jay and the other two members of Falco Secured Data Couriers would be bust before they even got started. If their only vehicle went down, it would sink the relatively new company faster than high tide coming in at Clear Lake.

With the bus turned away from the compact, Jay could not use the forward pointing laser. But he heard the big bore in the turret as his brother woke up and started clearing him a path. Slight shudders shook the transport as a drone took off between bursts from Kay.

A round hit the rear of the bus. The armor resisted, but spalling sent a fragment of interior metal zipping down the central aisle.

Jay swerved to avoid road debris the heads-up display indicated might hide another mine, and fought the urge to ask which drone his fiancée was planning to use to take the heat off of him. After all, she had options. The transport carried three rocket-armed drones and a stealth drone with a machine gun.

But bothering Dee with questions his mind created to distract him from their current danger wouldn't help any of them.

The well insulated bus kept the outside noise down. Cameras on all sides let the driver monitor in all directions. This meant Jay's first hint of Dee's choice was a stream of smoke on the monitor connecting a point in the air with the compact car.

Rockets then.

The big bore plus the rocket smashed into the little car in a one-two knockout punch. The armored shell gave, torn asunder by the rocket. An explosion of fiery red filled Jay's view, as the armed compact was converted to a burning hulk of twisted metal.

Over the audio from the turret, Jay heard his brother's deep baritone as Kay proved he was still awake by making asinine comments. "Well, I didn't want to get out and pull salvage anyway."

Dee laughed. "Got that right. Especially not with sensitive cargo. We might have had to leave you."

The clunk of the drone returning to its dock merged with the whine of the turret locking into its parked position. Kay would probably go back to sleep until he was needed again. He said it kept him sharp. Who was Jay to argue when Kay kept the road clean?

Jay spun the wheel, repeating his U-turn with barely a screech of tires. The new heading had them northward away from Houston, back toward Dallas once again. As they passed the smoking compact wreck, Jay looked back down the center aisle of the bus, checking the hidden embedded cargo safe, where their livelihood now rested. Their first cargo was secure inside.

Losing their first big cargo would be bad. There was too much competition on the Houston-Dallas route for someone to hire an armed courier who lost their cargo.

The contract for their first courier deal was small and pretty safe, he had thought. Just three small, flat boxes, 4.5 inches by 7.25 inches and five-eighths of an inch deep. High density hard drives. Their standard contract required the shipper to attest to contents and allow inspection, which kept small startups safe from stolen goods. Arbitration was by the American Auto Dueling Association. The AADA was big and everywhere, so it was worth their cut of a contract.

From what he knew, the drives contained designs for an antiviral that was supposed to be effective with one injection against almost any variety of virus. Jay could see how that would help with the new variants that came out of the Gulf every other year. Or the new one he read about, discovered in the algae vats.

Expensive, yes.

Important, yes.

But something was wrong. This compact made the third intercept attempt they had seen in less than an hour since the transport had started. That counted the mines and the armored compact together. But didn't cover the signal that occasionally appeared on radar, constantly hounding their progress. That was too much interest for just an antiviral. Too many people trying to intercept them.

And...

Dee unknowingly completed the thought for him. "That blasted aerial signal is back! Still can't tell what it is—a small helicopter or a large drone. Hide quick!"

The half-empty feeder road running along the side of the freeway gave no cover.

Jay scoffed, "Hide where? This is the Texas Gulf Coast. No caves. No tunnels. Hell, we barely have any trees."

But he continued to scan his surroundings for any cover beyond a cow byre. A deep green building with gray trim flashed in the edge of his vision to the west. A sign announcing another victory for the home team made him smile. Texas and high school sports.

Jay cut across the freeway, slamming up and over the median, and toward his own victory. "But we sure do know how to build an indoor high school arena! That will hide us."

He pulled the big dark blue bus up to the contestants' entrance of the New Woodlands High School Autoduelling Arena. He flashed a large bill at the young man at the entrance. "Let us stay for..." He looked at Dee who flashed him an open hand, fingers extended. "Five minutes."

The baby-faced kid wore a half jersey and a backwards baseball cap. His dark eyes zeroed in on the cash. He barely glanced at the blue bus, with its discreet licensing information for Falco Secured Data Couriers. "Dude. For that, you can stay five days."

"Thanks. Five minutes should do."

This time, Jay knew when the stealth drone left. He watched the slim black drone disengage and peel away. Before it faded out of view, he maneuvered the bus into the autoduelling arena.

Jay drummed his fingers across the wheel. The Japanese gods of luck tattooed on each finger danced for a minute. Shaking his blond hair, Jay popped his neck before slowly easing the bus into the perfect place. He had lined them up with the exit, giving a good view of the entrance. Jay knew he didn't need to take so much time. But the actions delayed having to deal with the more dangerous threat from earlier.

His fiancée.

All too soon, he shifted the bus into park and slowly turned his seat around.

Dee was already waiting for him. "Jay, you're not avoiding this conversation."

Behind her, Kay bolted out of the turret as if a napalm strike had breached it. "I'll be in back. Watching the drone cameras."

Dee didn't even register Kay's retreat. Her piercing blue eyes locked onto her fiancé. "We talked before getting engaged. You wanted kids then."

Jay didn't back down. Dee wouldn't respect him if he waffled or wavered. "Of course I want kids. Who doesn't? Just not right this second, while it's still just the three of us running around in this bus."

He raised a finger tattooed with the form of Benten, the red god of luck. "Amy's husband missed their kid's birth. He didn't even get to see his son until well after."

His fiancée's blue eyes glinted. "He was dead!"

Jay tilted his head sardonically. "That's not helping your case any."

He gestured at the interior packed with armor, electronics, ammunition, and the secure cargo vault hidden away toward the back. As if to underscore his point for him, the automated mechanisms clicked as Kay loaded a new rocket onto a drone.

Dee scowled and shook her head, electric blue ringlets bouncing. "There's always going to be something going on. That's the nature of life and why we pay for Gold Cross. That's no reason not to live."

"Dee, I want us to be there for our kids. If we're not. Well, you heard about the three children kidnapped in Houston—"

A banging on the outer hatch interrupted Jay's response. He hit a button, bringing up video from outside. The boy fiddled with the brim of his backwards baseball cap and cleared his throat.

"Dude, if it was up to me, you could stay all week. But I just heard. Mr. Vincent, the PE teacher, is bringin' a class out. He'd have my hide for letting you hang in the arena. Sorry, but y'all need to blitz before I get caught lettin' ya loiter here." He sighed and held the bill Jay had given him toward the camera.

Jay tugged his thin wisp of beard and turned to Dee. "Sorry love."

Shifting back toward the front, he hit the microphone button. "No problem. Keep the cash. We'll head out now."

Dee ran back to her station and peered over Kay's shoulder. "Any sign of the aerial signal?"

Kay shook his long blond hair. "Not currently. I think the drone caught a trace of it heading north as I got here. It's been clear for the last minute."

Dee pulled Kay out of her seat. "OK. Out of my seat, Snake Man, and back to the turret. Much as I like your pet snake Precious, you're a better shot there than I am."

"Aye, Aye, Ms. Blue Smurf." Kay flicked one of Dee's curls before bolting back for the turret and out range of her wrath.

Up front, Jay laughed, "Don't make me come back there and separate you two."

Kay swarmed up the ladder, looking like a Viking drummer resuming the stage. "See, you're just raring to be a father."

Jay took a breath to keep from growling at his brother to mind his own business.

He heard the noises of Kay settling into place, and then eased the bus out of the covered arena and back into danger.

A flicker of light caught Jay's eye, as Dee routed the signal from the stealth drone to the front monitors. It looked like she had set up a secondary broadcast trying to confuse anyone tracking the transport.

As the bus rolled away, a tall dark bald adult male in green fatigues entered the arena. He stopped and sniffed once. Exhaled. Sniffed again, making his mustache waggle. He shrugged his overly large shoulders. Dark sunglasses shimmered as he stalked into the arena. Behind him, like a gaggle of ducklings, followed a couple dozen gawky teenagers in green shorts and gray t-shirts.

Jay was weirdly and unexpectedly glad they had missed the PE teacher as he eased back into traffic on the feeder. With a few taps, he conferenced his brother and fiancée into an audio session and focused on the job at hand. "Dee, can you check the maps from Blue Imp? See if you can route us around known video cameras. Kay, I need you and Dee to inspect the cargo again. Is it really just hard drives?"

Jay could almost hear Kay's shrug. "Dee knows electronics better and she checked. Three hard drives. No place for drugs or virals."

Dee broke in. "Jay, avoid the toll road. If I didn't know any better, I'd say there was an APB on our bus."

Kay cackled from the turret. "Just what I always wanted to be, a high priority target."

"Shush, Kay. Dee, route me around the scanners." Jay swung the bus across several lanes of traffic, avoiding the ramp to the toll road.

He added, "It's impossible to stay off net videos all the time."

Kay grunted from above. "Impossible or not, it's worth trying."

Jay looked in the direction of a blast from a horn outside. "You're not the one cutting people off and getting the finger."

Dee's station made an obscene "brawk" as a monitoring program sent a priority alert.

She cursed floridly in response. "Net scanners just made us. New warehouse scanner a block back. Two drones going out."

Jay drummed his fingers on the wheel but kept from flooring it. He looked at the eight good luck god tattoos on his fingers. Maybe slow and inconspicuous was better.

They passed a yellow school bus, an El Paso Motor Corp Kidmaster 5000, clean enough to be heading out on a practical field trip. It had the older oval running lights. Kids' faces plastered themselves against the windows. The driver's face had the blank, far-away stare one saw on war veterans. Or parents. Jay shivered. His attention jarred back to the road as Dee released the drones.

Ca-chunk. One drone disengaged from the bus and flew out to auto-hold a half mile ahead.

Ca-chunk. Another drone away, falling back to hold a half mile behind.

Both drones scanned beyond the immediate range of the blue and yellow buses.

The wait wasn't long.

Less than five minutes later, Dee reported. "Three bogies coming up from the south... Road machines... looks like a mid-sized sport-ute and two motorcycles. I wish I knew who's behind these guys."

Dee sent the feed from the drone to the others' monitors.

From the turret Kay asked, "Are we sure they're after us?"

Smoke spurted from the green sport-ute on the monitor. The image flashed reddish white, before the feed turned black from a lost connection as the drone was blasted out of the air.

Dee scoffed, "What do you think?"

There was another thunk from the auto-service system in the drone compartment.

"Well, it could be worse," Kay commented.

In unison the engaged couple yelled back, "Never say that!"

Taking that as warning for incoming heat, Jay pressed down on the accelerator, trying to buy them time before the pursuers were within range. The yellow Kidmaster 5000 slowed and drifted across lanes, heading toward a toll road and out of danger.

The motor of their own bus roared to greater life, filling the relative quiet of the transport. Jay couldn't hear the clank of Kay rotating the turret or the click of Dee's keys. But he didn't need to as the motorcycles and green sport-ute grew larger in the rear monitor. The motorcycles swerved in and out of frame, while the larger vehicle blasted straight for them.

Over the rumble of the bus's Sam Houston Motors custom engine, Jay not only heard but felt Kay open fire. Whatever curses his brother shouted were covered by rattles and bangs from the turret. The bursts of big bore gunfire, audible through the armor, shook everything.

Instinctively Jay's grip tightened on the wheel.

In the rear monitor, bits of armor and rubber burst from a tire of the green vehicle. It jerked to the left, almost hitting one of the motorcycles that flanked it.

There was a tumble of dust and grit. First the motorcycle to the left and then the one to the right arced away from the larger vehicle. In their wake, a sport-ute tire lost cohesion. The now three-wheeled vehicle went through a short spin, before re-establishing a wobbly pursuit.

Both motorcycles accelerated around the green ute, veering out away from the larger vehicle, before they zipped around it. The red and white images almost merged into one as they bore down on them.

Jay saw a flicker of movement that looked like the motorcyclist on the white bike had leveled a single-shot grenade launcher at the back camera.

Dee's voice came along with the rushing hiss of the rear flamethrower. "Not today."

The white motorcycle on the left caught fire and swung away. The cyclist became a flaming torch of black synthetic leather armor. The burning two-wheeler crisscrossed the border grass before toppling to the side and spinning wildly out of control. The trail of smoke ended when it wiped out on the feeder road paralleling the highway.

Jay tried to keep his eyes on the road ahead instead of the swirling fire and buzzing pursuers on the monitor. Their current path wasn't arduous to follow, but he also didn't want to roll the bus over a mine. They were already putting more wear on the vehicle hauling this first cargo than they had wanted to in a year.

Gunfire from the second motorcycle rattled against the rear armor.

Kay fired back, but the cyclist had already leaned to one side, causing the burst to miss.

Jay observed in a bored tone. "Kay, that was an expensive miss."

A second shot was his only reply.

The driver simply disappeared from the seat. The red unmanned motorcycle continued on for a few seconds until the handlebars bounced back and forth causing the bike to skid before it hit a pothole and flipped over.

The green sport-ute swung around the downed bike. There was a blast of light that flashed across the back monitor as lasers from its turret sparkled against the bus. Jay wanted to yelp. Damage to the armor registered on his panels as each bit of armor melted or burst away.

Instead, Jay yelled, "Dee, laser! Now! Please!"

"On it," his fiancée replied with a chipper chirp. She was enjoying herself. There was another hiss as she fired the flamethrower at the green laser-armed vehicle. It was out of range, but the cloud of smoke now blocked the laser.

For a little bit.

From the turret, Kay fired a burst blind through the smoke. The rounds missed but must have distracted the driver who veered slightly wide before recentering. During the distraction, Dee triggered the oil spray.

Just as the sport-ute returned to their tail, it hit the oil and started to spin wildly. Dee, not believing in the concept of overkill, targeted the oil slick with the flamethrower.

There was a roar of tar colored smoke and a burst of yellow flames, as oil splattered tires became rotating torches.

Undeterred, the sport-ute regained control and continued after the courier bus. It sent short bursts of laser fire, carving off armor intermittently, despite Dee's work with the flamethrower.

Dee deployed another rocket drone. "Running low on flames. Switching to air support."

The explosion from the drone-fired rocket ate the back portion of their pursuer in a flash of red and orange, followed by a curl of black smoke. The driver lost control and banked hard to the left, hitting the concrete median. The sport-ute collapsed like an accordion in a hungry musician's hands.

Before the two brothers could say a word, Dee pre-empted them. "I'm bringing the drones in. And I'm calling the client. Something isn't right here. The hazard level is ridiculous for what this cargo is supposed to be."

Kay lumbered down from the turret and took over scanning for internet camera hits. "I should put a slide in for the turret. At least coming down would be easier."

Dee's fast, slender fingers dialed their contact. After a half-ring, the link clicked as it transferred over.

"This is the night service for Austin Pharmaceuticals," a cheerfully crisp AI voice sang out. "This is not a secure line. How may I help you?"

"This is DeeDee Durango with Falco Secured Data Couriers. I would like to speak to Mr. Hernández. We're getting way more heat than expected on this package."

Dee tapped a few buttons, her computer screen flashing a response, as she waited for the AI to respond.

The short pause of a few seconds was telling. The AI had to be consulting a human. "I'm sorry Ms. Durango, Mr. Hernández is in conference with his partners, and all are unavailable. May I take a message?"

Dee pursed her lips, her east Texas accent coming out. "Yeah. Tell him we aren't happy. We're seeing too much heat for what our cargo should deserve. Thank you very much."

The AI responded, "Noted. Message received, recorded, and routed to his inbox. Have a pleasant day, Ms. Durango."

The click off left her with a flat tone before she took a breath. Dee laughed at the disconnected line. "Did you hear that? 'Night service.' In the middle of the day!"

"That… doesn't sound promising." Her fiancé called back. His eyes, however, stayed glued to the road as he wove through traffic.

She turned back to her monitor where red text flashed on the screen. Aerial radar showed something incoming fast—a ring of circles at the edge of the screen.

"Dear, neither does this. The aerial blip is back. It's south of us this time."

After a deep sigh, Jay asked, "How fast?"

"Not too fast. I… think it's not sure where we are."

With a surge of power, the bus leaped forward. "That's a blessing."

"Well, it does appear to be hovering off to the side. My guess is it can't quite track us."

Dee felt the bus accelerate; she swayed in her seat as Jay took the bus through a decreasing radius turn without slowing. Then it steadied.

She took a breath and keyed in the private conference channel.

Jay's monitor flashed as Dee's face appeared in the side bar.

He raised a single blonde eyebrow, wondering why she wanted a private channel.

When she presented him with her best wicked smile, his stomach tightened. Once she had his attention, Dee winked. "Now, about kids."

"Really, love? Now?"

Dee's blue eyes twinkled as she laughed, causing her electric blue ringlets to dance around her heart-shaped face. "It's just like life. No reason not to keep going. And we're going to finish this conversation come hell or high water."

"But I'm driving!" Jay clenched the wheel tighter, the whites of his knuckles highlighting the luck gods adorning eight fingers.

"And I'm flying drones. And watching the internet. In case you hadn't noticed, your long-haired brother ran back into the turret, too scared to listen in."

There was a chunk as she launched the stealth drone to replace the two rocket drones being auto-serviced.

Jay's eyes flicked to Dee's smiling face, and he huffed out a laugh.

"Fine! I like kids, and—" he caught a glimpse of gray-on-gray movement in the middle of the road. He switched lanes as he scanned the pavement before him. "Why is there an armadillo on a freeway in the middle of The New Woodlands?"

Dee pushed her electric blue hair back. "So far so good dear. I'm still waiting to hear about why this is a problem."

"And I want to do my best by them." Jay took the bus through a curve over one of the water features the developers had added to the area.

"And?"

"I can't do my best if I'm busy—if we're both busy—hauling cargo all over Texas. Hang on a second!"

Jay strained as he took in the scene before him, trying to blink away what he hoped was a mirage. The text on the screen flashed a message almost too fast to read. Ahead he saw wet asphalt glistening in the Texas summer heat.

They were in for it.

"Dee, check the maps. Remember when you said, 'hell or highwater'?"

"Yes. And I meant it."

"Well, we've got both. The heads-up just said the road ahead is flooded. The news says someone blew up a retention wall on the drainage project. And I can see, just past the water, a Helltank."

Kay, who had been assiduously pretending not to hear, broke in. "A Helltank? I built a model of one of those back in high school."

Dee skimmed through screens blazingly fast. "No alternate routes. Let me guess. The Helltank can take us out with a single shot? And it's amphibious?"

From the turret Kay responded. "Of course. See the bit of pipe going straight up behind the main cannon? With the disk on top? That's the snorkel periscope. It was optional but it's been standard issue for twenty years. All the flooding you know?"

Jay downshifted manually, overriding the automatic transmission. The blue bus slowed in a scream of engine noises. Then Jay carefully and calculatedly swung the steering wheel.

The front wheels turned, the attempt to turn slowing the wheels even more. The rear of the bus was still trying to go faster than the front and swung around.

Screams from Dee and Kay blurred together. They hated being onboard during a bootlegger-reverse. Even the heads-up display gave up trying to process anything and just flashed confused symbols. But Jay had lost focus of everything except the road and the feel of the bus.

A bus which no longer had proper contact with the road.

And which came to a swaying halt, pointed back the way they had come. Putting the transmission back into full automatic, Jay accelerated, quickly passing through the curve and the construction zone.

"Dear. What about kids?"

The brothers spoke in unison. "Really?"

"Yes, really. And be quiet Snake Man, I'm talking to my fiancé."

Jay sputtered. "I believe I said we couldn't give kids enough time while hauling cargo."

Dee gestured at the packed bus. "It's tight, but we can take the kids with us. They can do remote learning while we're hauling cargo and go in for instruction when we're home."

"Dee, we get shot at!"

"And? I'd rather be with you, helping and knowing what happens, than at home waiting. I'm sure the kids would be the same. Drone footage on four."

The number four monitor at each station lit up with footage from the stealth drone back at the flooded bridge. The Helltank was just emerging from the water.

Dee interrupted herself. "Kay, how fast?"

"Fast enough. Faster than us."

"Well then." The footage shifted as the machine gun armed drone turned and headed back to the bus. The Helltank didn't disappear from the screen quite as quickly as one would have wished.

"Bring the kids?" Jay snorted while steering the bus up an overpass.

"Of course. We aren't usually shot at so much."

"How do you know that? This is our first cargo."

Nobody heard if there was a response.

The stretch of overpass before him simply stopped existing as it became a cloud of flying gravel. Jay downshifted and slammed on the brakes causing the bus to skid. The solid tires and inertia kept the bus moving, but the blue was scoured from the front quarter and the windows were partially frosted. Belatedly, the heads-up unit flashed an impaired roadway warning.

Jay struggled with the wheel. "Like being in a gigantic bead blaster."

Dust rolled up from the blast hole in front of them. Once clear, the couriers could see the steel and iron frame of the highway overpass.

Trapped. They were trapped. Pinned like bugs before a descending flame. Or between a collapsed overpass and an unstoppable tank.

Despite the heavy armor on the bus, Jay could swear he heard the roar of the Helltank loading a second round.

Dee looked up at Kay. "Nothing we have will even scratch the paint on the Helltank, right?"

Kay sounded excited. "Yup. The ceramics are nano-enhanced. And the reactive armor, even on older models, would take out the bus if we tried to ram."

"Dear?"

"Yes, Dee?"

"No ramming."

Even under the circumstances, Jay chuckled. "Noted. By the way, has anyone seen the aerial bogie that was following us."

As if responding on cue, a "bing!" sounded from Dee's terminal as a shadow passed overhead.

The reinforced windows of the bus rattled. A sonic boom, or something very like one, rang the bus like the giant bell at the Houston Ship Channel.

Kay had a great view from the turret. "Dadgum. I didn't think Texas had any—"

There was a blast of light brighter than a laser, as a mystery ordnance from the flying pursuer obliterated the Helltank. Jay's driver's screen,

Dee's monitors, and Kay's turret vision block showed them nothing but the fiery red explosion. Following this, a fresh rain of gravel brought darkness.

Jay gripped the wheel, blind and unable to maneuver the trapped bus as he felt the shifting surface of the overpass.

Shrapnel from the destroyed tank ballooned out, thundered against the bus, and scraped across the road. The overpass shook. But they could make out nothing as dust and smoke followed the gravel in a cloud of gray-brown mist that coated everything. Iron rebar whirled around the bus.

It took a while before the shaking stopped.

A last bit of wreckage hit, clipping the edge of the front wheel. What looked like it might have been the remains of their stealth drone assaulted the integrity of a front tire. Even solid tires had their limit, and this last insult was it.

The bus tilted, falling into the first hole the Helltank had made.

Jay spun the wheel and cranked the transport into reverse as it started to slip down.

"What are you doing?" Dee called from the back. "We need to go the other way."

Jay backed toward the flooded area and the Helltank graveyard. "Getting us out of here!"

Dee tried to interject. "But--"

Jay rolled onward. "Without the tank blocking the path, I can get us off this battlefield."

Just as Jay edged into the wreckage, light flickered from a moving object. The smoke from the smoldering Helltank cleared enough for him to make out a quadcopter hovering just beyond the remains.

A very large quadcopter—about the size of the compact car that had first saved Jay from Dee's discussion about kids.

Looked like he wasn't going to have to finish that conversation.

The black quadcopter probably had whatever weapon had taken out the Helltank trained on their bus.

The hair on the back of Jay's neck stood up. "Dee, can you jam the quadcopter?"

Dee didn't reply but he heard her tapping keys, just in case their new opponent was remotely operated.

The quadcopter rotated slightly. A royal blue stripe down its center shone menacingly.

Jay considered his two options; one led to a flooded bombed out overpass and the other to the crater surrounding the wrecked tank. He didn't need to have Dee pull up an electronic map to know they were trapped.

The telecom buzzed with an incoming call.

Jay grimaced but shrugged when Dee lowered her hand over the button. Her slender fingers pushed the accept call button.

The monitors lit up with an AI generated talking head of a middle-aged man with thick glasses, a big bushy mustache, and a cowboy hat.

"I am Techne. I am incorporated into this quadcopter. I do not wish to harm you. But we need to talk."

A mutter from Kay drifted from the turret. "Is it breaking up with us?"

Jay replied without thinking. "Only if it's your newest fling that you didn't tell us about."

Techne ignored the brothers' banter. "A Big Bill's Dine and Dash was observed a few miles back. I see you carry a Safe Haven subscription. Let us proceed to that location post haste. Being there should make you more comfortable with my presence. It also provides access to resources you will require to confirm my allegations."

Dee's eyes remained glued to her screen. "What allegations?"

"Your cargo is not as you were informed."

Dee didn't wait for elaboration. "Stolen?"

"Negative. Kidnapped."

Jay stood in the waiting area holding a list of damages about as long as Dee was tall for their company's one and only asset, the big bus.

Dee skipped toward him, her electric blue ringlets bouncing. Jay turned to smile at her. She was way too chipper to have lost the negotiations. At least something had to be salvageable from this wreck of a contract.

She started talking before she reached his side gesturing wildly. "The so-called Mr. Hernández had the three hard drives with Techne's children kidnapped. Hernández knew the people who'd stolen them were under observation, so he contracted the transport out to us."

Jay threw his arm over Dee's shoulder then gave her a side hug. "I take it you double-checked the story?"

"Of course I did, dear. I even contacted the Institute. We did a remote session. The three hard drives contain recently created—" She considered and finished, "—newborn AIs."

"So, that's why their design is so different?"

Dee giggled as she snuggled into his side. "Absolutely. Also, Techne sent three mobile chassis-bodies for the kids."

"Chassis-bodies?"

"Chassis-bodies. So the kids can interact with us while we take them back to Houston."

"Take them back? But—"

"Techne said AI kids get riled up when they're cooped up too long. He and Catherine, the mom, don't want to deal with three stir-crazy kids."

"So instead, we are?"

"You aren't going to turn down our first easy legal contract, are you?"

Jay stroked his wispy beard. "Of course not. So, where are they?"

A laugh answered him. "Where all kids are, if allowed. In the arcade. Don't worry, Kay is watching them."

Jay winced at the thought of his brother watching kids. "If they aren't careful, the kids will come back tattooed or draped with snakes."

"You mean like you?" Dee tapped the first god tattoo on his fingers.

"Hey, I am never draped in snakes."

Dee snickered. "Only because Kay keeps Precious in the turret with him."

Jay tugged Dee along to find the wayward childlike AIs and his brother. They rounded the corner to the arcade, which buzzed with light, rang from metal petals, and rattled with electronic music. The arcade was a throwback to the 1980s, with a few modernizations, but still had the same twang of pinball machines and beeps and buzzes from colorful quarter-devouring kiosks.

Jay scanned the room for his brother. One would think a tall, blond Viking bodybuilder with long drummer hair and three electronic sidekicks would stick out in an arcade. But there were a lot of over-muscled bikers crowded in.

Before they entered the din, speakers in the ceiling pinged and a polite voice stated, "Number eleven is complete."

Dee ran a finger along Jay's tattoos. "That's us. Don't worry, Kay was going to bring the kids to the bus when it was ready. I'll introduce you before we leave."

Jay sighed and turned back with her. As they exited the building, he leaned over and whispered to Dee. "I am not asking Techne about how AIs make babies."

Dee dimpled. "I already asked."

After chuckling, Jay responded, "You would."

She blushed and was still pleasantly red when they neared the bus.

The two-story bus had started out a professional looking blue. Now the paint was scraped, dinged, and dented, not to mention gravel-blasted at the front. But the reinforced windshield had been replaced, the dents pounded out of the armor, and a few replacement patches added. All tires had been replaced with fresh solids. It looked rugged.

Gone was the gloss of new steel and newer paint.

Just outside the hatch, Kay and three small metal AI chassis-bodies stood looking the bus over. The AI kids were all thin and about the size of a three-year-old human. Each thin, spindly chassis had two legs, two arms, and what Jay presumed were photoreceptors for a head. The chassis-bodies were colored in a range of human skin tones, with a variation in height so very little was uniform about them.

The black hard drives sat in the middle of the chests behind armored panels. The forms were unexpectedly graceful, although not quite pretty.

Jay silently bet himself the variations in height and tone between the chassis-bodies matched some statistical model Techne and Christine had picked out.

Dee walked forward and turned the tallest of the children toward him by placing a hand on its shoulder. "This is Ay."

She pronounced the name like the letter A.

Jay gravely shook Ay's hand. "Nice to meet you."

Ay replied with a voice that wavered at the edge of being child but undeniably tinged with adult seriousness. "And very nice to meet you. Thank you for rescuing us!"

Jay swallowed back a laugh. "We didn't exactly rescue you, so much as refuse to participate in your kidnapping."

The little AI nodded its oversized head, the reddish-brown photoreceptor lights blinking off then on. "Nonetheless, you have our gratitude."

Dee gestured toward the two AI kids on each side of Kay. "The two next to your brother are Bee, who has the green... eyes and Cee with the cyan ones."

Kay put a hand on each kid in turn.

Cee stepped forward; it was in the shortest of the chassis-bodies and had the smallest hands.

Jay knelt down to shake the cool mental appendage.

Cee spoke with a vibrant multilayered AI voice. "We are indebted to you."

Bee stayed next to Kay and waved. The voice was more old style digital, almost mechanical. "Please allow me to extend my appreciation. We must inform you of auspicious news. After conferring amongst ourselves, we have determined that your fiancée is our sister."

Ay took up the story. "The coincidence of naming was too felicitous to pass unremarked."

Cee finished with, "Once we've matured into male or female, we will let her know if she has sisters or brothers."

Dee laughed. "My first instinct was to tell Techne and Christine that naming their kids A, B, and C just wasn't done. Then they asked my name. And you and your brother's names."

Jay smirked at her but nodded gravely to the AIs. "Well, now that is settled. Let's get this circus on the road."

Cee glanced around. "Can I be the dancing bear?"

Jay opened his mouth and then shut it. He wondered if Cee's sense of humor followed that of its parents.

Situating everyone was easier than he feared, as a single child assigned itself to each human.

Once they were on board, Dee forwarded paperwork images to his monitor.

Her voice was crisply cheerful, "The AADA arbitration is finished. We got paid, plus damages, plus a reward. Falco Secured Data Couriers now owns this bus, battered as it is. We also have a nice capital account."

Ay was standing next to Dee. Both hands were, by direct adult requirement, locked onto Dee's workspace. "Yes. And I understand Mom and Dad are planning to hire you. Our kidnappers had horrible security— that's how everyone learned about you and tried to collect us. To sell on the black market."

Bee was similarly locked into the turret with Kay. Precious was wrapped around a particularly warm capacitor on its chassis-body. "The summary as I heard it, is that Mom wants to take out the kidnappers. Permanently. Mom and Dad are both financial analysts. Good ones too. They can pay well."

Cee looked up from near Jay's seat at the front. "Dad was very miffed. He wanted to sue them. Mom wants to bomb them. They are discussing the situation now."

Jay looked down at Cee, who was playing with a few wires on the console as it spoke. "Cee, hands! You know better."

Cee ducked its pale head and the chassis scrunched, drooping in an odd way to appear sheepish and chastised.

Compared to the trip out, the return to Houston was refreshingly uneventful. After dropping the kids and Kay off, Dee and Jay sat in the blissful silence of the bus.

Jay smiled and glanced around, noticing some additions the three AI kids had made. "Well, I will say having kids in the bus was an unexpectedly pleasant event."

Dee laughed. Her workstation was now decorated with odd AI symbols and at least one monitor was programmed for children's videos only.

Jay crawled out of his seat and lay in the middle of the floor of the bus, his hands outstretched.

"That's good, but what in the world are you doing Jay?"

"Measuring."

"Measuring what?"

"Well, we're getting married in a month. So, I need the dimensions. Special order parts for a bus like ours take time."

If Dee were a cat, her electric blue hair would have been standing on end. "Parts for what?"

"Parts for custom baby seats. I understand you need them for infants. Since we're starting a family right away, we need to get the order in now."

With a squee of happiness, Dee launched herself at him.

The Wheels on the Death Bus go Round and Round
By: Seth Taylor

It had reached a point where Gary actually wished raiders would attack. A man could only take so much torture, so much abuse, before mortal peril and the potential sweet release of death started to look inviting.

"The wheels on the bus go round and round! Round and round! Round and…"

Never mind. He couldn't depend on raiders. Bastards were too unreliable. Gary would be better off if he just aimed his bus at the flimsy guardrail, the only thing separating Highway 50 from the cliffs of Echo Summit, and floored the accelerator. The heavy, armored bus would blow through that guardrail like it wasn't even there, and the detonation of all the ammo aboard would ensure that the end was painless. Something to consider.

"Feeling suicidal again?" asked a sympathetic voice.

Gary turned to see a pretty brunette and grunted. "That and maybe a bit homicidal as well."

Daisy Wilson, or Miss Daisy as the children called her, grinned at him, which brought a sparkle to her blue eyes. "I promise to inform the board of your restraint if you do avoid running us all off a cliff."

"I'm holding you to that. No one said anything about a school bus driver having to consort with so many…" Gary gave a full body shudder, "children."

"They're not a bad bunch, really." Miss Daisy turned to smile fondly over her shoulder at her charges.

"Could have fooled me," Gary replied before turning to bellow at his passengers. "Quiet down back there!" He might as well have been yelling at the sky for all the good it did.

The boisterous busload of eight and nine-year-olds had just finished "The Wheels on the Bus" and had launched into a spirited, and off-key, rendition of "She'll be Comin' Round the Mountain". Appropriate considering that the bus was just rounding the big turn at Nebelhorn, at the crest of the pass. To the right was the old Caltrans yard that had been repurposed since the Blight into an armed checkpoint to keep raiders, reavers, revolutionaries, and other assorted riff-raff out of the Tahoe Basin. The California Highway Patrol and the Nevada State Police worked together to secure the mountain hideaway as a playground for the rich and connected. The beautiful people could ski the mountains of California and gamble in the casinos of Nevada, all safe and secure in the knowledge that no one too dangerous, or too poor, was getting through the security cordon. The mountains did all the work, leaving only six roads in or out. The glittering blue jewel of Tahoe Lake and the snowy mountains around it were amongst the safest places in the country.

"See?" he said, turning back to the young teacher.

"You just have to establish that you are in charge," she replied.

"Hard to do when I got no disciplinary power. Citations," Gary flicked the pad of orange notices, "are worthless and the kids know it."

"They're not bad kids, really," said Miss Daisy.

"Maybe not, but they are spoiled. This might be news to you, but most schools don't send their kids on ski trips."

The third-grade teacher shrugged. "John Sutter Prep is a destination school for the wealthiest and most powerful parents in Sacramento. The expectations are a bit different."

"Exactly how do you expect the child of a state senator to listen to a truck driver turned bus driver? I couldn't even convince the convoy lead to pay the gimme."

Daisy frowned. "The what?"

"Sorry, trucker slang. The toll."

"The toll for what?"

"For this road. Highway 50 ain't like Highway 80, that's the road we came to Tahoe on. On 80 the CHP keeps order and Caltrans road crews do the maintenance. All generously paid for by the taxpayers of

California. Highway 50 here was abandoned by the state decades ago. It was considered redundant to requirements. So, the locals have taken it over. They make sure it's somewhat drivable and not completely infested with bandits. You just got to pay the gimme if you want to use it."

"So why aren't we paying it?" asked Miss Daisy.

"The convoy masters said because it wasn't an official toll. Really, it's because they're greedy, and they think this convoy is so big that there is nothing these hillbillies can do to bother us." Gary shrugged. "This road doesn't normally get this kind of traffic, but with that avalanche shutting down Highway 80, we all have to go over 50 instead. I'm guessing they also want to set the standard that the foothill folk can't expect to skim off the traffic redirected by the avalanche." He tried to set his face into as neutral a mask as possible.

"You don't think it will work," said Miss Daisy after studying his face for a few seconds.

"I think everyone might be underestimating just how determined the foothill folk on the other side of the mountains can be. Have to be. They say California came out of the Grain Blight pretty well and they're mostly right. But the economic crash was still hard on the people out here on the fringes. Most of the jobs up and went away and the people living in these hills had to find other ways to make a living. They scratch food out of the ground, or haul timber out of the mountains, and the lucky ones work in the few vineyards that are still running. But most of the money 'round these parts comes from running protection. They call it a 'tax on contraband cargo' though it's as much an official tax as I am Devon Varity. On the 50, the tax is collected in Placerville and passed on to the folk further up the hill. Keeps them from going full bandit. Thing about a system like that, you need to enforce it. Let one convoy through and the rest will think they can get away with it too, and then the income stream disappears." Gary shook his head. "Nah, the locals are going to have to try something."

"But we will be OK, right? I mean we're part of a convoy, and we have this armored bus. We'll be fine." Daisy's pretty face scrunched up with worry and her voice climbed a couple decibels.

"That's right," Gary agreed quickly and patted the dashboard. "This baby is top of the line, a Kidmaster 5000 out of the El Paso Motor Company, and those Texans have to know their stuff, as bad as things are down near the border. Steel armor with a Kevlar backing, .50 caliber turret, side flamethrowers, a reinforced suspension, wreckage plow, and a nuclear reactor under the hood. I've driven rigs through hell that were less tricked-out than this Bessy. We will be just fine." He carefully did not mention the bus was designed to keep its occupants from being harmed by low-grade city violence, not to duke-it-out in road wars with raiders.

"Right." Daisy drew a large breath and blew it out again while nodding vigorously. "Like you said, we'll be fine."

"Why wouldn't we be fine, Miss Daisy?" piped a small voice immediately behind them. They both turned to see a small, blond boy standing in the aisle with a quizzical look on his face.

"No reason, Tyler. I was just worried that we might not make it back to Sacramento in time for the drop-off that I promised your parents. Come on. Let's get you back to your seat."

Gary watched them go out of the side of his right eye. Miss Daisy was a good gal. He hated to see her get worried. At least she had the good sense to be worried. The other teacher on the bus, Miss Worthington, was a dizzy dame who seemed to have no idea what time of day it was, let alone the situation they might be in. Miss Daisy at least had a head on her shoulders. And that was far from her best physical asset... Gary shook himself and turned his attention back to the road. They had at least a couple more hours before things got bad.

The highway descended from the crest of the mountain range in a series of smooth curves that kept the grade from becoming too sheer. They passed by the remains of one ski resort that was deemed too far from the patrolled areas of Tahoe to be worth defending, as well as dozens of cabins which might, or might not, still be inhabited. As a state, California had avoided some of the worst troubles that had befallen the country in recent decades. The outlying areas though, still suffered from many of the same blights as their less fortunate neighbors. On this day, that decay was covered by a blanket of pure white snow which rendered it a winter wonderland all the same.

The kids stopped their infernal singing and gaped out the window at the massive drifts, the snow-laden trees, and the half-buried cabins. They oohed and aahed and speculated on which magical creature might live within the dwellings. Gnomes or yetis seemed to be the primary suspects. In that moment they were nearly cute. Then some kid started singing "Dashing through the Snow" and it got worse from there.

"Five more hours…" Gary muttered. "Five more hours." Back in the day, this route probably only took an hour and a half to drive, but fifty rigs traveling bumper to bumper moved a great deal slower. Especially when they had to follow a couple of plows and blowers to cut through the fresh snow.

Excited shrieks interrupted his mantra as one of the kids espied a snowmobile race off through the trees. The rest surged to the windows to look after the mysterious vehicle, but it was already gone.

"And there's the spotter," Gary sighed. He had hoped it would take another hour or two before anyone saw the convoy. That snowmobile was likely racing down ahead of the convoy, which had no way to keep up with the speedy little conveyance in its own element. The question was, what kind of reception would be waiting for them? Some raiders nipping at their flanks? Like jackals trying to cut out the weakest member of the herd. Or a concerted attempt to take all or most of the convoy?

As the line of trucks crawled its way to lower elevations, the depth of the snow around them thinned from a quilt to a sheet, and soon was only patches on north slopes and the shady side of trees. They were well off the crest now and following the course of the South Fork of the American River as it wound its way down from the mountains that birthed it.

Gary kept glancing from side to side, his finger hovering over the ARMOR button. At any moment he expected a band of snowmobiles to sweep out from the cover of the trees and descend on the convoy like wolves on a line of sheep. The longer it took, the more worried he got.

His nerves were wound so tight that he jumped at the sound of a small voice from his elbow.

"What are you looking for?"

Gary turned to see that pipsqueak, Tyler, standing next to him. His eyes wide, blue, and infinitely curious.

"Go sit down, kid."

"But everyone else is standing."

Gary flicked his eyes to his mirror and saw that indeed most of the kids were out of their seats. He had been so busy scanning for threats, he hadn't even noticed.

"Hey!" he bellowed. "Don't make me tap the sign!" He reached up and pointed at a sign that proclaimed in big brassy letters "All Occupants Must Remain Seated When Bus is in Motion".

"It's all right, Mr. Kraus," called Mrs. Worthington from the back of the bus. "I said the children could leave their seats. We have already been on the road so long that they are getting antsy. Might we be able to stop soon?"

"No stops until we get back to civilization!"

"But I must insist. The children will need to use the bathroom."

"And I must insist…" Gary began, but he trailed off when he saw that the older teacher had already stopped listening to him. "What have I ever done to deserve this?"

"Deserve what?" Tyler asked.

"Deserve to have some question machine bugging me while I'm trying to drive. Go on, now. Go play with your friends."

"I'm bored of my friends. I want to talk to you now."

"No, you don't, kid. I'm just a grumpy old bus driver."

"Were you always a grumpy old bus driver?"

"Old, no. Bus driver, no. Grumpy, yes." Gary gave the kid his most ferocious scowl.

Tyler was unperturbed. "What were you before you were a bus driver?"

"I was a truck driver."

The kid's eyes somehow managed to get even larger. "You were part of the Brotherhood of Truckers?"

"Sure I was. So is anyone who gets into the life who isn't a damn idiot."

"Wow. Cool!"

Gary cast a skeptical eye over the boy. He was looking for any sign of sarcasm but could detect none. "Really? I figured a kid your age would be into the autoduellists."

"Autoduellists have rules and endorsement deals. The Brotherhood though, you guys are always out there fighting raiders and seeing far-off places. You're way cooler."

"Well… when you put it like that…" Gary chuckled.

"So why did you stop?" the kid frowned. "Being a truck driver has got to be better than being a bus driver."

"Oh, got into a bit of trouble in a convoy ambush in Utah. My truck got destroyed and I picked this up," Gary pointed to the scar on his face, "and a bum leg. My company, Sweet Carolina Carriers, recommended that I retire from the life."

"Oh," the kid seemed disappointed but rallied quickly. "Are we going to see any raiders today? Is that what you were looking for?"

"That's what I was looking for. I'm not seeing any though."

"So, we aren't going to see any raiders today?"

"I wouldn't say that. I think the only reason we haven't seen any raiders yet is because they are setting up something bigger for us, down the hill."

"Really? Neat!" Tyler pumped his fist into the air.

Gary frowned. He had hoped to scare the boy back to his seat, but it seemed to have backfired. Maybe he was going to have to get gorier? He opened his mouth to do so when Miss Daisy forestalled him.

"Tyler, stop bugging Mr. Kraus. Go back to your friends."

The boy wriggled past his teacher, and she took his spot. Gary regarded the change in company as an upgrade.

"Sorry about all of this," she gestured behind her. "I said that it was probably a bad idea, but Sandra is the senior teacher, and the kids really are getting restless." She leaned closer and whispered. "What are we going to do when they have to go to the bathroom?"

"I got some empty soda bottles," Gary suggested.

She threw her head back in a merry laugh that sounded absolutely wonderful to Gary's ears. She stopped once she got a good look at the bus driver's face. "Wait. You're serious."

"Completely. It's an old Brotherhood trick. We're often driving through places where slowing down or stopping could kill you. We had to learn how to improvise." Gary squirmed; maybe this wasn't the best thing to be talking about with a pretty young woman.

"Oh," she appeared to think about that for a moment. "That makes sense I suppose."

"You do? No offense, but I thought that might… shock you a little more."

"I work with children. I have to be inured to a whole bunch of disgusting things." Daisy's face screwed up. "What do you do with the bottles when you are done?"

"Me? I used to save them in case I did run into raiders."

"You drive trucks armed with guns, lasers, and flame throwers… and you throw bottles of pee at the bad guys?" Daisy raised an eyebrow.

"It's good for a laugh. Besides, you would be surprised how many big tough guys there are who would not hesitate to charge into a hail of bullets, but would run away like little girls from some piss." Gary indulged himself in a raspy chuckle but then caught the look on Daisy's face and stopped himself with a cough. "Not that we are going to have to do that today, or anything."

"We get to throw pee!" yelled a voice filled with childish delight. Tyler was back and had a pair of friends with him. The black-haired boy looked as equally thrilled at the prospect of hurling bodily fluids. The red-haired girl with the pigtails wrinkled up her nose and eyed her companions with a look that completely wrote off the male gender.

"That's not what Mr. Kraus said." Despite her normal calm demeanor, Miss Daisy's tone sounded exasperated. "He was just making a joke. Right, Mr. Kraus?" She shot the bus driver a look filled with equal measures of pleading and warning.

"That's right, just an old trucker's joke." Gary glowered at the children. "Don't throw your pee. Now, go sit down or I'm going to write all of you a citation."

The redhead twisted her face into a dismissive smirk. "My daddy says that citations have no force behind them and are just used as an imaginary power to trick us into behaving."

Crap, they figured me out!

Gary was about to respond with more bluster; it was all he had. But Miss Daisy cut him off. "Is my power to assign you more homework imaginary, Hannah?"

"No," the little ginger squeaked, her eyes wide as she realized she might have crossed a line.

"I thought not. Now go sit down. You too, Tyler and Ezra."

"Thanks," Gary muttered once the kids were a safe distance away. "I thought I was going to have to start threatening to strap them to the roof."

"You wouldn't actually do that." Miss Daisy's half smile said that she wasn't entirely sure if he was joking.

"If they annoy me enough, maybe." Gary tossed a half smile back at her even though he could feel the scar tissue on his face stretch uncomfortably. He just hoped he didn't look too much like a gargoyle.

"Then I had better go make sure they don't annoy you too much."

"You do that." A red warning light started flashing on the dashboard display in front of him and Gary's tone turned serious. "In fact, you had better make sure that everyone, including that dizzy dame, sits down and shuts up. I think things are about to start getting interesting."

Miss Daisy paled, gave a quick, nervous nod, and hurried back to start herding her charges into their seats.

The message on Gary's display told him the computer had flagged traffic on the convoy's CB channel that indicated potential danger ahead. Normally, Gary liked listening to the CB channel on long drives. The banter and jokes from fellow truck drivers was often the only social interaction you got on long runs through the Badlands. On this run though, he had the channel muted because it was a struggle to hear it over the kids anyway. He did make sure to have the bus's on-board computer (no AI but still pretty smart) listen for him. At the warning, he jammed an earbud into his left ear and put his finger on top of it so that he could hear over the chatter. He swiped a finger across the display to play back the relevant conversation.

"All vehicles. This is armored plow, *Snow Day is Cancelled.* Be advised that we just reached the end of snow cover on the roadway. We're handing off the lead to *Not Your Daddy's Breacher*. Me and the rest of the snow clearance vehicles are going to pull off to the side and let y'all pass. Good luck, we've seen a couple of snowmobiles ahead of us, but nothing big yet. *Snow Day*, out."

"All vehicles. This your friendly neighborhood barricade crasher, *Not your Daddy's Breacher*. Don't worry. We'll get you to Sacto alright. Ain't nothing in these hills that can stop us. Just follow us, and you'll be fine. *Breacher*, out."

"We'll see about that," Gary muttered as he extracted the earbud and popped it back into his charging station. He had never worked with the crew on *Breacher* before, but those guys on the barricade bashers were all the same. Cocky to a man, or woman, and sure that their rig was the baddest thing on the planet. Breaching rigs were tough, customized trucks with as much arms and armor as could be allowed before the government classified them as tanks. They were built to blow their way through any roadblock any enterprising bandit gang might throw up in front of a convoy. They weren't used much in northern California; the CHP kept the main roads pretty clear, but they were common on routes through the western Badlands and the Midwest.

The snowpack to either side of the road had dropped off to nothing. The storm that had buried the road and kicked off the avalanche on the 80 had been heavy and warm, so at least the snow line didn't creep too far down the mountains. Sodden greenery replaced the white snow and thick forest encroached on the road. With the plows and snow cutters out of the way, the convoy picked up speed as it barreled down the highway. In less than half an hour they passed an abandoned hamlet called White Hall, and crossed the bridge to the south side of the American River. That's where the grade abruptly shifted from downhill to uphill as Highway 50 climbed out of the canyon and up toward the town of Pollock Pines.

Gary kept examining the thick woods to either side of the road. Any number of ambushers could be hiding in those, but so far, there was nothing. Sometimes he thought he caught a glimpse of a dirt bike or quad zipping through the trees.

He stuck his earbud back in and tried to listen over the kids' interminable rendition of "Ninety-nine Bottles of Beer on the Wall".

"Tellin' ya. I keep seeing people in the trees."

"Any of them armed?"

"Nope. Just standin' there watchin' us."

"They're probably spotters. We should grease 'em while we still got the chance."

"They're just standing there. I'm not going to start hosin' down civvies on the side of the road just on the off chance they're spotters. That'll just make things worse for everyone."

Gary pulled the earbud back out. Figures. Truckers were an honorable breed. Men who put their lives on the line just to deliver cargo to those that need it (for a fee, of course, a man's got to eat). The Brotherhood even had a code it expected its members to live by. Amongst its precepts was an injunction against making things worse for those drivers and convoys who came after you. That included agitating the local population. You could turn peaceable country folk into raiders real quickly if you started shooting them up for no reason. Even if there were times when it might make sense.

The ambush came just short of Pollock Pines.

The flashing red light on the dash indicated priority traffic. Gary quickly inserted his earbud.

"… up ahead. Looks like it's just some trees dropped across the road. Looks like we got some logrollers. Don't y'all worry none. This is what the *Breacher* was built for. Ramming speed…"

Static burst over the radio, causing Gary to jerk the wheel in spasmodic reflex. The children squealed in joy at the sudden turn.

"This is *Big Bertha*, second rig. *Breacher* just blew the frak up! The bastards planted mines! Big ones! I gotta stop." The whole convoy ground to a halt and the radio chatter exploded into panic.

"*Wild Pete*, here. I got movement to my left. They're coming out of the trees."

"Same on the right. What the hell kind of trucks are those?"

"We have to bull through them! *Bertha*, get your ass moving!"

"Ok! Ok! Shit, I gotta go around what's left of *Breacher*. Passing on the right. Trying to get enough speed to break this barric…"

"Crap! *Bertha* just bought it. There must be mines every…"

"… got vehicles behind us…"

"… more over here…"

"… clear those mines! Or…"

The radio traffic dissolved into chaos as a dozen panicked truckers clogged up the airwaves with their observations, commands, and entreaties. Outside the bus, explosions and the crackle of gunfire reverberated through the woods. Columns of dirty, black smoke climbed into the sky.

Gary hit the ARMOR toggle and the whole bus vibrated as powerful electromagnets pulled heavy armored shades into place over the side windows with terrifying speed. The windshield was also covered with a massive armored plate that descended from the roof with the speed of a guillotine's blade, plunging the bus's interior into a darkness cut by the sharp shrieks of startled children. The darkness lasted for a fraction of a second before the projectors built into the dash threw the take from the external cameras onto the inside of the windshield plate. There were views of the front, back, and sides. Gary could see his surroundings better now than when he had windows. But he couldn't see any of the ambushers yet. They seemed to be concentrating on the head and tail of the convoy. They wanted the middle thoroughly bottled up and with no choice other than to surrender.

Suddenly a high-power radio transmission cut through the frightened chatter of the convoy. "Attention convoy. You have trespassed in the El

Dorado corridor without paying the toll. All of your rigs and cargo are forfeit. Surrender and you will be spared."

To hell with that! I might not own this rig, but it is still my rig! Besides, Gary knew how outfits like this worked. They wouldn't needlessly kill anyone in the convoy, but if they thought you might be useful, they would have no problem trumping up some charge for which the only punishment was several years of "community service."

The babble and screams of terrified and excited children filled the bus and caused him to rethink his priorities.

And I suppose I should get the kids home too. They would be prime ransom bait.

Gary flicked on the bus's speakers. "We're in an ambush. So, all of you. Sit down and shut up or I leave you to the raiders. Oh, and hold your little bladders. I'll get us out of this." Gary cranked his steering wheel to the right and smashed his foot to the floor.

Highway 50 in this area was once a major route connecting Sacramento and the Bay Area to Tahoe and had generous shoulders. Decades of little to no maintenance had allowed the forest to encroach on the roadway. Young pine and fir saplings up to six feet tall grew in a thicket on the old shoulder. A smaller vehicle would have been stopped dead by the vegetation.

Gary's school bus was hardly a smaller vehicle. It had mass and torque and near limitless power with its tiny fusion plant. It crashed through the saplings like they were mere paper cutouts. The cow catcher-like ram plate shoved most of the trees aside and cut others off at their bases. Greenery and splinters flew, and inside the sealed bus, Gary detected the tannic smell of tree sap. The bus jolted and vibrated as it rolled over the uneven surface of stumps and downed trees.

Gary saw a flash of movement on the displays for the front and right-side cameras. Several ambushers scattered out of the sapling thicket, fleeing the snorting beast of a bus that smashed through their cover. Though with its yellow paint job and black armor plates, the bus looked more like a fat, angry hornet from the outside than anything else.

Gary grinned and triggered the flame throwers on the right side, setting the whole thicket ablaze. *That should give 'em something to think about.*

He only had to drive through the trees for a couple hundred yards. He knew from his previous trips that there was an offramp ahead. One that would allow him to detour around this death trap. He was surprised that the rigs ahead of him hadn't already taken that route off the road.

"Where is it?" Gary's eyes raked the screens, looking for the break in the trees that he knew had to be there. Was he wrong? Was he further down the road than he had thought? His eyes flicked over to the map display. No. He was right where he should be. The offramp should be right…

Suddenly, the bus hit a cluster of small trees which were different from their neighbors. Instead of being rooted in the ground, they were freshly cut and placed in an artificial stand to obscure the offramp. These trees flew apart like nine-pins hit by a bowling ball, revealing an asphalt path leading away from the carnage on the 50.

"Clever bastards!" growled Gary as he cranked the steering wheel to the right and slalomed the bus down the ramp.

By sheer chance, a pack of dirt bikes and ATVs were coming up the ramp at the same time. Gary had just enough time to see the eyes widen on a helmetless biker in the lead before he plowed through the crowd. Most of the smaller vehicles veered off to the sides, either crashing into the embankment or getting hung up in the trees. A couple could not get out of the bus's way in time. Several light thuds reverberated through the bus and bike parts exploded into the air like confetti at a party. One rider was catapulted upwards and landed on the top of the bus. The sound of him rolling across the roof could be heard even through the armor. Gary was afraid that the rider might be able to grab hold of something and hang on, but he relaxed when he saw the unfortunate man fall off the back through the rear camera.

At the bottom of the ramp, he cut the wheel to the left and drove the bus under the 50 on Sly Park Road. There were a couple Fast Attack Vehicles, they looked like old Studebaker models, already on the road. The bus smashed one of them to the side, crushing it against the retaining wall of the overpass. Another, he designated as a target and the machine gun turret on the top of the bus started pumping .50 caliber rounds into the lightly armored two-seater. It brewed up after only a few shots. The road in front was clear.

Gary keyed the radio. "All vehicles this is…" he paused. He never officially named the bus. It wasn't his, after all. Technically, its call sign was *Bus 503*, but that hardly seemed appropriate for the vehicle that had just bashed its way out of an ambush. "…this is *Death Bus*. The offramp to Sly Park Road is clear. The bastards had camouflaged it. If you can make it there you can go south toward Jenkinson Lake and turn onto Pleasant Valley Road to go west." He repeated his message twice and managed to cut through the panicked radio chatter.

"Who the hell is *Death Bus*? This is a raider trick!"

"I was the school bus in the center of the convoy. And these raiders don't need tricks, they already got you dead to rights. You can stay in that death trap though if you want. *Death Bus*, out."

"It's no trick! *Truck You* here. I see the ramp right in front of me and I'm already going down it. *Death Bus* took out a whole bunch of putt-putts and tin cans on his way out. Watch the debris."

"This is *Wilma*, I'm right behind you."

Gary sighed in relief. At least he wasn't going to have to pick his way through these back roads alone. As bad as highways could be, and they could be bad, they were usually at least somewhat drivable. Back roads though, could be completely annihilated by a landslide, cut by a downed bridge, or blocked by felled trees. The only way to know if they were clear or not was to drive them. Pleasant Valley Road though was in pretty good shape from what he remembered, and it should take them most of the way back to Sacramento. He just had to hope the raiders did not try to get ahead of him.

"Mr. Kraus, where are we going?" yelled Mrs. Worthington from the back of the bus. "We're not going off of the highway, are we?" She made it sound like Gary had just taken a left turn into hell. Civilians had it drilled into them that leaving one of the interstates was certain death. Trust a dizzy dame like Worthington to hold to that, even in the face of an ambush.

"You can get out here," Gary shouted back. "I'm sure these raiders will give you a lift back to Sacramento. Unless they have need for an overbearing nitwit."

The children laughed like a pack of baby hyenas at that. Now that no one was actively shooting at them, the kids seemed to be enjoying the adventure. Their eyes were raptly focused on the screen at the front of the bus. Each likely hoping to be the first to espy the next barbarian who would gladly scrap their bus and hold them for ransom.

Mrs. Worthington's face split into a shocked gape. "Don't be ridiculous!"

"I'll stop when you do!" Gary slowed the bus as he saw several sharp curves ahead as the road climbed a ridgeline. "Now, would you kindly shut up and let me do my job." He took the turns a little too fast, and the bus tilted this way and that, eliciting squeals of terrified delight from the children. The Kidmaster 5000 was built to sedately take children to school with a basic level of safety. Barreling away from an ambush was definitely outside of its design specs.

Gary took the last turn fast enough that the wheels on the right side lifted and fell back to the ground with a thud once he straightened out. At least the road ahead looked a little less curvy and was now sloping downhill. Gary allowed it to gain even more speed as it rolled down. His bus might not have the armament he wanted, but by God, it had a lot of mass. Get it going fast enough, and no one would be able to stop it.

In the rear-facing camera, he saw other rigs from the convoy begin cresting the same hill and shook his head. *It's a fracked-up situation when a school bus is the lead vehicle in a convoy.*

When this was all done, he was going to force the board to let him take this thing to Uncle Al's and get it tricked out. At the very least, it needed bigger magazines. He had used the .50 cals for only a few seconds and already the ammo counter had dropped by nearly twenty-five percent.

He tore his eyes away from the display of misery on the dash and surveyed the landscape around him. If not for all the rednecks trying to kill him and steal his rig, this could have been a pretty nice place. Tall ponderosa pine trees framed the road, and to the left, Gary could see sunlight reflecting off the surface of Jenkinson Lake. Cabins and houses were tucked back in amongst the trees. Judging by the wisps of smoke coming from some of their chimneys, a lot of them were even occupied, likely by the same people who were dismantling the convoy. Which meant that their relatives were likely radioing his position to the raiders right now.

There was a major fork in the road and a faded sign helpfully informed him that the left fork led to Mormon Immigrant Trail and the right led to Pleasant Valley.

"Are we going to get out of this?" asked a quiet voice by Gary's right elbow.

He glanced over his shoulder and saw Miss Daisy standing there, her pretty face creased in a worried frown.

"Maybe," replied Gary with a shrug.

"The best you can do is a maybe?"

"Right now, yeah. We busted out of the ambush, but we are driving through these raiders' backyard for the next couple of hours. They'll have plenty of time to catch up to us or even set another ambush."

"I can't believe that scum like this can move so close to Sacramento." Daisy scowled at the trees around them as if the very landscape had become treacherous.

Gary chuckled. "Miss, these people didn't move from anywhere. They were always here. Many of them, their families have been here since the Gold Rush. This is just their latest way of making a living."

"But isn't all of this illegal?" The young teacher looked so earnest that it was all Gary could do to not burst out laughing.

"As illegal as strapping a 105mm to a rig." Gary paused for a moment before realizing that Daisy didn't get the metaphor. "It is very illegal. But I guarantee that every one of these bushwhackers has been deputized into the El Dorado County Sheriff's Office and what they are doing will be called a 'tax enforcement' or some such."

"You sound like you know a lot about these people." Daisy's voice held more than a hint of suspicion.

"I'm not from here, if that's what you're asking," Gary replied. "If I were, I would just call up a cousin or something and get us out of this mess. No, I'm from Sonora. A town to the south of here that's a lot like this one, only we charged convoys for going over the 108 instead of the 50. So, if anything, we are even poorer. That's why risking my life as a truck driver and risking my sanity as a school bus driver seemed like a good deal." He gave a short bark of laughter. "And now here I am doing both at once. Life is funny that way, sometimes. At least driving a Bessy still means that I am part of the Brotherhood even if I'm no longer a trucker."

"It's really that important to you? I mean…" Miss Daisy hesitated as if she was afraid that what she was about to say might offend him; she must not know drivers very well. "I mean, it's just driving stuff from A to B. No offense."

"None taken. Thing is, you're right. We are just taking stuff from A to B whether that's goods or goblins…"

"I think you mean children."

Gary shrugged. "Same difference. My point is that driving things from A to B is what keeps civilization stitched together. That's where us drivers come in. It's just a whole lot more difficult than it used to be. Speaking of which…" Gary pointed at the display which showed half a dozen vehicles racing up the road toward them.

They were a mile off and the only reason Gary could see them was because it was a relatively straight stretch of this twisty-ass road. Good ol' Sierra Nevada Foothills, where a straight road was something the locals came to gawp at like a museum exhibit. The raiders were in lightly armored fast movers. Something that he would have laughed at in his old rig, but the bus was unarmed compared to old *Gertrude*. He didn't particularly want to see how that would shake out in the long run.

Gary keyed his radio. "This is *Death Bus*. I got half a dozen crunchies just ahead. Who's following me?"

"*Truck You* here. I just pulled onto the same stretch as you. You are about five hundred yards ahead of me."

"Great, what kind of weaponry you got? I don't have much on this thing."

"I wouldn't call her a tank, but I got her rigged up for a run through the Wastes."

"Then you got more than I do. I'll be just about clocked out after taking these assholes…"

"Mr. Kraus, language!" shrieked the senior teacher from the back of the bus.

"Not right now, Mrs. Worthington!" Gary bellowed back over his shoulder as he designated the two lead vehicles as targets for the auto turret.

The twin gun turret started hammering away at the targets, though more rounds missed than hit. Damn computer-guided turrets were never as good as human beings; Gary didn't care what the eggheads had to say on the matter. Still, the rounds were big enough, and the auto guns scored enough hits, that one car veered off the road and into the bushes, and the other's engine abruptly belched smoke and died. Gary moved the target designators onto the next two. Before the guns could reengage, the remaining vehicles abruptly turned, using a wide spot in the road to flip a U, and headed back in the opposite direction.

"Huh," said Gary to himself before turning to the radio. "*Truck You*, be advised that the baddies have turned around."

"Maybe it was just a scouting party?" the other driver replied.

"Must be. But there is a wide spot here where you can pass me. My ammo levels are at ten percent."

"Roger, wilco."

Gary pulled his bus right into the turnout that the raiders had used and waited for *Truck You*. He could also now see at least two other rigs from the convoy on this stretch of road. Good. Two rigs wasn't much of a convoy at all.

"Mr. Kraus, look!" Tyler and his friends were back. Apparently, everyone had taken the stop to mean that they were now free to move about the cabin.

"Kids, you need to sit down."

"But look." Tyler pointed at the screen showing the view ahead of them where the wreckage of one of the attacking vehicles was still smoking. It shook as someone moved around inside the cab. One of the doors wrenched open and a dazed-looking man with a handle-bar mustache and a mullet poked his head out.

"Finish him!" shouted Tyler's friend Ezra. His face lit with an atavistic bloodlust.

"No." Gary shifted the bus back into gear and pulled out behind the *Truck You*.

"Why not?" whined the three kids in unison.

"He's no threat to us anymore."

"They do it in the arena," grumped Ezra.

"This ain't the arena, kid. There's no points to be got by mowing down someone helpless, and the rules are way harsher than the ones you find in the arena. The only thing that killing him right now would get me is a blood feud with his relatives."

"But what about the guys in those other FAVs?" asked Tyler. They were passing the other wrecked car and the blood sprays inside the cabin were evident.

"Oh, that's just business. Not going to say that their friends and family aren't going to be sore with me, but not enough to try and track me down later. Just the way things work out here."

"Oh," the girl, Hannah, wrinkled her nose in thought. "So, they're not going to try and kill us?"

"No. They are *definitely* going to try and kill us. Or kill me, anyway. You guys, they will probably just hold for ransom. Though they will probably call it 'protective custody' until your parents can pay the appropriate fee to 'bail' you all out." Gary turned away from the trio and allowed a small smile to crawl across his face. "That could take years though, and until then they'll probably put you to work picking apples or dragging logs or something like that." He schooled his face back to neutrality and turned back to the children.

All three kids were noticeably paler.

"They can do that?" asked Tyler in a small voice.

"Sure. Ain't no rules out here. Of course, there's the chance a family up here needs a new kid and just adopts you outright. Been known to happen. I hope you kids are ready for a life with no electricity or television."

The expressions on the three little faces moved from shocked to utterly horrified.

"Yeah, that's what I thought," Gary gave them a wink. "Don't worry, I'll try my best. But I hope I'm not distracted by someone during a crucial moment…" The three turned and fled back to their seats.

Gary grinned to himself and turned his attention back to the road. It was comforting to see the rear end of the *Truck You* in front of him rather than just empty roadway. It assured him that he was not all alone out here.

Suddenly, the brake lights of the *Truck You* blazed to life and the big rig swerved in the roadway.

"Watch out," squawked the radio. "The bastards put thumbtacks in the road."

The tires on the *Truck You*'s left side all popped simultaneously and the rig slewed off the road to crash into the trees. It plowed twenty yards into the greenery until it got unbalanced on a tree trunk and toppled onto its side.

Gary had seconds to react and jammed his finger down on one of the buttons on the dashboard. The wedge-shaped crash bar fell to the ground with a clang. The whole bus slowed and shuddered as the weight and speed of the vehicle pushed the improvised plow into the top layer of the asphalt. Despite the added friction, the nuclear reactor at the heart of the bus's engine kept the vehicle grinding forward even as it removed the top half-inch of roadway, along with any tire popping spikes that might be in the way. The more the bus pushed along the concrete, the more it slowed and shuddered. From the back, the children shrieked and Mrs. Worthington squawked. Gary kept at it for a hundred yards before relenting and pulling the crash bar back off the ground. The bus shook again as its rear end settled fully back onto the pavement.

"Mr. Kraus, was that necessary?" warbled the senior teacher.

"Absolutely," Gary hollered back. "There were thumbtacks in the road."

"You nearly wrecked us over something so trivial! Are you quite mad?"

"Trucker speak. That's what we call tire-popping spikes. Now, shut up before I pull over and leave you on the side of the road."

"You would not dare!"

"Try me!"

Before Gary could make good on his threat, the lightly armored cars he had seen earlier came whipping around the next curve ahead. Five other vehicles roared along behind them. None of them looked particularly heavily armed or armored, but Gary was driving a spitball special himself, and there were a lot of them.

He set the cannon on the roof to target the lead vehicle and pressed the accelerator to the floor. The motor surged as bottomless amounts of electricity poured into it from the nuclear reactor. As a fighting vehicle, *Death Bus* had many problems, but lack of power certainly was not one of them.

A red icon on Gary's dashboard flashed, helpfully informing him that his autocannons were out of ammo. He cursed, the last few shots of his primary weapon had not even earned him a single kill and he still had nine raiders barreling down on him.

"This is *Death Bus*. I got nine, count-em, nine raiders driving up the road ahead of me. Is anybody nearby to give support?"

"Negative, *Death Bus*. *Wilma* caught one of those thumbtacks you missed and is jackknifed across the road. Gonna take a minute to get everything here unstacked."

"Copy. Better get moving soon. They'll get to you not long after they finish me. Catch you at the nap trap, brothers. *Death Bus* signing off." Gary ended the transmission and tightened his hands on the wheel. On this straight section of road, the bus had built up a good head of speed and the gap between him and the oncoming cars closed rapidly.

The raiders began firing at the bus. It was mostly small caliber weaponry and most of it ricocheted off the bus's heavy armor. There was a lot of it though, and soon it sounded like they were driving through a Midwestern hailstorm. With that many bullets in the air, it was inevitable that something fragile would eventually get hit. Sections of the display started to go dark as the bus's front-facing cameras were knocked out one by one. It took only a few seconds before the view forward was gone. Gary had to use the view from the side cameras to keep the bus on the road. He knew from his previous trips this section of road was straight for at least a mile and half. He kept piling on the speed.

"Now these assholes have to consider the downsides of playing chicken with a blind man," he muttered to himself. Though he couldn't see it, he imagined the panic taking hold amongst the raiders when the bus didn't stop or even slow. The jostling between the pack of cars as the more nervous of them looked for a place to pull off. Some would start to slow, and others would keep firing, hoping that at the last second, they might hit something vital and stop the armored monstrosity hurtling toward them. Finally, their nerve would break. Some would dive off the road, and if they were lucky, avoid hitting a tree or rock. Others would crash into each other instead, and probably one unlucky bastard would be too boxed in to do anything.

BAM!

The bus bucked into the air and back down again, eliciting yet more squeals and shrieks from the kids and warbling from Worthington. From the side-facing cameras, Gary could see several raiders flash past to either side and in the rear camera the remains of one coupe that the bus pancaked. One down. A little further on, he saw another raider wrapped around a tree on his left side. Two down. That left seven, and in his rear camera he could see them turning around to follow.

The bus still ran, though there was now an odd shudder coming from the right front wheel, but Gary was completely blind to the front. He flicked a switch and raised the armor plate over the windshield, keeping the armor over the side windows in place. Just in time too; a curve was just ahead and he would have driven right off of it.

"Isn't that dangerous?" called Miss Daisy from the behind him.

"Not as dangerous as driving blind. I'm kinda running out of options here." Gary flicked his eyes down to the rear-view display, which had shifted to a smaller screen in the dash once he retracted the windshield plate. The seven remaining raider vehicles were gaining on him fast.

"They're not shooting at us anymore," remarked Daisy.

"That's because they know we are out of ammo," said Gary. "They're going to board us."

Gary swept his eyes across the dash in search of some sort of deterrence. A button to deploy landmines, or an oil slick, or thumbtacks that he had somehow missed during the last several hundred times he drove this bus. Of course he found nothing. The only weapons he had left were the side-mounted flamethrowers and they didn't project out the rear. If he survived this, he was going to have a major customer complaint for the El Paso Motor Company. Maybe they would make a design upgrade to the Kidmaster 5001 and name it after him. Far more likely that he was going to die in the next couple of minutes.

The two lead vehicles nudged up close to him. Both were upgraded pickup trucks with half a dozen men riding in the back of each. He tried brake checking, but they were expecting that. Those smaller rigs were far more maneuverable and easily avoided his little trap. They both tried maneuvering around to either side of *Death Bus,* but a couple blasts of the flame thrower pushed them back. Instead, they nosed up to the back of the bus and their boarders shimmied across their hoods and started climbing. Gary tried braking again and giving the steering wheel a shimmy but nothing worked. Soon he could hear boots thumping across the roof.

"This is *Death Bus*, I got flies on my back. Anybody nearby who can give them a swat?"

"Negative *Death Bus*, we only just got moving again. Any way you can loop back toward us?"

"Nope, if I slow down too much, I die."

"*Vaya con dios, hermano.*"

"Thanks." Up ahead, Gary could see a large oak tree overhanging the road. He veered toward it and was rewarded with several screams overhead. Through the side and rear cameras, he saw several fall from the roof. The ones still up there started thumping at the side windows and the roof hatches, but Gary knew that the electromagnetic locks would hold those closed tight. The only way in was through the windshield.

Seconds later his would-be hijackers figured that out as well. Soon a grinning mustachioed face poked into view at the top of the windshield. The raider dropped down to the hood of the bus, took a shotgun out of a scabbard across his back, and tapped the glass in front of Gary's face. The meaning was clear. As was the leer he gave Miss Daisy who still stood behind Gary's shoulder.

The bus slowed as Gary took his foot off the accelerator.

"You're not going to let them take us, are you?" Daisy's voice was shrill with barely contained panic.

Other raiders dropped down onto the bus's hood. One, two, three raiders were awkwardly standing on the front of the bus even as it sped along. The hijackers had to use one hand to steady themselves, but they used their other to aim their guns at Gary. All of them grinned like the fox that had just caught the chicken. They had him dead to rights. They knew it, Miss Daisy knew it, and judging by the terrified silence in back, even the kids knew it.

They were all wrong.

Gary jammed his foot on the gas and the bus lunged forward. The raiders stumbled into the windshield. Bumping into it and then pressing into it as the bus accelerated. They wore looks of shock which slowly transformed into anger. The one with the mustache raised his gun to blast the impudent bus driver.

Then Gary hit the toggle to drop the windshield armor back into place.

The massive armor panel fell with the speed of a guillotine.

Blood splashed across the windshield as hijackers were swept aside, crushed or delimbed by the improvised weapon. Gary raised it again so he could see the road, but the mess left behind on the hood of the bus made him wish he hadn't. It was also hard to see through the blood smears. He quickly turned on the windshield wipers, which tossed two fingers and what he thought was part of a butt cheek over the side.

The terrified silence of the children turned into screams. Even kids desensitized to the violence of autoduelling weren't ready for something like that. Behind Gary, Daisy retched loudly into the aisle, and she was not alone.

Seeing that the road ahead was clear, Gary turned in his seat. "Now that is why you always listen to your bus driver and stay in your damn seat." He was answered with a terrified silence. In the back, it looked like Mrs. Worthington had fainted. Gary gave a satisfied nod and turned back to his displays.

Behind *Death Bus,* the remaining raiders backed away. Though they still kept up desultory fire at the bus's armored rear end, it was obvious that they had been cowed by the spray of blood and body parts. If only he could find a way to get rid of them.

"This is *Death Bus*, I'm still mobile. You guys gotten moving yet? I got half a dozen tin cans following me but I'm out of ammo. Can someone come scratch my back? I just passed…" Gary checked his map display, "Thorson Drive."

"*Death Bus*, *Wild Pete* here. I'm gaining on you fast. Just hang in there."

Just as Gary drove past an abandoned elementary school, the raiders made their next move. Two of them upped their acceleration and made to box him in from either side. Gary triggered the flame throwers but they sputtered and died as their fuel ran out after only a second.

"*Wild Pete*, I sure hope you are close."

The keening wail of an alarm sliced through the bus as the computer detected the launch of a missile.

"Everyone brace yourselves!" Gary hollered. He gripped the wheel and prepared to jerk the wheel to the side in a last-ditch attempt at evasion. Then one of the raiders blew up in a pillar of flame. The concussive thump of the explosion vibrated up through the padding of Gary's seat.

"Somebody order a can opener?" *Wild Pete* radioed.

The rest of the raiders scattered like roaches, dispersing off to the numerous side roads.

Gary slowed *Death Bus* and allowed *Wild Pete* to pass him. "Thanks for the assist."

"What the hell happened to you?" asked the rig's driver when he could finally see the mess on Gary's hood and windshield.

"My Bessy got hungry, so I had to feed her some raiders," Gary replied.

"*Death Bus* is a good name for her."

A new voice broke into the radio. "Convoy vehicles, this is CHP Captain Wallen. We have a checkpoint set up at Diamond Springs. All vehicles, head to Diamond Springs."

"Where's that?" asked Miss Daisy. The teacher discreetly dabbed at her mouth with a wipe.

"Only a couple miles away. Look." Gary pointed up at a cloud of drones that had suddenly appeared overhead. "The newsies are already on to us. We made it."

"Thanks to you!" The pretty young woman gave Gary a smile that nearly made him drive off the road. "You're going to be famous now."

"Famous enough to ask you out for a drink?" Gary responded without even thinking about it.

"Maybe." This time, Daisy's smile was a soft and inviting thing.

Gary's grin was so large it hurt when it pulled at the scar tissue on his face. "Yo, Tyler."

The blond boy appeared at Gary's side as if by magic. The look on his face was nearly worshipful.

"Let's have a song," Gary commanded. The boy beamed at him and scurried off. Soon the bus echoed with young voices bellowing out lyrics to a simple children's song.

"The wheels on the *Death Bus* go round and round, round and round…"

SNAFU on Snake River
By: William Joseph Roberts

"Uncle Albert's sure to have your every desire," a perky little blonde in a tiny bikini top and urban camouflage pants said as she stepped into view on screen. She toted a light machine gun, holding it in both hands with two belts of ammo that she wore crisscrossed over her chest like bandoleers.

"Don't settle for those imitation brand names. Uncle Al's guarantees the largest selection from coast to coast!"

Dozens of weapons systems flashed across the screen. Autocannons, flame throwers, machine guns, mines, lasers, and rocket launchers faded in and out of view. "If it's in stock, we got it!" she shouted, then bounced in place. "Uncle Albert gives you the weapons, gadgets, and accessories you need! But don't take my word for it!"

The screen suddenly flashed to a pair of autoduellists standing in front of a battered and bruised Fnord Motors Smokin' Joe. "Uncle Albert has saved our tailpipes more times than I can count. Without his overnight delivery and dirt-cheap prices, there's no way we could ever keep up with the corporate teams no matter how much of socket-brained slushboxes they are."

"Thanks, Uncle Albert," the gunner said, then fired off a round into the sky.

The perky little blond reappeared, this time stroking the tail fin of a mini rocket that rested across her lap.

"Guaranteed, you won't find prices lower than ours for your autoduelling needs."

The scene shifted again, and she appeared suddenly in mid-bounce over the backdrop of the original Uncle Albert's shop. "And don't forget to ask about our fast-fast-*fast* delivery! Don't wait! Come on down and find exactly what you never knew you needed at Uncle Albert's Auto Stop and Gunner Shop in all of these fine locations."

The perky announcer vanished from the screen, replaced by a fast-scrolling list of addresses for all of Uncle Al's locations in North America to the twangy tune of Uncle Albert's theme song. The screen momentarily faded to black before the logo and theme music for *Arena Side* returned then shifted to two announcers sitting at the news desk.

"Can you believe that match, Nathan?" Kim Moorland asked, turning in her seat to face him. "Not only did the Beltway Bruisers take first place, but their sponsored teammates, the Coal Burners, took an astounding second place leaving their bitter rivals, Team Scarlet Skulls, smoking in the ditch."

"You aren't kidding, Kim," Nathan Stoker said, turning back to his co-host. "In my thirty-five years of reporting on every sort of autoduel imaginable, I don't think I've ever seen someone handle a car on the *Sasquatch Slog* quite like what we saw from Sargon tonight."

"Sargon and AbsentEmpathy have got to be the luckiest team out there, or they're some kind of idiot savants, Nathan. How they managed to slip through death's fingers one more time has got to be something close to a miracle."

"It wouldn't surprise me in the least if Apex Asphalt pulled their sponsorship from the Scarlet Skulls, Kim. They've been known to make knee-jerk decisions at the slightest blemish to their image."

The vid screen exploded, raining chunks of glass and plastic to the ground from the impacting gunfire.

Austin Matthews calmly sat his semi-automatic hand cannon in front of him on the boardroom table. Placing his hands palm down on the cold stainless steel top, he breathed in and released a slow, deep breath.

"Mister Matthews," a sniffling weasel of a man seated halfway down the table said as he stood and straightened his suit jacket. "Even though we have lost the Pac-West circuit, the Scarlet Skulls still have an opportunity to win the Southwest regionals. Once our technicians have completed repairs and upgraded the Skulls' vehicle, they will be better prepared to win this next set of matches.

Mister Matthews glared at the small man then slowly took in the other faces that stared back at him, waiting for their moment to agree, grovel, or otherwise kiss his ass. He thrummed a slow heavy beat with both of his meaty hands.

"I am sick of these fracking failures. With the number of losses the Scarlet Skulls have racked up, one would think they were taking a dive, or for some godforsaken reason, they are attempting to make us—their benevolent sponsors—look bad."

An older gentleman at the far end cleared his throat and leaned in. "Perhaps, sir, it is time to find another team that better represents the interests of Apex Asphalt and our customers."

Mr. Matthews let out a gut-shaking laugh. "That, Mister Martens, is probably the first bright idea I have heard sputtered out of any of your mouths." He reached over and tapped a button on a small control panel near his seat.

"Yes sir, Mr. Matthews," a young, seductive-sounding female voice answered over the intercom. "How may I be of service, *sir*?" The way she purred "sir" left very little to the imagination.

Nearly every eyebrow around the room raised in surprise at the young woman's tone. Austin Matthews flashed the others a knowing smile and chuckled to himself before pressing the button once more.

"Natasha, would you please send Mister Shrader in?"

"Shrader?" Someone asked in a hushed voice followed by more excited whispers. Several others glanced about, panic showing on their faces.

"He is on his way, sir. Will there be anything else?"

"Not at the moment, Natasha. Why don't you go ahead and take the afternoon off. You deserve a little break with all of the extra hours you've been putting in."

"Yes sir, Mister Matthews. Thank you."

Austin Matthews turned his attention back to the gathered men. "Can any of you fine gentlemen tell me what our contract with the Scarlet Skulls states?" The large double doors leading into the boardroom opened, interrupting the blank stares and worried glances answering his question. A broad, blond-haired man stepped into the room and closed the door behind himself. He straightened his suit jacket then stepped forward beside Austin Matthews, standing at ease with his hands folded in front of himself.

"Reporting as ordered, Mister Matthews."

"Not one of my colleagues seem to know what is written in the contract we have with the Scarlet Skulls. Would you mind enlightening them for me?"

"Would you like a full recitation of the contract, or would you prefer I summarize it, sir?" Mister Shrader asked in a calm, smooth tone.

"A summarization will suffice."

"Very well, sir," Mister Shrader continued. "The currently active sponsorship contract between Apex Asphalt and the Scarlet Skulls autoduelling team details the terms of their support, in exchange for no less than six wins in the current season."

"And what is the current standing of the Scarlet Skulls for this season, Mister Shrader?"

"The Scarlet Skulls record is currently standing at zero wins and nine losses, with one match remaining in the *Sasquatch Slog* and four matches in the upcoming *San Carlos Southwest Circuit* to wrap up this season."

Austin Matthews chuckled. "Zero to nine, with five matches remaining. Let me see," he said, counting on his fingers, then smacking himself on the side of the head. "Mister Shrader, I have to admit that I'm terrible with math. If the Scarlet Skulls were to win every match remaining, what would their total be?"

"Five, Mister Matthews."

Austin Matthews shook his head, acting confused. "But doesn't their contract state they must win a minimum of six matches?"

"It does, sir."

"Well, I guess that means The Scarlet Skulls are now in breach of contract, doesn't it Mister Shrader?"

"It does, sir."

Austin Matthews nodded, looking down as if in thought. "I suppose that doesn't leave me with any choice. Would you be so kind as to execute our contractual agreement and remove the Scarlet Skulls from our employ, Mister Shrader?"

"It would be my pleasure, sir."

As the enforcer turned to leave the room, Austin Matthews raised his hand. "Wait. I seem to remember one other small line of fine print that extended beyond the Scarlet Skulls themselves, should an issue like this arise. Do you remember what that stipulation mentioned, Mister Shrader?"

"I do, sir."

"If you would please humor me, Mister Shrader. Please summarize that portion of the contract as well."

"Gladly sir," Shrader responded, taking up his previous position. "Should a failure of the Scarlet Skulls exceed more than half of the matches during the season, the management committee in charge of the Scarlet Skulls would be held as accountable for the failure as the team itself, to include up to all penalties and punishments agreed upon within the signed, registered, and certified contract."

Austin Matthews nodded to himself again. "Mister Shrader, if it wouldn't be too much trouble, would you please execute that portion of the contract as well before you leave?"

"Gladly sir."

Shouts and murmurs erupted as panic set in, drowned out by sudden gunfire. Jeffrey "The Shredder" Shrader's dual-wielded hand cannons rapidly barked a cacophony of fire and noise that silenced the room.

Austin Matthews giggled with excitement. "God, I love the smell of gunpowder in the morning!"

Shrader returned his pistols to the shoulder holsters hidden beneath his jacket and turned back to Mister Matthews. "Will there be anything else before I leave sir?"

"Actually, yes, Mister Shrader. I want you to eliminate those fracking upstarts racing for Vanguard Hot Mix. It's about time they saw some of the losses we're experiencing this season. Go do what you do best, Mister Shrader."

Shrader smiled wide. "With pleasure sir."

"Dammit, John!" Big Ed slammed the driver's side door of *Red Death*, The Coal Burners' Hotshot. He caressed the crushed rear quarter panel. Large flakes of the green ablative coating fell away to the garage floor as he passed his hand over the crumpled sheet metal. "What the hell was that out there? Were you even fracking thinking? Larry worked all night to fix the damage from the last match, then, BOOM, you had to go and do twice the damage anyone else managed the last three matches. We'll be lucky if Larry doesn't skin all of us alive."

"It's called evasive maneuvers, Ed," John said as he pulled himself from the driver's seat of *Doris*, the Beltway Bruisers' Slipstream, stoic and unfazed from the match.

"If you hadn't kept getting in our line of fire, maybe we would have finished that round ten minutes sooner and before they blew out our napalm tanks," Christopher Robin shouted back at Big Ed as he climbed out of the gunner's seat. "Do you know how long that'll take the tin techs to repair?"

Big Ed chuckled. "Are you really that lazy? It'll be faster and cheaper if we do the work ourselves."

Christopher Robin looked taken aback. "You know damn well the company forks over a small ransom for Gamer and Knuckles to be our tour techs. They're bought and paid for. Let them do their job, and you do yours."

"Every penny we spend on repairs," Trevor "The Real" McCoy interrupted as he slid out of the passenger window and sat there looking over the roof of the car, "just adds to our debts with the company store."

"Oh, frack me," Christopher Robin shouted back. "Really? I don't know where you come up with that hillbilly bullshit, but that's not how it works out here on the *real* autoduelling circuits."

Big Ed charged forward then skidded to a halt as John stepped directly into his path.

"We'll need to do repairs on the road if we're going to be ready for the next match," Knuckles said as he entered the garage area.

Larry "Knuckles" Southard was one of the best-damned arena techs to ever enter into the business of autoduelling, and was being kept on retainer for the Vanguard Hot Mix team along with Kim "Gamer" Schoeffel, who followed Larry into the garage.

They both proceeded forward to their respective vehicles, clipboards in hand as each began their post-battle assessment.

"Wait," Christopher Robin said, turning toward Knuckles. "What do you mean we'll have to do the repairs on the road?"

"He means," Kyle Roberts, the team's truck driver, said as he hurried into the garage area, "y'all need to get your asses in gear and get these rigs loaded up. Word just came down from the company CEO. We have to make the time trials for the *San Carlos Southwest Circuit* down in Tucson Arizona in two days. So we gotta get gone like yesterday."

Everyone let out a low groan.

"Don't they know how much of a pain in the ass it is to work on these things while we're on the road?" Trevor blurted out.

"If you didn't break them so bad, it wouldn't be such a problem, now would it?"

Trevor turned to find Katherine "Cutthroat" Eudy, the team's personal PR liaison standing right behind him. Her bright-red skirt suit nearly matched the hair on her head and the fire in her temper. "I don't care how you make it happen, just get there and keep the winning streak rolling. The bosses and the fans love you guys. Don't make them change their minds."

Trevor and several others took an involuntary step back, retreating from the evil scowl she was so well known for, which was currently directed at Trevor.

"And exactly how are we supposed to do that? Are you going to help us get them up and running?" Big Ed held out a greasy shop rag, offering it to her.

Katherine blurted out a chortling laugh that took her a few moments to get under control. "Maybe you should be a comedian instead of an autoduel driver. You might make your fortune, because that was hilarious. No! I'm not going to help you," she snapped at Big Ed. "That's what *they* are for," she said with a snub of her nose, motioning toward Gamer and Knuckles. "I will meet you in Tuscon." She glanced at her watch. "And I'm afraid that I need to be on my way. My flight leaves in an hour. Don't be a second late," she threatened.

She glanced at everyone present as she backed out of the room, stopping beside Kyle. "No deviations or special shortcuts. Get them there on time," she said, digging a bright red fingernail into his chest, "or I'll make sure you never drive for anyone ever again. Got it?" She gave him a knowing wink before storming away through the garage door.

"Frack me," Kyle said under his breath.

"Can we make it?" John turned to Kyle, his visage as serious as ever.

"Yeah, if we leave like yesterday and I put the hammer down. With the extra power packs on the rig, it should last that far, but just barely." He nodded to himself as he thought. "Yeah, we'll just make it if we go east along the Snake River before cutting south. But it might be a little bumpy along the way."

"Then what are we waiting for?" Trevor smacked his hands together, rubbing them vigorously. "Let's get 'em loaded up."

A scream followed by incoherent shouting reverberated from the alley outside the garage. Everyone in the garage drew their sidearms at the sound of heavy-booted footfalls approaching. Mike Ford, the Vanguard Hot Mix team's number one super fan, sprinted into the garage.

"Holy hell, guys!"

"Mike!" Everyone shouted in unison, letting out a sigh of relief.

"I just ran into some crazy lady in red who wouldn't let me walk past her in the alley," Mike continued.

Everyone laughed.

Kyle snorted a laugh then waved to get Mike's attention. "So, what did you do?"

Mike shrugged, looking to the side like an innocent puppy. "I wasn't actually going to do anything but wait on her to pass. But when she screamed and put her hands on me, I might have nudged her into that big deep mudhole out there at the end of the alley."

"Bless her heart…" Trevor chuckled as he spit a mouthful of tobacco juice into a plastic bottle that he capped then tucked into his back pocket. He walked over to shake Mike's hand. "I don't know what we'd have done if you hadn't been out there, brother man. You saved our tails more than a few times with that ringside .50 cal."

"Isn't that what a super fan is supposed to do?"

"Well, yeah, I suppose so. But that's an awful lot of cash to spend just to fire a .50 cal from the sideline. You've at least gotta let us buy you a drink or something."

"Naw," Mike said, waving it off. "It was my pleasure. Besides, they had me on the big screen seven times. I want to see Marcus top that."

"Either way," Kyle said, interrupting as he headed for the door. "The drinks will have to wait till we've checked in down in Tuscon. I'll get the rig ready to load up and roll out."

"Time to get gone," Ed said as he climbed back into *Red Death.*

"Pretty much," someone mumbled.

Mike slapped John on the shoulder as he passed by. "I'll catch you guys in Tuscon before the next match. I heard they have RPGs and mortars for rent at some of their arenas."

"Let's load 'em up," Big Ed yelled.

"Ugly Duckling to Mother Goose. Everything alright up there?" a voice squawked over the radio. It was Tommy, the convoy's tail gunner.

"Shit," Gamer said. He hurriedly sat his plate down on the workbench and turned to the small computer console at the forward section of the trailer. "I'm so sorry for the interruption. I completely lost track of time and missed our required check-ins." He smacked himself on the side of the head as he slid into a seat at the console and keyed the mic.

"Go ahead Ugly Duckling. Mother Goose hears you loud and clear."

"Your tail feathers are crystal clear, Mother Goose."

"Copy that, Ugly Duckling. Little Bo Peep, this is Mother Goose. What's your status?"

"Dark, empty, and lonely up here, hot stuff," Kelly Beck, the convoy's point guard responded from a few miles ahead of the other vehicles.

"Why don't you ever want to ride up here with me instead of back there with those stuffy old cars, you handsome devil, you?"

Gamer looked taken aback. Color ran up his neck and he flashed an uncomfortable smile at the others in the repair bay.

"Sounds like someone's got the hots for you, Gamer," Big Ed said, laughing.

"Good thing she isn't into tall, dark, and loathsome, or she might be stuck with you," Christopher Robin said, chiding Ed.

"Oh, ha-ha." Big Ed flung an algae cube at Christopher Robin that bounced off his head and onto the floor in front of Trevor.

"Waste not, want not, right?" Trevor leaned down, picked up the cube, gave it a quick blow then popped it into his mouth.

"You know," Knuckles started to say in one of those dad-like tones. "Isn't that how you got worms the last time?"

"Meh." Trevor waved off the question. "Minor inconvenience."

"More like a major inconvenience to everyone else because you were camped out in the lavatory for days."

Trevor chuckled. "But think about how squeaky clean my innards were after that detox."

Gamer loudly cleared his throat. "If you don't mind, I'd like to finish the check-in."

"Oh, no, we don't mind. Go on ahead," Trevor said, before turning back to his dinner. Gamer flashed him a sidelong glare then turned back to the console.

"Copy that, Little Bo Peep, all clear on point. Little Red Riding Hood, are you still with us?"

"That's affirmative, Mother Goose," Margaret McNabb, the team's supply truck driver responded. "Little Red is right on your tail."

"Roger that Little Red," Gamer replied. "And last but not least, your turn, Muffin Man. What's our status?"

Kyle keyed his mic and responded. "We are eastbound and down, making damn good time, and the power packs are holding up well. Otherwise, all is quiet up here."

"Excellent," Gamer said, jotting down notes in the travel log. "Next check in three hours. Maintain radio silence until then."

Breaks sounded over the speaker as each of the convoy vehicles keyed their mic in affirmative response to his last statement. He slid out of the seat and immediately returned to his dinner.

"So, like I was saying," Trevor said, picking back up where he'd left off in his story. "Me and my buddy Bobby thought we were just coming up on a raccoon or two in the brush, but it turned out to be this big assed sow and about a dozen little piglets that had hunkered down in the brush at the base of an old elm tree. Talk about lighting a fire under our asses. We both high-tailed it out of there just as soon as we heard that first grunt and made for the closest tree. If you ain't ever been chased by a pissed off mamma hog, you don't know what scared is."

"Bunch of fracking bullshit," Christopher Robin said, laughing.

"I swear to god," Trevor defended. "I ain't shitting you. You could have put a lump of coal up my ass and it'd turned to a diamond," Trevor said with a snap of his fingers. He took the last bite of his sandwich and washed it down with a bottle of water he'd gotten from the rig's galley.

Gamer laughed, finishing off his chips. "I sure am glad the company hired me for this team. You tell some of the best stories I've ever heard."

"Telling a story is one thing," Knuckles started, "what I want to know is how are you still alive?"

"What do you mean?" Trevor picked a wad of tobacco from a small pouch and stuffed it into his cheek, adjusting it before he spit a stream of viscus brown liquid into the water bottle he'd just emptied.

Christopher Robin let out a chuckle. "This should be good." He stood, stretched, then laid down on the floor and shimmied his way under the rear end of *Doris*, the Belt Way Bruisers' Slipstream.

"It seems that almost every hunting story you've told us ends with something trying to kill or eat you."

"Oh, that." He spit into the bottle again and shrugged. "Luck, I guess."

"Little Bo Peep to Mother Goose. Danger ahead," Kelly shouted over the radio. "I repeat. Danger ahead. Come in Mother Goose."

Gamer rushed back to the terminal and keyed the CB mic. "Go ahead Little Bo Peep, we read you."

"You might want to pull it over for a minute. The I-84 bridge crossing the Snake River at Glenns Ferry is gone. Looks like one hell of a fight happened here and the bridge came down as a result."

"Mother Goose copies." Gamer activated one of the screens on the console that displayed a twisted charred mess of steel and concrete that used to be a bridge crossing the river. He rubbed his eyes then turned to Knuckles. "We're already tight on power, but protocol calls for all defensive systems to be online."

"Protocol is protocol for a reason. We have some flexibility to deviate, but if we're attacked while defenses are down, then we'll be in breach of our contracts."

"We might have to get creative to make Tuson in time."

"Then we get creative. They can't get upset at us if we're following their rules to the letter."

"Agreed." Gamer nodded then reluctantly activated several switches across the control console. Servos on the rig's automated defenses whirred to life. Gamer keyed the mic again. "Muffin Man, bring us to a stop, all hands to defensive positions. Kelly, can you turn on your brights so we can better see what you're seeing?"

"Sure thing, dreamboat." The darkness surrounding the bridge suddenly receded, highlighting the charred damage to its superstructure.

"Dang," Trevor said, spitting into his bottle again. "She wasn't lying, was she?"

"No, she wasn't," John replied as he leaned in to see the screen better. Everyone turned to listen as he continued, breaking his normally silent demeanor. "There's entirely too much damage for a simple firefight. Look here, here, and here," he said pointing at several locations on the screen. There's cratering in the riverbed. I'd be willing to bet there was artillery involved to cause this much damage."

"You might be right," Gamer agreed.

"Muffin Man to Mother Goose," Kyle interrupted.

"Go ahead."

"Looks like we can bypass this bridge by heading north through King Hill along old US Highway 30. It'll be a slight detour and a few extra miles, but it looks like our fastest option."

"That's if it's still there," Christopher Robin added.

"Better than backtracking, though," Big Ed said.

Knuckles tapped Gamer on the shoulder. "Agreed. Considering our timetable, I think it's worth the risk."

Gamer keyed the mic again. "Little Bo Peep, return to base. Course change to US Highway 30 through King Hill."

Jeffrey "The Shredder" Shrader looked down on the Snake River from his position. Perched on the hood of his Hammer at the top of a small hillock, he could see for miles. The night breeze was crisp, and the sky was clear. Stars gleamed and twinkled high above in the near-pitch darkness.

"When I retire, I might consider coming back to this part of the country," he said to Tim, his driver.

"Why? It's desolate."

"Exactly," Jeffrey replied. "Near total isolation and silence." He closed his eyes and inhaled deeply when his phone started to ring. With a disappointed huff, he retrieved his phone from the inner pocket of his jacket and looked at the number. He knew it was the forward scout they'd deployed when they arrived. He tapped the screen and answered.

"Go."

"The target is in the box, Mister Shrader."

"Are you sure it's them?"

"Yes sir. The tractor-trailer has Vanguard Hot Mix plastered across the sides of the trailer."

"Time to firing solution?"

"They aren't rushing it. Maybe ten minutes."

"Understood. Get the men ready to intercept any vehicles that survive the initial barrage." Jeffrey disconnected the call and dialed a new number.

"Yes sir, Mister Shrader?"

"Target is inbound. Ten minutes. Get the mortars ready. Fire as soon as you have the shot." He disconnected the call, tucked the phone inside his jacket, and stared up at the sky. He smiled. "It is beautifully quiet here." He closed his eyes and enjoyed the night breeze.

"Can someone tell me why in the hell we were using ablative armor in a lead-slinging fight?" Big Ed hammered at the thin metal underlying the ceramic and composite armor of the Coal Burners' Hotshot. Fine dust fell away with each strike.

"Because it's the most effective defense against lasers," Gamer answered.

"But no one else had lasers. In every match, we've been more or less up against conventional weapons. Plastic doesn't work well against stopping lead."

"Statistically," Knuckles said, interjecting himself into the conversation, "the rival teams had a ninety percent chance of using energy-based weapons over any other during that last three matches, based on their previous season loadouts." Kim brought up statistical graph charts on the console display. Examining the readouts on the screen, he pointed at several peaks.

"Each of the rival teams primarily relied on energy-based weapons in their last six matches prior to our encounter."

"Then that means someone caught wind of what we were up to and planned to literally shred the competition," John said, wiping his hands on a grimy shop rag.

Christopher Robin joined the others around the console. "Well, that's just lovely. So what do your statistics say about the southwest circuit?"

Knuckles tapped at the console and brought up another screen. "Missiles, gauss cannons, recoilless rifles, and other heavy long-range weaponry will most likely be employed."

Trevor and Christopher glanced at each other. "So we get in close, hit 'em hard, then dip back out?"

Christopher Robin nodded in reply. "That's what I would do. Go with a lighter physical armor and retune the power plants for higher speed."

"Float like a butterfly, sting like a bee," John asked.

"Exactly," Trevor said, spitting in his bottle again. He suddenly froze in place, eyes wide. "Did y'all hear that?"

"What?"

"It was like a couple of thuds and a high-pitched whine."

Everyone in the bay froze and listened intently.

Christopher Robin shook his head. "You should probably get your hearing checked. I don't…"

Several nearby explosions shook the trailer and the rig suddenly rocked, leaning hard to the left then back to the right.

"Fire fire fire!" Kyle shouted over the radio. "We've got some live ones out there, and Kelly is toast. That first salvo came down right on top of her."

Rapid gunfire sporadically peppered the outside of the rig, but nothing penetrated the light armor.

"Y'all hold on back there," Kyle said. "I'll get us out of this as quick as I can." The rig accelerated.

"Oh, god, Kelly…" Gamer rushed to the control console and keyed the mic. "Is there any chance Kelly survived?" His voice quavered. Tears threatened to escape as his face contorted with worry. Larry hurried over, taking his seat at the console. The two tapped at the controls, activating the surveillance cameras and automated defenses.

"That's going to be a big fat negative unless she has more than nine lives."

"Auto-defenses engaged," Larry announced.

Another explosion rocked the rig. The rear-view cameras flashed white, then slowly returned as they put distance between them and the burning vehicle obliterated by a high explosive incendiary round.

Big Ed pushed Gamer to the side and grabbed the mic. "Tommy! Come in. You still with us?"

"Yeah, just barely. Took a good bump to the head and I'm pretty sure my car is out of commission, but Margaret is toast. Her truck took two direct hits in that last strike. There isn't anything left but a pile of burning slag."

"Ya know, I try to be a good-hearted soul, but why don't we just forget about Jesus for five minutes and deal with this *problem*," Trevor suggested, curling his fingers into air quotes. "Time for some unadulterated vengeance if you ask me."

"Sounds like a good plan to me," John added as he hurried to climb into *Doris*, the Beltway Bruisers' Slipstream.

"Sit tight while we deal with this, Tommy. Kyle, get ready for a hot shot, then punch it and get the rig out of here," Ed shouted into the mic, then ran to the aft end of the trailer and squeezed into *Red Death*.

"Buddy," Kyle came back over the radio. "You really want to drive out the back of a moving trailer?"

Big Ed grabbed the mic in *Red Death* and keyed it. "Sure do. They won't expect it, and you'll be harder to hit as long as you're moving."

"You're bat shit crazy, ain't you? But it's your funeral," Kyle said.

"What about the damage? We haven't finished the repairs," Gamer said.

"Is what it is," Christopher Robin answered. "We'll have a better chance of surviving if we divide their fire."

"Do we have any idea where the shots are coming from?" Big Ed asked over the team channel.

"Scanning," Knuckles said.

Gamer smacked his fist on the workstation. "Gotcha! Thermal is picking up heat signatures on a hillside ahead of us."

"There's also tracer fire coming from that hillside," Kyle added.

"Send in the dragonfly kamikaze drones?" Knuckles turned to Gamer with a questioning look.

"Frack yes, send in the dragonflies," Trevor shouted. "Hit 'em' hard and we'll pick off the stragglers."

Gamer flashed a wide smile. "This is going to be fun. I've been waiting for a chance to test these."

Knuckles laughed and punched Gamer in the shoulder. "You and me both."

"Hey," Trevor hollered. "How about before you two get wrapped up with those drones, you open the back door so we can get out."

"Oh, right," Larry said and tapped at the controls. "Done. Good hunting."

"You too," Big Ed replied.

"Weapons online," Christopher Robin announced. "You ready John?"

"Absolutely."

"Then punch it and get out of our way," Big Ed said, breaking in.

"Dragonfly one away," Gamer announced. "Round inbound. Evasive maneuvers, Muffin Man."

"Dragonfly two away," Knuckles said.

"Let's go already!" Big Ed floored the Coal Burners' Hotshot, smoking the rear tires.

"Just as soon as the door is opened," John cooly replied.

Sparks flew from the rear of the truck as the rear ramp struck pavement. John floored *Doris* and the Beltway Bruisers' Slipstream leapt forward, launching from the rear of the trailer, followed immediately by *Red Death.*

"Little Pigs are out of the pen," Christopher Robin shouted over the channel then whooped as the two arena autoduellers rushed ahead, launching from the moving truck. More rounds peppered the trailer but failed to penetrate the armored sides. Sparks flew as the Slipstream, followed by the Hotshot, hit the pavement, skidded, and bounced before each of them pulled a high-speed U-turn.

"What do you think we're up against?"

"Probably just some rag-tag raiders looking for a quick payday," Trevor answered.

"Maybe, or maybe not," Big Ed replied. "Either way, the faster we end this, the faster we can pick up the pieces and get back on the road."

Tracer fire exploded from a bluff that jutted out from the small hillside to the north of them.

"Hot damn," Trevor shouted. "We've got contact."

"We see them," Gamer responded.

Three more large flashes lit up the night sky.

"Mortars!"

"Copy that," Kyle replied, then slammed the brakes on the massive rig. Wheels locked and tires squealed, quickly slowing the massive rig.

"Let's light 'em' up," Christopher Robin shouted. "Range, fifteen hundred feet. Missiles away!"

"Five seconds," Knuckles added.

"I got nothing to hit that kinda range," Trevor groused.

"Don't worry, kid," Big Ed answered. "I doubt these guys are alone."

Both missiles from the Beltway Bruisers' Slipstream slammed into the mortar emplacement followed closely behind by the Dragonfly drones. Secondary explosions spattered the hillside, igniting the prairie hillside like a fireworks display.

"Taking point," Big Ed said. "We'll see if there's anything else up ahead."

"Right behind you," John responded.

"Whoa, hold on, John," Christopher Robin broke in. "Any signs of life from our friends up there?"

"Negative," Gamer responded, only to be proven wrong by more heavy machine gun fire. "I take that back, one contact."

"We're out of missiles," Christopher Robin replied.

"Not to worry," Knuckles said, chuckling. "I think we can handle this."

Gamer giggled like a giddy schoolgirl over the open mic. "Oh, baby. Should we break out *Ivan*?"

Knuckles looked at him with concern. "*Ivan* is an awful big gun."

"And overkill does get the job done," Gamer said, grinning.

"Even with the power drain, I believe so," Knuckles said. "Activating drive and feed motors."

"Targeting sensors onli— Damn, that was quick." Gamer chuckled. "Target acquired."

"Nerds," Trevor poked over the channel.

"Two new contacts," Big Ed reported. "Just saw headlights pull onto the road ahead from what should be a small side spur."

"Fire in the hole!"

"Firing!"

The rig abruptly rocked hard to the right with a thunderous boom. The cacophonous report of an artillery round striking home reached them a moment after a third of the southern face of the hillside ceased to exist.

"Holy hell, people," Kyle shouted. "Warn a man next time. That shot nearly flipped us!"

"But the threat is neutralized." The sound of excited laughter and slapping high-fives from the techs flooded the comms. Machine gun rounds impacting the trailer quickly disrupted the celebration.

"That was it for our big guns," Gamer admitted. "We're down to point defense machine guns. The ball is back in your court, Little Pigs."

Both teams responded with a solemn "Roger!" simultaneously over the comms. Trevor chuckled at the light peppering of lead. "Are these guys stupid or something? Those guns aren't any good for long range."

"Looks like a pair of Joseph Specials," John added.

"Gotta be raiders or arena wanna-be's using what they've got handy. The only ones dumb enough to use those outside the arena would be the **Scarlet Skulls.** They love those shit boxes for some reason."

"Wouldn't that be funny as hell," Trevor said.

"Kyle! Put the hammer down and keep going," Christopher Robin ordered. "We'll part the way and take care of these two ratchetheads before we go back to pick up Tommy."

"Copy that, good buddy. Hammer down and rolling!" Kyle let out a loud rebel yell that crackled the comms.

The Beltway Bruisers and the Coal Burners rolled headlong at the pair of charging Joseph Specials.

"Hey John," Christopher Robin said. "Feel up to a game of chicken?"

"Sure. Staggered or stonewall?"

"Stonewall. Better chance to split them and clear a path for the rig."

"Roger," John answered, accelerating to bring the nose of his vehicle even with that of the Coal Burners' Hotshot.

Miniguns flared to life, flinging lead in their direction. Tracer rounds ricocheted from the team's battered armor and the surrounding pavement. Damage warnings flashed across the Bruisers' dash.

"Little Pig two, your forward armor is failing and about to go critical," Larry warned over the comms.

"Well, no duh," Trevor replied. "It's not like we're Irish Spring fresh or anything. We were already pretty chewed up from the arena."

"If at all possible, I'd suggest evasive maneuvers," Larry said matter-of-factly.

"That would be nice," Big Ed shouted. "Primary power pack is hit. We're down to half speed, and I'm getting fire warnings."

"Drop back and cover the rig," Christopher Robin ordered. "We've got these frack heads."

"Sure do," John said plainly before the Beltway Bruisers' Slipstream leapt forward with a burst of speed.

Big Ed let out a bestial roar. "Not like we have much choice in the matter, but I'd rather cover your rear even if we might be slow getting there."

"Roger that," John said into the comms.

"You still wanna play chicken?" Christopher Robin asked, looking over at John.

"Dunno." John grunted a laugh. "What's the worst that could happen? We have a head-on with these frackers?"

"That's what your Gold Cross is for," Gamer reminded them over the comms. "You were updated just a few days ago."

"No surrender!" Trevor let out a loud whoop over the comms. "You two split 'em and I'll light 'em up while they're trying to recover."

John floored it, barreling head-on toward the pair of Joseph Specials. Rounds danced across the hood and bulletproof windshield of their Slipstream. John returned fire with their forward-facing machine guns, focusing his aim to the car on the left.

"Get ready to hit this guy on our left with the Wasps as we zip by." John disengaged the automatic traction and antilocking brake systems.

Christopher Robin looked up from his controls to John. "Sliding Joe?"

"Yup."

"Estimated speed when we break?"

The car lurched forward with sudden acceleration. "Ninety."

Rounds continued to pepper *Doris's* nose when the tone of the strikes suddenly changed. Warning lights flashed across the dashboard.

"I'm picking up minor damage to secondary power pack alpha," Larry announced over the comms. "Nothing major yet, but it could be."

"Understood," John replied, then jerked the wheel, shifting lanes to throw off the enemy fire.

"Rockets!"

John pulled the emergency brake and cut the wheel hard to the left, intentionally throwing the car into a skid. He floored the accelerator and brought the nose of the Slipstream back around to bear on his targets, dodging the rockets, one of which grazed the roof of their car as it zipped past.

John aimed for the Joseph Special on his left, angling to ram them head-on, keeping the accelerator buried.

Christopher Robin looked up from his controls to John. "They aren't turning, John."

"They'll turn. Speed correction, one hundred and five."

"John…"

"They'll turn," John said again calmly.

"JOHN!"

The car on their left swung to its left, bumping into its companion before cutting hard to the right. The Joseph Special on the right soared off the roadway and over an ancient set of railroad tracks to the riverbank below.

The remaining Joseph Special scootched over onto the broken shoulder, skidding slightly over the dusty ground.

"Now!" John shouted, pulling the emergency brake and cutting the wheel hard to the right, sending the Slipstream skidding out of control. Christopher Robin fired the twin, rear-mounted wasp cannons as their rear came around to bear on the target.

The ancient Joseph Special's side armor exploded from the impact of the specialized shredder rounds from the wasps. Sparks flew from the rear drive motors as the remaining opponent limped away.

Trevor laughed over the comms. "You just fracked the hell out of their evening!"

"Hold on, we aren't done yet." John cut the wheel hard to the left, tapped the e-brake, then gunned the throttle, spinning the tail end of their car around to pursue the wounded vehicle.

"Where the hell do you think you're going," Trevor said, chuckling. A high-pressure stream of liquid fire lanced forward from their Hotshot, falling just short of the Joseph Special. Big Ed maneuvered the Hotshot to block the enemy's path. "Let's get him off the road so the rig can get by."

"Agreed," John said, redirecting their momentum so they accelerated toward the enemy vehicle. Machine gun fire erupted from both teams, bathing the Joseph Special with incendiary tracer fire.

The driver's side wheel soared through the air onto the railroad tracks alongside the road as the Joseph Special's quarter panel and rear fender exploded.

"Frack yeah!"

"Bet they had a mine dropper in the rear that we just set off," Christopher Robin said.

The Joseph Special slid off the road and onto the railroad tracks where it skidded to a stop.

"All targets neutralized," Gamer announced. "I'm not picking up any other power signatures on the scanners."

"Kyle, bring us to a stop, please," Knuckles asked. "We can load the cars here."

"We'll run back and pick up Tommy, then check out the wrecks while you get *Red Death* loaded. No sense in turning the rig around if we don't have to."

Big Ed limped the Coal Burners' Hotshot up alongside the Beltway Bruisers' Slipstream.

"Let's check out these wrecks before we roll out to see if they need any medical attention," Christopher Robin said.

"Frack that," Big Ed shouted. "These ratchetheads just tried to kill us for no good reason."

John stepped out of the Slipstream. "Would you want to be left to die on a deserted highway?"

"No, but still," Big Ed replied.

"Ya know," Trevor started to say as he climbed out of the Hotshot. "I knew we were joking about the Scarlet Skulls loving these slushbox Joseph Specials, but isn't that actually their car?"

"There ain't no way," Kyle said, laughing into the comms.

"Why would they be all the way out here?" Big Ed scratched at the back of his head.

"You have been destroying them in the arena," Knuckles added.

"I'm more curious about how they got ahead of us so quickly," Christopher Robin said.

"Airlift?" Gamer suggested.

"That's the only thing that makes sense," John said.

Christopher Robin drew his sidearm, checked the load, and started for the smoking Joseph Special. "Whatever is going on, we'd best be on our toes from here on out. Let's check the wrecks and get out of here. We've got an event to get to."

John checked his sidearm, following in step behind Christopher Robin. "Sounds like a plan to me."

Smoke suddenly roiled from beneath the wrecked Joseph Special that flared to an instant blaze. An acrid black mushroom cloud of fire and smoke rolled high into the sky above the vehicle. Metal slag melted away, igniting the surrounding vegetation and railroad ties.

Another explosion of roiling flame from the riverbank farther down the highway lit up the night.

"Damn..." Trevor gasped.

"Yeah, kid. Damn." Big Ed swallowed hard. "No way anyone could survive that."

"Doubtful," Christopher Robin said. "All we can do is hope they were already dead."

"Listen," Kyle broke in over the radio, bringing the rig to a stop nearby. "If we're going to make the next match, we need to get, and I mean in a big way. We'll have to make up time where we can and the nerds will have to slave in some extra power, but we can still do this."

"You heard the man," Christopher Robin said. "Let's move. Get the Hotshot loaded, and we'll go pick up Tommy."

"It doesn't surprise me they lost again," Jeffrey said more to himself than anyone else. He adjusted his binoculars, focusing on what was left of the Scarlet Skulls. "It would have been ironic if they'd won outside the arena."

"It would have, Mister Shrader," Tim replied.

"Has any of the mortar team checked in?"

"No, sir. There's been no word from any of them."

Jeffrey stared up at the star-filled sky. "I can't get over how peaceful it is out here." He let out a long sigh. "Time to liquidate the assets," he said, turning to Tim.

"Yes, sir, Mister Shrader." Tim retrieved a transmitter from his trouser pocket and entered a code into the keypad.

"Activate," Jeffrey ordered, and Tim pressed another button on the controller.

Sudden flashes of light illuminated the valley below. The sound of the explosions reached them as the foul cloud of flame and smoke rose skyward.

Jeffrey reached inside his jacket and in one fluid motion drew a hand cannon, aimed, and fired one of the high caliber rounds into the side of Tim's head. He slumped to the ground beside the Hammer.

"I'm really sorry about that, Tim." Jeffrey shrugged and let out another sigh. "Nothing personal. Just business, you know. A man can't disappear if he leaves witnesses." He turned his gaze back to the star-filled sky. "It really is peaceful here."

We hope that you enjoyed this title and look forward to many more to come. Please, leave us a review! Reviews matter to all of our authors.

Check out the latest in the Car Warriors: Autoduel Chronicle fiction series.

https://threeravenspublishing.com/car-warriors-autoduel-chronicles/

And don't forget to check out the latest edition of *Car Wars*

http://www.sjgames.com/car-wars/

Or the other amazing titles from
Steve Jackson Games

http://www.sjgames.com

Take a look at some of our other award-winning series at
https://threeravenspublishing.com/series-universes/

Visit us at https://www.threeravenspublishing.com and sign up for our newsletter for the latest and greatest news on upcoming titles and events.

Other series and titles you might enjoy.

AVAILABLE ON
AMAZON
JOINT TASK FORCE
13
HOLDING THE LINE
BETWEEN HEAVEN AND HELL

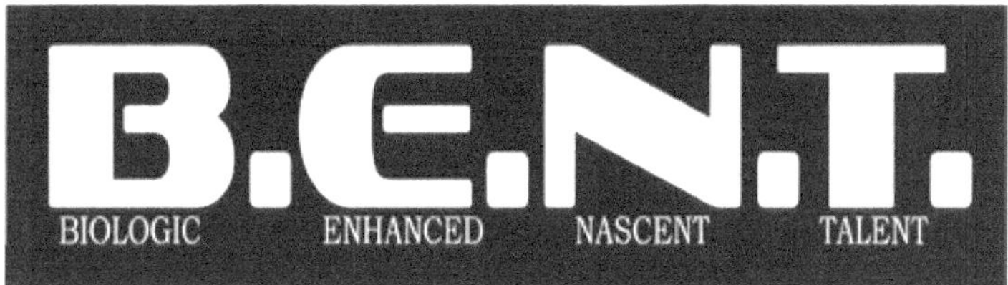

B.E.N.T.
BIOLOGIC   ENHANCED   NASCENT   TALENT

STARFLIGHT

IT CAME FROM THE
TRAILER PARK

You can also keep up to date with our latest release announcements on Scifi.radio and get some of the best fandom programing on the planet.

Scifi for your Wifi

And don't forget to check out our other Sponsors and Affiliates

A southern Appalachian jewel for craft beer lovers, Buck Bald Brewing offers something for everyone.

To discover more visit us at buckbaldbrewing.com

Revolution X is a testament to the power of collaboration, blending four unique styles into a cohesive, revolutionary sound. When these four individuals unite, the result is nothing short of musical Revolution!